Four
Nails

G.J. Berger

Also by G.J. Berger:

South of Burnt Rocks West of the Moon

Four Nails

G.J. Berger Publishing
San Diego, California

ISBN: 978-0-9883982-3-8 (hard cover)
          978-0-9883982-4-5 (soft cover)
          978-0-9883982-5-2 (e-book)

Printed in the United States of America for Worldwide Distribution

For Eugene and Justin, each with broad shoulders, a strong spirit, and deep integrity. In their own way not unlike Ashoka, and I am blessed for that too.

Praise for *Four Nails*

"Epic historical fiction…"

"A treat for ancient history buffs… Spanning more than a decade and far from being a tired history lesson, the story flows naturally and never feels rushed. It's full of interesting facts… fortified by Berger's simple yet rich descriptions of battles and the struggles of war. However, Ashoka's nuanced, personal narrative drives the novel."

"A highly entertaining, sophisticated look at the Second Punic War through the eyes of an unlikely hero." *Kirkus Reviews*

"Berger's unpretentious prose weaves a brilliant tale of heroism and cowardice, love and heartache through the special relationship between a glorious animal and its trainer." Sharon Robards, *A Woman Transported*.

"A compelling story about an Indian *mahout* (elephant trainer) named Ashoka, who went from a slave to becoming a key member of Hannibal's incredible army. One of the fairest depictions of Hannibal and Carthage that you will see in print. One of the best fiction reads you will see this year." Jonathan van Helsing, *Cyber Loves' Illusions*.

Praise for *South of Burnt Rocks West of the Moon*

Chosen as the Best Published Historical Fiction Novel of 2012 by the San Diego Book Awards.

"A spare and intense novel of a people half-lost in the mists of history, resisting to death and beyond the conquering power of Rome." Elizabeth Loupas, *The Second Duchess* and *The Flower Reader*.

". . .G. J. Berger has written the stirring tale of a Celtic girl at a time when bravery was a child's first weapon. *Burnt Rocks* is a heart-stopping read." Elizabeth Cobbs Hoffman, *Broken Promises, A Novel of the Civil War*

". . .Captivating debut historical fiction. . . Smartly written, the novel moves quickly, building prose with quiet strength unencumbered by the heavy style. . . The simple yet powerful narrative relies on a commanding cast of characters, many of whom are indeed women, celebrated for their resiliency and constitution. . . A wonderfully crafted balance of Roman-era drama and the fierceness of battle." *Kirkus Reviews*, September 2012

"[W]ell researched and engrossing novel. . . enlivened by Berger's outstanding talent for stirring set pieces and gripping action sequences." *Historical Novel Society Review* (2015)

Chapter I

Brothers

Every evening as the sun slid down behind far-away trees and big cats reclaimed the land, the same unease crept in. His fear did not leave until morning, sometimes not until he sat high on the back of his favorite elephant.

Near the end of this day, Ashoka stood at the edge of the river meandering past the elephant camp. He called out, "Come, Red Eyes. Night does not wait." Most times when he called, softly, she came to him without delay, but all was not right with her now. She shook her head, dipped her trunk into the water, and raised up as if deciding whether to drink or spray her back one last time. She blew out in the direction of the river's flow.

Ashoka waded in to face her. He locked his gaze on the center of her forehead and quieted his insides so that her big ears heard the power of his heart, so his breathing told her that he meant what he said. He reached out to her cheek, and it trembled. That too was wrong. Red Eyes never trembled at his touch. He patted and stroked her face then her trunk down to the sensitive tip. "Tell me what you hear, what's out there."

Red Eyes leaned over to him and rumbled from deep in her throat. Ashoka knew whatever troubled Red Eyes came from down river, but that was all she told him. He waited with her, both looking south, she flapping her ears and raising her trunk, he listening and watching for any sign at the river bend, in the dense growth on both sides, in the sky. He saw nothing, sensed nothing to alarm him, but Red Eyes did not play games about such things.

"You hear something, don't you?"

She rumbled again.

"Well, you can't stay out here. I won't leave, and we'll protect each other." He prodded her cheek, and she turned slowly. He tapped the back of her leg, and she moved up the bank, across open space and into her pen.

After Ashoka cajoled Red Eyes, one by one the other elephants followed into their own pens. All the men in the camp had carried out the same ritual many times, as had their fathers before them from a hundred years back when Alexander invaded their lands with his elephant army. But now the other men also struggled with their charges, to calm and settle them for the night.

Some men grabbed long poles tipped with spiked ends. Others set torches alight and stuck them into the ground. Then they all lined up at the path out of the camp to their village. Three men at the rear tied on white and black painted face masks. The masks made them taller, and the painted faces stared backwards. That way, predators did not attack the last in line. When ready, the group would walk home fast but never run. Hungry meat eaters chased down anyone running from them.

Most nights two trainers stayed at the camp and slept on platforms high in the trees. Their quiet talk and songs calmed any restless beast. If a fire came through or the river flooded in the night, the trainers released the elephants.

But on this evening no elephant trainer or laborer made any move to leave. No elephant lay down on the clean straw in the pens. None ate the young bamboo shoots waiting in their food troughs. All ten, two in each pen, faced south, heads high, ears straight out to catch every sound and trunks held up to capture every scent.

Wooden posts deep in the ground anchored the pens, and heavy logs made up the rails. One anxious elephant and then another pushed at the posts with their foreheads or leaned hard against the rails. Ashoka thought the posts would not hold much longer. If they broke down the fences... and all got out in the night... what then? Everyone in their village would laugh about this one time Father let Ashoka's older brother, Govinda, run the camp for one day.

The elephants not leaning on fence rails or posts pawed at the straw and dry red dirt. They blew out of their trunks, then one and more let out trumpet sounds. These sounds would be heard by big cats a half day's travel away and warn them to not come near. They never did that all together, not even when a tiger prowled or a cobra built a nest nearby. Something bigger than tigers and perhaps deadlier than the cobra was out there.

Govinda spoke first. "Onto the platforms and into the trees. Maybe we can see whatever they smell and hear." The men scrambled up into the trees and platforms and peered south.

It felt right to Ashoka that Govinda ordered the men, most older than Govinda, into the trees and safety. Only Ashoka, nearly as tall as his older brother, trained elephants faster and better than Govinda, faster than anyone at the camp. From two years before, when Ashoka was eleven and his voice changed and he grew hair where adults grow hair, he felt the older mahouts watch how he talked to any elephant, how he stood and held his shoulders, how he breathed when he approached a new one, how he stroked and rewarded them. Yet this evening no gaze, no prods or hard slaps, no quiet talk or shouts from either brother calmed their beasts. The snorting and trumpet blasts grew stronger.

Full darkness came quickly, but no strange light appeared against the black sky. A distant fire heading this way was not it. The dry season had barely begun, and for days the prevailing breezes blew south from far away high mountains at the northern border of India.

The elephants snorted, rumbled and now trumpeted so loudly, steadily that whatever was out there must be getting closer, must not be moving away, must be moving at them and fast.

All at once Ashoka understood. Through the din of his own elephants, he heard distant peeps like from a chick, then the whistles—wild elephants, many of them bent on moving into the camp. They talked to each other through these peeps and whistles. Those rogues were clever, wanted to approach quietly on their soft feet, perhaps surround the camp, before announcing their presence and closing in.

Suddenly, the wild ones trumpeted back at the camp elephants.

On a platform two trees away, Govinda shouted through the blasts, "You all hear them, yes?"

Many faces turned to Govinda. "Yes..."

"A wild herd... close... not stopping..."

"What shall we do, Govinda?"

Govinda did not respond, did not move.

Ashoka knew that a big wild herd could make the men stay in the trees for days while it flattened the storage hut, cleaned out the stacks of honey-soaked balls of rice treats and broke down the pens. After this night, Father's reputation would be worse than a monkey with boils on its backside. No one would buy an elephant from this camp or send them another elephant to train.

Light from the torches stuck in the ground fell on the eyes and tusks of the intruders. Ashoka spotted fifteen, and there were more he could not see. A large female strode into the edge of the camp clearing. She stopped, moved her head down and around, raised and lowered her trunk to sort out the new smells and measure the strength of the human kind.

Silently Ashoka begged Govinda to lead the men, to shout out instructions. His brother doing nothing, saying nothing, made Ashoka's chest cramp up. Soon the wild ones would smell that fear and have their way in the camp.

Ashoka didn't have to think through the choices. He felt, then knew what to do, was sure of it. It came to him out of stories told by his father and old men when he was little and pretending to sleep. *Remember the first rule of the herd for wild elephants. Find the leader—the matriarch. Control the leader and you control the herd.* Quickly a plan formed inside him for how to stop the coming chaos.

Govinda only stared down into the gathering rogues. Ashoka's insides screamed for his brother to shout out, to act, to lead, but Ashoka had to stay quiet, had to respect his elder and camp leader.

The wild matriarch moved farther into the camp. If Govinda waited another moment without challenging her, she would signal her rogues to move in and not let the men down. If a big male waited out of sight, he would charge any man on the ground, shake the men out of the trees and not stop until he had stomped them to death or run them off.

Govinda, on his knees, leaned over the edge of his platform a bit more but not in way that said he was about to jump down, more like a rabbit crouching lower and trying to hide from a big hawk circling above it.

Ashoka could not wait another moment. He clambered down his tree and onto the fence railing of the pen underneath his platform. He hopped to the ground, lifted off the rope loops holding the gate shut, and climbed onto the neck of Red Eyes. She did not resist. He felt her shift as if to welcome him, as if she did not want these invaders any more than he did, and he knew he and Red Eyes could do what needed to be done. He motioned for a mahout from his tree platform to follow him, then another and one more. He rode Red Eyes out of her pen and straight at the nearest torch cluster stuck in the ground not yet surrounded by the intruders. With his free hand, he signaled the other three to grab a torch and follow him to the wild matriarch.

Right away she noticed the four elephants and mahouts carrying torches, shuddered and snorted then backed up. Her own herd crowded in behind her, also backing up, tightening up.

Other camp mahouts now helped from either on their elephants or on the ground, jumping and waving hands or poles at the wild herd. Ashoka spotted his brother running closer to them than any other mahout or helper. Govinda, without any pole or torch, lifted his arms high and shouted for them to get back, get out. And that made Ashoka relax, focus on what he had to do.

Ashoka shouted over the noise and growing dust, "The empty *kedah*, into the *kedah*." Pointing, shouting, he led the four mahouts on four elephants up to the matriarch from both sides. They waved their torches back and forth close to her face and eyes. Her own elephants did not help her. Some backed away from her, allowing the four camp elephants to close on her. The matriarch moved to one side then the other, trying to find her own way out. It was too late. Two elephants on both sides of her and fire torches near her face left only one way open—not backward and away but forward into an empty pen. This pen held two elephants easily, allowing them to eat and drink from the water trough, move about or lie down. But now the pen held five elephants, the matriarch and two tight on both her flanks.

Ashoka yelled, "Keep your torches close, keep tight so she can't move." He jumped off Red Eyes, closed the gate behind and sat on the top rail.

Some of the wild ones realized what had been done to their leader. They trumpeted and ran up but stopped short of the blocking elephants, the men and fire torches. Ashoka knew these wild ones would not gore one of his father's elephants. They wanted to join them not hurt them. Elephants rarely hurt their own. And he felt they had never been among shouting men carrying fire. The rogues, now without their leader, did not know what to do.

The wild elephants milled around aimlessly. Some snorted and squealed then crashed off into the jungle. The boldest still ran up, but slower now, and always stopped before colliding with any of the camp elephants or men. After a time, they stood around at a distance facing the pen that held their leader.

A different worry welled up in Ashoka. Would Govinda hate him for what he had done, for saving the camp? Would the other mahouts and helpers shun one or both brothers after this night? The new fear helped him find his next words, made him yell across to his brother, "Govinda, what do you think? Is it time?"

Govinda's answer, the strength in Govinda's voice, let Ashoka know, let everyone know, he was again the leader. "A while longer, little brother. On my command."

After what seemed like a good wait, long enough for the rogues to calm some more but not become desperate, Govinda shouted, "Release her now and chase her like she's a dirty thief."

Ashoka opened the pen gate, jumped onto Red Eyes and backed out. The three other mahouts followed and then the wild female. She spun around fast and ran south, trumpeted once and tore into the bushes and trees. All her rogues piled after her.

The mahouts and helpers nudged their own elephants back into the proper pens, poured fresh water into their troughs, talked to them, patted them, calmed them.

After the camp quieted, Govinda motioned Ashoka to his platform. "You did well, little brother."

"I was closer to the leader, could see her better than you."

Govinda tousled Ashoka's hair while laughing softly. "Little brother, you tell stories, but maybe that is what happened. Next time we wrestle, I'll beat you until you cry out."

At that moment Ashoka knew he would always love his only brother, would let him rule the family when the time came, and stay near him for all of this life.

+ + +

Their father arrived in the morning with more workers. He asked each mahout alone, one by one, why none had come home the night before. Then he sat at the edge of the river for half the day as if in deep thought, while the elephants carried cut-down trees to the river and played in the water when done. They settled for the night without any protest.

That evening he ordered Ashoka and Govinda to watch the camp for seven nights straight.

The wild herd never again menaced the camp, but Ashoka's worry from that night did not fade out. Disaster had nearly touched him, Govinda, his whole family.

Chapter II

Powerful Strangers

Near the end of the dry season, traders from the region and far away arrived at Ashoka's village. They rode in carts pulled by mules or oxen. A few walked, carrying bundles across their backs. Armed soldiers rode with some groups. Outside of the village, they formed camps protected by fires, big dogs and thorn bush cuttings.

Ashoka watched them and wondered. From the dusty paths in front of shops and outside the village walls, he listened to the banter and bartering but moved on when an adult caught him staring. Did the wealthier traders hail from huge cities, perhaps even Mumbai on the western sea and a caravan ride of more than thirty days? What precious things remained hidden in their boxes and baskets? The traders came every year, but Ashoka noticed them more than he had in the past. This year they unsettled him.

Father had said, "They sell fake silks, and their trinkets break the first time we use them. And... sometimes they snatch up our children." His mother ended the talk about traders with, "They bring foul sicknesses."

Ashoka believed most of that, but not all of it. He knew his father sold elephants to traders who paid the best prices, called *Syrians*. They did not come every year, but villagers often talked about them. This year rumors swirled that the giant Syrian trading caravans were not far, that they might send traders to his village.

Early on a morning when the sky thickened with the promise of new rain, a stranger trotted up to Ashoka's group as it headed for the elephant camp. Ashoka did not notice him until he was on them.

The stranger wore clothes unlike any Ashoka had noticed before. A black tunic hung over black trousers. Little stitched flowers and patterns of red and yellow ran along the seams of the garments down to black boots. But the skin of his face and hands reminded of dried-out leaves, and his blue eyes remained fixed on Father leading the group. A carved scabbard hanging from his waist held a long sword, longer than any sword carried by the village soldiers. As the man passed close, Ashoka caught the odor of unfamiliar meats cooked over a smoky fire.

When the stranger reached the front of the line, Father smiled, and his open hands signaled a welcome to the stranger as if greeting a friend. The two walked on and talked quietly with their backs to the others. Father raised his hand for those behind to stop and turned. "Govinda, you know what to do. Must get the wood in from Simha's forest before the heavy rains. I may come later."

After the stranger and Father were out of sight, Ashoka worked his way to the front and next to Govinda. "Who was that? I've never seen anyone like him."

"A Syrian."

"I know what they want. They come again for our elephants."

Govinda strode on ignoring his little brother.

After a time, Ashoka said, "I won't let them take Red Eyes."

"No one refuses them. They're the only ones allowed to come here from outside our emperor's India—pay the best prices."

"I won't trade with that one. He stinks."

"Little brother, don't talk like that—prideful as the prancing peacock. You show only pretty feathers."

"I won't let him take Red Eyes." Ashoka was not as sure as he sounded, but saying it tamped down his worry.

"You'll do as our father tells you." Govinda shook his head and picked up the pace in a way that told Ashoka to stop his questions, to get away from him, to take his place at the back of the band of elephant trainers and laborers.

At the camp the elephants were ready, anxious to begin the day. Red Eyes snorted and made noises in her throat as if trying to talk. She ran the tip of her trunk up and down Ashoka's shirt, not probing for a treat, but sniffing out new smells on her master. She too noticed the Syrian's meat-eater stench carried by Ashoka.

+ + +

Four of the camp elephants, their mahouts and helpers labored in a forest a long walk uphill from the camp. Wood cutters felled the tallest, straightest teak trees and sawed the hard wood into sections. The wood cutters must have already worked for days. Many heavy wood sections and piles of smaller logs lay on the ground. The big beasts rolled the cut logs up ramps into waiting carts. They hoisted smaller branches and eased them into the carts on top of the log sections. Later the elephants pulled the carts to the river or all the way to the village.

Red Eyes, with Ashoka on her neck, worked as well and quickly as any. Without him telling her or pointing, she found the wood slabs ready to roll up into the carts. When none were ready for her, she found the branches and smaller logs to pile into waiting carts.

In the heat of mid-day when the forest rested, Father and the Syrian arrived. The two rode on one big stallion with the

Syrian in front. Three soldiers, each on a horse, came with them. The soldiers carried those curved long swords and wore shirts of hard leather. The five dismounted, but the soldiers remained in the shade with the horses. Everyone knew that big cats smell horse flesh from far away.

Now and again Ashoka glanced at the Syrian. Through the afternoon the Syrian said nothing, and his face gave nothing away. His horse carried a water pouch, but he did not drink. Unlike other elephant buyers, he did not approach the elephants, did not inspect the pads of their feet for cracks or rot. He did not look into their mouths or check the wear on their teeth. He did not study the color of their eyes. He only watched the elephants, mahouts, and loggers work.

The stranger caught Ashoka's glance and stared back out of that unmoving face. Ashoka turned away quickly but then and later sensed the Syrian's gaze on his bare shoulders, on his legs and arms, on his moves with Red Eyes. Ashoka felt a power from this Syrian he did not understand, a power without kindness.

The Syrian came to the camp the next day and the day after that, but did not stay long and again said nothing to anyone.

+ + +

At the evening meal on the last day of the stranger's visits to the camp, Ashoka's mother served her husband first. Father ate only one bite of the hot rice mixed with bits of egg and mango fruit but stayed seated on his cushion while his two sons ate after him. Ashoka waited for the usual talk of the day, of questions about what the brothers had learned, what they would be doing tomorrow. But their father said nothing, and that made Ashoka look at his father more closely than he had in many days.

The candle in the main room of the house cast long shadows, but Ashoka saw well enough. All at once Ashoka knew that his father had in this one dry season grown into an old man—only nibbling at his food, his hands shaking, the knuckles swollen but the fingers thin and too white. Head down, his shoulders and chest had collapsed. His cheeks lay pale and hollow. Not long ago their father had held his strong shoulders back, his chest out, head high—the proud ruler of his family and business, a warrior caste elephant trainer, owner of the finest elephant camp in central India. Now he sat like a grey old dog, too weak and too tired to gnaw the bone lying at his paws.

Father broke the long silence. "I must tell you about the Syrians and what they want." He waited, as was his way, and his waiting made Ashoka listen, but he thought, *they can't have Red Eyes.* Govinda waited too, his hands in his lap, breathing easily, while Ashoka fretted like a wet hen. And that told Ashoka his older brother already knew what the Syrians wanted.

Since the night they chased off the rogue herd, Ashoka noticed that Govinda and their father often walked off by themselves and talked quietly. They did so at the camp, out on the street away from the house, and outside the village wall. Since that night Govinda won every wrestling match easily, had not let Ashoka throw him down one time. Govinda's commands rang harsher, and he gripped firmer, came at Ashoka far rougher. The other mahouts no longer studied and tried to copy Ashoka's handling of Red Eyes, no longer cheered for him after he escaped Govinda's wrestling holds. Ashoka was again merely the youngest mahout.

Ashoka knew he brought on these changes, had insulted his elder by six years and their leader. Many times since that night he thought he should have waited for the rogues to have their way a while longer. Maybe Govinda would have sprung out on his own and led the mahouts and tame elephants. On that night, without a word, Ashoka had declared to the whole

13

camp that Govinda was a coward. Since then Ashoka grieved that he had done that, that he might never restore what he had with Govinda before the night of the rogue herd.

The old man put his hands together and directed the ends of his fingers at Govinda.

"The Syrians don't want one of my elephants. They want to take..." his voice broke for an instant, "you. They want to take my eldest son."

After a long silence, Govinda said, "Yes, Father. Is it done, then?"

"No, my son, not done. They have not set a price... nor have I." Govinda exhaled loudly enough for Ashoka to hear. Father continued. "Other empires far from India use our elephants for work and war. Ours are the best but must be trained and led by our best mahouts. I will learn what I can before I set my... my price for you. They want my answer no later than the morning of the seventh day. They'll leave a day or two after that."

Oh, on all the offspring of Vishnu, Father will sell Govinda—to them. Only the price remains. Ashoka let out, "For how long... how far away... why?"

Silence for a long time, and Ashoka was not sure if they had heard—better that their father had not heard, better he should control himself and not make a sound.

Govinda responded, "The Syrians trade with people of almond eyes in the East all the way to the yellow hairs in the West. Syrians become rich by trading what others make, what we make. They have for two thousand years. A Syrian caravan bigger than any around here waits a day's ride off on the Emperor's Road. All the shop owners in Lalput are bartering with them and getting the best prices. But Syrians are no fools. They only buy what they can sell for many times more."

Ashoka knew the little lesson was directed at him, though Govinda did not look at him. He felt small and young and ignorant that he did not know this.

Their father said, "None of that matters. Only the price matters. And one more..." He stopped in mid-sentence as if to catch his breath or to think. Ashoka could not tell which.

Govinda said, "Say it, Father, one more what?"

Ashoka heard a choking in Govinda's question and that made him sad. Govinda knew the answer, and the answer made Govinda choke up.

The old man responded more slowly than Ashoka had ever heard him talk, in a voice flat and dull, as if he did not believe what he said but had to say it, as if there remained little life in him. "The... the Syrians say that mahouts who serve well, who ride for victors and share in great plunder at battle's end, may buy their freedom... may come back home... with gold... enough gold to buy their own land."

Silence, again for a long time. No fly buzzed.

All at once Govinda stood up fast, made fists and held his muscled arms by his side. "Father, if you get a good price, I will be one who returns with gold. When I come back, I'll buy much land for a princess, and she will be my wife."

Their father looked up at Govinda standing as if saying, *Good, my son. May the gods bring you back.*

Ashoka thought everything at once, too many thoughts, and none brought order to the jumble. Sell Govinda to the foul-smelling Syrians, Father not well, might not stay much longer in this life, if he lived... too weak and sick to rule the family. And if Govinda left with the Syrians—Ashoka closed his eyes—him as the head of family, the guardian of his younger sisters until they moved to the homes of their husbands, protector of his mother. He tried to let be what he could not change, to quiet his insides, as his guru had taught him to do in times of turmoil.

Sounds of soft clothes moving came from the door to the other non-sleeping room in the small house. His mother and three sisters had been so quiet Ashoka had forgotten them. Govinda did not move, did not turn to their mother, and neither did her husband, but Ashoka could not help look at her—for her comfort, for a sign that everything would be all right, for her to stop this talk.

On other nights, her eyes laughed when she served her men, and they smiled back at her and thanked her, sometimes with words, sometimes with hand gestures. On some nights she bowed as she set banana leaves holding the steaming meal in front of her husband and sons and made them all laugh— *Oh, do you see? I must take it away and cook it some more. Or worms will tickle you from the inside.* Sometimes their father looked up at her and smiled back, their hands touched, and their fingers, one on the other, lingered.

Ashoka thought her the most beautiful woman in the village, that she looked younger than all other mothers of seven children, of any number of children. Her songs were the sweetest, her bearing the most proud. On other nights the three daughters still at home helped, brought cups and jugs of water and tea or juice pressed from many kinds of fruit. Often his mother and the three sisters hummed songs in the kitchen area of the next room, though they always stopped the instant the men started talking.

On this night their mother rustled in fast, grabbed the leaves roughly so that Father's heaped food almost spilled, and left quickly. The three sisters did not show themselves and made no sound. They all must have known. Women always knew about family matters before the men. She knew she would lose her older son and did not hide her anger, her sorrow.

+ + +

Long before he and his brother fell asleep, Ashoka heard their father snoring. He whispered, "Mother knew. You knew? When did you know?"

"Ah, little brother, you are young. I knew that first day the Syrian came to our camp. He is no elephant buyer. Yet, he watched and studied us working like a buyer watches and studies. And... I'm the second leader of the mahouts. I have no wife and babies to keep me here... If he came to buy a mahout, and this one did not come to buy teakwood, I had to be the one."

"When our father gets his price, you will go?"

"Oh, little brother, the best mahouts come from India... our family has trained the best mahouts in all of India for many lives past."

"But you will go, will leave us?"

"Little brother, you must listen and not talk so much."

Ashoka wanted to ask what Govinda and their father had talked about over the last days and months but dared not. It did not matter. At last he said, "I will try."

"You don't understand, do you, little brother?"

"What do I not understand?"

"The Syrians know our father trains the best mahouts and in the end will give him a good price. Then I must go... will come back with much gold. Sleep now, little brother."

Thoughts of losing Govinda did not let Ashoka sleep. Anger at their father, at whatever had made him grow old so fast, mixed with that slight hope from Govinda's last words kept tears from spilling out.

He stayed awake until many roosters crowed the morning in.

Chapter III

Journey's End

Six days after the arrival of the Syrian trader, Ashoka's group of mahouts and laborers returning from the camp broke out of the forest into the clearing around their village.

Underbrush smoldered at the forest's edge. Smoke hung on the ground, and ash mixed with dead leaves swirled on the path to the main gate. In places, leaves and ash covered Ashoka's feet. That day farmers had set the dry waist-high grass on fire. Ashoka knew they did that at the end of every dry season to enrich the soil and stop the jungle's advance.

A hot darkness fell early on his village.

"Ashoka, is that you? Come quick," said his mother. She stood silhouetted against the firelight outside the family house. "He's not with you? And his mongoose got out."

"No, Govinda's not with me. He's checking our youngest female ready to drop her first calf. He ordered me to tell you that he'll come in with the group from the lumber camp."

Standing next to her, looking down into her face, Ashoka caught the pleading in her dark eyes, and he understood. "Don't be troubled. They'll find her. New mothers hide to give birth, but not far. He'll be here soon."

"What do you know about giving birth?"

"I know our elephants."

"Today of all days, Govinda should have come in early. He knows he'll be gone from here after tomorrow."

Ashoka realized she had a mother's worry about her first-born son, a worry far greater than his. "Govinda will see places far away and..."

"I'd like it better if I could see him every day."

"And he'll come back with enough gold to make us all rich."

"No one brings back anything when the caravans take them. No one comes back. Not ever. Right now I must feed him. Soon I won't..." She stopped. Only the gods and high priests who talked to the gods knew what would happen tomorrow.

Ashoka stretched up to full height, raised his chin, and would make his mother feel better. "Govinda's strong. I'm the only one he can't throw down on first try. He's leaving because he knows I'll best him before the next dry season."

"Oh, Ashoka, you've no time for wrestling, or a child's pride."

He pretended to not hear. "Someday I'll wrestle for the emperor. What do I smell?"

"Your brother's favorite stew. Your father twisted the head off an old chicken before he left to barter more with the Syrians. Lord Buddha will let us feast on one chicken to honor your brother's far journey. Won't need as many eggs when your brother's..."

"Mother, Govinda knows. He'll be here." Ashoka believed Govinda would come in soon, would want to spend every last moment with his family.

Ashoka sat down on the wooden steps leading up to the open door of the family house. He scratched patterns on the dry dirt with one of the walking sticks propped against the wall. His three youngest sisters came to him from inside.

Sanjushree, five years old, wrapped her arms around his bare legs and rested her head on his knees. Her long shiny hair, her small body again made Ashoka think of the coming days, of their father's sickness, and he grimaced inside at the burden he would soon carry. Since that last meeting with their father, seemingly small events over the past months fell into place. Their village priests and doctors had visited too often. Reddish powders and sprinklings of what looked like sand often covered their father's evening meal, but none of it had stopped his sickness.

His mother now stood over Ashoka still sitting, and they all looked up the pathway in the direction from which Govinda would come home.

A thought made Ashoka stand up. "He's at the house of one of his friends, must be. He told me so. I'll find him."

"Yes, go. Tell him I'll pummel his ears if he doesn't come with you." His mother laughed with the lilt of a young woman and flicked the back of her hand for Ashoka to go.

He reached around his sisters to grab a piece of warm bread from the stone plate inside the doorway then bounded into the street between rows of dwellings.

Children played everywhere, some almost bumping into Ashoka. They were never allowed outside the walls when darkness neared. Young children absorbed in their play always made him feel better, even now. Women tended outdoor fires and cooking pots under roof overhangs slotted to release smoke but deflect rain. The aroma of many spices hung in the air. Dogs roused. They too became nervous every evening and barked at noises their masters could not hear. Peafowl searched for night perches. Shopkeepers shuttered their narrow store fronts. Peddlers hawked the last of the day's sweets pointing at Ashoka, at anyone nearby. Carts pulled by oxen clanked into their paddocks for the night. Most of the traders had left.

Ashoka waved at villagers he recognized. "Have you seen Govinda?" None had. He closed on all groups of young men and searched for his brother. He looked into the taverns on the main street. Govinda never went there, but he might have on this evening.

In the quieter wealthy section, Ashoka hailed young men leaning out from a second story balcony. "Is Govinda with you? Have you seen him?"

"Not here. What'll your father trade with the Syrians this year? Elephants? Tusks? Mahouts? Where'll he hide his new gold? Come, tell us."

Ashoka moved onto side roads and alleys, back to the open gate he had entered earlier. Its two sentries were not in their place, but that did not worry him. They never strayed far.

He waited for the last torch lights coming in and asked the last groups if they had seen his brother or any others from the elephant camp. None had.

In near darkness he walked along the raised path into the ashen field. Birds squawked in the tree line. Far away a big cat grunted once, followed by the bark of sambhar deer and screeches from monkeys. Ashoka held his breath to listen hard, but no human sound from outside the village reached him.

He thought to run through the field, into the jungle across four streams to the elephant compound, to tell Govinda about the waiting stew. He knew every fork and turn, in darkness could feel the path with his bare feet and the openings in the bushes with his hands. He stepped farther up the trail—and hesitated. On many mornings big paw prints lay in the wet ground over human footprints from the day before. If he reached the camp and did not find his brother, he could not return alone at night, and their mother would worry more. Be still, his guru had taught. In times of trouble, quiet the mind, and allow the way to show itself.

"Ashoka, is that you?" One of his friends ran up, shouting. "He's back. Govinda's back."

"Ah, thanks to Krishna!"

"No, Ashoka. Go home."

"What is it?"

"Go home fast."

The two sentries, returning from the direction of Ashoka's home, looked away.

He heard the crowd before he saw it, heard the shouted names of many gods mixed with Govinda's name and crying. He pushed at the back of the throng, and it parted for him.

Low wailing came from the dark corners on the far side of the main room—his mother and sisters, and aunts and their daughters.

Father's voice jolted, "Ashoka, stop. Wait outside. I forbid you to come closer."

He heard Govinda, barely audible. "No, Father. I want Ashoka. I must... talk to... him."

Father, down on one knee in the middle of the room, stood up. Two other adults moved aside, and Ashoka knelt in the place left by Father.

Govinda lay on straw mats next to light cast from candles set in bowls. A white cloth bound his right thigh. Blood seeped from two clean gashes on the calf, and Govinda's mongoose lay at his bare feet, one normal, the other foot swollen to the size of a leather water sack. Eyes half-closed, he breathed rapidly, then slowly, panted, slowly again, gasped. He raised his nearer hand for his brother. "Ashoka. . ." He took a breath.

"Don't talk. Save your strength."

"The fires, the grass fires." Another breath. "The fires burned its nest." Two shallow breaths. "It... waited by the path... We didn't see it..." Three hard breaths. "Wouldn't let go..."

Ashoka knew the rest. Every boy and girl had been taught many times to look out for and avoid all contact with the cobra. When a full-grown cobra, as long as three men lying end to end, bites, there are only two outcomes. Their guru said he had heard of some immune for life after such a bite, but confessed he had never met a survivor.

The village surgeon, who must have cut the leg, stood on the other side of Govinda next to the village priest, both silent, helpless.

Ashoka closed his eyes for a moment and begged the beautiful goddess Vishahara to take the poison out of his brother. Only she could do it now.

"I'm here." Ashoka gently squeezed his brother's hand. "Sleep now. I'll stay here."

Govinda thanked his younger brother with his eyes and breathed hard gasps.

"Be still, Govinda. Our guru has told us of those who recover."

"I'll not be one." His brother panted.

"Tomorrow or the next day you'll start your journey."

"No, Ashoka. My journey... ends tonight. You... go in my place."

"They'll wait for you. Don't talk."

"No Syrian waits for anyone. Promise me..."

Ashoka interrupted before Govinda could make him promise, before he would have to deny the promise his brother struggled to ask. "If I can, I will."

Govinda persisted. "Say you'll go with them..."

"They know I'm not you, not ready, and they will beat me and..."

"Not... if you're good... at what they need. And they need... our elephant drivers—"

23

"Quiet, Govinda, quiet. Save your strength."

"Promise me you'll... for the honor of our family."

"Quiet, Govinda."

"Promise... you'll go with them and become the greatest elephant trainer from here to the far side of Macedon."

"I'll try. Quiet now."

"Promise."

"I'll try."

"I... must have your promise."

"I promise," said Ashoka.

Govinda closed his eyes, clenched his teeth then opened his mouth wide.

Two strong hands of Uncle Vasavedu pulled Ashoka to his feet. "Go to your mother and sisters. You can do nothing here."

Ashoka backed up, turned and wrapped his arms around his mother. The three sisters, sobbing quietly, clung to his legs and chest. He forced himself to not shake, to not give way now, to not give way ever, to hold steady as long as they needed him. *Oh, Lord Vishnu, help me be strong. I need all the strength you may give me.*

Govinda rolled his head from side to side on the dry mats, and that made the sound of women thrashing rice. Ashoka tried to shield his mother's ears with his shoulders and arms, but she tensed at each gasp from her older son.

The throng faded away, and the main room grew quiet. After a time only the last shouts of children and random barking of dogs drifted in.

Late in the night the sound of wind joined the familiar taps on the thatched roof, on the hard dirt outside the open door, and, louder, on the four window ledges of the house. As the life-giving monsoon rains began to fall for another season, Govinda's journey in this life ended.

Chapter IV

The Barter

Ashoka woke out of deep sleep to a damp morning and sounds of water dripping from many places. "Ashoka, get up. I must find the advance riders from the caravan, the *sudra*, and the priests. You're in charge until I return," said his father but not loudly. His father could summon only a raspy, strained voice. Ashoka jumped to his feet.

Govinda lay in the middle of the main room on fresh mats. He wore clean clothes and smelled of flowers. Their mother knelt next to him, and the three sisters stood behind her. All four wept, their weeping turning to sobs and then quieting again. None wore any paint or powder on their faces. Their hair hung knotty, uncombed, flecked with straw and dirt. Govinda's mongoose lay in the same place as the night before by his master's feet. Ashoka did not know what to do, to say, how to comfort them. He too now knelt next to Govinda's body but refused to sob, to cry.

They stayed there until early afternoon when four strange laborers entered the room, shaved Govinda's pale body and head, then slid a robe of white silk with bands of gold and red around the body. The strangers worked quickly and without effort. The sisters looked away, but Ashoka and his mother watched as much as their tired eyes let them. The only time Ashoka had seen any family member wear silks this fine—any silks—was at the weddings of his two oldest sisters. Those two did not come to the house but stayed in the homes of their husbands, who owned them since their marriages.

The laborers carried the body out the front door. A long line waited. It must have collected and formed quietly. Ashoka had no idea when or how, had not heard it. The laborers moved to the front between the village priests. Somehow Ashoka knew to take his place next to Father behind the priests and Govinda's body.

The procession marched to an open area outside the village north wall next to the cemetery, where a pyre of logs, branches, and dried twigs waited. A roof of palm and banana leaves protected the top from the light rain.

The laborers carried the body up to the top of the pyre. The four took up Govinda's favorite short pole for prodding elephants and a bronze bowl filled with his untouched stew of the night before. The priests knew how to make torches and build mounds of branches and logs which caught and burned in all but the heaviest rains. As the head of the family, Father carried a lit torch to start the fire.

Ashoka gave thanks his brother had not married— even a daughter of one of the wealthy families with a great dowry. Some years back, his family had been approached by an intermediary for another family in a village not far from Lalput. The intermediary asked if Govinda might take their daughter as his wife. The two families knew each other, and a fine dowry would come with their daughter. At an evening meal, Father hinted at the union. Govinda threw up his hands and let out a derisive laugh. "Have you seen her? She has teeth of the wild boar. You will not do this to me." The overture faded away.

Had Govinda taken a bride, his father might have forced her to go up there with her husband. Ashoka had seen mothers of infants resist until, overpowered by men of the husband's family, one on each arm and leg, they gave up and lay down next to their dead husbands. The fire noises never muffled the screams, and the flames never hid them when they stood up searching in vain for a place to jump off the pyre. Ashoka had heard that some widows fled before the death ceremony, never again to live in a handsome house but to beg for food, scavenge scraps of cloth to cover their bodies, and sleep on the ground in a far away city for the rest of their days.

Ashoka did not know what more to think, to say to his father, about Govinda's new life, about his own promise, about what next. A tired sadness drew him to the rising warmth as the pyre caught fast and burned hot. He felt many people close behind him but did not want to make eye contact with any. The pyre burned down to a mound of ash, hunks of burned wood and charred bones.

+ + +

That night Ashoka and his father again sat cross-legged on the floor of the family house. The three sisters served them warm vegetables. Uncle Vasavedu's family cooked the plain meal and would bring food every day. Mother, wailing, lay where Govinda had slept since a boy.

New widows usually fasted for at least ten days, and Ashoka thought his mother would not eat for ten days or longer but would not starve to death. The three unmarried sisters, especially Sanjushree, growing fast, needed her. In a few days, he would try to talk to her, cheer her.

Ashoka forced himself to watch his father's shaking hands trying to work bits of clustered rice and spinach into his mouth, to chew the few morsels. His skin hung loosely on his forearms, and its color had turned reddish. Not long ago that skin had stretched tightly across strong muscles. Ashoka was now sure he would soon have to rule this family.

"The Syrians will want to leave with all haste."

"Yes, Father."

"Two days at most. They've paid for all their cargo and only need to collect and load it. Their caravan must leave before the rains soak the Emperor's Road."

Through the haze of last night and this day, Ashoka began to believe that his mother had been right. None of them would have ever seen Govinda again, would ever have known what became of him or where he found the end to this life. At last Ashoka said, "I will help, Father. I cannot help like Govinda, but I'll get better, stronger, and do whatever you ask."

"You're always a help, my son." The old man shifted and reached under his coarse cotton shirt. "You will help me more than you know."

Ah, Father will now show me the colored cloth strip of the family ruler, thought Ashoka.

"I did not send this with your brother. He—and I—wanted you to have it." Father brought forth no colored cloth but an ivory-handled dagger, the blade in a leather scabbard which trailed long leather laces. His shaking hands set it in front of Ashoka. "Metalworkers and ivory carvers in the city made it many years ago. It does not turn brown and never needs sharpening."

"I can't..."

"Tie it on where you can grab it but where no one will notice until too late."

"Big men will take it from me."

"You'll need it."

"You've said this village is safe, Father."

"You will go in Govinda's place, as you promised him."

He wanted to say that he could not train fighting elephants for wars between strangers far away, but it came out,

"We must follow *ahimsa*. Buddha teaches to not take any life without just cause or for food."

"Ashoka, you are insolent. You know nothing. *Ahimsa* is a curse. Our Emperor was once a great fighter, but has grown weak and cries like a baby every night, cries for all lives he ended. He, not Buddha, decreed *ahimsa*. I can't kill my elephants and sell the ivory until they die of old age and their tusks are broken and brown. War elephants... no use here. But far from here our elephants fight in many wars, and our mahouts have greater worth than soldiers."

Ashoka bowed his head. He had heard these things before but had never thought about how they affected his family. When he looked up again, he saw newly graying hair on his father. "You need me here..." He could not get out all he wanted to say—too much to think about and Father not looking at him, not listening to him.

"You'll take Govinda's place."

"Father, the Syrians... they do terrible things. You've told me so. I am too... young."

Father's raised shaking hand told Ashoka to be quiet. "Ashoka, you knew the ways of the elephants before you could talk. When the rogue herd came through, my best mahouts stayed in the trees, even Govinda. Elephants obey you like they obey no other man, not even me. The Syrians will keep you unharmed, will not allow a mark on you, to sell you for a high price."

"I'm not ready to fight strangers with only this knife."

"This dagger belonged to a warrior and a wrestling champion of all India. He was my grandfather."

That brought a tiny smile for a brief moment, and then, "This is a warrior's dagger. We are not warriors."

Father shifted. "You must go for your sisters and mother. Take this dagger for them. You are of the warrior class and will be so for every breath in this life."

Ashoka wanted to scream that he had to stay here for his sisters, to run the elephant camp, to protect them as they grew into marriage, to gather suitable dowries. Surely his mother and sisters wanted him to stay. He studied the black scabbard of soft leather, etched with a design of three men hunting a tiger standing on its hind legs. But he kept his hands in his lap. If he removed the knife, he would signal he had taken ownership and would go with the Syrians. "If I leave, who will work Red Eyes?" As soon as he said that, he knew its foolishness. Red Eyes would obey any kind mahout.

His father rose up to his knees and slid closer. "Red Eyes will work for me until I can't..." Father dropped his voice and bent over next to his last son's ear. "The gold they paid for Govinda... allows us to go on. I spent everything we had for... the funeral, for his silks, ashes now." He paused. "The Syrians asked everyone about you and learned you're my best. They'll take you in his place, and we all shall thank them."

"If I don't go..."

His father spat out in a hoarse voice, "They'll kill us."

"The Emperor's soldiers..."

His father laughed, a laugh cut off with a grimace of pain in an angry face. "The village soldiers can't kill a fawn. If a few Syrians die at our hands, the next month or year other Syrians will come here with many more soldiers."

Ashoka had not realized these things, not ever, these unreal things. "Our Emperor cannot let them do that."

Father shook his head and tightened his lips. "Did you not hear your brother?"

Ashoka did not know what that meant. "Our Emperor will let them do this to us?"

Father scoffed, coughed onto the back of his wrist, leaving specks of blood. "The Syrians are most-wealthy traders. They pay for the best soldiers, wield the finest swords, ride the swiftest horses." He stopped and coughed and waited, but Ashoka could tell that Father was not done. "One band of Syrians soldiers could slaughter everyone in this village in a day."

"But, our Emperor—"

Father again raised up a hand for Ashoka to stop. "I must talk to your guru when you are gone." He slapped his hand down on the cushion. "All rulers welcome the Syrians... and the things they bring, for the prices they pay. The Syrians have friends close to our Emperor and pay him great sums to have their way as traders in our land... He will let them do what they want with us—"

Father coughed again, and Ashoka kept quiet, regretting that he had made his father strain so much, that he had not learned better.

After a long silence, Father said, "So, it's done. If I'm not here... my brother will take care of this family until you come back to us."

Ashoka's last plea came softly, slowly. "Have you asked Mother?"

"That's not for you to know."

Father sat again, and his trembling hand pushed the knife closer to Ashoka. "Before you leave, I'll show you how to use it, on a man if you must."

Chapter V

Leaving

Ashoka's last hope ended with light rain in the morning. During a restless night, he had prayed for rain so heavy that the Syrians moved on before the Emperor's Road became too muddy, moved on without waiting for the last loads of cargo from his village. But he knew better. The monsoon often came in on bird feet, and heavier rains would stay away for a few days more.

He glanced back into the house, ran his fingertips down the family seal etched into the front door.

Father had left with his mahouts and laborers for the elephant camp without taking his last son, had no use for him there. Ashoka would have no final parting exchange with Red Eyes, but that was wise. Any parting had no purpose, only added more sadness.

Ashoka looked out in the direction of the camp and said into the misting air, "Oh God Ganesha, ruler of elephants, please protect them all, let Red Eyes stay healthy and strong, and, if it pleases you, let our father stay in this life a while longer." He thought, but could not say out loud, let him live until I come back home.

His mother and sisters were inside but quiet. Mother had spent the night on Govinda's old straw mat. Ashoka had heard her snore, and that was good. She and his sisters needed to gather strength.

Ashoka caught himself gently rubbing his left wrist, as if tracing a bracelet, though he did not wear one. Memories swirling below awareness made him do that. His guru taught to let past joys and sadness sleep. Waking them cannot help the present journey, but now those memories of the last brother-sister festival flooded in…

+ + +

Barely five years old, Sanju had made her first *Rakhi* strip for him. She tied it onto Ashoka's left wrist and chanted in her little girl voice. He knew the words by heart. "I tie you, the *rakhi* that was tied to King Bali, the king of demons. O *rakhi*, I pray that you never falter in protecting your devotee."

Her strip of red and silver beads on cotton threads was not elaborate, not like those made by older girls or the daughters of wealthy families, but she had made it for him alone. He never took it off, traced it around and around just as he had done now, and admired it every day. In time its threads frayed, and then one day it was gone. He looked everywhere and finally realized he must have lost it in the river while washing Red Eyes. That evening after he told her, Sanju thought for a moment, looked up at him, patted that empty wrist, and said so only he could hear, "Next year, I make you another, better, stronger, so you never lose it." Her little hand snugged his empty wrist, her little fingers wrapping half way around, and she smiled. He would take better care of her *rakhi* after this coming festival—

At that last festival, his next older sister, Madhu the quiet one, placed the Tilak mark on his and Govinda's foreheads. His oldest sister, Paavai—meaning beautiful girl—presented the brothers a hand painted plate filled with sweets of many kinds and shapes. Unlike earlier years when his family had more money, this last year the sisters had painted the plate themselves. But it was the finest of any. A medallion of flowers in gold and hues of red held the middle and was ringed by repeating patterns of little elephants, tigers and snakes.

Govinda selected the first treat from that plate, then Ashoka, and then the brothers took turns until the plate was empty. When done, the brothers promised their sisters they would stay by them, protect them so long as they were part of this house. Their parents looked on not needing to say a word, joy and pride on their faces.

Rashka Bandhan, when all of India celebrated the bond of protection between brothers and sisters, and he would be gone at the next one. He breathed in deeply and held it, thinking, hoping that this house, his sisters, this village would stay inside him until he might find his way back to them.

Barefoot, he stepped out to feel the red dirt, to feel the dirt's pleasure in drinking new rain. After the throngs around Govinda's dying and burial, the village seemed empty. Dogs and pea fowl had found places out of the rain and made no sounds. Ashoka knew that most village men were in the fields shaping the ground to make the new water flow where it should, preparing trails and work camps for many days of rain. Women and children stayed inside most houses—sewing garments and blankets, checking walls and straw roofs for bad leaks, preparing the evening meals. Children of the upper classes would be gathered in lessons from their guru.

Again he found himself in the wealthy section, even more quiet there, and near the estate of Uncle Vasavedu. On that evening after Govinda's pyre, Father had said, *My brother will take care...* Uncle Vasavedu did have the duty to take in his mother and sisters when Father passed to his next life. That was the way with families, but...

From when Ashoka was little, the two families visited on feast days, four or five times a year. Uncle's house, that some said was the grandest in the village, sat behind a wall far back up a winding path bordered by trimmed bushes and trees. Its two stories had indoor drains and water basins upstairs that servants kept filled. Uncle let the older children play outside on the grassy areas leading to the stables but never let them near his animals. Most men of wealth enjoyed showing off their fine horses and cows, their roosters and pigs, let children ride, but not this uncle.

Uncle's festival food was plentiful and elaborate, but no one laughed or sang in that house. On most visits, Uncle's wife, Aunt Durga, joined the servant girl watching the youngest children. Sometimes Aunt Durga wept quietly, though the young children gave her no cause to weep. Ashoka pretended he did not notice, but he had noticed her crying and other things about the big house, the land around it, its horses and dogs, and the people who tended the estate.

Now soaking everything up one last time, Ashoka remembered more about Uncle Vasavedu, his many servants, more than he needed for his eight children and to keep the main house running well. His house servants were all women, young ones. From visit to visit some were gone, and new ones quietly hushed down the halls and through the rooms, to be replaced by the next time Ashoka's family came. Aunt Durga, wearing a proper veil and attended by a male servant, often ventured out of that estate to shop for food, garment materials, bedding and furniture. Sometimes she asked Ashoka's mother to go with her, and Mother never refused. At other times, no one saw Aunt Durga for many months.

Perhaps uncle would let them stay in their own small house, send the sisters off with good dowries, and help find worthy mahouts to run the elephant camp. Ashoka shook his head in helplessness and disbelief at his own foolish longings. *Lord Ganesha, please protect them from him...*

Along the village main street ending at the largest gate in the village wall, most shops were shuttered. The shops would open later and through the evening when the village filled again. For a few moments this empty street took away his sadness and fatigue, brought up a tinge of excitement. In dry weather on some mornings before most shops opened and the day's work started, boys of all ages raced here.

Ashoka did not remember when first he outran everyone his age. Like his way with elephants, one day he just did. In recent times, no older boys challenged him for fear they would lose face when Ashoka outran them. Younger ones, whose honor would remain safe if they lost, still ran against him but never won.

Shop owners and their first patrons of the day watched and clapped. Beggars cheered too. Men and boys of the upper castes yelled at the beggars to get out of the way, even though they could easily see over the stooped and broken bodies. That never seemed right to Ashoka. The beggars did them no harm.

Ashoka often caught one cheering voice through all other cheers and shouts. It came from a tanner's daughter. She, the youngest in her family, lived with her mother and father behind the tanner's shop. Across the seasons and years, Ashoka had glimpsed her, caught her looking at him from when they were both smaller and into this past dry season. She had grown into a young woman, likely soon to be sent off in marriage. Ashoka had never entered that shop, had not much noticed either the father or the mother. The upper castes never set foot inside that shop. They bargained for the leather goods at one of the markets.

Ashoka paused at the tanner shop's shuttered front doors. No singing, no noise of any kind, reached him. That was good, good that he would be far gone from her, from her making him notice her. She, who must tend to foul dead animals and one step above the untouchables, had no right to even look at Ashoka much less cheer for him. She was rude, and her parents should have taught her better, taught her to not disturb boys of the Warrior Class. Her father was gone to his next life, but mother and daughter kept their shop going. Her rude boldness could bring her great shame—and for an instant Ashoka was sad for her.

He made his way to the main gate and its two guards. He wanted to say something to thank them for keeping their village safe from bandits and predators but kept quiet and turned back. His guru taught attachments were for the weak.

The smell of spices wafted at him again from many dishes cooking over indoor ovens. He made himself feel the hot vapors coming off their pots, see them, taste them—turmeric, cinnamon, paprika, flowering spinach, peppers of many kinds— and tears came. He had not cried on the night Govinda died, not when the pyre took him or when their father explained what Ashoka must do, but now, shuffling along the nearly empty wet streets of Lalput, he had to scrunch his eyes shut. *All living things leave us. Crying at their leaving will do no good, will not help, will not change what I cannot change.* Ashoka swallowed hard, then once more, and the tears stopped.

+ + +

The next morning while the sky was still dark, Ashoka, his family and many villagers gathered in the open area outside the main gate. Syrian soldiers finished loading three village wagons. Ashoka watched them pile on rugs and cotton mats then sacks of rice and cassia. They placed glass jars filled with perfumes and spices in corners of the soft cloth. When done, the cargo sat so high the wagons looked like they might topple over. Ashoka thought he must be the only human cargo in the little caravan. The headman of the Syrians pointed at Ashoka to mount one mule harnessed to a cart.

Ashoka spotted Uncle Vasavedu standing out past his family with two men unknown to Ashoka. When his family came near to these three, they did not interact.

The moment before Ashoka mounted the mule, his father stepped forward and grabbed his shoulders. "The strength inside. You have it. Listen to it and to our gods. Honor our gods, and they will keep you in their sheltering hands, and, if they are kind, bring you to us once more."

His mother, Madhu, Paavai, and Sanju moved a bit closer but not close enough to touch. His sisters and mother tried to put joy on their faces, to send him off with good thoughts about his journey, but no joy came. Their faces twisted like they wanted to cry.

His family headed away through the misting rain to the only house Ashoka had ever known. Only Sanju looked back at him and waved her little hand.

Chapter VI

New Rules

Near day's end, they found the main Syrian caravan. The wheels of these carts were as tall as Ashoka, and each cart was longer, bigger than the three carts from Ashoka's village all together. More men, bullocks, and horses than he had ever seen in one place crowded inside circles of carts and around campfires. The men spoke in strange tongues. The same odor of cooked meats as from that Syrian trader covered the camp.

One of the soldiers who brought Ashoka motioned for him to follow. As they passed clusters of men, the men stopped eating. They studied Ashoka, some out of green or gray eyes, a color he had never seen. Laughter followed him. The soldier shoved him to a big tent and campfire surrounded by familiar looking men. These men were older than he but of his region.

The soldier said something he did not understand and left.

An older man with long white hair pointed for Ashoka to drop his bundle in a small cleared space on the floor of the group tent. The white-haired man said, "He says, obey all rules of the *sarthavaha*, our captain," and then, "I'm the cook for your cart. If you want something, ask me. Don't talk to other men unless they talk to you first."

All the next day, Ashoka and the others from his tent walked beside their cart. He had never seen oxen as big and strong. The wheels turned easily on the raised Emperor's Road.

Their cart's place, fourth from the last in a line of twenty-eight, made him wonder about more valuable cargo up ahead.

Only the tall slaves had darker skin than Ashoka or his countrymen. One slave who seemed to be assigned to Ashoka's cart stood taller than the others, taller than anyone in the caravan. The slave helped fold their tent and hoist it onto their cart, covered waste holes out away from where they had set up for the night, and brought around a big jug of water during the trek. He had a calm face but active eyes. At their first eye-to-eye connection, the tall black man smiled and nodded at Ashoka as if greeting him, then glanced at Ashoka often on that first day.

The slaves shouted strange words to each other from cart to cart. But Ashoka's cart's slave watched everything silently. After their work the slaves huddled around their own campfire, chanting to the sounds of distant thunder they pounded out on hand drums.

Scars from diseases and fights marked the skin of most caravan men, and many had no front teeth. At night some men played games with bones or dice, laughing as they played, as they ate. Ashoka sat back from the circle of his camp. He watched the cook, the roaming soldiers and their long swords.

He tried to make himself small but could not hide, could not disappear. Father said the Syrians would keep him unharmed, unmarked, to sell for a high price. He thought to run away, to become a beggar in a strange village until he grew into full manhood. He could not return to his village and to Father. Better stay—for a few days more.

The second night at the group meal, their cook said, "Ashoka, I'm told you're the youngest freeman in our caravan—seventeen years old, I'm told?"

Ashoka shrugged as if saying, "Sure". Father had told him to lie. The Syrians must believe he and Govinda were close in age.

The cook said, "I'm Madan. I know your village. I know of your family. Your family has trained elephants since the time of Alexander."

The cart mates nodded and grunted. Elephant trainers held the warrior class, and caste said much about a stranger. No others from his region looked as if they were mahouts or soldiers, and Ashoka wondered about them, their families, what the Syrians planned for them. His dread of unknown men, what they might do, eased a little.

Still, he fought sleep until after the last Syrian soldiers bedded down, and only the sentries peering out into the darkness remained awake. If a Syrian came at him with a sword or spear, his cart mates could not protect him. Their captain took away the weapons of all his passengers. No one had asked Ashoka for weapons, and he guessed no one expected him to carry a knife on his thigh under his loose-fitting *dhoti*. He tried to keep one hand on his *kukri* as he fell asleep. On that and every night, he prayed to Ganesha, slayer of evils and guardian of new journeys, *help me stay alive to see clouds and rain again after the sun wakes.*

Deep in the night Ashoka heard women talking in his language, quietly as if in mourning. He thought the dream would end if he blinked hard. No dream, the voices—sad and low—came from a tent or a cart near his. He rolled over onto his stomach and slid to the side of the tent until he could stare under the flap edge but saw nothing. That and the next night, he heard the soft footfalls and small steps of women along with grunts and crunching of heavy soldier feet. He wished they were only going to one of the waste holes, that the women might be precious cargo for trade and not for the Syrians' use. He saw no sign of any women in daylight, but those sounds in the night told him about the foot soldiers and riders always with the last cart, far more protection given to that cart than to any other.

+ + +

As the days fell away, the land changed. The mature shade trees lining the road ended. They left behind rest turnouts with their roof-covered shelters beside man-made ponds stocked with fish and fresh water for the travelers and their animals. Dense jungle growth now mixed with wheat grass, nut trees, shorter hardier bushes, and many palms. The rains lightened. Small wagons and groups of traders no longer met them throughout the day to sell spices and food from villages near the road. Most other travelers on the main road headed into the Indian empire, not out.

One mid-morning at a long curve in the road, the caravan ground to halt, its entire length bathed in bright sunlight. Everyone looked to the front, to the Syrian captain, garbed in black carrying a sword, wooden bow, and leather quiver filled with arrows, riding slowly down the curved caravan line past Ashoka's cart to the end and back to the front. He repeated that ride. On each of the two passes, he shouted an angry jumble of three languages.

Ashoka understood some of the Greek and his own language, enough to make out the sense of the enraged sermon. "Girl crawled... out of tent in the night... snuck back to village. Now... I must post many sentries around the women... need them looking for wild tribes... out here and later... not for stupid women in caravan wanting leave... bargain, a bargain," the Syrian bellowed from behind the last cart. "Obey me and become rich. Disobey, you die."

Two foot soldiers jumped onto the back of the last cart, raised the wooden bar which locked the rear gate and swung the gate open. Heavy cloth covered the last cart's latticed sides. No one could see its cargo from the road. The soldiers pulled out a young woman. Quiet fell along the length of the caravan. Even the horses and bullocks stopped their snorting and stomping, and the whole caravan waited, staring at the hunched form, head down standing small in the bright sun. Ashoka eased closer to that cart.

She broke the silence. "I will obey. I'll obey..." she cried over and over, louder each time, in the dialect of Ashoka's region, then stood straight but with head down.

Taller than most men near him, he saw her well. A rope bound her hands behind, pulling tight the top of the white garment pressed against young breasts. She was as alluring as Ashoka had ever seen, fairer than his grown and recently married sisters, than even Paavai.

Something more than the Syrian's rage and her desperate beauty grabbed him—her face, the voice, her stature. That could not be. He had never been around strange girls that way, never close enough to know their wailing sounds, to study their faces, to care how they cowed, how they begged—except this one. But she could not be that one. No Syrian would have traded for her of no value. She must be another one, or his mind played tricks in its yearning for home. He shoved those thoughts away.

The Syrian yelled commands Ashoka did not understand and laughed a cackling laugh. The soldiers brought out another woman, gray-haired, stumbling from the cart, hunched over with age, head down.

"The female dog's mother. Hid the young bitch. We pay gold. Ours now." Ashoka caught the cause of the peculiar laugh. The Syrian did not look as old as he sounded, but through missing front teeth he laughed like an old man.

The captain maneuvered his mount so the sun stood high behind him, and his shadow played across the two women. He stared down at mother and daughter. "Look at me!" He pointed to his eyes.

The two women straightened up and squinted at the furious Syrian and the sun above him.

From behind the women, a guard drew his sword and in one slicing stroke—so quick that neither woman flinched—drove the blade edge through the neck of the mother, sending the head tumbling onto the road stones and sand.

Those close by gasped. Screams came from the women's cart. Murmurs ran the length of the caravan. Unchained bullocks trailing at the end of the caravan behind the women's cart backed up.

Ashoka looked away from the mother's body slumped on the road. As the daughter collapsed partly on top of the older woman, her black hair brushing against the headless neck, he dropped his hand to feel the dagger resting on his thigh, felt its uselessness.

Laborers dragged the daughter back into her cart and tossed the body into dense brush by the side of the road.

They picked up the head by the hair, drove it onto a tent stake and, with vines, tied the stake upright to the rear corner of the last cart. They turned the dead face to the front, so all who looked homeward might see the open eyes, white, rolled up into the forehead, and smother any urge to flee.

The Syrian reared his steed, cantered to the middle of the caravan curve, and signaled for a soldier to sound the conch shell used to rouse them every day before dawn. He shouted in three different languages, "Move, move, hurry."

For two days the old woman's head stared forward from atop the last cart, where Ashoka could see it easily. Flesh-eating birds circled but, as if sensing the accuracy of the archers, never swooped down to tear at the dead face. In time the vines could not keep the head from toppling onto the road where the trailing bullocks trampled it.

The head of the old woman made Ashoka forgive. His father had no choice but to sell the last son, send him away before they could make the trek to the Great River and scatter Govinda's ashes on the holy water. A bargain with these Syrians had to be honored. Ashoka added Father to his nightly prayer, a prayer to see him again and tell him.

Chapter VII

Where Caste Means Nothing

Three nights after the beheading, an older Indian of their caravan, Purna, asked Madan, "Eight days to cross the desert and we'll be rich?"

"You'll get a few brass coins if you live long enough, serve your new masters long enough. The sponsors of this caravan get rich."

It was a quiet night except for the shuffling, snuffling of oxen and horses, the low grumbling of men. No laughter came from around other campfires on this night.

Purna said, "If we get there?"

Madan said, "We'll get there. Our captain's the best caravan driver I've known."

Purna said, "He takes the head of the old mother in front of her daughter and laughs."

"He's Syrian, wields Syrian justice. But the same slaves and soldiers have been with him for many caravans."

Madan raised his index finger. "Under other masters, slaves live no longer than horse flies. The tall Numidian with no tongue has been with him from the first caravan many years back."

"What Numidian with no tongue?" three cart mates asked.

Madan shook his head. "The tallest one who brings our food I turn into a feast for you swine, the one who does all things you're too high caste to do for yourself. He hears and smells and sees better than any of you. Who among you even knows his name?"

Ashoka had noticed other slaves look up to their cart's slave and not only because he was tall. They asked him things he answered with his hands and head and eyes. They called him a name that sounded like Nu.

One of them said, "And no tongue? He told you about that?" The cart mates stifled laughter.

Madan scowled at each man circled round him. "Never ever laugh at Nuur. Never disrespect him. Watch how the horses and bullocks make way for him, how the soldiers leave him alone. His first master took his tongue for telling the truth, but his powers grew stronger, stronger than all the soldiers with all their swords. He and the captain will get us through the Great Desert. But... it will be the hardest thing you've done."

The listeners were shamed, and they drifted to their sleeping places without saying more, Ashoka too. His guru had taught about the Great Indian Desert. They called it the *Thar*, a word related to *thul*, ridges of sand.

For days his cart rolled in a cloud of dust, flies, and the increasing stench of bullocks, horses and men. Daily washing ended. At every rain shower the soldiers unfolded large cloths to collect and funnel water into earthen jars carried by every cart. That water was for drinking only, animals before men. After a rain Madan filled his own jar and made hot meals with rice or barley.

On a night when Madan cooked alone and no other soldiers cared to watch or talk to him, Ashoka approached. He stood still, looking at the large pot.

Madan said, "You want something?"

Ashoka wanted to ask many questions but said only, "Master Madan, will we need the gods' protection from here on?"

"Yes, always."

"The wild tribes?"

"We're beyond them and too strong. The cargo they can see us carrying is not worth losing any horses or men. The wild tribes fear the Syrians too."

As if in a new thought, Madan turned to Ashoka and said slowly, deliberately, "Young Ashoka, worry about our captain and his rules. Let him and the gods worry about things you cannot control. If you disobey our captain..." Madan ran his thumbnail across his throat, "Then tomorrow or the next day, like the old woman... from your village, the mother of our most precious cargo."

From your village flashed at Ashoka. He pretended ignorance. "The old woman from my village?"

"Don't say you did not know."

Images crowded in—cheers and that cry in the same voice. He was forbidden to let them in. The harder he tried to block them, the more they came, the clearer they came. "I haven't seen anyone from Lalput."

"Ashoka, my friend, at home you'd never notice a *sudra*. The young one, named Radha, came out of Lalput, on a cart two days before yours, buried in the blankets."

"I wouldn't know... her."

"They took her to her tent after the men slept and hid her with the other women. She has a fire spirit. That very first night, alone she ran back to your village and her mother. Not many could do that. You could not, Ashoka."

Madan raised a spoon at Ashoka as if asking him.

Ashoka had thought about fleeing back to his village—but didn't have the girl's courage. "My father told me about the Syrians. Must all be true, what he said."

"Yes, the Syrians are too strong for anyone in their way. They sent soldiers back to find the young one. Her mother

48

tried to hide her. They brought them both back. Clever, yes?" Ashoka nodded. The daughter would not flee again with her mother in the cart beside her. "They waited until we reached that place on the Emperor's Road where everyone could see the lesson and learn. They waited to kill the mother until we were too far away for the daughter to run off again."

Now at last, far from his village, he dared to let in more memories. Many times he had looked over at the daughter and wondered how someone of such a low caste could be so fair. Here and there she had looked back at him and, caught by her, he had looked away. Sometimes when he looked into her shop and rested his gaze on her, she started humming, then sang with the joy of a young life—in the same voice as on the road. The husband had been a leather worker, and often they worked side by side. When the father died, the mother took his place—but must have struggled if she had to sell her last child. Now the bones of that mother lay scattered far behind them. "Where's she going?" spilled out of him, and he realized he cared—about that dead father and mother, and now about the girl—that he felt a new sadness for them all.

"Who knows?"

"No one will want her." Ashoka knew he had lied, said what he wished, and what he wished could never be. From a hundred stories, he knew strangers in other lands would wash her long hair, scrub the dust and grime off her young body, rub her with scented oils, knew that a thousand men would not care about her caste and bid a high price to own her.

Madan shook his head, looked directly at Ashoka. "You, young Ashoka, know this. She can't help you drive elephants, can't help you live, and return to your village. Think only about elephants you must train for battle. You won't last three nights away from this caravan if your thoughts rest on her."

"I will not train elephants for war."

Of the more than one hundred words and expressions for elephants, Ashoka used his favorite—he who drinks twice. It came from sucking water into the trunk and then squirting it down the throat.

Madan stomped a sandaled foot on the ground hard enough to startle Ashoka. "Ashoka, you'll do as you're told. Generals in Greece and Carthage will bid a high price for one mahout to sit on the neck of a fighting elephant and drive it to trample soldiers and scatter horse riders. You are the lucky one. No one else in this whole caravan can drive an elephant."

Ashoka felt the blood rise into his face. Madan was right. The tanner's daughter made him crazy and disrespectful of this wise elder. The girl made him forget his—his promise to Govinda.

He looked away. "Forgive me."

"The finest mahouts are more precious than a hundred soldiers, more than a general. Be one of them and live."

Ashoka closed his eyes and listened to the scraping sounds made by Madan's big spoon. Ashoka moved closer to the fire under the pot of now steaming rice, cane sugar, wild honey, and peppers. He let the heat push away thoughts of her. After a time, he said, "I pray the elephants in far places will do what I ask."

Madan looked directly at him and grinned. "That will be up to you and them, won't it?"

Ashoka didn't know how to react, didn't want to say he always found a way for elephants to listen to him, to do what he asked them. He managed, "How can they at the market tell I am worthy?"

"Oh, they have ways. Patience, young mahout."

"I will pray for more patience, for an obedient elephant and..."

Madan interrupted his thoughts. "When I was young, younger than you, my family had nothing for me. They too sent me away. We Indians serve wealthy masters in all the great cities west of here." He tapped his head. "We learn well and quickly and know how to obey, how to fade away until needed, and, most of all, how to help each other. I followed all orders and kept quiet—and lived. My last masters had many children and a big house. But when all their children left, they didn't need a cook and released me. This caravan, cooking for my countrymen, pleases me. Remember what I've said, take these words, hold them until they are part of you. They are my gift to you."

"I'll try, Master Madan. And I thank you for them."

"Ashoka, for your age, whatever it is, you have some wisdom. Leave me now."

Ashoka backed away. Something new stirred in him. Another outcast from his country lived to old age and freedom. Another from his village, low caste though she was, traveled with this caravan.

Chapter VIII

Secrets of the Desert

For days no cloud sheltered them. The trail descended into warmer air until they hit soft sand. The hot sand raised blisters on bare feet. They had entered the Great Indian Desert.

At night the slaves built no campfires. They had no water for cooking and did not need the warmth. They ate dried fruit. The lookouts with the keenest eyes no longer searched for strangers. They rode out to scout for clumps of bushes, wild grasses or lines of trees that might mark an oasis. In some places stubby grass grew in the sand. There, water might soak the sand not far under the hot surface.

On the third day in sand hills, the caravan arrived at the last wells. White flags on the tops of tall bamboo poles in a grove of palm trees marked the last water until the other side of the desert. All the men helped fill every water jar and let the animals drink until they stopped. Then the men made them drink more.

The caravan left the last oasis in the light of a new moon and from then on traveled only at night. From that day the soldiers guarded the water jars and brought around all water for animals and men. A rumor spread that some of the perfume merchants in one of the front carts offered sticks of precious spices for extra water but were rebuked and one beaten for his attempted bribe.

In the middle of the sixth day in the desert when the sun stood nearly overhead, only the carts and open tents provided shade. No water ration had come around since the start of their last night's trek. The scouts would not search for water until near sunset. The caravan could not move until they found water. A number of bullocks lay still, dropped where they stopped in the middle of the night. Vultures circled in the bright blue sky.

Madan, seated on the shady side against a cart wheel, said for anyone who cared, "The gods still favor us. There's no wind, and the sky has been high. The scouts can see far. They'll soon find the next oasis."

Purna, in the hot shade under the cart said, "The scouts take water for themselves and their horses. They'll ride off and leave us. Old man, your caravan captain is no better than any other. And he surely takes the most water for himself. In the next life, I'll find him and tie him up for vultures to feed on him—as they will soon on us."

No one responded to Purna, though they all lay close by in the shade of or under the caravan.

It hurt to blink. Ashoka's swollen tongue made it hard to swallow. He did not perspire. His remaining saliva tasted bitter, and his head hurt. If the animals gave up, the men and women would have to make their way on foot carrying what they could. He thought they might walk through one night but not survive the next day. He had not slept in two days and nights.

Promises not kept—to Govinda, his father—and the end of his family's proud line of elephant men kept him from closing his eyes, closing them for perhaps the last time. Were the women in the last caravan still alive? Did they get extra water, or none? Did the girl's mother begin her new life in a better place—or as a bird's egg in a nest built by Govinda? These thoughts did not help. His face, his head hurt too much.

+ + +

In the evening's lengthening shadows and hot orange light, a warm breeze stirred some men to stand up, to take a few slow steps before retreating to any shade they could find. Not able to avoid the sun and hot dirt, rocks and sand, more animals had lain down. But the scouts and their horses strode around the caravan camp. Purna might have spoken the truth. The scouts and their horses must have taken more water than anyone.

A fluffing of sandals approached. Nuur poured water out of an animal skin into the same cup for each of Ashoka's cart mates, one by one taking their turn at the one cup. After Nuur finished pouring, he moved his big hands with long fingers low over the sand. He pointed at the animal skin holding the water, then at the sand. And he left.

Most of the others looked annoyed. But Ashoka thought that Nuur told them water lay not far under this hollow place in the big hills of sand. He said to himself, *live one more night and day. Nuur hears and smells things others don't.*

+ + +

The scouts found no water that evening or the next morning. Some of the horses which stood still all day under canopies on tent poles now slumped down. Healthy horses slept standing. A rumor spread that a number of older paying travelers died in the night. In the strongest heat of the afternoon, Ashoka could no longer fight the urge to sleep.

Shouting of men and bellowing of animals brought him back. "The wind... the desert wind... cover up, fast," yelled many.

Slaves and soldiers tossed large cloths out of every cart. The tents came down. Some of the oxen which had seemed dead stood up, turned to face north away from the wisp of wind and from the midday sun.

A dark cloud rose from the land and covered the sun. The cloud stretched across the southern sky from one end of the land to the other. The cloud billowed higher and higher, closer.

A blast of sand and darkness hit before they were all in the best places. Every part of exposed skin took the sting of hot sand blowing. Ashoka shut his eyes, held his hands over his nose and mouth, and curled into a ball. He glanced back into the wind only one time, the stinging sand too painful. He glimpsed the sun—like a faint rosy moon in the black sky.

Men and animals crowded together ever tighter. Strong men pushed down from both sides of Ashoka. The crush of other bodies comforted. They were alive.

After a long time of black heat, wind noise so loud it blocked out thoughts, a clean evening sky returned. The big wind left as quickly as it had come. The men on either side of Ashoka rolled away, stood, and shook off sand. Ashoka did the same slowly, little strength left in him.

From somewhere behind came a cry he did not understand, then more, then, "Grass, grass! We have grass."

Ashoka trudged fast in the new sand around the cart and to the other side. A hill of sand covered the south side of his cart, but from the base of that new hill in front of him, a flat expanse of scraggly grass tufts still green stretched as far as he could see through his dry eyes. Instantly he understood the wind had blown off the sand that had covered the scrub grass.

Far away at a low place in the flat area under another sand hill, a tall black man dug, faster, stronger than when digging any waste hole. Many trudged toward him. The horses and bullocks had already turned to face the laboring man. Some of them scraped at the low spots in the sand with their front hoofs—as if they knew, had seen this digging in a desert before, as if they wanted to help.

A wordless scream like out of a giant bird arose down there. Nuur held his shovel high above his head and pointed into the hole he had dug.

Others shouted and grabbed shovels, ran down to the low point and began digging near him. The Syrian captain led many to look into Nuur's hole and into holes dug by the others. Each hole filled quickly with the muck of sandy water.

The caravan remained in the hollow five more days. Every able man squeezed water out of sandy muck wrapped in cloths, drank some and let the rest run into jugs. At the end of each day some of the water holes dried out but filled with water during the night. They squeezed out enough water to top every jar after all men and animals drank enough.

When the caravan pulled out of the hollow, it left behind the carcasses of seven bullocks and four horses but not one human.

In less than three full days they reached a strong stream that soon reached a larger river.

+ + +

The mighty River *Sindhu* flowed south in shades of silver under a gray sky. Ashoka's guru had taught about melting snows from India's highest mountains feeding this river at the western gateway of India year round. Ashoka knew they were headed ever westward, soon to places conquered by Alexander, ruled by generals he left behind and now governed by fierce tribes too independent to stay under his rule or ever unite with each other.

He wanted to strip and dive in, swim while barges carried the carts, horses and bullocks across. But that would be reckless, too like a child. No one else in the caravan was so foolish, and the wide river flowed too fast.

He had to think of elephants, not of a river swim. He had to find them, follow them. Elephants were the only thing that mattered, the only way home.

Father made his sons swim in the river upstream from the family elephant camp. He said, *Elephants take to water like fish with legs. They swim stronger than the tiger. They smell the land on the far shore and will swim to it even where men cannot see it. If you let them play in water every day, if you wash their hide, they'll do what you ask for all time. You can't serve them if you can't swim.*

Great-grandfather picked the land by that river for the family elephant camp. He paid the land owner three tuskers and seven females for the right to use the land as the elephant camp—but only as long as male offspring ran it.

There, Ashoka cleaned Red Eyes every day, twice on hot days of hard labor. But now, his journey barely begun, Ashoka knew if he did not soon return home with gold in his bundle, the family elephant camp would end. Women were not allowed to run it, and Vasavedu never spent any time with elephants. He feared them, and they smelled his fear.

On the morning of the forty-second day after crossing the *Sindhu*, the advance riders shouted when they returned. The caravan's beasts at the front plodded faster, and the whole caravan sped up. The caravan reached the heights above the first town since the *Sindhu* valley. The town sat in an open plain amidst green fields and straight lines of trees planted by man. A white wall protected the town and all its inhabitants.

They camped at the low point outside the wall so that their odors and waste would not foul the air or water of the village or the stream winding through it.

Every campfire group whistled and laughed. Caravan men slapped the town wall with open hands and yelled at whoever might hear them on the other side. The caravan's armed riders chased them back away from the wall.

After a quickly devoured meal, Madan said to his cart mates, "Listen now to our captain's orders for this encampment."

Some grumbled, "When can we go in?"

"Not tonight."

Purna said, "Why not? We'll scale the walls and teach them Indian hospitality. No town in our country makes us wait outside after a long journey—like beggars."

Madan said, "You'll wait. If you look at them twice—or their women—they'll cut you down. Alexander's men built the wall and inner city. They deserve your respect."

"We drove him out. Show me his grave, and I'll piss on it."

"Quiet. Stupidity comes out of your mouth."

The others hissed, but Madan pressed on more loudly, deeply. "None of us will touch the women here—unless you marry them first."

Everyone laughed, even Ashoka.

Purna said, "Now you're the stupid one, old man."

Ashoka knew the same urges, the same freedom. No mother or sister would report what he might do here.

But he felt relief when Madan said, "Ever you stand victorious over unarmed women, pray you keep your honor by honoring theirs."

"What do you say, Old Man? Alexander showed no mercy."

"He allowed none of his men to touch any local woman until marriage in this and all other towns that bear his name."

Purna said, "This town's Exandahar, Old Man."

"You know nothing. The locals can't pronounce his name, Alexander, and call this place Exandahar."

That quieted them. Perhaps Madan was right again.

"Tomorrow, in groups of five or less, you may visit the village. If you don't obey, you'll stay outside the walls."

Madan turned to Ashoka. "You must stay near me or Nuur. Can you ride a horse?"

"Yes, but not like I ride elephants."

"Nuur will teach you how to ride like a Numidian."

Later in the night, a cold breeze from the north swirled over the village, over its walls, and through their camp. Out in the open under a high starry sky, Ashoka thought he caught familiar odors from cooking pots. After those faded away, not sure whether out of dreams or awake, he caught the smell of elephants.

Chapter IX

Four Nails

Someone shook him awake before the sun climbed over the mountains. "Get up. You ride with Nuur today. They'll meet you by the wide stream closer to the mountain." Madan's look invited no questions, though Ashoka had many.

The townspeople watched them from the top of their village wall. They laughed and pointed at the pair riding one horse. Ashoka sat behind Nuur, like a child hanging onto an adult. Young boys with blue eyes and hair the color of dry grass ran to Nuur's mount. They touched the black skin of his legs and scrambled away talking fast and giggling. Ashoka tried to pick out their words but could not. Stray dogs barked at them but did not come close.

On the far side of the village, lay fields of grain, groves of fruit trees and a line of wells. Beyond them a trail led around the shoulder of a rocky hill to dense stands of acacia and pine trees and the sounds of rushing water. Ashoka felt its presence now stronger than the night before, and then he saw it—a male Indian elephant.

It ate the wild grasses not far from its heavy fenced *kedah*. Its hide was healthy, neither too loose nor tight. Its tusks, thick and shiny white, had grown out more than an arm's length. Its massive thick head, slightly oversized compared to its body, told him this male was not fully grown. Yet he had never seen a bigger bull, even an adult bull. Soon this one might be a giant among giants. Its front feet were tied by thick ropes, so it could not run or even take one normal stride. The bull ripped the grass and low bushes out of the ground with its trunk and stuffed its mouth. When chewing, it held its head high like the animals most desired for processions.

Their Syrian *sarthavaha* with four of his soldiers stood at the edge of the field next to the enclosure. Five others stood in another cluster several paces away from the first. Ashoka did not recognize this second group. Ten horses were tied to trees beyond.

The captain yelled as Nuur and Ashoka jumped off and tied their horse to the top pen rail. "I ask Nuur bring you. These men don't know with that beast. You can help them, yes?"

They all waited. From their looks, Ashoka realized they understood the language, Ashoka's language, spoken by the captain. Nothing came to him to say, too much to take in, to figure out. Help to do what? Would they leave him in this village with this young bull? Until the bull was grown and then sold? Until the bull was trained and for what?

The captain did not wait. "He come as calf with mother, drop out of cow on your Emperor's Road many years back. Mad, they say." Pointing to where the elephant ate, "You see, yes? Mad, mad beast, yes?"

Sensible words did not want to come. Ashoka looked at Nuur and got no sign. He had to answer. "Yes, Master Captain, I can see him. But he does not seem mad."

The Syrian grunted. "They say beast is mad."

The locals' open mouths and frowns, their slouching stances, their refusal to in any way greet Nuur or Ashoka said everything. They thought him a dark, smooth-skinned boy from the warm lowland. Predators pick out and stalk the young first. And these men sensed his true age, barely fourteen. The men would have laughed and shooed him away or killed him if the Syrian captain, his soldiers, and the giant Nuur did not protect him.

Now and again the bull's alert eyes looked over at the gathered men. Its large ears turned to them. Its raised trunk sniffed for scents of hostility and fear or of kindness and confidence.

Ashoka's questions piled in. Had this elephant ever been guided by a tame mother, or only by men who did not know elephants? Why did they think this elephant was mad? He blurted out a safe question. "Where is the mother?"

A local responded in Ashoka's language, with a strong accent and Greek words stitched in, but Ashoka understood. "She can't help you, Indian boy, unless you talk to the dead. Can you Indian boys do that?"

"How many days may I have to help with this one?" Ashoka pointed to the bull, tried to study him closer and still saw no signs of madness.

The captain said, "You not need many, tomorrow, next day enough."

Ashoka bowed. "To train him or show you he is not mad, I will need many days."

The locals scoffed, and the scoffing rose to laughter mixed with mocking. The captain said loudly, over the laughter, "You come with when we leave. You have until when we leave show these people to kill that mad beast."

Ashoka felt struck as if by fire flashing from a big storm cloud or by a cobra like the one that flashed at Govinda. Nuur, their captain, the whole village wanted him to kill this wonderful animal. Nothing in all his time with elephants troubled him more than the few times Father organized the killing of an old sickly one. The animal trusted and obeyed humans for many years, but, now betrayed, it lay bleeding out from many deep cuts, crying and thrashing against ropes and posts.

Nuur looked off in a far direction, avoiding Ashoka's eyes. But all the others bored in on him, expected him to agree to help, to show them how, to lead them in the killing. He managed, "And when might that be, when might we leave, honorable *Sarthavaha*?"

"When my oxen, horses fat, carts fixed, barters done. Ten days, ten and five, no more."

Ashoka looked at the elephant for help so he might say the right thing, or say nothing but do the right thing. The big beast seemed to look right back at him and turned to the side moving its head as if inviting him to come over into the field, to come closer. That gave Ashoka the courage to say, "I need many months, perhaps two years, to train an elephant—or to take the madness out of him."

He looked away from the men. What he just said was so foolish, so impossible, so disrespectful. But he caught them gesturing that they agreed with him. It would take two years to change this animal's nature, take the madness out of him if he was mad. The only way open was to help these men kill this animal.

Not today though, not today. He had ten days, and maybe some more after that. One of his guru's many lessons seeped in. *A trek over far mountains begins as the walk down to the river in the morning—with a single step, and then the next. Take the first step and the next and do not trouble about the one after that until it is before you, until you must.* The next step, the next step, what should it be? He must take it today, right now. The day had much light left. "I must fetch my things."

The captain said, "Stay. Nuur brings and another horse. You sleep with the elephant or at my camp, as you wish."

"I'll sleep here."

63

Nuur mounted and rode away. Ashoka approached the elephant and counted out loud in a flat voice. When he got within twenty paces, the bull looked up and around, head high, trunk tip raised, flapped its ears, and then looked straight down at this newcomer.

Ashoka stopped for the animal to smell him, let it feel that he did not threaten, and to take in the power of this beast. After standing with ears flapping for a long time, the bull's breathing slowed. He lowered his head and gently swung the trunk from side to side and up both sides of his face—signs of play, no threat in them. Ashoka moved closer.

"I'm Ashoka. I've helped train many of your cousins."

He moved within touching distance, but on flexed legs. If the elephant lunged at him, it might snap the tethers on its front feet, knock him down, pin him with a knee and gore him. He spoke as he moved in, again spoke in his deepest voice, and it was indeed a bit deeper than the last time he spoke to Red Eyes. This animal shuddered and rumbled but did not back away. It let him touch its cheek under the left eye, pat back to the shoulders and over to the trunk.

Ashoka did not look at the two groups of men. But they must have followed behind him, close enough that Ashoka easily heard their grunts of surprise and approval.

Ashoka pushed and stroked and patted the hide. The animal blinked, raised and lowered and waved its trunk. Ashoka sidestepped the swipes of the trunk but kept his hand on the hide. The elephant stopped moving its head and trunk, stood still, and let out a low rumble of contentment. This bull had at one time accepted human touch. Ashoka thought he might in time control and train him—not kill him—but never in ten days, fifteen at most.

Without looking back, he said, "May I speak to this animal's *kavadahi*?" using the word for apprentice trainer.

One man stepped forward and yelled, "This mad animal is mine, but I'm no *kavadahi*, and you're no mahout." Then more quietly, "Not far back, I lived in India, teaching your soft boys how to fight, and they taught me all about your elephants. I keep peace for our council, peace in our town and with this beast. This mad beast must die. Yes?"

Ashoka kept his hand and eyes on the elephant. Its reaction to him gave him the courage to say, "You're right, Master. This one must die, when the gods will it."

Some grunted at his disrespect for the leader of this little band. Their leader spat. "You don't see, Indian boy, its feet tell us he's mad."

"I know about four nails."

"Everyone knows, Indian boy. If you will not kill him, go back now. Go back to the caravan and clean up the shit behind your oxen and horses. You're no use to us here."

The Syrian captain raised his hand to quiet the little man. "Master Vishpar, your council ask I bring a mahout help kill him, show you how kill him. You have my mahout until we go." He smiled. That smile of no front teeth did not signal friendship, but a dare to the local men to challenge him.

Vishpar responded, "The four nails. We must kill him before he kills our horses—kills us."

Ashoka knew the myth. Most Indian elephants have five nails on each forefoot. The myth said that only four nails signals madness. The adult with only four nails will gore its kind and stomp any man who comes close. *Father laughed at this. Elephants know what we think about them better than we do. They will react like a child reacts to parents who hate the child. If the mahout believes a long tail, or missing nails, or white eyes ruin the animal, it will feel the scorn and remember. When least expected, it will take revenge.*

Vishpar, thin, wrinkled, dirty brown hair dangling from under a turban, drew up near Ashoka. The bull backed away, grunted and stomped, but not freely in the tethers on its front feet.

Vishpar said, "Every night I need more men to drive him into the *kedah*. He used to go by himself like a horse. He eats too much. I have to make the *kedah* stronger. We have to move to places of new grass. No caravan coming through will take him back to your India. We have asked them all." Vishpar turned to the other men and the captain. "The council ordered I cut him up before he has to mate. When he has to mate, the madness will come out." The captain raised his hand and started to say something in response, but Vishpar cut him off. "I asked for a true mahout from the caravan, not a soft boy. I asked for a mahout to show us how to cut up this beast and let the poor of our town feast on its meat. We have all the ropes and long knives we need, if this boy will not show us a better way."

No one responded, but again they looked at Ashoka. He did not know a better way to kill an elephant. He managed, "What's its name?"

Vishpar shrugged. "Have you not listened, boy? Why should it have a name when it feeds our poor in days?"

Ashoka would not let go. The next step was a name. If it had a name, it might sooner follow commands and remember any training from long ago. "I need to know if it can respond to a name."

"Call it what you will." Vishpar shouted and waved his arms.

The bull moved back farther, and Ashoka understood this animal held no respect for the smelly leader of the locals. "Call it Four Nails. Four Nails, that's a good name for a mad elephant." He looked at the caravan captain as if he wanted him to agree. The captain smiled, signaled for his men to follow him to their horses, and they all left Ashoka alone with the locals.

Ashoka said, "Master Vishpar, after it obeys simple commands, I'll teach you how to teach it. Let me try, please. Let me try alone, I pray, Master Vishpar."

Vishpar turned back to his men. As he mounted up he yelled, "Help us kill him before your caravan leaves—or we will kill you both." And they rode off.

At sundown Ashoka and Nuur had little trouble getting Four Nails into his pen. They slept on the ground next to the *kedah* where Four Nails spent a quiet night with a real elephant man close by.

Chapter X

Running Free

In the morning as soon as Ashoka opened the gate, Four Nails ambled as fast as the tethers allowed down to a place where the mountain river quieted. Ashoka waded in beside him. He scrubbed the hide with rough stones. After a time, he could no longer bear the cold water and retreated to sunshine warming the little beach and a sheepskin coat Nuur brought. Four Nails followed him out of the water and listened to this new human, to the repeated words, but followed no command.

The trail from above ended at an area of sand, flat and soft enough to lie on and warm up in sunlight. The water lapped at the edge of the beach gently and formed a pond away from the river's main current. At the river's edge away from the beach, tall grasses, bull rushes, fir and acacia trees protected from winds sweeping the plateau above. On sunny mornings, this hollow below the mountain plateau warmed up quickly but made a fine place for an ambush.

On the second morning deep in the water, Four Nails allowed Ashoka to climb onto his neck and back. Ashoka started to gently rub the hide with two rough stones but stopped. There, on the only soft spot at the back of the skull, sat a gouged hole. The multiple ridges at its edge told Ashoka the wound had opened and healed again and again. Scar tissue jutted out in all directions from the wound in the middle, like a wheel's spokes without a rim. But it was not red, not yellow with fly worms or puss.

No elephant could do that to itself. No elephant will try to pull a man off once on its back or drop to its knees and roll over him, not even to stop the gouging jabs. Men made that wound, and Four Nails had not allowed any man to climb on its back for many days, for time enough that the wound healed and scarred over. Ashoka knew that Four Nails already trusted Ashoka more than he had any man in a long time.

Out of the water, Ashoka repeated the first commands—forward, stop, right, left. He signaled with hand motions, his own body position and voice inflections, taps with a switch on the front legs, hind legs, trunk, or chest. Nuur had brought apples, salted celery, and balls of millet soaked with honey. Ashoka held up treats after each command but did not give them up.

That second afternoon Four Nails obeyed a single voice command to stop. Ashoka clapped, placed an apple in the end of the trunk and patted the hide.

Vishpar and his band arrived at odd times, sometimes on foot, other times by horse. He carried a long pole with a three-pronged black metal spike at the end. He said, "You can use it if you want."

Ashoka said, "We must teach it to respect us and not our weapons."

"Indian boy, do you respect the tiger with no teeth and claws?"

"An elephant may fear the weapon but not respect the man who uses it."

Some days Vishpar and his followers did not come around at all.

When sure they were not near, Ashoka rode Four Nails through the tall grass, into the trees and up the rocky hill. He let Four Nails pick the trail, let him sense the best footing. The third time they made it to the top of the hill above the river as the sun slipped behind distant mountains. An urge from deep inside Ashoka made him do this, made him think about the day when the caravan had to take him away, made him think of the only way out. He prayed Four Nails read his thoughts.

On the seventh morning, Vishpar came by himself. "You're doing well, better than any of us thought. But you don't know this beast. It's clever, too clever. You kill it today, tomorrow?"

"As I'm learning his ways, he's learning from me."

"Be careful, boy."

"I do not fear him."

"You will when the thickness runs down his face and he goes mad. We all will."

Ashoka knew about that too. Male elephants did secrete a thick smelly fluid from spots near their eyes, did show signs of madness at those times. But four or five days of fasting and no water always cleared that up and settled the elephant back to its normal behaviors. "We watch for the thickness and know the way through that in a few days."

Vishpar scoffed. "I've never seen that. Four Nails'll bash your head on the rocks down by the river. I've warned your captain."

That last made Ashoka think all the harder about his next step. Four Nails was far less likely to bash Ashoka's head on river rocks than were Vishpar and his men. Ashoka said, "Master Vishpar, Four Nails will need to follow your commands after I'm gone."

Vishpar looked at the elephant heading down to the river. "Your first cut to kill will be easy. He trusts you. After that, you'll need my men to finish him."

Ashoka heard fear in the voice, saw fear in the eyes, face and shoulders, the fear of whether Vishpar could round up enough men, if they could keep Four Nails down while they finished him. Elephants despise the man whose courage comes from sharp metal spikes that gouge flesh on the back of the neck at the base of the brain. Vishpar had it right. In time Four Nails could turn into a killer, and Ashoka would not be here to save the bull or the man. "Master Vishpar, allow me to teach you how to make him pull and lift. He'll do the work of ten horses and will live three times longer than any horse. Painted, he'll lead your processions."

After appearing to think, Vishpar growled. "We have no processions."

"Master Vishpar, I meant no disrespect. This valley and your town... can use his strength."

"If you don't do what I tell you, we will take care of him after you leave, after you show us where to take the first cuts. They say your caravan leaves in two days. I and my men will be back before it leaves. You can show us how to kill him best, yes? You will lead us in killing him, yes?"

Vishpar turned to his horse, mounted slowly, and rode into the mountain morning. Ashoka saw his next steps, and he needed help.

+ + +

Four Nails responded to new commands every day. By the ninth day, the bull followed all easy commands without Ashoka repeating—go, go fast, stop, back up, turn left, turn right, hold it still, set it down, bend knee, lift it. Someone in this or another lifetime had once trained Four Nails, and he remembered commands as only an elephant remembers.

Sadness filled Ashoka. That morning Nuur had scratched numbers and small cart wagons on the dirt. Ashoka sounded out what the pictures showed him. Nuur nodded when Ashoka said their caravan would leave the next day, or the day after at the latest.

Ashoka asked Nuur to stay for a while, to listen to him. Ashoka told Nuur everything. He told the tall slave with no tongue about Govinda's last night, about his father and the family elephant camp, about his sisters with no dowry, about the only thing he could do when Vishpar and his men came back—or if they did not come back—about how he had to do it before the caravan took Ashoka away.

Later that day the *sarthavaha* visited, stayed a while, and just watched like that other Syrian at the camp far away. The captain came alone, and that puzzled and troubled Ashoka. Had Nuur drawn pictures and gestured about what Ashoka had confessed? Had the captain figured out that Ashoka could never help kill Four Nails?

Before the captain left, he tugged at Ashoka's arm, pulled him close. "Tomorrow when the locals come, kill big mad elephant. Yes?"

Ashoka turned away but knew he had to leave with the caravan. The Syrians had paid Father too much gold for him. Vishpar or others in the town would not hide him, would not let Ashoka live if he stayed here. The wilderness around the village was too vast, too bare, too unknown for a lone man without a horse to survive even if the villagers did not hunt him down.

The next day for the first time on this caravan stop, a cold mountain rain hung in the morning air and soaked the little beach by the stream. Alone with Four Nails, Ashoka listened for every noise, every footfall. If Vishpar and his men decided to sneak down, Four Nails would tell him before they could get close and before Ashoka might sense them. Only night's darkness provided good protection down here.

Near the limit of Ashoka's tolerance for the cold water, Four Nails lifted his head and trunk and turned his ears in the direction of the path.

Distant talking and sounds of horses, then Vishpar and helpers rode to the narrow beach. They made no effort to hide or sneak up. Vishpar again carried the long pole with the three-pronged end. He came with more helpers than usual, nine in all. They carried clubs, heavy ropes and long knives across their horses or hanging from their belts.

Vishpar shouted, "Teach us, Indian boy, on this your last day." Then he laughed, and all his helpers laughed with him.

Almost shoulder deep in cold water, Ashoka slid his left arm under Four Nail's ear. The powerful mass, the thick hide, the senses keener than his own calmed him and let him listen for what to do next. He said quietly, "I pray I've trained you well. Obey me now so that you may have a long life."

He turned to the nine at the water's edge. All were off their horses. "Master Vishpar, thank you." For a few moments more, the deep water would shield him from strikes with knives or clubs. "I must clean the nails of his front feet before we come out."

Those peculiar words slowed the three already sloshing toward him in water up to their knees. Vishpar yelled, "You mad too now? Dead elephants can have dirty nails."

Ashoka dropped into the cold water and slid his hands down to Four Nails' front feet pressing on the river bottom. With his *kukri* he sliced at the heavy ropes tethering the front feet. The last uncut threads parted easily for the sharp blade. Ashoka had started to cut into the ropes before, a little more each evening, but never enough for the ropes to part and always in a place not easily seen. When he came up, the leading three men waded closer.

Ashoka said, "The river's too cold. I can't teach how to scrub his hide today. We'll come out."

The leading three stopped. Ashoka saw that the front man carried a black club of iron wood hard enough to crack rocks open.

Vishpar yelled, "We know how to scrub. Today we carve meat for the beggars, meat of a mad elephant that crushed the head of a poor Indian boy." He cackled. "We tried with all our strength to save the boy from the mad beast."

Four Nails had turned in the water, his left side facing the charging three. Ashoka said into his ear, "Knee, knee, give me your knee."

The big male dropped his head closer into the water and bent his front knee. Ashoka stepped onto the knee and swung himself up.

Sitting high, he took one long glance at the gathering men. They had all stopped as if not sure what to do next, as if afraid at the size of Four Nails with Ashoka on his neck. He leaned over to Four Nail's ear. "Go now. Go, go, go with all your mighty speed." He slapped Four Nails hard on the upper belly. Four Nails surged through the water to the tall grass and trees.

Ashoka thought the water served them well. On open ground, that first surge, suddenly without heavy ropes tying his front feet close together, might have made Four Nails stumble. The water allowed the big animal to get used to his free front legs.

As the water became shallower, Four Nails surged ahead faster. At the tall grass he found the path he and Ashoka had started in prior days and broke into a run. He ran with a big rolling gait through the trees and beyond them up the rocky hills. The cut tethers flopped on his front feet, and his gray muscled mass pulled uphill stronger with every long bound.

From almost out of sight in tall grass, Ashoka heard Vishpar yelling in the local dialect, and Ashoka only made out, "Get him... time to die, Indian boy."

Ashoka felt more than saw the men. At first they did not know what to do. They had never seen Four Nails run. They had never seen any grown elephant run flat out, did not know a healthy elephant can outrun any man and, on rough ground, any rider on a horse.

Then the noises of men and horses faded, leaving only the sounds of big soft feet landing on dirt and rocks, some of the smaller rocks and stones rolling away, heavy breathing through the mouth and trunk beneath him, and an increasing wind.

They crested the rocky hill—where Nuur and two horses waited at the spot marked by Ashoka's bundle left there by Ashoka at first light.

Ashoka jumped off, slid his trailing arm down the big ear, the cheek and tusk, and said more to himself. "Four Nails, you must go now. Go and don't stop until you find a good herd with many females that will take you." He stepped to the back of the elephant, slammed a flat hand onto the upper thigh, and shouted. "Go, go fast, go, go."

Four Nails obeyed. He broke into a run again and ran free.

From their horses, Ashoka and Nuur saw the last of Four Nails, his big shoulders and head rising and falling until they blended into the brown and gray land lying under high mountains. He trumpeted once, again, and then all sounds of him were gone.

They had to outrace Vishpar's men back to their caravan and the protection of its soldiers. They made it easily, saw no rider trail them, saw no rider chase after Four Nails.

+ + +

At their cooking fires on their last night outside the town wall, out of hearing of other cart mates, Madan said, "Our god Ganesha cradled you in his hands today."

"I pray he protects my elephant and Red Eyes too."

"Pray Vishpar and his men were cruel enough to that wonderful animal that he will run away from here through the night. They won't chase him then."

"And then they will forget about him, and he will live."

Ashoka turned away. He belonged with elephants and they belonged with him, this one more than Red Eyes, more than any elephant he had known. This one had shown him where to go, what to do when the only path he saw at first led to a brutal killing. This one had given him more than he had given the noble giant. But this one, now called Four Nails, was gone.

He thought to ask Madan if he heard of what happened to Vishpar and his men. It did not matter.

Madan said, "You handled the big bull with skill, and our captain knows it. He will guard you until he sells you for a good price."

"That's why he let Nuur help me?"

"That's why he let Nuur watch for the men who came to kill you and gave Nuur two horses that are faster than any horse in this valley, two horses that only the scouts ride."

"What will happen to Four Nails?"

"Ashoka, that is a foolish question don't you think?"

He felt the sting because it was so true. Only the gods would know the answer. Madan said, "If no big pride of lions sets on him, he'll reach swampland down by the endless sea. There a herd may allow him to sire many offspring, and he may live a long life."

"I wish he finds such a herd."

"He may follow our caravan. He may want you to scrub his hide every day and teach him to serve man."

"I wish that also," said Ashoka, meaning it more than he had meant anything since leaving home.

Before the sun broke over the mountains, the caravan was under way again. Many villagers looked out from the white walls. Some waved, whistled and shouted. The men of Ashoka's cart said the town's people were pleased with the spices and blankets traded for fresh fruit and the labor of woodworkers and blacksmiths to help repair the caravans.

No one said more about the elephant called Four Nails.

Chapter XI

Seleucia

In the late afternoon heat, Ashoka's deeper breaths made him cough. The odor of tar rode on the air. Tar oozed out of low-lying wet ground. Larger clumps splotched along both banks of the river which split this city, called Seleucia, the first city Ashoka had ever seen and the final stop for his caravan.

Noises of uncounted men, horses and donkeys, dogs, and long lines of other carts rolling on cobble-stones smothered the usual sounds of Ashoka's caravan camp all day and through the night.

Over the last two days, most of his caravan's soldiers and traders, horses and bullocks, carts and all their cargo disappeared into crowded streets flanked by buildings rising to four stories. By the end of the second day here, the other Indian men from his cart collected their belongings, and they too all departed. Ashoka did not ask where they were headed, who owned them now. From their quiet talk, most left for the main auction ground, where bidders from many lands shouted out the value of their lives.

Sometimes a stranger waited for an Indian man in the gray-brown mist at the far end of the dirt and scrub where they had camped. The stranger called out the Indian's name, and he scrambled to collect up his few belongings and leave. No time for parting or good wishes, no time for Ashoka to learn if his countrymen began their new lives as servants or, perhaps, soldiers. If asked, they would have known only that someone else owned them now.

By the end of the second day, only four carts, the Syrian captain, his attendants and a few armed men, six horses, Madan and Nuur circled up together. The latticed cart sat with them, watched over by the remaining guards.

Where would he be when darkness fell tomorrow? Ashoka saw an opening to ask Madan, a moment when no one else was near the cook, and Ashoka could help him unload a sack of rice.

Ashoka said, "What will happen to us?"

Madan shrugged, pulled the sack out of Ashoka's hands and said as he turned away, "Be ready. Be ready for elephants. Tomorrow they auction servants and concubines, the next day elephant drivers and elephants."

The words *elephants* and *concubines* jolted Ashoka. Though he had not seen Radha since that day on the road, tried not to look for her, he thought she must still be in the latticed cart. And then he forced himself to think only of elephants.

Later on that second night outside the big city, Ashoka said, "Nuur, in the morning take me to the auction place." Nuur looked at him and scowled, and Nuur seldom scowled at Ashoka. He waved his hands palms down and shook his head.

Ashoka said, "If you don't take me, I'll go alone. Or our captain will have to put me in chains. I must prepare for when they sell me."

Ashoka and Nuur arrived in the central square at dawn. The auction had already started with the youngest, so young that in the weak light any bidders away from the platform could not see whether they vied for a girl or boy. They based their bids on the names and ages shouted out or on what they learned on closer inspections in prior days. Ashoka silently thanked all the gods of India that Father taught him to train elephants, or else the Syrians might have taken his sisters to pay for Govinda's funeral. After the children, came young women, darker ones from jungles in far off places, lighter ones from the north, mixed with brown ones from his country.

Over the long morning, a mob crowded around him in anticipation of the most enchanting virgins, always last. Ashoka listened as best he could for their names, ages, their homelands, whatever truth or lies the auctioneer shouted out in Persian and then in Greek. As the auction wore on, he hoped she had been bought before this auction or fled again, that he would not ever again hear her name, have to think about her.

Now, near midday, he suppressed the urge to cough, tried to not attract attention, to hide in the many men. But the throng did not care about him or the tall black man next to him.

She stumbled out the open door flap of the cloth enclosure on the raised wooden platform. From behind, two guards, their bare upper arms glistening in the heat, pushed her forward, and she stumbled again. At the far end of the platform the auctioneer yelled, "And next, feast your eyes on and ready your loins for the last, the best we've brought you." Many, it might have been several thousand, cheered and shouted and whistled. "Her name's Radha," shouted the auctioneer, "for the Indian beauty taken by a god."

The delicate yet strong ankles on the platform at a level with his chest caught his gaze, then the unblemished brown skin of long slim legs, her white gown, cinched at the small waist and draped over the torso's curves in a manner to ignite desire, to the glistening black hair pulled back from her face, tear-streaked in helplessness.

Men tore off their reeking turbans or plain head coverings and waved them in high circles. Ashoka, though near the front at the edge of the platform, stood on his toes and shifted from side to side to see. He winced at that name and berated himself for wincing.

The two guards pushed her forward to the front edge of the platform. Hands bound behind her as on that day on the Emperor's Road, she froze, a white rose presented to screaming, whistling men locked on her, their beards streaked with spittle, in the center of the main square of this tar-stinking city.

The whirling turbans and other head covers settled down. Ashoka, not three paces from her, looked away and closed his eyes shutting out the shoulders and backs and sweat-soaked heads. But he could not block the cries of lust and laughter out of unnumbered men, a laughter tinged with futility and a knowing that none of the laughing screaming men would in the end claim her.

The guard standing by her raised high his massive arms for silence. The auctioneer, off to one side, yelled, "No matron has worn her out carrying water or suckling the baby." He grabbed her chin and pulled up her face, her eyes scrunched shut, her mouth tight. The raised head and line down the chin and neck led to her young breasts pressed against the white cotton top fastened at the left shoulder, leaving the right shoulder bare. "Take note of her modesty. She refuses to look at any man until one of you makes her his own."

The whistles exploded again with shouts in different languages. "I'm that man... Me... Over here. Give her to me... Now. I'll mount her... in front of you all when I win her." Laugher erupted again. The auctioneer waited, and they quieted once more.

"Look, all of you. The sun will not blister her brown skin, but it is not too dark." From behind, the auctioneer placed his hands on her hips. "She's thirteen and one half years old," he yelled out over her head.

Ashoka flushed at the lie. Radha was his age.

"She has all her teeth, is free of disease. See her belly, small and flat, but the birth chamber wide for many children. No man has taken her." This last brought the loudest cheers and whistles of the entire morning.

"She's the finest, the most precious of all. The bidding starts at ten daric of gold or one hundred drachmas of silver."

Ashoka could not watch any longer. He nudged Nuur to leave. They squeezed out of the throng filling the square, it too paved with large brown bricks made of the mud from the River Tigra and set with black bitumen. The strongest odor of tar sludge rose here in the city center.

They headed down one of the wide roadways and tried to hug the dusty shade of many buildings, taller than Ashoka had ever seen, and the shade of date palm groves in open areas. Men on foot, riders, and carts drawn by oxen or donkeys cluttered the straight streets, laid out in a grid extending into the desert beyond the houses and irrigated croplands or running up to the Grand Canal that divided the city.

Ashoka walked slowly, all energy spent. Suddenly he wanted to turn back, not to see her but to see the man who won her, follow him, ask about him if he ruled over a good household. Many from the auction caught up to and swept around them, the bidding ended. Nuur did not stand out among the other tall black men from lands south of Egypt. Ashoka and Nuur attracted little attention in this trading hub for empires.

Here, as in Exandahar, no honorable unattended women appeared on balconies, walked in the streets or public areas. In

Ashoka's village, only untouchable women hid from plain view, and young mothers carried their babies on their hips while shopping for food or fetching water. Perhaps, thought Ashoka, the absence of women in this city caused the frenzy for one long look at Radha and the other women before they too hid for the rest of their lives, never again seen by men except those who owned them.

Only prostitutes waited in plain view. They stood in doorways or leaned out of window openings, legs splayed or breasts partly exposed. They leaned against garden walls and down from balconies, ready to relieve those who had failed to claim a prize.

More than one yelled in broken Sanskrit, "Handsome Indian boy. Come here. You not forget me. I make you forget her. I make you harder and longer than tusks on your elephants... I give you my white-skinned daughter."

At home Ashoka never paid attention. On this day, he slowed and listened to their taunts, glanced, then stared, at their eyes, faces, bodies. He held out his open palms, signifying he had not a single coin. They laughed, but several beckoned him. He turned to one standing in a doorway. Her youth, close to his age, her clothes covering her completely, and a soft perfume, all pulled him and smothered Father's admonitions and his respect for Mother and sisters and all other women in his life.

Nuur's strong hand on his neck snapped him out of her spell and stayed on his neck until they neared their camp.

"Ashoka, sit," said the Syrian from his rugs and pillows under a tent canopy set on a rise north of the city.

Nuur eased down to the hard ground in the shade of a lush palm and patted the dirt for Ashoka to do the same—but not on the rug.

An attendant brought a jar of cool sweet tea he poured into cups for Ashoka and Nuur. He returned with plates of dates, flat bread, and bowls filled with chunks of meat from a sheep cooked in raisins and topped with melted cheese. Nuur ate like a hungry man.

Ashoka knew it was rude to refuse. Even Buddha ate meat when served by gracious hosts. Many days had passed since he had eaten anything this fine, and never presented by his captain's servant. He drank the tea and nibbled at the bread, his insides too knotted to try more.

"You... like my food? Madan good cook," said the Syrian.

Nuur bowed from his sitting position.

Ashoka said, "Yes, very good."

The Syrian changed to his own language. Madan translated. "The money from all the cargo is in my clients' counting house. They're pleased, have rewarded me well." He drank from his cup of a yellow metal. "In five days I leave for Damascus. I have been paid enough and will not lead another caravan. This city is too big and stinks. You like this city, Ashoka?"

If he told the truth—the bad air, the local language, a mix of Persian and Greek, he could not follow—what then? If he said he liked it, would the captain sell him to someone who lived here? "I am at your service, Master Captain."

The Syrian leaned in. "This is true. You are my reward from my sponsors. Come closer," the voice gruff and commanding. "Come here."

The Syrian's gaze allowed no delay. If he angered this man, he might lose his tongue or his head. No one in this city would care about the body of a slave who had angered his master. Ashoka stood up and took a step closer to the captain.

The Syrian laughed. "My four wives wait for me. Four is enough." He paused for Madan to translate, leaned forward, grabbed and shook Ashoka's elbow with a leathery hand. "You like come to my house? Play with my wives? They like you."

Ashoka did not pull away, did not resist. The answer came easily. "Master Captain, I serve best when I teach elephants."

"We Syrians trade elephants."

"I'll help train your elephants so they get a good price."

The Syrian let go of Ashoka's arm. "Everyone at the compound talks about you and Four Nails. Not possible, what you did with that beast. They say I lie about you, you too young. You bring a high price tomorrow, yes? If the elephants down there follow your commands, maybe you bring a good price? Only one other head mahout at the auction tomorrow."

Ashoka breathed deeply. That's why Madan had said so little, why Nuur was so relaxed, why he, Ashoka, was the last of the cargo to leave. Tomorrow... a chance to command elephants once more. He caught a tiny sign of agreement around the mouth of Nuur and laughed inside, from relief and excitement. But he had never seen those elephants, didn't know where they were. If they refused to follow his commands... His insides clenched again.

The Syrian stood, stamped his foot on the rugs and pushed Ashoka away. "Not bring enough money, I keep you. You good to play with. Be gone now. When the sun is so high," the Syrian set his arm a third of the way to vertical, "at the compound."

Thoughts of Radha faded. He had to prepare for his own auction tomorrow.

+ + +

Nuur knew where the elephants were kept, and Ashoka made Nuur take him as soon as the captain released them.

Ashoka watched the herd from the levee that held back the River Tigra. Two large side-by-side rectangular areas and five smaller pens made up the compound. The far wall of each pen was the levee holding back the river. Thorn bushes and rings of sharp metal spikes covered the inner three sides protecting a flimsy fence from any angry elephant. A cluster of squat palms grew in the center of the first rectangle. Cracked and brown chunks of tusks lay scattered on the ground outside.

The larger of the main two enclosures held eight adult elephants and two calves. The other enclosures were empty.

Inside the elephant enclosure, stone troughs, filled with water dripping from stone pipes, ran along the base of the levee barrier. Two adults stood side by side at the trough, drew up water and sprayed the water over their heads and backs until the hides were soaked. Then they backed away for the next pair. Mercifully, the elephants had enough water to drink and cool their hides in the dry air. They flapped their ears without stopping. Under the sun without shade, they were hot despite the constant water sprays.

Away from the two large pens, tents topped by bright yellow flags provided cover for a steady stream of serious-faced men. They too studied the elephants but ignored Ashoka and Nuur.

Ashoka gave each elephant a name easy to remember— Tall One, Little Girl, Long Tail. The adults' front feet were roped together loosely. The top edge of the ears of the two oldest curled over like a dry banana leaf. Ashoka wondered if they all suffered from parasites in the water. At least the two calves seemed to be with their natural mothers.

After all the visiting men had left and the sun began to drop, Ashoka became restless. *If the elephants... follow your commands*, the captain had said. Only two lead mahouts were up for sale, and that was good—unless no one came to bid or bid too low. Then the Syrian who had taken the head of the old woman might remain his master for the rest of this life. He didn't know what the captain meant by "lead" mahout, and guessed the captain had spoken of Ashoka's stature that way. Father was the only lead mahout in his village, and Govinda—had he lived—might have become the next one.

Ganesha show me the way, the first step and then the next. And it came to him.

He said to Nuur, "Stay here. Don't help me. I must do this alone. If I fail, let the guard take me or the elephants trample me."

Nuur let him go.

Ashoka slid down the levee and squatted at the fence opening, large enough for a man to crawl through but too small for any elephant to get out. A solitary guard holding a long spear stood outside the fence. With hand gestures Ashoka asked if he might go in. The guard motioned with his head and hands for Ashoka to enter. These elephants must not have been of much value for trade, and this one unarmed dark-skinned boy must not have seemed any threat to the guard.

Ashoka stooped through the opening, stood up and waited. He peered at each elephant to see how they stood, how they leaned into the next one, how soon they noticed and turned to him, how they swayed their trunks and flapped their ears. A familiar calm entered every part of him. He was with elephants, and they were with him. He waited for them to tell him they were ready for him to approach.

They turned to him and held their ears still. The two cows with calves backed to the opposite side of the pen. Two elephants came close but with ears spread, not snorting out of their trunks, not stomping. They ran the tips of their trunks around his hands as if searching for a treat or weapon. He had left his *kukri* in his bundle back at the camp and was glad. A hidden weapon could alarm these beasts.

He patted each trunk and let the elephants take in all the scents from his fingers and arms, his shoulders and head. They were accustomed to men, to treats for following commands. He said, "I'm sorry I have none, but please do what I ask now."

When he talked, the lead elephants quieted their breathing, slowed the flapping of their ears to better hear his voice, his words.

He tried the first command—stop—and the second— go. The closest one, then the next and others did as he asked. These Indian elephants had been trained by an Indian. He patted and stroked them each time. "I wish I had a treat. In our next life I will."

One by one, he cajoled seven of the eight, even the mothers with calves, to form a rough line behind the first two. As the red sun dropped into the dark haze over the city and shadows covered the whole pen, he got the seven and two calves to move around the pen in one direction.

The oldest-looking one stood off alone. Her eyes followed Ashoka, and she shifted to always see him. He kept clear a straight line away from her to the opening in the fence or to the palm trees. This one might no longer care about being punished after she hurt a man. He named this one Clever Old Woman.

With more time he might have tried to ride on the necks of the leaders, but in this fading light that was too dangerous. Most killer elephants strike in darkness. With more time he would have worked with Clever Old Woman and perhaps learned more about her anger, her sadness, or whatever made her stand off. But he had to leave now. Seleucia was no place for Nuur and him to lose their way at night.

Chapter XII

The Elephant Boy

Ashoka and Nuur returned to the compound as the sun came up hot and orange yellow. The herd had been moved into the other large pen.

Soon more men collected on the levee. This time they approached close, looked into Ashoka's eyes, at his sandaled feet, his hands and the outlines of his limbs through the cotton garb. One by one or in pairs they went down to the largest of the tents, came back out and looked him over some more. They were the bidders and he the prize.

One group of three men stayed on the levee far from Ashoka and Nuur. Ashoka caught glimpses of another young man from his country with them, had to be that other lead mahout.

The Syrian captain, two of his soldiers, and Madan arrived last.

At mid-morning more men emerged from the main tent. The other dark-skinned Indian, now carrying a long pole, came out with them. Ashoka had not noticed him go down there, but that did not worry him. Only the elephants down there mattered.

Someone shouted out in Greek, and Madan translated for his little group. "You'll bid for two lead mahouts: Ashoka Gopta out of India, and Naja Kaniska from the island of Lanka. Mahouts, come down here."

That fit—Naja had the same name as the snake which took Govinda. The two men followed Naja down to the headman, one of them also quietly translating.

"Take off your head coverings and shirts," said the headman and motioned for the two to stand side by side.

Both mahouts stripped to their *dhotis*. Ashoka handed Madan his clothes, bundling up the dagger. The sun felt hot on his bare shoulders, hotter than in Lalput. The waiting men surrounded and gaped at them.

This Naja didn't have the body of a snake. About Govinda's age, he had big arms, a thick waist, and more powerful legs than Ashoka, like a young bull. But Ashoka was taller, felt quicker. *Can I best this one in wrestling? Maybe... Doesn't matter. The elephants, only they matter now.*

The headman yelled, "Bidders take note. Their skin is clear and free of boils." Murmurs of agreement. "Each mahout must find the lead elephant, mount it, and move the herd from its pen out to the roadway and buildings to that man with the flag on the far side over there, bring it back around the tents and into the pen. Ashoka will go first."

The most precious thing is always auctioned last. Ashoka knew that. They thought him less worthy than Naja. Perhaps the Syrian captain had bragged about Ashoka too much, and they didn't believe what the Syrian said about Ashoka and Four Nails.

The headman turned to Ashoka and Madan. "Does this mahout wish to use a *kohle* of any kind, or a club? We have many in the tent to choose from. Treats and knives, other cutting tools are not allowed."

Ashoka shook his head. Two guards pulled open a section of the thorn-covered fence into the fresh pen, and he entered.

He stood still for what must have seemed a long time to those who came to judge him. But Ashoka did not care about what the men thought now, about how much gold or silver he might bring, or how they measured him against that other mahout with the name of a snake.

The two lead elephants came to him right away this time. They moved quicker, as if to greet a friend. The two searched him again, and again he told them he was sorry he had nothing for them.

Clever Old Woman did not move from back against the fence but watched him.

He lined them up as the evening before. On his voice commands and finger prods, the one at the front dropped onto her knees and allowed him to climb onto her neck. With toe and heel touches behind her ears, Ashoka made her leave the enclosure. Six other adults and two calves followed. Clever Old Woman did not.

He led the line toward the street, tall buildings beyond, and the flag man far away. Still Clever Old Woman did not leave her place. He heard some men, now on both sides of the line, talk and then snicker, but was not troubled. No elephant wants to be left behind by the herd unless giving birth or preparing to die. The looks from the men told him he could not wait half the day for Clever Old Woman to follow. Perhaps she would never follow and knew all the elephants had to come back to her.

He jumped down, told his elephant to stay and the other six in line to not move. They would not run off. The leader was too tired, too beaten to try to run stumbling over the ropes on her front feet into this strange stinking city, away from the only nearby water and food.

He strode back into the pen. Close to Clever Old Woman he slowed, giving her time to tell him what was wrong. He took her in with his eyes, his ears, his insides. Neither anger nor sickness made her stay back. Sadness came from her, from the way she stood making tiny little scratches on the hard ground with her front foot, came from the gentle flapping of her old curled ears, from how she held her head and eyes. She blinked often, as if about to cry. Ashoka had seen elephants cry when one of their own died, when men took a calf from them.

And he understood. Clever Old Woman yearned to take that first place in the line of elephants, not the very last. A long time back, she led her own herd, perhaps a large and powerful herd, and wanted to lead again. Now, on this day, in this hot stinking city, she was too slow, too weak to force her way up past the younger elephants.

He reached out to her. She came to him, placed the tip of her trunk in his hand. He caressed the trunk, stroked it back up to her cheek, and patted the cheek. He looked into her eye on his side. "I know, I know. Far back, you were the matriarch. It's a little thing here now for you, after the years of the great herd you led back then. Help me now, please, and you can be first again."

He stroked the stub of her tusk. Without him asking, she bent the leg on his side for him to step up on her thigh and hoist himself onto her neck. She rumbled from deep in her throat at the pleasure of carrying him, lurched forward and out the pen to the line of elephants waiting. Ashoka guided her to the head of them all, and the other elephants did not protest.

The men stopped talking, snickering. Some nodded at each other, as the elephant line followed Clever Old Woman out to the noisy street of carts and curious strangers and the man with the flag, then back around the main tent and to the pen.

Ashoka jumped down. He said to her, "Thank you. May you know kindness in your last days." She caressed his arm and shoulder with her trunk.

He patted and thanked each elephant. He was sad now too. After today he would never again see any of these good elephants. He lingered too long perhaps but did not care. Then he walked to Madan and the captain.

The headman motioned to the other mahout.

Naja moved at the herd quickly, as if he expected to repeat the easy little test much faster than Ashoka. He carried a long stick ending in a metal prong sharpened at the tip. He pressed on the lead female, the one Ashoka rode first. She backed up. He leaned to one side, jumped to the other side and nudged the back of her front knee with the point of the stick. She did not follow the command to bend the knee to let him climb onto her.

Naja shook the stick close to her eye and nudged the back of her leg once more. She backed up tighter into the others, a snorting line of protection and defiance.

Clever Old Woman positioned herself next to and slightly behind the lead female. But Naja seemed to take in none of this. He yelled. "Kneel. Kneel, or I'll stick you. If you don't obey, they'll take you away, and your flesh will feed many tonight."

The leader stood taller, held out her ears straight, raised and lowered her trunk, snorted loudly.

Naja slid to her right side and raised the pointed stick over his left shoulder as if readying to thrust it downward at the back of the front leg. Ashoka wanted to look off, did not care to witness the coming chaos, these good animals getting rebuked and hurt.

Clever Old Woman did not let Naja finish. Her forehead caught his bare shoulders and upper back square on. The short powerful thrust made Naja stumble sideways. He tried to turn to the attacker, but the lead female he menaced caught him with a swipe of her trunk and head. He tripped toward Clever Old Woman. The lead female caught him again with her trunk. Naja fell at the front feet of Clever Old Woman. As he staggered into a crouch, she stepped on the side of his left leg at the knee and leaned forward.

From up on the levee Ashoka heard the tendons rip and a bone break. Naja screamed and rolled away. Madan took a firm hold of Ashoka's arm. He must make no sound.

The headman raised his hands for no one to move in, not the guards or onlookers.

Clever Old Woman backed off. Naja, his bare chest covered by the sandy dirt of the pen, rose to his good leg. Using the pointed pole as a walking stick, he stumbled toward the elephants and wailed, "Obey now, obey me."

The elephants parted out of his way. He tried to cut them off, with thrusts of the long pole tried to keep the leader in front of him but could not. After three shaky hops, he fell onto the dirt face-down.

The headman motioned for the guards to take him. They pulled Naja out and dumped him at the feet of the men who brought him. His teeth were clenched, and lines of tears or sweat streaked his cheeks. The two who came with him grabbed him under the bare shoulders and pulled him to his feet. They yanked him up the path to the road on the levee and away.

After a time of serious talk and shaking heads among all the men, the headman spoke again. Madan translated. "I give you Ashoka. He's from the family that trained the very elephants which defeated the Macedonian. He got that clever old one to obey his every command." Ashoka knew that last was a lie, every Indian knew. Alexander rounded up the best elephants outside all of India, trained them better than anyone, and defeated the elephant army of the Emperor. Ashoka closed his eyes to not look at any of the men, to not give away any of his thoughts.

Sounds of appreciation rose from the circled men.

"Ashoka is in his prime, only seventeen years old but has helped train elephants since he was four, a mahout since age twelve, one of the youngest ever." More approving grunts. "Next to him stands his caravan's guru, who speaks the language of Greece, Persia and India. Through him, you can ask any questions."

One of the onlookers yelled, "Has this Ashoka ridden elephants into battle? He looks to be a boy, not a man. India has fought no wars in many years. He's not seventeen. I'm sure of that."

One of them shouted, "How old is he?"

Ashoka knew he could not hesitate, that this question would come again and again. "My captain and Madan know I was seventeen when I came to their caravan. I must be coming on eighteen soon."

The headman said, "This boy—this man—is unafraid. And... we know Indian men. They're all older than they appear."

Some men smirked at that last.

Another shouted, "What does the mahout say about the health of these elephants?"

Ashoka's response came easily. "They have not eaten enough for many days. Two are old. The mothers are still making milk but not much longer. The pens are too small, and the sun burns their backs. One season in the jungle, in fields of grass, bathing in unsoiled river water, rolling in the muddy banks will bring them back. The old one that knocked Master Naja down protects the leader of this herd. The old one and the leader might be mother and daughter."

Grunts of surprise at his confidence, at his knowledge.

"Let the bidding begin. We start at two daric or twenty drachma."

The hand signals and shouts ended moments after they began. At the last upraised hand, they all cheered. The headman motioned Ashoka to a man waiting on the levee.

95

Madan gestured for them to wait. He handed Ashoka his belongings—the dagger bundled in the shirt and head covering, and another bundle with the coat Nuur gave him in the mountains, leather foot coverings, water gourd, combs, metal toothpicks, and a few other bundled-up clothes.

Madan said so that only Ashoka heard, "The man who bid for you is out of Carthage. It has been a mighty power for six hundred years. He bid more than for many soldiers, enough that he'll watch over you."

Ashoka took the bundles. "What will happen to Naja?"

"If his gods are kind, his master will keep him and allow his leg to heal. If not... they've dumped him in the streets and left."

"I should have shouted at him to go slowly."

"Then you would have been rebuked by these men and returned to our captain."

"Master Madan," he said, looking off over the river from the levee. "The auction man said you're the caravan guru. Is that so?"

"I am a cook. Yesterday means nothing. Only the lessons we take from yesterday, the promises we made yesterday have meaning."

"I pray I remember your many lessons. I wish you could be a guru where I now go."

Madan responded as if in one of their unhurried exchanges over the caravan fire, as if to delay their parting. "Cooks are wanted in many places but not as much as elephant drivers. Go now. Go with the song of Lord Krishna in your ears and heart."

"He gave us many, but I don't remember..." Ashoka was not ready either, did not want to leave. The caravan had been his village and refuge for months, ever watchful silent Nuur, wise Madan, who treated him like a son, and even their captain, his protectors all. Without thinking, he dropped to his knees at the older man's feet.

Madan placed his hand on Ashoka's bare shoulder. "Look upon friend and foe with equal regard, be not lifted up by praise or cast down by blame, regard heat and cold, pleasure and pain, honor and dishonor with the same quiet inner eye in harmony with all creation."

Ashoka tried to repeat the words, to remember them.

"Do this, and you will meet your destiny as the gods intend and light a path for others who come behind you. Go now. It's not wise to test your new master so soon."

One of the men beckoned Ashoka to follow. Ashoka rose and turned away. He feared his eyes might water, but they did not. As he walked up to the path along the levee, he passed the captain and Nuur. Both stood relaxed, satisfied at the bidding, at Ashoka's performance. He bowed at them. They, even the captain, returned the gesture.

Part II

Land of Smiling Children

Chapter XIII

Different Elephants, Different Gods

The twelve mastiffs raised their snouts as high as a man's chest, sniffed the air, and strained against the leather leashes. Ears cocked forward, the dogs quieted. The biggest male growled and started barking, then the others. Sounds carried far on the dry wind pressing down from the mountains, across the cultivated fields and orchards, and into their camp on the northern coast of Africa.

Ashoka tried to see what the dogs saw or heard.

Tilaka, the head mahout here, limped toward the orchards and yelled, "The dogs tell us he's coming."

A short time later he yelled again, "I hear horses and hooves and stones tumbling on the trail. Line up at ready. Mintho's coming. If it's not Mintho, prepare to fight."

Ashoka, the other nine elephant trainers, and six helpers scrambled into their stone huts. Wooden boxes held full-length wool robes and head coverings, the standard clothes of men in Carthage. They all knew what to do. In Ashoka's four months at this camp, they had often talked about and sometimes practiced for the day when High Senator Mintho would arrive. Dressed in the heavy clothes, they formed a straight line on the orchard side of the huts. The laborers, naked to the waist, fell in behind the elephant men.

The camp guards struggled into leather cloaks, boots and caps. Their hair and beards were mostly gray and white.

Some had only one eye. Most missed one or more fingers, and none could run fast on their worn-out misshapen legs. But they knew how to handle a fighting weapon. Each grabbed a sword, axe or short spear. They repeated, "Mintho's coming... Pray it's Mintho."

Soldiers strung wooden bows and laid out arrows on the dirt in shade cast by the huts and taller wooden storage houses. They mumbled, "Mintho will inspect us, our weapons... we must be ready... pray it is Mintho."

Women and young children scampered into their own underground shelter, its entrance concealed by scrub brush. The mothers did not have to say a word to their children. Every time the dogs or men warned of danger, women and children knew what to do.

The dogs jumped up in excitement. Their leashes, tied to metal hooks set in buried cement blocks, snapped them back down.

Now Ashoka and the men with good eyes saw horses and riders on trails down from the hills. Behind them older horses, mules and donkeys carried packs, and two horse-drawn chariots carried men or supplies he could not yet see. The little army wound down the switchback, closer through the fruit trees and orchards, then over the wooden bridge across the stream and on the narrow trail into camp.

Ashoka counted sixteen horses and riders in the line through the gathering dust before the lead riders blocked his view.

Four riders near the front stood out. The day's last shafts of sunlight bounced off their wide bracelets and necklaces. Clean white cloaks, striped with dark blue, contrasted against the dirty robes of the other riders.

The lead rider of those four on the biggest stallion broke out of line and cantered to the waiting men. He jumped off and strode along the lined-up mahouts. One of his other men led the horse away. He took off his cone-shaped hat and shook his long hair, graying at the temples. He hugged Tilaka. "How are my giants and their good keepers?" he said in Greek. Unbroken teeth gleamed in the black-bearded face.

Tilaka spoke in the language of Carthage. "*Adoni*, my master, well, very well. We rejoice at your safe arrival."

"Shed your cloak. Every time I must tell you not to wear the heavy cloth for me."

"Thank you, Master."

Tilaka bowed, slipped out of the garment, and handed it to a camp laborer. He backed up on unsteady legs. The other mahouts and helpers and all camp soldiers behind shed their coats. The women and children came out of their hiding place and drew up close behind their men.

Mintho said, "Do they fight better than last time?"

"Yes, Master. Some of them no longer run away when the guards shout and shoot arrows at the ground in front of them."

Tilaka had lied, and the lie puzzled and angered Ashoka.

"Excellent. My new mahout? He's here, they tell me."

Ashoka stepped forward out of the line. He looked into the brown green eyes, the face, of the man who owned him. Mintho was old, older than Father—if Father still lived—and that unsettled Ashoka. Old men died suddenly for no reason. What would come of this camp and its mahouts then?

Mintho said more softly, so only Ashoka and Tilaka could hear, "Do the elephants and the other mahouts heed him?"

"Very well, Master, even the Libyans. He's not afraid."

"Then we're ready for more elephants. We can't get enough worthy ones out of India." Mintho shook his head and let his shoulders and chest slump in disappointment.

Ashoka understood. This camp needed worthy elephants out of India, not these small beasts from the mountains above the camp. They fled when men ran at them. They backed away at the first smell of fire-tipped arrows. When the men who bought these elephants from Mintho found out, this camp would shut down. And someone did buy Mintho's elephants. At Ashoka's arrival the camp held thirteen, but only the six most docile were left. This camp didn't need nine mahouts and six helpers. It needed real elephants, Indian elephants, fighting elephants.

Mintho said, "The Greeks steal all the worthy ones, or they die before they get here. We don't have enough fighting elephants."

First Tilaka, then Ashoka and the other mahouts bowed deeply from the waist as if they wanted to take the blame for the camp's shortage of worthy beasts.

Mintho laughed. "Stop. Stop." He fixed on Ashoka. "You're not to blame. I won't pay what they ask for the pus-covered used up beasts in Seleucia. The army of Carthage still takes mine for a good price. I want to keep it that way. My men bid only for slaves last time."

Slaves. The word jarred Ashoka—high-caste mahout, now slave tending frightened little elephants in a strange place far from any war. And Mintho had it wrong about the elephants in Seleucia. They were mistreated by men who didn't know better, not used up, not the younger ones. If fed well and bathed every day, they would have taken the training to charge strange men throwing spears and fire sticks. Clever Old Woman and her offspring proved that much.

His bearing once more upright, head back, Mintho turned to Tilaka. "The drought has not let up. My advance scouts report Moth drives them to the very highest meadows, closer to us than in many summers. Tilaka, take this new mahout and six others. Tomorrow we'll get fresh fighting elephants. If Baal El favors us, you will train them to fight, and if he favors us more, he'll allow Tanit to bring rain."

"Yes, Master. We'll be ready."

Mintho pointed at Ashoka. "What do you call him?"

"I'm Ashoka," Ashoka said quietly and then regretted he had not waited for Tilaka to answer.

"Yes, after your mighty Emperor." Mintho smiled. "I knew your name, but sometimes others do not use their given names. Do you deserve that name, Ashoka?" Mintho's eyes said he did not want Ashoka to answer. "And you speak Greek?"

"I know some Greek—if spoken slowly, Master."

Mintho reached across and grabbed Ashoka's chin like a father might grab a child not listening. "Do you know how to ride a horse, Ashoka?"

"Yes, Master."

"Indians can't ride horses. You're too young to ride a big horse. How is it that you can ride?"

"A man from North Africa taught me."

"A man from Carthage?"

"No Master."

"Then you must learn to ride properly. We will teach you."

Mintho pushed Ashoka's face away as if to say, I'm done with you, turned to the side, and shouted, "Feast and drink and rest. Double the sentries and put the dogs on the perimeter. At sunrise we'll hunt elephants."

Mintho strode past the waiting men, who all bowed, past the huts and fire pits where some of his men were building fires. His tent of three sections already sat on the beach close by the lapping waves and the cooler air of the sea. The locals called it the Great Inland Sea, so wide that a long ship with a big sail needed many days of good winds to reach the other side. Ashoka and cargo for the camp had arrived at this camp on such a ship, but this was the first time he had been close to his new master.

The mahouts and helpers held no wrestling competition this evening, too many strangers, too much to do, too much to eat. Besides, none could throw down Ashoka. He was too strong for the small quick ones and too quick and slippery for the strong ones.

Mintho's cooks prepared slabs of smoked tuna, wild pig and sweet biscuits made from wheat flour. The camp children stood in line first for the biscuits and came away with a big one in each hand. After the meal, fathers and mothers played with their children, splashing down at the sea's edge, and huddled in family clusters as darkness deepened. In the idle days at this camp, Ashoka came to know some of the wives and children. He feared for them, defenseless to drunken soldiers. But Mintho's soldiers left them alone.

When the camp quieted, Ashoka said, "Tilaka, who's this Moth that chases elephants up the mountains closer to us?"

"He's heat and dryness that turns skin to black leather."

"Tilaka, heat and dryness come from the wind and a sky without rain. Every guru in India knows this."

The second mahout in seniority, Ganesha, said, "Moth is the death god."

Tilaka's usually happy voice turned flat, hard. "Enough lessons for one night. We rise before dawn. Ashoka, you will lead us on the hunt."

"Don't choose me."

Ganesha said, "You must go. Mintho wants to test you."

"Ganesha, I don't want your place."

"We, you and I, will jump and roll in the dirt like his dogs when Mintho orders us. Mintho has ordered you to go and will make you lead the hunt."

As they headed for their sleeping places in the hut, Ganesha pulled Ashoka away from the door opening. "When the fire arrows hit and the Romans run flaming pigs at them, our elephants will flee and trample any of our men standing in their way. They show no more courage than when I came. Mintho bought you to make fighters of them. Tilaka and I can't."

Until this moment Ashoka had never said anything about the docile beasts. It was not his place to complain. Keep quiet, stay in the shadows, remember Madan's lessons. But from his first day here, he knew they could never be trained for war. All the mahouts knew, and Mintho knew too.

Ganesha said, "We pretend to train them for battle, and Mintho sells them with the promise they'll fight."

"It is our place to serve Mintho," said Ashoka.

Tilaka cut in, "I'm done, my legs worn out. He paid for you to replace me."

"I can't replace you. Ganesha must replace you. I don't understand these elephants, the scorpions... this language."

Tilaka said, "Moth has dried me out. One morning when you wake, Mintho will send me to the place of dried up slaves of Carthage."

Ashoka searched for the right thing to say to this kind mahout, who reminded him of his father and of Madan. "Where is that place?"

Tilaka snorted. "Perhaps up in the hills with the lions and hyenas. That's no worse than the streets of the city with its beggars and packs of wild dogs. Lions would kill me quicker."

"I'll go with you then, Tilaka. You and I will stay together," Ashoka blurted, and realized he said too much too soon. If Mintho took Tilaka away, he, Ashoka, could not stop him. But he meant it too. Tilaka had the wisdom of many years. He knew the language and people of this land, knew its gods, knew elephants as well as Father knew them. Without Tilaka, Ashoka would be a stranger in a strange land. He had to keep Tilaka near.

"When Mintho shows his other side, obey him no matter what happens to me."

"His men follow him. For an old man he rides a strong horse. He and his men have built a good camp, have chased all the big cats far into the hills so they do not pester us. He seems honorable."

"I've known Mintho for longer than you have lived in this life. There's a cruel madness in him that we can never understand, a madness that grows bolder with his power." Tilaka waited for his words to not lose their effect. "I must sleep now, you too."

The mahouts opened their tightly-fastened bedrolls and shook them out over the fire in the pit outside the open door of their sleeping hut. Red and black-banded cobras and yellow sand vipers lived here. No mongooses protected the huts. Scorpions hunted at night, but when day's heat left the dry night air, scorpions crawled into any blanket. A water-filled stone basin in the dirt threshold guarded the door to the hut, but the hard-shelled crab-like creatures sometimes found their way across. When scorpions swarmed at night before a rainstorm, the ground turned deadly. Parents left no child out of sight. Not many days back, a single sting in the open mouth of a sleeping infant brought death. By his second day here, Ashoka never walked on bare feet.

They lay down on their open bed rolls. The southern breeze blocked the cooling air off the water. Drowsy in the heat of the crowded hut, Ashoka said, "Madness, power?"

Tilaka whispered, "He wields the power of a god in the City of Carthage, in the whole empire of Carthage wherever he and his army go."

"Power of a god?"

"Gods end any life whenever they please. Gods are both cruel and kind, and only another god can stop their cruelty. On the north coast of Africa, this man, who owns us, is the most powerful god and the most cruel. Sleep now. I command you."

Chapter XIV

Big Dogs Hunting

Before full sunrise eight handlers tied the best eight dogs to leashes and ran them three times round the moat in the center of the camp. These dogs knew what came next. They had hunted many times before in this life and in a thousand years of the hunt bred into them.

The camp elephants huddled on the other side of the moat. The dogs frightened them.

Mintho, already mounted, waited at the head of the forming line. He looked back, checking the soldiers and mahouts mustering behind him. Then in the increasing light, Mintho spotted Ashoka mount his assigned horse. It was Mintho's own, ridden the day before, a strong horse that obeyed only one master, never let anyone else on its back. Mintho, laughing inside at the coming embarrassment for his arrogant new slave, watched his new mahout and horse.

As Ashoka grabbed the mane and pulled himself up by ropes coiled around the horse's belly, the horse circled at him, then away, then back and tried to bite him. Ashoka avoided the snapping teeth, pulled himself up quickly, and leaned forward on the bare back. The horse bucked, kicked and snorted, and tried to shake him off. Ashoka stayed on easily, better than Mintho's best riders. The horse bucked and squealed again, once more, but then quieted. Mintho nodded in admiration and surprise.

He glimpsed Tilaka struggling to mount his smaller horse until two others boosted him up. "Where is Tilaka. I want my lead mahout here with me." Mintho signaled for the little army to move out. At the front the dog handlers jumped onto their horses and let out the long leashes. The dogs exploded up the trail.

Mintho mused how long it would take Tilaka to drop back, even fall off his mount, and Ashoka to move up next to him. Mintho decided he would not halt the ride to collect up Tilaka if Tilaka fell off—maybe on the way back if lions or hyenas had not collected him up first.

After a short way out of the camp at a switchback on the first climb, Mintho had a view of those who followed. Tilaka had fallen far back in line, but here came his own horse with Ashoka, passing others at every chance. A tree branch hanging across the trail threatened, and Mintho's horse veered into it. Ashoka slipped to the horse's side. He hung on with one hand on the neck and a foot across the back, another correct and quick rider's move that pleased Mintho.

Ashoka's mount reached Mintho, nuzzled his leg, and stayed close. Mintho mumbled in Greek, "You have indeed learned to ride."

"Thank you, Master. Yours is a proud and strong horse. I could not hold it back."

That made Mintho laugh. "How did you know?"

"Master, you rode this one yesterday... and it wants only you."

"Tell me, how did you learn to ride like that?"

"In the high plateau above a town called Exandahar when our work was done, a Numidian slave taught me."

"Oh, tell me more, how a slave taught an Indian to ride so well."

The mahout did not answer immediately, looked as if he collected his thoughts, as if he wanted to pick his words, and then spoke slowly, deliberately. "We rode in a cold wind and laughed while we rode, laughed at the high snows in the distance, at the fine beasts under us, at the narrow trails carved by many riders over many years before us, trails we could not see until we were on them. But our horses knew, never stumbled. Sometimes we jumped up onto their backs as they came running at us, then rode them over on the side—as I did down there. We rode until the sun dropped behind the mountains, and we had to get our elephant in." He reached over and patted the neck of Mintho's horse. It did not mind. "Master Mintho, your horse is like those beauties."

So it might be true, Mintho thought. "That's the elephant with four nails, yes, the one you let free?"

"Yes, Master. But I did not free that great elephant. The gods freed him. I was only their instrument."

Mintho did not respond, no need to. This young brown mahout told him enough, perhaps too much, but he was now convinced his buyers had not paid too much for the one who called himself Ashoka. Ashoka could easily take Tilaka's place, might even turn his remaining elephants into fighters, into more than big cows.

After a half-day ride with one short rest, the army reached the forests and meadows below the highest rocky crags. The dogs pulled them up until any sign of a path for men or animals melted into dirt, scrub grass, rocks and trees. Near the crest of the coastal range, the dogs stopped their weaving from side to side low to the ground, stopped their sniffing. They formed into a single line and lifted their snouts off the ground. The handlers jumped off the horses and released their charges. The dogs sprang silently through dry grass, dirt and rocks, and raced up the slope vanishing into evergreens. The dogs' barking rolled across the mountain valley and drew the little army to them.

Mintho approached from downwind and stopped where he could catch sight of a crouching dog or gray hide dappled by the light. The dogs had found a herd resting in the coolest stand of shade trees in this mid-day sun. Mintho raised his arm to halt the riders behind. Until the elephants were encircled, disoriented and unable or too tired to run, his army must move no closer. They had to wait for the dogs to do their work and only then select the best ones to take.

No one, not even he, taught the mastiffs to carry out what he once again watched. No human had trained them in the patterns to run, to snap at the backs of the hind legs where the elephants cannot see, to make the big beasts turn circles until they no longer noticed the riders and ropers moving up. If one of the adult elephants slipped off into dense brush, the dogs followed, cut it off, and brought it back to the herd. Yet they knew to not chase the old or sickly. No mortal had shown the dogs how to spot and challenge the leader, how to cut out the elephant the men pointed to, and, through it all, stay clear of tusks and trunks and padded feet as big around as tree trunks all trying to kill them. A spirit superior to any man moved in the dogs singly and together. Baal El, god of gods and rider of the clouds, surely chose these dogs to experience life on firm ground. As Mintho took it all in, he once again felt the deep tingling in his whole body, the tingling of a kinship with the supreme god of Carthage.

When all the gray hides appeared to mill in a tight circle and all the elephant heads hung low concentrating on the snarling pests at their feet, Mintho nudged his horse forward.

It too knew its role and remained in shadows, behind trees and rocks, and froze when once or twice an elephant raised a head and trunk and flapped its ears toward them.

This herd's leader was not the healthiest female but a male. Its tusks, curved forward at the tips, were so heavy he could not for long lift and hold up his head. Three dogs danced around this one even before Mintho gave the signal to isolate it. It had lived many years. Mintho guessed over forty. He had to take care. This one was smart and brave enough to evade or defeat all who hunted for tusks such as these.

Mintho and his men could not have chosen better terrain. The land, wooded but not so dense that the dogs and horses could not follow, maneuver and surround, assured quick and safe capture. His dogs had found the first herd to reach the coolest and highest areas of untouched grass in an early but dry summer. It must have been the strongest herd in these mountains. He let the dogs keep pestering and tiring the elephants, take turns rushing in and backing off and snapping at the hind legs. A good half-day of light remained, more than enough time for the hunt's first stage and to prepare for a safe and quiet night. He sensed that this was perhaps too good but did not know what bothered him.

Mintho signaled for Tilaka, Ashoka and the other mahouts to move up to him, slowly. He mouthed to Ashoka, "Have you restrained elephants with only ropes?"

"Yes, Master," Ashoka mouthed back.

"Have you tied their feet to trees?"

"Yes, Master, bigger elephants than these."

Now the elephants looked up and stared out past the dogs pestering them low to the ground. Mintho whistled twice and shouted in the language of Carthage, "Let's take the big one with the tusks. We have him, and the herd will be ours."

Then in Greek to Ashoka, "Have you hunted with dogs?"

"No, Master."

Mintho wanted to ask how, then, had Ashoka hunted elephants at all. No time, later perhaps. He motioned to the dogs. "They'll keep him busy. You and any of the mahouts you want must tie his legs. Can you do that?"

"If the gods will it."

Mintho hissed, "I will it." He wanted to shout it, but shouts from him might break the dogs' concentration, their teamwork, might startle some of his men.

Ashoka pointed to Ganesha and the two youngest mahouts. The four rode closer to the dogs and the elephants, the little army pressing in behind.

Mintho wanted to ask why Ashoka took two of the youngest and least experienced mahouts but soon saw—they were the nimblest, most fearless and most eager. He wanted to say, *Do well, young Ashoka. I can have only one lead mahout.*

He pulled his horse's mane to stand still so he could watch this great bull, the biggest elephant he had seen in thirteen hunts in these mountains, almost as big as an adult female Indian elephant, defend against his dogs and mahouts. The tusks would sell for enough to provision his army for a year with more left over to pay the section leaders a few coins.

One of the dog handlers on horseback pointed to the bull and shouted, "This one, this one."

The three dogs converged tighter on the bull, barking, snapping, bounding and lunging from opposite sides and the rear, teasing the bull to move at them out from his herd. The bull held its place. Two dogs rushed in, the first straight at the lowered head and trunk trying to swipe it, and the second from the other side at the back leg. It bit hard and hung on. The elephant lurched away from and then spun at that second dog. The third dog grabbed the other hind leg. The three

114

dogs worked the leader from side to side ever away from the herd to an area where the mahouts might approach. As the bull separated, the small army of riders, through shouts and pointed spears, kept the other elephants from their leader.

Mintho now saw what was wrong. The dogs ran in too close to the old bull, bared more of their teeth than ever before. The pitch of their snarling and barking was lower, louder, angrier. When they caught the back of a leg, they bit too deeply and hung on too long, risked getting flung away and breaking their teeth or jaw. They had turned from hunters to killers. This herd did not respond as usual either. Fewer of them faced out toward their leader or tried to follow him than on other hunts. Something besides calves in the center held the elephants' attention.

Mintho counted three dogs barking, leaping, and teasing the bull and four more around the herd, and knew. *Mother of all leech eaters. They must have gored my beauty, tossed it high, and surrounded it, stomped it to death. . . and now pushing and kicking its carcass.*

Mintho decided to carry on as if nothing had gone awry. The angry bull and out-of-control dogs made a good test for Ashoka.

The four mahouts jumped off their horses and unrolled their coiled ropes. Crouching low, sometimes partially shielded by trees, boulders and bushes, sometimes in plain view of their target, they scampered and crawled into position on the four quarters. On the way each tied his rope twice around a tree where a soldier waited and carried the other looped end toward the bull, still turning left and right and all the way around at the crazed dogs.

At a moment when one of the dogs had the bull's full attention, Ashoka sprang out of his crouch and slipped the free looped end of his rope up and around the elephant's hind foot. The soldier at the tree end of the rope yanked it taut and slung multiple loops around the tree. The other three mahouts each did the same on another leg, and soldiers pulled those ropes tight around three other trees. The bull stood helpless, its legs splayed in four directions unable to drive on any foot.

Mintho had never seen better coordination among mahouts, soldiers, and dogs. Ashoka and the others would not have done as well had they known about the dead dog, of that he was sure. Both little Ganesha and tall Ashoka worked quickly and well. For an instant Mintho turned to look back and around, look for Tilaka, but did not spot him. Perhaps the old cripple fell off his horse and sat on the ground back out of danger's way.

Another worry seeped into Mintho. Elephants from India and from Africa south of the great desert never allowed mere dogs to round them up or footmen to restrain their legs with ropes in open terrain. No man tried to capture and train the monsters from the south of Africa, with their massive shoulders, oversized ears, strength to push down any log fence and a rage no man knew how to control. No African or Indian adult bull would allow four unarmed mahouts and three dogs to trap him. A wild goat ram fought harder against capture than these elephants. If Carthage ever tried to use these docile beasts in battle... no time to think about that, about what might happen to its army and to him if that Barca upstart found out.

The dogs and men isolated and bound five larger females in the same manner. The remainder of the now leaderless herd scattered, leaving behind the carcass of the lead dog, a slab of wet hide, broken bones protruding through the hide, mixed into a thick sticky mat of pine needles on the forest floor.

Mintho's men cut down trees and by sunset built an interlocking barrier of logs around each captured elephant, preventing escape even if one of the leg ropes loosened in the night. That rarely happened. Once bound, these elephants soon gave in to a superior master.

He would have liked to have roasted the muscles and heart of his lead dog in olive oil, rubbed the hot cooked meat in crystallized honey and shared it with his best soldiers while they talked of their greatest battles. All men of courage in Carthage ate the flesh of dogs. The bull and its herd deprived him and his soldiers of the finest dog any of them might have taken into their bodies. All the more reason he had to teach the old bull and his new mahout hard lessons.

His men slaked their thirst from the streams and springs that fell away from the high forests and ate well. His dog handlers grieved, though not for long, and he praised his section leaders for the good hunt. He took his bath in the leaky wooden tub brought and assembled for him, donned clean garments slightly scented, and summoned Ashoka and Tilaka.

Chapter XV

Master and Slaves

Seated on cushions covered by a soft leather mat, two of his entourage standing on either side, Mintho spoke in Greek but looked at Ashoka while he said, "Tilaka, your mahouts performed well, my new one too. The captured elephants are healthy and strong and soon will bend to our will."

Ashoka responded, "Thank you, Master. Your lead dog had great courage."

Mintho focused harder on his new mahout. In the dark light of the tent, his eyes had weakened. "Ashoka, do you know how my dog died?"

"Yes, Master."

"Tell us."

This new mahout stood straighter and taller than Mintho remembered, looked Mintho directly into the eyes and talked without fear in his voice. "The tip of the right tusk—had fresh blood and black hairs. The herd kept the body. Indian elephants do the same when they kill a tiger."

"You did not delay. Weren't you afraid?"

"The bull's hatred of your dogs blinded it. After its tusks ripped the dog's belly, the bull wanted to do the same to the other dogs more than it wanted me."

This new mahout noticed the important things in the melee, perhaps even before he did. This mahout recounted them without fawning, but that agitated Mintho. This Ashoka showed no fear of power, and surely he knew of Mintho's power, had learned to respect that power, bow to it. If not, he would learn, perhaps beginning now.

Mintho reached an open hand to one of his attendants standing to the side. His man produced a dark metal hammer, the kind used by ironworkers to pound hot steel, and a spike as long as seven hands, one cubit in the measure of Carthage. "Ashoka, in the morning when the bull has quieted from its sleepless night, my men will force it into a narrow section of its pen where they have built a platform. You know about that?"

"Yes, Master. Tilaka told me, to hold its head still. Once locked in, it can't move its head."

Mintho handed the hammer and spike to Ashoka, who took them without any sign of bewilderment. This too surprised. "You've done this before?"

"No. Tilaka has told me how Carthage kills captive elephants for their tusks, or the sick ones before the sickness spreads. I don't know a better way."

"Ashoka, we know a lot that is better than in your India." Mintho tried to say it with kindness. "One strong blow behind the ear to the brain brings death quickly and with less pain than the many deep cuts used in Seleucia and in your India."

Ashoka bowed. "When I go back, I'll tell them of your better ways."

When I go back... Mintho's elation at Ashoka's skill turned to instant anger—but he held it in, must not show it, not yet. No slave of his must be allowed to dream that he would ever go home. He waited and watched this Ashoka for a long time, wanted to make him nervous, afraid, but the tall Indian just stood there relaxed showing nothing, waiting for Mintho to say more. Mintho forced a smile. "Excellent. Go and in the morning and do what you must. We'll take his tusks and leave the carcass to foul the mountains, not our camp. This bull deserves no better, don't you think?" Mintho waved his hand for Ashoka to leave—now.

Ashoka did not move. "Master Mintho, if you permit me..."

"To kill him for his tusks and honor my finest hunting dog. Go."

Ashoka did not leave. Mintho noticed him more closely now, handsome in the soft light of the candles flickering on the floor of the tent, the brown skin finer than his own at the same age. It did not blemish, burn, and wrinkle like the skin of white men and women. He thought Ashoka fearless almost, but not quite, to the point of rudeness.

"Do you question my order?"

Tilaka reached for Ashoka's arm before he said any more.

Mintho suppressed a laugh. Better to wait and let Ashoka try to explain and thereby set the punishment. Mintho, too pleased by the newly captured elephants, the skill of this mahout, and his plan for Tilaka, did not let Ashoka's resistance spoil his good spirits. He had paid too much for this mahout. Better to let him live, sell him if he caused trouble, or keep him if he learned to respect his master. "Leave. I'm done with you."

Ashoka refused to move, to let Mintho laugh and drink wine and rest. "That bull, Master Mintho, might show the way to teach your camp elephants to fight. If your men kill the bull in front of the others, the others will never obey a single command from your men."

Mintho motioned with his hand for Ashoka to explain.

"My father's elephants help train new wild ones. If your elephants will ever show more courage than sheep, they need one of their own to lead them."

That did it. Mintho could take, would take, no more from one of his slaves. He had cut out the tongue, crucified men, for lesser insubordination. Mintho forced his worst scowl and bellowed, and the bellow made Ashoka move back. "My elephants fight—they are no sheep, not sheep."

Ashoka still did not seem afraid, did not move away. He said very quietly but very surely, "If you leave some of your soldiers at the camp, the ones who built the fence of logs that now holds him, we might teach him how to fight. The bull will remember the voices and smells of the men who cut down the trees and penned him. If he charges those men, the others in his herd might follow and become real fighting elephants."

This made sense—let him try, no harm in that. In time, that upstart Barca might learn that Mintho's elephants were as docile as sheep in a fight. Then Mintho would have to deal with problems far greater than one insolent slave. But, perhaps, if he delivered real fighting elephants, that day would never come. Mintho relaxed his face but kept his voice strong. "What you say... do it. Teach the bull, but kill him before I next come to the camp if he doesn't obey. Leave now, before I don't let you leave."

Ashoka and Tilaka left. Mintho again noticed Tilaka limping out. The muscles of one or both legs must be ripped, or bone rubbed against bone in the knees. Carthage could not survive under leaders who could not lead. Macedon had lost its leader and crumbled. While the Senate argued and the generals squabbled for influence, afraid to battle, Rome had nearly brought Carthage to its knees in the last war. That must not happen again. Leaders who could not lead had to be put out. When the two mahouts were beyond hearing, Mintho said to no one and everyone, "Ashoka will bend to the will of the gods of Carthage, and it will be good. Ashoka is my best mahout, don't you think?"

His attendants did not respond.

Through the night, the mahouts sat on the logs that fenced in the frightened animals and talked to them, softly, musically.

By the end of the next day, all the females took water from leather water sacks, and not one lunged at or tried to knock over any of the mahouts. One by one the captured elephants took treats—balls of millet and honey, dried sweet figs, dried grasses brought into the mountains by the army, and their favorite, celery soaked in salt water. They accepted the will of man, as had their stronger, bigger relatives in India for many generations.

By the fourth day, each of the captured elephants allowed its front legs to be untied and only loosely tethered together, the hind legs freed, and a mahout to climb on its back from the top of the makeshift fences. The bond between mahout and elephant had begun.

Tilaka said, "Master, the six new elephants are ready to take down to our camp."

"Yes, I can see that."

On the way back, the remaining seven dogs again took to the front following a new leader selected silently by them. They knew no other way.

The captured elephants followed far behind the lead riders and dogs. The bull with the tusks that nearly scraped the ground and that had slain Mintho's best dog led the five females to the main camp, Ashoka riding by its side when the trail permitted.

Chapter XVI

Dried-Out

The grasses turned yellow and stopped growing at the height of a man's knee. Figs dropped to the ground before they turned plump and sweet. The stream down from the mountains feeding the irrigation ditches and moat year round slowed to a trickle. Cobras and yellow vipers drew closer to the camp. A third year of drought had clasped onto the north coast of Africa tighter than the hawk clasps a rabbit before it takes flight with its prey.

The camp men slept by day and tried to stay awake through the night. After dark leopards and lions growled and huffed ever closer to the camp. Only the fires, the armed sentries, newly cut barriers of thorny bushes, and dogs kept them out.

During the day guards looked out from high up in different trees outside the camp. A small band of outlaws could easily overwhelm them all. Not much left here to fight over, a few chickens, horses, two cows, and lesser weapons. But outlaws did desperate things when easy mountain game vanished.

The four remaining Indians—Ashoka, Tilaka, and two helpers—had little to do since the last sale of Mintho's worthiest men and elephants more than a year back. Most of the able-bodied men, all their women and children had left with Mintho's sale of the best elephants. The four old cow elephants still at the camp stood in the shady area of their little island inside the moat.

"Ashoka, help me here. I need your legs." Even using the stick, Tilaka limped on both legs. "Reach up there." Inside their hut he pointed to the top of the wall under the sloped roof of cedar boards covered by flat stones. "Look if it's still there."

Ashoka found the bag and handed it down. Tilaka pulled out a bronze coin. "Long ago when he had more to give, Mintho paid me something. I kept them all. Look at this one. It's her best likeness."

Ashoka took the unevenly round bronze coin. A raised profile of the head, facing left, appeared on one side. The nose was straight and delicate, the chin strong, and the neck long and of clean lines, neither too thick nor too narrow. Her hair, high in curls that sloped forward at the top, gave the effect of a crown on the head of a young queen.

"Tanit, the goddess of life and rain and every growing thing, isn't she beautiful?"

Ashoka couldn't help laughing. "Tilaka, you've been here too long."

"I know, I know. A poor metal worker copied the head of the noblest woman from his region, and she became our god Tanit on this coin."

"Our god, Tanit?"

"She is ours now. Do not forget that. Whatever she looks like, she must help us now. We've nothing to give her, to sacrifice to her. She allows Moth to have his way. Only the senators and high nobles have what she wants."

Ashoka turned the coin over. A stout horse and a palm frond appeared on the coin's other side. The locals said the god of war came to earth as a horse. The locals called the god of war Haddad. "Tilaka, these are not our gods. Our gods help us if we live worthy lives."

"Our gods are too far away to help. Forget them."

Ashoka did not know what to say, what to think—other than, Tilaka was right. Only idleness, stupidity, and a dying spirit honored his promise to Govinda. Thoughts of returning home rarely flickered in him and then not for long.

"These coins will help you more than any gods of India. This camp will close, and... these coins will help you more than they would help me." Tilaka put the bag in Ashoka's hand and folded Ashoka's fingers around it.

"Keep them. Our gods still provide what I need." Ashoka lied, more to himself than to Tilaka. Many nights in his dreams, he walked eastward with another Syrian caravan. If he were older, stronger, knew the local language better—had more courage—he might have fled this camp, lived on shell fish along the shore until he reached the City of Carthage. There he could have found work tending horses or cattle and in time a ship heading east. But always he remembered his mother's last scolding, about his foolish pride at wrestling for the Emperor. He knew Mintho's army or lions would find him long before he reached a safe place, and his short knife would not do against an attack from a big cat or many men.

Tilaka still had Ashoka's hand wrapped around the bag of coins. "He knows you're his best trainer but takes other mahouts out of here with the worthy elephants. And you trained them all."

The bull captured in the local mountains had indeed chased the men who fenced him in, charged those who brandished swords and spears against it. Flaming arrows did not deter it. The captured females followed its lead, then other females of the camp did too. But they were long gone with the other mahouts, sold to an eager buyer unknown to Ashoka. Mintho had not organized another hunt for elephants.

Tilaka took Ashoka's arm. "Help me out to the orchards. He's near. I feel his madness, his cruelty."

125

They passed the sleeping dogs, the guards playing a game with bones, and laborers snoring in the shade of cedars and twisted junipers. They stopped and waited near the dry grass at the end of the olive orchard.

"Hear the horses on the trail, Ashoka?"

Soon Mintho and his army, this time much smaller, arrived. The remaining men again put on their best garments of wool and stood at attention in the heat, but any excitement had dried up. The high senator strode directly at Ashoka and motioned for him to walk away from the others. "Come with me, Ashoka."

Out of hearing of the others, Mintho continued, "In the morning, we'll set free the last of my elephants and you will leave with me. My scouts have told us for a long time there are no more elephants in the near mountains. This camp is finished."

Ashoka caught every word. Mintho had said nothing about Tilaka or the two helpers, the remaining broken down guards, the camp dogs. Ashoka wanted to ask, but Mintho walked off.

There was no feast that night. Mintho and his men ate by themselves down close to the sea. Ashoka and Tilaka did not talk about the camp closing. They and the others all knew they were at the mercy of Mintho and could do nothing in the night. Ashoka asked the God Ganesha, the spirit of Buddha, the family spirit in his *kukri* what to do. He remembered Madan over the big pot and what he had said about patience, about helping his countrymen. Patience and finding a way to help his countrymen was the most he could do.

The next morning at sunrise, Mintho's army rounded up the camp's useful implements, chickens, goats, the two cows, and horses. The men released the elephants from their tethers and walked them over the moat bridge, but the elephants did not move out, did not stray from fresh water, easy food and the safety of the camp. Mintho's men had brought extra horses and now assigned each camp member to a horse. But no one had said anything to Ashoka or to the other three from his country.

Mintho found Ashoka, "Ride behind me on that free horse made ready for you."

"Thank you, Master. Tilaka and our two helpers also?"

Mintho looked away and then directly at Ashoka. "You haven't learned yet? You still question my commands? Must I leave you at this dead camp too? Look over there."

Ashoka looked but did not see what Mintho intended.

"Those old elephants will need Tilaka and your helpers more than I will. They can keep my dogs, stay here, live out their lives here, or follow the elephants. They are of no use to me."

Ashoka tried to quiet his insides. Leaving the four elephants did not worry him. Lions might attack one, but never four, and these elephants might soon find another herd. But leaving Tilaka and the two Indian helpers, defenseless to predators and bandits or to die here alone in this camp, would dishonor them in this life and for all lives to come. Ashoka dropped his hand by his thigh to feel the *kukri*. Only one other way came to him. Ashoka said loudly enough for all around them to hear easily. "Master, I will not leave them. If they are ripped apart by lions and hyenas or dry up behind these thorn bushes, that is my karma too. So it will be. Each has served you well, has honored you for many years. Our Buddha and our priests teach that to mistreat those who work for a master dishonors them but their master far more."

As Ashoka talked some of the soldiers on horseback moved closer and patted their mounts to quiet them. The remaining dogs cocked their ears at Mintho and Ashoka. The elephants turned toward them too. Tilaka and the two Indian helpers moved back but not out of hearing. Mintho looked around at all of them, walked away from Ashoka and shouted back. "Mahout, you choose the wrong master, you honor the wrong gods."

Ashoka was ready for that. "I meant that I, their master here at the camp, cannot leave them. I know well you are my only master here and now, and by leaving these men here, I do not serve you well either."

That stopped Mintho. Everyone fixed on him. He looked at the sky, then ahead at nothing. Slowly her turned to Ashoka and walked straight at him. "Indian, your ways are not our ways." Then, leaning over to Ashoka and in a lower voice so those watching could not hear, "I'll enjoy peeling off your skin after a hundred leeches take your blood. That might teach you loyalty, yes?"

Tilaka limped up to them. "Master, the drought has dried Ashoka in the head." He shrugged. "We can stay here and let him go with you."

Mintho ignored the old man. "Ashoka, do you refuse to go with me?"

"No, Master, as long as Tilaka and our two helpers leave with us. They will serve someone if you no longer need them."

Before Ashoka got it all out, Mintho grabbed his horse's mane and swung up onto its bare back in one movement like a man forty years younger. He yelled, "Ashoka, you shall have your Tilaka and helpers. If you or they delay us to Carthage City, your and their flesh will feed many hungry animals." Mintho laughed a laugh that said, I'm not done with you, Indian boy. Mintho pointed at his soldiers. "Let these worthless Indians ride on the camp horses, double up on the horses as you need, and let us leave this dead camp."

The camp dogs followed them out, but the camp elephants only looked at the men as they turned and rode off.

The elephants turned away before they were out of Ashoka's sight. He thought they liked the smell of freedom, that their keen hearing might have already located sounds of a wild herd far off in the hills.

+ + +

On the fourth day, they came upon cows grazing in the green grasses of riverbeds running to the sea. Tilaka, holding on around Ashoka's waist, said, "The pastures are smaller than the last time he took me to the city."

At cultivated plots of land, farmers looked up from their work. Children picking olives in scrawny trees stopped and looked at Mintho and his men. Women came to open doorways of houses made of rough stone or stood up from their washing and cooking pots outside the huts. Their faces remained quiet, without joy.

Ashoka pulled on the mane to slow his horse and create a gap between the riders in front of them. "Tilaka, if they had weapons they'd kill us," he said over his shoulder.

"All this land belongs to Mintho. They pay him so that they may be his slaves."

Ashoka tried to sound cheerful but could not. "We don't have to pay Mintho."

"Soon you will, in ways you don't yet know. They'd have nothing if he didn't let them work their land."

"You said it was his land. Now you say it's their land."

"Most are Libyans. More than three hundred years ago Mintho's forebears came from the eastern shore of the inland see, found the harbor of the City of Carthage, settled in and took the land from the local tribes along the whole north coast of Africa. Now Mintho lets their locals tend his crops, and they pay him tribute, a share of all crops, one of every litter, in some years a fine bounty."

"He steals from them and from the land that has been theirs for a thousand years... that's why he needs his army?"

"Yes, Ashoka. You begin to understand."

They traveled east in a straight line past ever denser farms and clusters of huts to the City of Carthage on the hill. Most of Mintho's soldiers left them. The soldiers took the camp animals, tools, laborers and camp guards. By midday only Mintho and three riders remained together with Ashoka and Tilaka on their one horse.

They passed through gates in one massive wall and then another wall protecting the city center. Cheering men and children ran up to them and parted in a continuous shouting flow. Ashoka caught the chorus yelled over and over, "Hail to Mintho. Hail to the senators... Hail to the great festival..."

The riders followed a cobbled road north out of the city into large estates and lush open spaces. The drought had no effect here. They came to a high plaster wall on a street lain with smooth flat stones. The street wound north through estates hidden behind walls so high only treetops hinted at the wealth of the owners. They stopped by a solitary wooden gate in a long wall. It swung open at a signal Ashoka did not see or a command he did not hear.

Inside the wall, cedars, junipers and thick palm trees shaded the wide main path. Narrow tiled walkways led away through fig trees, bushes blooming in many hues of red, flower beds, and ponds connected by trickling brooks. Black birds with long necks played in lily pads.

One of Mintho's entourage led the two Indians down a separate path to a long two-story house next to a stable. Ashoka guessed all the estates of all the wealthy families in Lalput could fit inside these walls.

Ashoka and Tilaka, each helped by a man servant, bathed

in a stone tub with an internal drain built into the floor, combed their hair, put on clean garments, and ate sweet rice cooked in milk and dried figs and dates. They sat on a softer, deeper mat than Ashoka had ever known.

Ashoka said, "Why does he bring us here? There are no elephants here." He wondered if Mintho cleaned, dressed, and fed them to kill them. He had only his *kukri* for protection.

Tilaka said, "He brings us here to show you, Ashoka, his might, his power. He brings us here for the festival tomorrow night."

"Why... what... festival?"

"Patience, Ashoka. You will see and never forget. Then you will know his power and obey him in all ways."

"I will not obey to do things I cannot."

"Ashoka, do not talk such foolishness until you know more. Sleep now. Tomorrow night you will not."

In the night, through the window openings of their room, Ashoka heard voices of women, animated, happy then angry, crying. He could not make out the words or where they came from, but the voices scraped at his insides harder, louder than anything he had heard since Govinda's last gasps for air and life.

Chapter XVII

The Holiest Festival

On his second night in the city, an early moon crept up red and full. He and Tilaka bathed again. Servants made them spread perfume over their bodies, gave them fresh garments and a collar of many colors. Tilaka said the colors signified they belonged to Mintho. Without it, they could be enslaved by another wealthy family or set upon by thieves. As Mintho's possessions, they were safe in any part of the city.

"But we are safe here? We don't need this collar."

"Ashoka, you think he would dress us in fine garments and slather our skin in sweet oils to stay here? No, tonight we gather with everyone from this city and other places far from here."

"Oh, for what? This is no time or place for any harvest."

"I told you yesterday, but you did not hear me. For the festival of the Molk." Tilaka's voice invited no questions.

"What is that? I heard you but thought it nothing?"

Tilaka waited, exhaled, shook his head. "You'll know soon enough. This festival does not happen every year—only when the gods of Carthage are angry at its people. They must be appeased now, or the drought will suck the little life that's left out of this city and its empire."

Ashoka scoffed. "You believe that? Droughts are made by the sun and no rain, not by these gods. Appease how?"

"Ashoka, the empire of Carthage is ruled by gods of a different persuasion."

The door to their room opened and a servant motioned them to follow.

Tilaka tugged Ashoka's elbow. "Stay close to me until the morning." Tilaka's voice and look told Ashoka that the two must stay together, not to help Tilaka hobble around but for Ashoka's protection.

Ashoka, Tilaka, laborers and slaves, men, and women from Mintho's estate streamed into the street. It seemed the whole city had come out, more women and children than men. Torches and the light of the moon rising in a clear sky allowed Ashoka and Tilaka to keep their places in the throng of Mintho's servants. Ashoka thought he spotted several of the soldiers from the elephant camp limping along, looking forward and smiling at something Ashoka did not see, did not understand.

Many adults carried wooden musical instruments of various shapes strung with horsehair, some very fine, some crude. Others carried conch shells, hand drums of animal skins, and rattles painted various colors. Some played flutes. Some wailed songs Ashoka had never heard and did not understand, the beats ragged and the tunes off key.

The masses, joyous and laughing and smelling of sweet perfumes, came together from all directions heading toward the center of the city and down to the harbor. They packed tighter and tighter. Off to the sides in the darker alleys, Ashoka spotted armed soldiers and thought they must have been stationed to keep beggars and thugs from setting upon the throng or any of the throng from sneaking away. The songs of the assembled merged to make the sound of wind, as loud and deep as the sandstorm in the Great Desert of India.

The whole crushing mass slowed to a shuffle until his group, and only his group, seemed to free itself and moved faster than the rest. His group slithered through a narrow opening between buildings on one side and idle hulls sitting high and massive on bare ground out of water on the other side. His throng made its way past many warehouses and up a dirt ramp to an empty roof, flat and large enough for them all. Once Ashoka's group was all at the top front of that roof, standing there three or four deep, the other areas on the roof filled in quickly. The newcomers seemed to know when to stop before they pushed off those at the front, or their leaders made them stop.

Taller than most of the others, Ashoka had a good view. Torch fires, bigger than he had ever seen, sat in a line in front of him on a wharf. Past the wharf dark water caught and reflected the torch fires. Many wide eyes and teeth in laughing faces on the roof strained to get a view of the torches and wharf and whatever else was down there.

In the clearing between Ashoka's building and the water, robed men and women stood at attention on both sides of a rock. Ashoka counted the robe wearers, seventeen, each in a different color with tapered head coverings the same color as their robes. Ashoka had learned Carthage worshiped seventeen gods, each associated with a unique color, and he guessed these were the highest priests connected to each of the seventeen gods.

The rock's waist-high square top was as flat and smooth as a table. Ashoka noticed grooves across the flat top and crude stick figures etched into its sides. Beyond the rock stood two black metal ovens, their bases of stones and cement buried in the ground. The ovens' tapered chimneys reached higher than the heads of Mintho's group on the roof.

Though he could not hear them above the din, fires roared in each oven, and sparks flew into the night out of the open chimney tops. The ovens each had two gates at ground level. Laborers next to a hill of cut logs and a mound of black bitumen fed the ovens' back gates.

One of the seventeen men at the rock approached the building that Ashoka stood on. He beckoned at someone Ashoka could not see. A man and woman together came out of one of the buildings on ground level. The woman carried a bundle, its top against her cheek. The masses sang louder and cheered when the couple emerged. Those around Ashoka started to jump up and down, then harder and higher until the roof flexed with the jumping but held.

A hand squeezed hard above his elbow. It startled him— enthralled like all the others. Tilaka shouted through the din, "It begins. Close your eyes and don't listen, else you'll never find sleep again."

The man who had come forward to beckon the couple spread his arms high and wide. The masses quieted. Only the sounds of moths and insects exploding in the torch fires, the crackling from the furnaces, and babies crying competed for attention. Many bats chased insects in the fire lights from torches and oven chimneys.

This priest's small head and face, striped with a brown pigment, seemed stuck to the top of his dark brown one-piece garment covering his body from chin to feet and hanging from the length of each arm. The priest, arms outstretched in this wide brown raiment, waiting, small head barely moving, reminded Ashoka of a giant bat preparing to take flight.

He shouted to the man and woman who had come out of the building, "Senator Luli, Carthage honors and thanks you."

The masses cheered again.

The priest raised his arms higher, the crowd quieted. "My god, Haddad, thanks you. He will bless your house and all your kin and will favor the horses and riders of Carthage in battle. Lift up thy treasure to Haddad, god of the horse."

Luli and his woman remained motionless, heads slightly bowed so Ashoka could not see their faces. The priest reached toward her. She moved the bundle off her shoulder but did not hand it up. The priest snatched it from her. He unwrapped the bundle to let the blanket drop at his feet, held high an infant male, and turned the small body from side to side for all to see. The sound of the insects snapping mixed with the cries of the baby boy in the night, naked, its arms and legs resisting the stranger, and sobs—deep and choked—from the woman. Luli's head drooped farther.

The priest walked to the rock table. Ashoka noticed the knives, one on each corner, and understood all. He reached for the dagger on his thigh under his garment. He could change nothing, not even by taking his own life in this place. From the priest's stance, the sound of his voice, his confident movements, Ashoka knew this priest had slaughtered living beings before many times.

And Ashoka obeyed Tilaka, closed his eyes and tried not to hear.

The crowd grew even quieter, making the lone woman's sobs louder, and then she too quieted.

Suddenly, the masses resumed their songs and cheering. Many shouted the names of the infant's father and of the god of the horse. Ashoka dared to look again.

At the base of each oven door, a shovel waited. The priest pulled the shovel out of the nearer fire and rested the hot end on bare ground. He placed the tiny naked body on the shovel giving it the effect of reclining on a flat bed tilted up at the head. The young skin hissed in the shovel's embrace. The priest poured a thin amber fluid from a plain ewer over the shovel and body. The hissing grew louder. As shovel and tiny body entered the oven's mouth, white-hot flames roared around and through them. Down on one knee, the priest peered at the conflagration.

After a time, he and a laborer pulled out the shovel a black mound in its center. The laborer doused it with another liquid, releasing white smoke. Cheering and shouting smothered any noise made by the cooling.

Thirty large glass jars waited in two rows at the right of the ovens. The priest and another man carried the flat shovel holding the charred mound to the first jar. With small hand tools they transferred the remains into the jar's wide mouth. Smoke and vapor rose from its mouth after they finished.

The mother, alone, sobbing again, followed behind the priest. She fell to the ground in front of the jar until other women took her away.

The priest turned to the masses and spread his arms high and wide for total silence. He shouted, slowly deliberately, in the language of Carthage. Ashoka understood enough. "I saw it, and it is good. The child smiled as the flames freed him for his ascent to Haddad. He'll be happy in his new life, and Haddad will have a new son. Haddad thanks Senator Luli, his house, and Carthage and will bless them and keep them strong all of Senator Luli's days."

Before he finished the masses again broke into cheering, clapping, singing and jumping, and shouting. Luli, youngest senator of Carthage, and Haddad, ruler of the horse and god of war, were forever joined. Ashoka felt the roof under him vibrate once more. He did not see Luli again.

The ritual repeated twenty-eight times until dawn began to glow in the eastern sky beyond the ovens and the high chimneys. At times two or three children were slaughtered and cremated through both gates at opposite sides of the ovens. Some of the mothers refused to come forward. Their senator husbands, with the help of other men, wrested sons or daughters from their grasps. Some children had no mothers to present them—fathers only. Other mothers laughed and danced and shrieked and aided the priest in placing their dead babies onto the shovel and into the fire and the remains into the burial jars. Some of the sacrificed children, older, old enough to understand, staggered forward between parents as if drugged. Four young toddlers wore blindfolds.

Blood, black in the night, covered the stone altar top and ran along the grooves and onto the ground from the corners. The masses became exhausted. Many collapsed and were revived with splashed water.

The priest of Tanit, covered in a robe of deep blue, summoned the last senator. Mintho emerged from the door below Ashoka and the others of his group. As soon as they saw Mintho, the exhausted masses began to sing and moan with an energy as if Mintho were the first father of the night to offer his child.

A mature woman came out behind Mintho. She, with her gray hair showing at the side openings of her linen head covering, displayed no emotion. She too carried an infant on her shoulder but strode forward faster than many of the mothers before her. Ashoka wondered if the child were hers or her child's child. The sacrifice would be no less. He wondered if her strength and bearing came from having done this too many times before.

The infant boy, near the same age as Luli's, slept, deeply, mercifully. When awakened by the din, he burrowed his face into the woman's neck and shoulder, eyes closed, trying to turn away from the light and noise.

When unrobed and naked, the color of the infant's skin, brown, made Ashoka gasp—and this time watch through squinting eyes. At the same time, above the mounting wails and shouts of adoration, he heard a shriek by a woman on his roof from behind him. The shriek was snuffed out as if someone had clamped a hand over the woman's mouth or struck her down. That shriek jarred Ashoka through his fatigue and wretchedness as never before. He had to hear it again, look for her, find her. He trembled and knew he trembled because his body knew that shriek. He looked around but saw only tightly packed laughing, smiling, singing faces, no one in agony, no one down low or lying on the roof, or crying. He wanted to move away, back to where that shriek came from but could not. The crush on the roof packed him too tightly.

Again the crowd quieted. This time the blue-robed priest talked to Mintho and the woman next to him quietly, placed his free hand on each of their shoulders and bowed to them.

Then he turned to the slaughter stone, and the crowd wailed and shouted again but not long. It again grew as still as the morning.

As Tanit's priest used one of the knives on the brown infant, neither Mintho nor the woman next to him reacted. But at the instant the knife touched the child, through the dead silence came that high-pitched shriek again, close enough now and long enough that all of it entered deeply into him, this one of a terror and rage from the darkest place of any living being. Through the shriek came words—deliberate and slow, each enunciated clearly but spoken in his own language in a dialect that only someone from his region of India would easily understand. The shriek and words came out of a throat and with a voice Ashoka knew.

"Mintho... You merciless monster... May you drink at the teats of a pregnant sow... and when you're fat, may you be fed to the lowest of sewer cleaners and defecated out of them with a foulness black flies won't touch... in every one of your wretched lives for all eternity."

The cry and words came from directly behind Ashoka on the same roof, behind the crush of Mintho's people who did not hear, who again started to cheer and shout and jump, or if they heard did not understand, or if they understood did not care. The voice was of that girl, now a woman and mother—Radha.

Chapter XVIII

Yearnings

Ashoka staggered off the warehouse roof after the others. Patience. He spat it under his breath. This life wasted, trapped, waiting for a child-killer to call on his Indian playthings yet again. His promise to Govinda was now a curse on Ashoka for all eternity.

In the early light, Ashoka saw many boats and much larger ships tied up at the harbor out past the still smoking ovens and more ships waiting in the farther distance on the water. Would Tilaka's coins be enough to buy passage on a ship heading east? He glanced at the brown skin on his own forearm, on Tilaka. He touched the colored collar signifying he belonged to Mintho and shut out thoughts of going home, but knew those yearnings would come back.

He and Tilaka did not talk as the throng swept them into the city center, where celebrations had already begun. Long tables under tent tops sat covered with bread, meats, fruit and goblets of water, juices and wine, one table for each senate family. When Ashoka and Tilaka arrived, long lines had already formed at each table. Many people not in one of the lines meandered about in tired dances and sang tired songs.

Ashoka and Tilaka avoided the dancing clusters and the dispensers of wine. They averted their gazes from old toothless women beckoning in doorways and window openings of crowded bottom floor flats. They tried not to notice couples, sometimes of differing skin colors and various ages from young to old and graying, in the shadows of buildings and behind bushes, their legs and arms wrapped, inhibitions eroded by fatigue and a collective permission to mate with whomever they wanted on this one solitary morning after the festival of the smiling children. They might not have this collective permission for another generation.

Ashoka and Tilaka did not join in the cheers and shouts every time a senator and his entourage passed by. In the mid-morning heat, Senator Luli and his wife, faces puffed and eyes red, came to their own family's celebration tent and managed to wave at their adoring citizens. The line to Mintho's tent-covered feast table was the longest of all the lines. Ashoka and Tilaka hung in the shade of a building off to the side, did not eat or drink. Ashoka looked for any sign about what Mintho would do to them now. Mintho and his grey-haired woman, busied by many people wanting to touch them, hug them, talk to them, clapping and shouting as they passed by, did not seem to notice any of their servants.

In the late afternoon's hot shimmering air, the crowds dissipated, and the thirty senator families retreated to their homes north of the city and country villas across the bay. Now representatives of the senators distributed to every one of their private soldiers and each head of household a cloth pouch filled with salt. Ashoka had heard that in years when no winter caravan from the south made it across the great desert to the north coast of Africa, salt traded for the same amount, by weight, as gold. Mintho and the other senate families knew how to draw a loyal crowd.

Mintho's servants, all Indian, collected and loaded into many carts every left-over food item, every table, tent cloth and pole. They worked together without wasted motion or useless talk. Tilaka spoke softly to some, embraced one or two. Ashoka exchanged glances, too unsure of what to say to his countrymen or what trouble he might bring on them if they befriended him. He didn't see Radha or any young woman belonging to Mintho. They must have been assigned only to Mintho's big estate.

Ashoka and Tilaka lugged hunks of roasted pigs, dogs, chickens, and slabs of beef into brine-filled tubs and up onto flat carts headed for the smoking house on Mintho's estate. By this time on the next day, maggots and rot would infest cooked meat unless dried and smoked or heavily salted. They helped load bones and food scraps into bins and hauled the bins onto other carts bound for places outside the city where birds and small animals quickly cleaned up anything edible.

When done, one of Mintho's armed soldiers motioned for Ashoka and Tilaka to leave with other servants back to the main estate. They were sent to the same room and told to stay there. No one brought them food, let them bathe, or gave them clean clothes. A jar of water sat in the room, and the door remained unlocked. They could not sleep but did not talk, too fatigued, too jolted by what they had seen, had heard, and their thoughts of what would come next. Radha's cry had taken hold of Ashoka, a cry he knew would never leave him. The big ships in the harbor, his work with other Indians brought up memories of his mother and sisters, of his father and uncle, of his village, and the now constant thoughts of how to find a way home. *God Ganesha, God Vishnu and all the gods you talk to, please give me a sign, tell me what to do.*

Long before any rooster crowed, Ashoka said, "I know her."

"Who?" said Tilaka.

"The brown child's mother."

"You know the old woman, Mintho's wife—too old to birth a son? I know her, but surely you do not."

143

"No, no, the one who cursed Mintho in our tongue."

Tilaka said, "I heard her too but guessed—hoped—I had fallen asleep and dreamt while you held me up."

"You didn't dream it."

"I know that now, Ashoka. You and I could not have had the same dream at the same time."

"She knows me too."

"How do you know her?"

"She's from Lalput, a tanner's daughter."

"You wouldn't know a tanner's daughter."

"She came on my caravan with other girls from my region."

Tilaka's silence, his changed breathing in the dark, told Ashoka that Tilaka grasped all—the woman's caste, Ashoka's longing that wrestled against barriers instilled from a parent's first shooing away and scolding. No Carthaginian cared about these barriers, not an old man married to a dried up gray-haired woman, an old man near this life's end but able to take whatever he wanted.

Barely out loud, as if only to himself, Tilaka said, "And she must have been one of the fairest virgins in your village."

"I'm not to notice anyone of her station—," mumbled Ashoka.

"Ashoka, you're right. She is Mintho's and a *sudra*. Don't think of her ever again. She'll be the death of you, and you'll be reborn to handlers of dead animals." Tilaka laughed a laugh that said he knew Ashoka could not stop thinking about her.

"Her cry must not go unheard."

"It didn't. You saw the other Indians on the roof with us and today at Mintho's tent."

"None of them is from her village or will return there."

Tilaka rolled over on the straw mattress. His voice told Ashoka that Tilaka now faced him. "A kind master might release us now, might let us use those coins for a passage home. But not this one. The only way he'll set us free is to kill us."

"Our gods and the spirits of my ancestors will guide me home." As Ashoka said the words, he heard their foolishness. He didn't know how to get out of their building, past the guards, over the wall that ran around the estate, and down into the city. But he kept talking, wishing. "Every day one of those big ships must head to the east…"

After a time Tilaka said, "Ashoka, I'll try to find a way."

"It is not my place to stop you, but—"

"Oh, Ashoka, listen to me now. Mintho has no more elephants, no more need for us. The festival has pleased him, but he'll soon turn, and when he turns he'll kill us, both of us. I must try."

"Had he wanted to kill us, he would have out at the camp, would not have brought us here."

"Ashoka, he brought you here—to show you his power, to let you see him sacrifice a child out of a woman from your country—that much I know. Don't you think he knew she was from your village, that you knew her? Her cry when Tanit's priest slaughtered her child must have pleased—"

"Tilaka, stop, I beg you. Retelling it does no good." Ashoka shuddered and tried to think. Radha's scream must have excited the old monster all the more.

"Ashoka, I retell it, so you see his evil, so you know he'll kill you. That's what slave owners in Carthage do when their slaves are used up. The kind owners let their used-up slaves go free to become beggars and set upon by street dogs."

"The masters can't do that—all the slaves will rise up as soon as the killing starts."

"Oh, Ashoka, you know so little. Before I came here, the masters ran out of money. Servants and soldiers from other countries did revolt. The masters won—had enough loyal men that they slaughtered fourteen thousand, wounded and chained many more, then slaughtered them…"

Ashoka gasped. "I didn't know. Didn't know anyone could do that."

"Killing a few servants now will be easy for them, for Mintho. I must find a way before his killing begins."

"Then I'll go with you."

"It's better I go alone. If I don't come back by the end of tomorrow, you must flee this place on your own. Easier to kill us both if we are together. I'll draw less attention on my own."

"Tilaka, I'm a coward if I let you go alone."

"Ashoka, you're no coward. Mintho, his soldiers and servants know that. I have my ways, my friends, here, in this estate, in this city."

"What ways?"

"Mintho's first camp was on these very grounds, only two elephants then, and I was his first mahout. The older servants remember me well. You saw that."

"His servants cower."

"My old friends... will help if there is a way."

"I forbid you to go." Ashoka laughed at the audacity of him forbidding his elder to do anything his elder wanted.

"Ashoka, the trying makes me young one last time. I've been useless. Your journey is long, mine near its end. Allow me to find a way out for us."

"You can't free her, can't bring her to me and free us both, and find a ship to take the three of us away."

"Ah, Ashoka. I know Mintho's wife. I saw her watching me, remembering me from the old days. She has power over Mintho... and if he kills me for trying to get us out, I will die with honor."

Ashoka did not answer, nothing more to say.

"I must go, find my friends still in their sleeping rooms and not scattered around the estate."

Through his misery and fatigue from the night before, Ashoka saw no other way, nothing else to do. "Tilaka, if you must leave and will not allow me to go with you, I won't chase after you. But come back fast at the first danger... Together, we'll do something."

Tilaka limped out as soon as enough light allowed him to see. Ashoka looked after him from an opening in the second story wall. Tilaka, moving faster than Ashoka expected, passed the stables, where handlers soon would lead horses to water, then huts of weavers and metal workers not yet rising from the celebration of yesterday. Tilaka vanished down the main path into lush gardens surrounding the largest estate buildings.

The deep barking of a big dog smothered the gentler sounds of dawn. Ashoka prayed to his gods for Tilaka's safe return, for Tilaka to find a way for them to leave Mintho's estate, to get out of the City, to go home.

Chapter XIX

Summer Rain

Rain started after Tilaka left, came on a cold north wind and lasted all day. A servant set flat bread, dried fruit, cheese, and a jar of water outside Ashoka's door and was gone before Ashoka noticed. No sounds other than the falling rain, no cry of women, no shout of children, only an occasional barking of a dog and nickering of a horse told Ashoka he was still tucked into a room next to stables on this estate waiting for Tilaka to return, waiting for Mintho. Darkness fell and, though he tried to stay alert and ready for anything, Ashoka slept deeply.

Late in the afternoon of the next day, an armed stranger marched into the little room. "Mahout, come with me. Take your belongings." This guard spoke in proper Greek. His right hand rested on the hilt of a broad sword under a long cloak, and the left hand clenched a leather and metal glove and held another cloak. He tossed the cloak at Ashoka. "Put this on."

Ashoka's response, the boldness of his voice, surprised him. "Who orders that?"

The guard snorted out of a flat nose, broken many times. "Your master orders that."

"Where am I going?"

"Far from here."

"Where is Tilaka?"

More of a snarl than words, "Gather your things." One blow from his gloved fist could split open a man's face.

Ashoka said softly this time, "We're going to get Tilaka?"

"You, come now... or I'll tell Master Mintho you fought me, and your belly ate my sword."

Ashoka obeyed. He rolled his coins, comb, razor, one clean tunic, sandals, one blanket and elephant tools into the thick sheepskin coat, tied the roll with rope lengths and followed the guard.

They walked fast in rain that ran cold off their robes and caps. Torches under small roofs cast enough light, yet Ashoka saw not one other person or animal. He warmed with worry. Perhaps they all still slept from the festival and feasts.

At the top of four flights of interior stairs, they entered an open door to a large square room. Oil lamps on a ledge running at shoulder height along the left and right walls cast an orange glow into the room. Mintho and the gray-haired woman sat at opposite ends of a backless sofa. Another of the big black dogs dozed on the pelt of a male lion between their feet. The lion's open mouth and bared teeth faced Ashoka. Two more sofas hugged the right and left walls, and deep red cushions arranged in seating areas lay on the floor. A white life-sized statue of a naked woman posed for all time against the far wall next to a closed door.

Mintho's skin sagged under dark eyes and on the sides of the neck not covered by the full beard. "Ashoka, remove your wet garments, drop your bundle by the door, and sit." Mintho pointed to the floor in front of the dog and lion face.

Ashoka sat on the stone floor and felt the cold draft low in the room.

"I've sold you. Want to know where you're going?"

Ashoka's mind stopped. He would not die on this day.

Where did not matter. He would find out and could not change it. He recovered enough to say, "Please, Master, if I can take only Tilaka and if my other two are safe, where I'm going will not matter."

Mintho shook his head. "I've sold you to a general in New Carthage."

Sold to a general in New Carthage, the empire across the Inland Sea, the training ground for the elephants from his camp, the staging area for the army gathering in the region the locals called Iberia and others called Hispania. Ashoka felt a shout of joy rising in him, but had no one to shout to and too many questions. Was it a trick?

Mintho talked on. "Your new owner has many elephants." He held out his hands, palms up, as if presenting an offering. "He paid well for most of mine, the ones you trained too. Now, he's paid well for you, more than you cost me. A ship leaves with the morning tide. In this wind and rain, our vessels can outrun any Roman war galley." Mintho leaned down to him as if imparting a happy secret. "The priests and senators of this city made a great festival to our gods and feasts for all our citizens and servants. Our gods smiled, and our god Tanit brought rain for me, for you, and for all of us. You must thank her for the summer rain and for your good fortune, Ashoka, don't you think? " Mintho raised an eyebrow. "Did you like our feast?"

If Mintho had told the truth, he was safe and could speak. Mintho would not harm a mahout who belonged to a general in the most important colony of Carthage. If Mintho had lied, nothing Ashoka might say would make any difference. Ashoka's mood changed to boldness fueled by relief, by joy, by whatever would be. "I must take Tilaka with me. I must know the other two are safe."

Mintho sat up straight as did the woman. "Ashoka..."

Ashoka, standing up as he talked, looked down directly at Mintho and then the woman, held up his hands palms out for Mintho to stop talking. "If I left him here, my gods would be as angry as Moth and Tanit and Haddad and your Baal El all together."

The woman, barely perceptibly, stretched up her neck, breathed in and held it—waiting for Mintho.

"Ashoka, you did not answer me. Did you like our feast?"

"The faces smiling as they burn—I will not forget them—I could not eat."

"Ashoka, your impudence knows no limits, does it?" Mintho shrugged and spat what must have been a date pit to the side of the room. "Before I send you off, tell me why Tilaka has angered me. Did you make him do that?"

Ashoka bowed but not deeply. His bow gave him time to sort out what to say next. "Tilaka meant no disrespect."

Mintho stood up, turned half away, as if to address the open door in the wall. "Tilaka asks about caravans leaving my city, about big ships heading east. He asks when the servants of my house will leave. He asks about a low caste girl from your village. I bought that one for my wife." He nodded at the woman on the sofa. "Why did you make him do that, Ashoka?"

Was Mintho's talk of a sale to a general in New Carthage a trick after all? One thought to grab and hold, one next step. "Master Mintho, I must take Tilaka away and go to the one who has bought me and help that one with his elephants."

"Did you make your broken mahout turn all my servants against me, against my wife?"

All courage, all joy, all pride suddenly gone, Ashoka again felt like that night with Father, not being able to answer directly, afraid to tell the truth, afraid to lie. "You don't need him any longer, don't need our two helpers."

Mintho smiled a thin smile. "Who are you to tell me I don't need them? But I will tell you what you want to know before you leave here." Mintho paused. "Then tell your new owner I am an honorable man."

Mintho looked at the old woman sitting next to him. She clapped twice, not loudly, but the beats echoed.

"Yes, Mistress, I'm coming," a voice said in Greek—the same voice as in the tanner's shop, as on the caravan road, as on the night of the festival.

Soft footfalls on the stone floor, then Radha entered from the side of the naked woman statue. Her black hair was longer, shinier than he remembered. A white toga, clasped on the left shoulder, draped her body, a body stronger than on the caravan. Her eyes were puffed and her breasts full for a baby no longer in this life.

Ashoka let all the memories in unchecked. She had more than sung and clapped from inside her shop, had come to the doorway and watched whenever Ashoka raced. She laughed and cheered loudly for him, always just for him. When walking on that street, he listened for her, looked into the shop when the front door stood open. Sometimes she sat cross-legged near the front and sewed or carved designs into leather. And each time he watched her far longer than he should have.

Instantly he saw that this house had worn her less than if she had remained a tanner's daughter, married a low caste and brought new lives out of her body back in India. After one long look, Ashoka gazed at the cold floor. How could he... take her with him... to his new master... to make leather garments for others?

Stop. Madan's voice piled in. *But... she can't help you to drive elephants, to live, to return to your village. Think only about elephants that you must train for battle. You won't last three nights away from this caravan if you dwell on her.*

152

It was not his to decide that she needed to be saved, needed to leave this great house. He, standing unable to look anyone in the eye, unable to answer simple questions honestly, was the one who needed saving from whatever came next.

At last the gray-haired woman spoke, also in Greek, slowly. "This is the man who wants to know about you. Tell him about your time as my handmaiden. In your language if it suits you."

Radha, still facing her mistress, said in their village dialect, "Please, elephant driver, my mistress says you will leave here soon, that you will join many elephants, that your new master is a great general, and, if the gods of Carthage are kind, you may journey back to the place of my birth."

Journey back to the place of my birth. It was too much, too big, too impossible.

"If the gods allow this, tell anyone who asks, though I don't know why they should ask about a tanner's daughter, tell them I am well."

"What may I say about this house?" said Ashoka more to the lion's head in front of him than to her. He had to know if Mintho had taken her as another, younger wife, or if that now dead baby was fathered by someone else. And he hated that he had to know this, about which he could do nothing.

"Yes, please. This is the greatest house in the city of Carthage. My mistress provides better than any husband who might have bought me in our land." Radha's voice caught, and she blinked. "I don't want for anything, tell them." She stopped. "Now go and tell them and ask no more. Buddha teaches it's rude to pry into another's life without permission and good reason."

Radha bowed at her mistress and, still bowing, turned to Mintho. "I have told him everything. He will go now."

Ashoka could not let it go, could not let this moment end, so soon and for all time... in this life. He had to ask her one more thing. He raised his hand, and the other three stared at him. "One last question, if I may." He bowed and raced through his mind the many ways to ask without Mintho knowing why he asked.

Mintho looked at his wife, and she nodded.

"Are you allowed to watch races in this great city? What may I tell others in the tanners' shops about that?"

Mintho took on a puzzled look. His wife frowned.

A tiny smile flickered in Radha's eyes, and her voice picked up. "Ah, yes, Master Elephant Driver, tell anyone who asks, though no one will ask, that this city has far greater races than any in our village. It has other sport contests of many kinds, as in Greece. Many thousands watch and cheer. Sometimes we are allowed to go, and, tell them please, I always cheer for the swiftest runner—I'm allowed to do that here. That is all they might want to know..."

Silence for a long time, broken by Mintho deep slow voice, "Ashoka, what secrets does she tell you about these races, why did you ask about our races?"

Oh, on all the gods of India, I have been too bold... but I must say something. Help me now... Ashoka tried to laugh as he talked, to make it seem his was a small question of no consequence. "No secrets, Master. Our village has one long straight street. In the mornings and on festival days, our village has races on that street. All the shop owners look on and cheer. And the tanner shops have the best place to see the end of every race. All tanners of our village cheer from their shops. They will ask me—if the gods allow me to go back."

Mintho leaned forward toward Ashoka. "Tell me, were you the fastest runner on that street?"

"That street was... many years back when I was younger, I did win one or two."

Mintho now laughed, slapped his own knee, and leaned back as if satisfied after a good meal. For an instant Ashoka wondered then understood. Mintho had caught Ashoka's yearnings for this slave girl and her yearnings for Ashoka. "Radha, leave us now." Radha left as quickly and silently as she had entered, then, "Did she cheer and shout for you?"

Ashoka could not let Mintho or his woman see his eyes and looked over them in the direction of the statue. "So many voices, so far away, so long ago." He shrugged.

Mintho stomped hard on the stone floor. His wife started a bit, as did Ashoka, even the big dog. "I know your caste system better than you do. She did cheer for you, for only you—and for that she could have been stoned, banished from your village if she lived. And... she risked all that for you."

Mintho waited. But Ashoka had run out of ploys, evasive answers, pleas. After a long time, he said, "Yes, Master."

Mintho laughed once more, this time a laugh that said he was done, had caught his prey. He waved the back of his hand at Ashoka as one waves at a fly. "My guards will take you to the place where you can wait for the ship."

"Thank you, Master and Mistress. I will ask my master in New Carthage to let Tilaka help me. Let me take him, and the two... His voice sounded like a street beggar asking for coins. He felt as weak.

Mintho said, "Yes, go. Take your old cripple. I won't touch your two helpers. But one thing more."

"Yes, Master."

"Swear to never come back."

Mintho yelled something out the main door that Ashoka did not understand except for Tilaka's name and a plaza.

Three guards appeared and beckoned him to leave with them.

"Swear it, Ashoka."

"I will never come back, Master Mintho—unless the gods or you summon me to come back."

"Ashoka, you stupid, insolent Indian, I will never summon you. Get out of my sight."

The dog, its large brown eyes atop those of the lion, fixed on Ashoka. It shifted its head and growled.

"Obey your new master. He's not as merciful as I."

"Thank you for selling me and letting me live. Thank you for letting me take Tilaka."

Mintho growled like his dog, then talked loudly, and yelled the last, "You'll obey your new master. If you don't, he'll send me a message, and your village slave, the one who cheered for you, and all her offspring will live and die with the beggars of this city. They treat girls worse than street dogs treat a bitch in heat. Do you hear me, Ashoka?"

Ashoka shuddered in every part of him and turned away, collected his cloak and bundle, and headed out of the room with three guards surrounding him. His pride and elation at being sold to a general in New Carthage were now swamped, crushed by his foolish pride, by things he could not control, by his yearnings for the impossible. *May all the gods of India protect her from my foolishness.*

Chapter XX

The First House of Carthage

*L*ord Vishnu, *he needs your help,* thought Ashoka. He stared up into the rain pelting his face, up the thin legs bound at the ankles to the upright heavy board, stared higher to the caved-in stomach and ribs heaving with slow breaths, but barely. Sinewy arms spread out as far as they could reach, the hands bound to the beam. Above the arms and hands, the face of Tilaka tilted down, his eyes closed. He hung on one of two crosses upright in the largest square of the city. The square was empty except for two crosses, Ashoka, the three guards, and weakly flickering torches off to the side under cover.

The guards brought two ladders from a nearby building, untied the leather straps, and eased Tilaka down onto sheets covering the wet stones of the plaza. They set him on his side. Bloody swollen welts covered his back. Hard leather tails at the end of a whip cracked against flesh by a strong man must have done that.

One of Mintho's men shoved a water pouch at Ashoka and beckoned him to give some to the man on the ground. Tilaka turned his head to the side and up, sipped and coughed and drank and coughed again. He opened his eyes and shut them. The same guard produced a jar of thick ointment smelling of honey and garlic. He motioned Ashoka to apply it. Ashoka knew these salves. After the bleeding stopped, they helped heal any burn, cut or scrape.

The other two guards held a large cloth over Tilaka and Ashoka. Ashoka smeared the ointment onto each open gash. Tilaka did not react. His back must have been dead to pain. His breathing remained steady. He took more water and bits of bread soaked in honey and salt brought by one of the guards. Ashoka thought these men knew how to free a man from death's grasp after whipping and time on a cross.

Tilaka mouthed, "Ashoka?"

Ashoka turned to face the guards. "His wounds must dry. If he dies, the general in New Carthage will be angry."

One guard said, "If you want him, carry him."

He lifted Tilaka onto his right shoulder, a lighter burden than expected, and carried his roll of belongings under his left arm. Leaving the plaza, he noticed the other cross and its man, limp, lifeless.

Ashoka spent his last night in the City of Carthage in an empty horse stable on Mintho's estate. Curled in a hollow of dry hay, he listened for Tilaka's breathing against the sounds of wind and rain. In darkness he gave Tilaka water and more fat-soaked bread. Tilaka slept, sometimes deeply, and this life flowed back into him.

By morning, Tilaka managed to sit, stand and walk a few steps, then sit again.

"Ashoka, I dreamed of the lake below the mountains when I was a boy. With my dreams, the cross wasn't bad."

The old man, his voice, his presence comforted Ashoka. "Don't talk about that. Let strength come back."

"I must tell you—before I can't."

Ashoka sat next to him in the straw, put his arm around him and pulled the coarse blanket the soldier had left over them both. "All right, tell me."

"Mintho did not want me to die," a faint smile in the voice. "My old friend would not let her husband kill me. Leather straps bound me to that cross, not the usual nails. If I passed over, he'd tell her it was the way of the gods, not his doing. Men have hung on the cross far longer and lived."

Ashoka was not sure about any of that, not yet. Perhaps Mintho's guards would drown them in the harbor on this day. Perhaps he had not been sold to another. He said, "Was the man next to you one of his servants?"

"Yes."

"He's gone to his next life."

Tilaka's head and shoulders slumped lower.

"Sit up, Tilaka, or lie on your stomach. Your back must not touch the straw. Don't talk and keep still until they get us for the ship to Hispania."

"Hispania, ah, that's where you are going?"

"Quiet. That's what he said. You'll come with me."

"Ashoka, let me tell you what I learned while I am able, before they come for us. I will never get back to India, but you may. And if you do, someone may ask you about the greatest house in Carthage. I must tell you about the slaves from our country who do all things their masters need done."

"When you have strength again… not now. They told me what I wanted to know."

"Who told you?"

"Mintho and the one who screamed when her child was slaughtered, the one we talked about."

"What did they say?"

Ashoka told Tilaka everything of his meeting in Mintho's house.

Tilaka said, "There is more."

Ashoka wanted to know more about her this one time. Then he vowed to forget her. Maybe… he would look for her again in another life when they both lived as big cats—or elephants. He wished for that. "Tilaka, tell me then, tell me."

"Mintho and his wife are the most powerful family in North Africa. He's the head senator of the thirty senators that rule over the empire. They have many children and grandchildren but have lost many too. Some perhaps fight with the army in Hispania. Others who knows? None of their children or grandchildren lives in their estates any longer. They don't know where they are, how many are still alive."

"Why do they need servants then?"

"Ah, Ashoka they don't. That is why I left you. I had to know if a caravan or ship heads for Greece or Rome, perhaps where a big house might take them in, take us in, had to know if he would kill us or let us live on the street."

"Well, what did you learn?"

Tilaka shook his head. "This city is like an old dead tree rotten on the inside, ready to fall over. Everyone who can has left for New Carthage and the army or for mines south of there. This city has more people from other countries than true people of Carthage. The senators fret about what will happen—if war with Rome will start again, if Rome will invade."

Ashoka thought, *and the servants fear what will happen to them when the tree falls... Can I take her? How... can I take her?* He thought of Madan again and became angry at his own mad thoughts.

"When Mintho bought me, I lived in the servant house where you and I stayed. Dido, his wife, was young then, young and wealthy beyond what you and I can imagine... and grew up in the next house over from Mintho's. She brought a dowry suitable for a king of the greatest nation. You and I spent those nights at her estate. She came into the marriage with that estate, part of her dowry. Her wealth gave him his power. He was no senator back then, a mere trader of modest means and a good fighter. After the marriage Mintho led his private army on hunting trips and dreamed of an elephant camp with many fighting elephants. He bought or hunted for elephants but with her money. It's ending now. The tribute his farmers pay is less every day. The drought and the army gathering in New Carthage have hollowed this city out, have hollowed him out."

"And that is why they whipped you and put you on the cross?"

Tilaka chuckled and coughed and breathed but without stress this time. "No, no. He did that to me because he could not do that to you—and he had to send you off with more lessons of his power, his cruelty."

"He whipped you to death's doorstep... to ease his anger at me. That is past madness."

Tilaka chuckled again, coughed and coughed some more, then settled. "No, no, Ashoka. He had good reasons inside his madness. Dido would not let him harm you as long as your village girl serves her. But... you are the first and only servant, the first and only slave who has spoken rudely to Mintho and not lost his tongue. You are the first who has ever disobeyed him and lived, not once, but three times. All his soldiers and servants talk about you, about your foolishness. And then they laugh at Mintho for letting you, his slave, have your way each time."

Oh, all gods of India, help me—Tilaka whipped and put on the cross, and another dead, because I was rude and stubborn. It was true, from the evening in Mintho's tent after the elephant hunt, then on the morning Mintho closed the camp, and yesterday in the great room. "But you look pleased, Tilaka?"

"Dear Ashoka, you have let me live, saved me from a lion's belly or street dogs. I am broken, used up. Mintho doesn't need me. No one does." Tilaka stopped. Each word came out slower than the one before. "By whipping me in front of the others, by whipping to death my old friend on the cross for laughing about him, Mintho reminded everyone to bow only to him, that he is their only god, still has power and will use it."

"And the other servants, what will happen to them?"

"You mean, the girl from your village?" Tilaka laughed until he had to stop because it hurt. "As long as Dido lives, she will keep the girl alive. Radha is her best and most beautiful servant, the only one who knows how to make the softest leather." Tilaka's voice turned serious. "His other servants will try to flee, or let be whatever happens to them... and pray for a better life in the next one. Dido may leave him. When all his power has dried up, she will have no use for him."

"I wish all the servants find a better house in a better place. I wish Dido takes her away from him. I wish that in her next house, they let Radha make things of leather. For the army if she must." Ashoka thought, *and I wish Mintho does not make more sons or daughters with her.* He knew his wishes were weak breaths against a cold wind, that Mintho would mate with Radha as long as he was able. And Ashoka knew he had to stop thinking about her. "A general has truly bought me?"

"Yes, Ashoka. His servants know Mintho has sold you. You leave today."

"We'll both leave. Tilaka, you will help me more. You here, talking to me helps me now. Rest until the soldiers come for us."

Tilaka bowed his head and in a short while dozed off, and one last question came to Ashoka.

After Tilaka woke, looked around, took more water and bread, Ashoka said, "On our first night here when you slept, I thought I heard women talking, children's laughter, then crying."

"Ah, Ashoka, you ask too many questions. But... at the festival every house of Carthage had to give the gods something of the highest value, to win back their favor. And the senators each had to give their most precious thing—or the people will vote them out. A horse or cow would never be enough from the wealthy senators."

The skin on Ashoka's arms, his neck, raised the bumps of a plucked chicken. "Women and children crying the night before, shouting, then on the next night the brown baby slaughtered for the rain god, Tanit, and Radha screaming as I've never heard? How?"

"If Mintho had young grandchildren here still, he might sacrifice the last born, perhaps he would. But… he chose one of his own out of the servant girls, yes, out of Radha—I think to show you his power, his meanness."

"But?" Ashoka could not finish, his question both too obvious and useless.

"Thank our gods, Ashoka, thank all the elephants you have ever known. You'll be gone soon, and do not, not ever, look back."

+ + +

Ashoka paid for Tilaka's passage on the ship with some coins Tilaka had saved. Someone else had paid for Ashoka.

The vessel moved away from the wooden wharf, eased out of the narrow harbor, turned north and around the cape protecting the City of Carthage against winter storms or invaders from the north, and out to the open, gray and wind-whipped water.

Everyone knew Roman ships of war were a danger only if they came close enough for their great spike on a beam to lock the two ships together.

No other ships appeared to challenge them. By midday the captain stood relaxed under the giant wooden swan's head at the bow.

Ashoka said, "Tilaka, don't leave this spot, don't lean your back against anything. I'll be back."

As Ashoka approached, the captain said in Greek, "Indian, speak kindly about me to your new master. Pray your new master will let you keep the old man."

"Tilaka is the best elephant trainer in all of Carthage. If my new master will not have him drive elephants, I'll take the old man as my helper."

The captain raised an eyebrow. "Your new master moves fast, faster than any of his soldiers, sleeps on the hardest ground in snow without a blanket, and tolerates no weakness in any of his men. You with that old one hanging onto you won't keep up."

"Who is this general?"

"You don't know?"

"Only that he bought me."

"His family is Barca. His father conquered Hispania and built New Carthage on its five hills, built its harbor, the best in the empire. But everyone calls the son by his first name. You don't know it, you say?"

"I've lived in an elephant camp many days from here, and before that in India. Nobody tells me about generals far away."

"Indian, the men of the great army chose the one who bought you to be their Supreme General. Those soldiers came to him from many countries and know he's the best fighter and leader, better than any other."

Ashoka waited, hoped this ship captain would tell him more about the general. But it would be rude to ask.

The captain looked out over the foaming waves for a long time, then said, "The Senate has confirmed him. If it did not, the army would lay down its arms and many soldiers from other lands would go home—or sack Carthage as they did before you were born."

"Then I should call him Supreme General?"

The captain laughed. "It doesn't matter what you call him. You'll never come near him."

"He paid well for me, owns me, but won't let me come near him?"

"He has maybe a hundred mahouts, and will take only the best ones into battle."

"And if he should happen to speak to me, how shall I address him?"

"Call him by his first name, as do all his soldiers. In our language it means, 'beloved of the Great God Baal.' Your new master's name is Hannibal."

Chapter XXI

Monster Out of India

On the morning of the ninth day after leaving the City of Carthage, the men straddling the mast spar high above the main deck yelled, "Over there, the hills, the yellow sky."

Ashoka, standing on that deck, smelled the animals well before he saw the faint outline of hills. "Tilaka, how many horses must there be on that land?"

"More than we can know."

Soon white buildings and walls shimmered through a thick haze. But their ship could get no closer. Ashoka counted more than forty ships ahead of them riding at anchor on gentle swells in a loose double line. The line slipped closer to the shore only when another ship came out of the harbor.

As they crept forward, he studied everything, nothing else to do, no other place to go. Cargo piled up in front of warehouses and out onto the dirt and stone unloading areas. Rugs and animal skins, cages, furniture and chariots, battering rams of wood, the ends covered by dark metal, and coils of heavy chain choked the wharves. Unbroken strings of tanned laborers and black slaves unloaded the ships. Women dressed in full length garments striped yellow, orange, and red, sometimes looked up from hauling cargo, peered out at the waiting ships as if searching for their men.

166

Yelling and cursing in different languages carried from vessel to vessel. The clang of ironworkers hammering metal floated out on the water day and night.

Tents, like a forest of low white trees, rolled part way up the five hills surrounding the harbor above the city. Behind the hills, dust and smoke rose into the sky, but nothing suggested elephants, and Ashoka wondered.

+ + +

"Listen to me now, new boys." The man Ashoka and Tilaka had been told to find in the flat land beyond the hills stood with his back to them. "You're assigned to one of the five herds. When the lead mahout tells you to jump, you jump. Or we'll send you to the mines."

Behind this man elephants gathered in herds of roughly equal numbers. They stood about or walked slowly among bare bushes, clumps of cactus, and twisted trees stripped of leaves and bark. Ropes tied their front feet. All were of the North African mountain kind.

Tilaka said, "Our old master told us these elephants are trained to fight. Those out there have no more fight in them than cows."

The other man turned toward them but still did not look directly at Tilaka or Ashoka. By the set of his uplifted chin, he asked Tilaka to tell him more.

Tilaka said, "This old man requests but one day to work with real fighting elephants and a mighty army."

The stern expression faded, and this other man's eyes now looked at them, and he grinned. "I know that voice. Tilaka of Mintho's camp. That is Ashoka with you, yes it is."

Tilaka laughed. "Yes, yes. Young Ganesha... they feed you well here I see. How goes it with you, with Mintho's elephants?"

Ganesha started to bow but stopped. "Master Tilaka, I thought my eyes played tricks, but then you spoke. He let you go at last—."

"Ganesha, that story will take too long and makes my back bleed again. Tell us about our elephants."

Ganesha shook his head and gestured out to the herds. "These only pull and carry. The greater number of Mintho's war elephants and the few we could get out of India from the Syrians train far from here."

Tilaka said, "That's where we want to go."

Ashoka said nothing, tried to show nothing, but his questions spun. How many other mahouts from Mintho's camp had arrived here? How would they react to their former leader Tilaka, now a helper? How would they treat him, Ashoka, once a new prize but now without influence or elephant of his own, and still one of the youngest among them?

Ganesha said, "Hannibal and his head mahout have chosen all the war elephants, their trainers, and mahouts to ride them."

"Then why buy Ashoka?" said Tilaka.

Ganesha sighed. "Master Tilaka, men are wounded every day in the fierce training. And if there's war with Rome, mahouts will become the first targets. In time, you'll be needed—here or in the mines not far from here."

Later that night Ganesha said, "You're nothing here, two more bodies. Tread on quiet feet."

"Never seen so many men, horses, elephants, tents, everything. Mintho didn't prepare us for this," said Tilaka.

"Mintho worries about his little army and influence with other senators. Hannibal prepares to save the empire with sixty thousand men, more."

Ashoka tried to conjure up that many fighting men in one place but could not. Then again, all those tents could

168

shelter many thousands, and the wharfs and ships held enough supplies for that many.

"Tell him we came to help right now, not later when he's lost half his mahouts," said Tilaka and laughed.

"Every mahout will kill for a chance to ride an elephant to war... and freedom." Ashoka thought he might too. "You've arrived late. Don't draw more looks than you have already. Don't ask for anything, wait your turn. Hannibal and his advisors choose the best men for all tasks. If you're the best, they will find you."

Ashoka thought that Ganesha was sounding like Madan, and Tilaka said, "And you? Do you want your own war elephant and a chance at freedom?"

Ganesha pulled his shoulders back, raised his head. "I have a wife here. She wove the most glorious silks in our home country and now makes coarse woolen togas for soldiers in the garment huts. Hannibal allows his men to take wives. It's said the Supreme General's wife and young son are at this camp. I'll stay here and tend the horses and mules left behind when all the elephants are gone."

+ + +

Every day Ashoka and Tilaka shoveled elephant dung out of empty kedahs, lugged broken chain to blacksmiths, offloaded fresh grass, fetched tools from storage boxes for the real mahouts, rode carts to the city with sickly small farm animals, and brought back new clothing, tubs of food and medicines for men and beasts. At night they formed balls of rice, honey and animal fat, just like the balls of treats Ashoka had made as a little boy for Father's camp. They washed clothes of other men. Ashoka had never before washed clothes for others—women's work.

The mahouts yelled at Ashoka when he approached their elephants. He had known some of them at Mintho's camp. Ashoka nodded and bowed. A share of the spoils from a wealthy beaten foe might buy freedom and a passage home—but only for those who rode out to battle. And not one would give up his elephant.

Ashoka took his food with the last group at the communal evening meal. It was good—boiled oats with fruit, smoked or freshly roasted meat. The ground was free of scorpions and killing snakes. Elephants were close, and one might find him. He was alive, and Mintho was far away.

Sometimes when he woke before the others, he faced the sun coming up out of India and softly said, "God Ganesha, thank you for bringing me here, for rescuing me from Mintho. If it pleases you, show me the path, show me an elephant or mahouts who need me, and after that, if it suits your purpose, show me the way home."

+ + +

Deep into winter of his first year in Hispania, a rainy winter, Ashoka caught words from the other mahouts in tones of reverence, disbelief. "It's bigger, taller by six hands than our tallest."

The next evening another said, "It smashed the *kedah* in the night and let out the whole herd but did not make them run off."

"It's from our country?"

"It can't be one of ours. Never has a male Indian elephant reached Hispania. Someone must have brought one of the monsters up out of Africa from south of the desert."

"It's just talk. The talk will die out."

The talk did not die out. New stories about the monster coursed among the mahouts every night.

"They say it follows in darkness as quietly as a cat, nudges with its trunk begging for treats. It does not harm any—unless they try to mount it."

Ashoka had never spoken one word to the group here. The talk of this monster out of India or Africa, a whisper of hope, and memories overrode his manners and Ganesha's warnings. He said loudly enough for many to hear, "Elephants that have lost respect for man must be watched. They play with men before they stomp and gore them."

"We know, be quiet. From your first day here, I remember you, Ashoka. Mintho's new pet until you refused to obey him. It's right you wash my clothes."

"I serve you willingly. I serve even children who soil their clothes." That quieted them. "Who here has seen this rogue?"

"I've seen it. It's as big as the big African elephants," said one of them.

"All the other elephants, even the well-trained males, move out of its way but then try to follow it."

"Hannibal will cut off its head if it disturbs his trained elephants," said Ganesha.

A new voice said, "If Hannibal wants to do that, let him try. They say he wants to ride this one, not cut off its head."

"He doesn't need another elephant. He's beaten all the tribes. What more is there for him to rule?"

"Hannibal insists he rides this one," said Ganesha.

"To where? Around the camp?" They all laughed.

Another said, "Maybe he's getting them ready for Rome to attack us and will ride against them on that one."

Talk of an attack by Rome was constant. Ganesha said, "He's getting ready for Rome. We all know that. But he wants to ride this one all the way there, to Rome itself."

To Rome. . . to Roma, they uttered in all its pronunciations, in disbelief.

"It's true. He plans a charge down the back of the mountains to shock the Romans with our elephants. His bone readers say the arrival of this monster is his omen."

"I don't believe there's a Hannibal, anyway. I've never seen him."

Ganesha said, "He's here, the same Hannibal who killed two lions with a short sword and his bare hands when he was sixteen. Another time by himself he drove off twenty Romans who trapped him in Trinacria."

"He must think his men are fools with stories like that," said the first mahout.

"True or not, he wants to ride the new elephant. But the beast casts off every mahout who tries to climb onto its neck. That makes him want all the more to show us how to do it."

Someone said, "Enough talk of a beast none of us has seen, of Hannibal who is a myth. I want to sleep now."

Others murmured agreement.

After a long silence Ganesha said, "Hannibal has ordered three new mahouts and helpers with no elephant to get ready, wants them on the war training ground tomorrow. Riders with extra horses will arrive before the sun crests to take them to him." He grinned quickly at Ashoka. "In this camp, that's you, Ashoka."

"Ganesha, you should go," said Ashoka.

"When you come back with a broken leg, I may. Until then, someone needs to run this camp—and these mahouts."

The others hissed and laughed but did not protest that Ashoka should have his chance. They were all Indians first, rivals for the spoils of war second.

Several said to Ashoka, "The gods be with you."

"Come back and tell us if you see Hannibal, if you see the monster out of India or Africa, or wherever he's from."

"Remember us if you win Hannibal's favor."

Chapter XXII

A Common Soldier

Ashoka rode last in line of the six riders. Many tent villages, each village's tents of a different color and shape, covered the flat land behind the hills on the backside of New Carthage. Smoke rose out of hundreds of fire pits from the night before and dirtied the sky. In the center of the tent villages, big dogs barked low and continuously. Here, at last, Ashoka saw the great mass of the army, and it astounded him, took away all thoughts other than the enormity, the many men, tents, noise, fires, power. And one more thought followed. If he got an elephant, he would have to fight with these men, their horses, their dogs, and he tried to take it all in.

In open areas lightly armed men jousted with wooden swords or spears. Archers shot arrows, and sling shot bearers flung stones at straw and wooden targets shaped to resemble men or horses. Bullock-drawn carts delivered food and water throughout the flat land.

Ashoka's riders arrived at a place of many dogs, the same breed as Mintho's and each on its own leash. Ashoka estimated five hundred. The dogs stood or sat in rows of pens, with water troughs and bones making parallel lines. These were better trained than the dogs scattered through the tent villages. Not one barked or growled or seemed anxious. Ashoka sensed one emotion from those dogs, an urge to fight, to be let loose, to attack—but only if commanded.

As the sun crested the hills to the southeast, Ashoka's group stopped at a plain brown tent in one more tent village.

A common soldier, wearing the same dusty white tunic and leather skirt as all the other foot soldiers of Carthage, emerged from behind a flap. The lead rider of their little group jumped off his horse. The new man swung onto that horse's back. A long pink scar from below the new man's tunic down his right thigh did not slow him. Mounted, he waved for the five others to follow.

The little column rode through a low area and up a ravine embankment on the other side. What Ashoka next saw and heard brought his father's voice about the Macedonian's reaching India with his elephant army.

The opposing lines, each one hundred strong, marched head on. When they smelled and heard the other line, both lines broke into a run and charged with all fury. The beasts trumpeted as they ran. They outraced the advancing foot soldiers. Only the horse riders kept with them and urged them on with shouts. The two lines of giants smashed head-on and locked tusks. The stronger ones turned the weaker ones around and gored them in their exposed bellies, and riders lanced and cut them in the exposed places. The wounded elephants fell or ran back and trampled their own advancing men. Thus the battle was lost. Our soldiers were slaughtered and people of our Sindhu valley enslaved.

As Ashoka looked out on the flat plain, he felt no fear, no doubt, nothing out of his small self. He was a leaf swept along by a current larger, wilder than he understood or could resist. His only goal was to stay on top, to not go under.

He looked around at the other five riders. They were real and also looked at the giant training ground, and brought him back to the present, the now.

Fence lines of sharpened wood stakes, angled outward, rolled away in random directions. The closest men had painted faces and wore light armor of leather and chain. Their helmets were shaped like those of what Ashoka thought to resemble Roman helmets. They carried full-length bowed shields to resemble shields carried by Roman soldiers marching in tight groups. The nearest group of soldiers yelled and threw stones and spears at tethered elephants not far from them. The elephants had a mahout on each neck and one archer on each back. They formed up a line. The mahouts gave the cry to go, go fast. The line of elephants charged the pestering men. Only the tethers of heavy metal chains on the front feet allowed the mock Roman soldiers to outrun the elephants and duck behind the sharp-tipped fence stakes.

Ashoka recognized some of these elephants. He had trained them well after all—at least for mock battles without pain, without wounds flowing blood, without real fire too close, without the stench of real Roman soldiers.

Farther out on the flat land other lines of elephants, not hobbled, ran after shouting riders. Here and there groups of elephants milled tightly, to get ready or to rest.

One by one the nearest men not caught up in exercises of war set down their shields. Those running and shouting a little farther away stopped too. The nearest line of elephants stood still and the mahouts and archers on their backs turned and stared at the visitors. Soon everyone within shouting distance grew still and stopped all their elephants, all their horses and faced the lead rider of Ashoka's little column.

The rider on the lead horse shouted out in Greek, "Where's Hannibal's beauty—not escaped again, I trust?"

A nearby soldier gestured out to the distant riders. "He runs by himself chasing the riders—as he did the other morning."

"I like that," said the lead rider. He laughed with the joy of a warrior and turned on the back of his horse. "You mahouts, can you tame him?" He did not wait for an answer. "Let's find him." He cantered out in the direction of a dust cloud and riders in the distance.

No one could miss it, its size so much bigger, its power so much greater than all the other elephants. The rogue stood under the first clump of palm trees at the far edge of open ground. As tall as two horses and heavier than the two largest North African bush elephants, tusks gleaming, it slowly turned to face Ashoka's group. The six riders stopped a good distance away, and still their horses backed up.

One of the mahouts said, "Master, the ears and back and head and legs—it is from our land."

The lead rider said, "The finest elephant I've ever seen. It's well trained but allows no man to mount it. I will be that man—but I need your help."

Only one man in the entire army would proclaim to a group of mahouts that he would mount this elephant but also ask for their help. Ashoka said, "Master Hannibal, this elephant is a worthy prize. I too have never seen a better one."

"How did you know my name?" His laugh said he did not want an answer. "I must get a better disguise."

"Forgive me, Master."

"Nothing to forgive. Your Greek's not bad for an Indian. He is indeed a worthy prize, worth the sum I paid the Syrians."

But Ashoka did not hear what Hannibal said next. The wisp of hope, then the realization, then joy flooding through him so strong that he heard nothing, saw nothing, felt nothing other than the bond to this animal from his country. He sat up as high as he could, didn't hear the others, what they said, didn't follow where they rode. Nothing... just this wonderful beast.

Hannibal's nearly shouted words broke through, "... hurt fourteen of my mahouts already, but only those who tried to mount him. Who among you is next?"

One of the three mahouts said, "It will not be trained. It must be killed before it kills other elephants or your men. The tusks will sell for a good price."

Hannibal turned on his nervous horse. "Get out of my sight before I send you to the silver mines."

The mahout rode away.

The giant faced them, pawed the dirt with its front left foot, flapped its ears and rocked its head from side to side, then raised it and trumpeted a blast that carried far over the plain.

The horses reared and walked backwards, Ashoka's too. He leaned forward, talked to it, and patted its neck. He felt safe, and his horse calmed quickly. He searched for the one moment to let the beast hear him, smell him but not in a way to insult the Supreme General.

The third mahout, on a horse next to Ashoka, said, "It doesn't charge foolishly. It moves its head and trunk in mock anger, playing. May I mount it to serve you?"

Hannibal said, "Never ask a man to do what you won't. If I fail, you two who are not afraid can help me."

Hannibal heeled his horse's flanks, telling it to move up. It hesitated but then walked in a wide circle to approach at an angle from the side and behind. The elephant seemed to understand, stopped pawing, held still its head, laid its ears back, and blew out of its trunk. Hannibal nudged his mount closer and closer until he could almost touch the hide behind the ear. His horse nodded nervously.

The rogue shuddered, flapped its ears, and spun at the horse and rider. The horse reared, dropped its head forward and away, and bucked kicking up its hind legs at the elephant again and again. Hannibal let go his one-handed grip on the mane, the other hand on the reins, and jumped off. He landed on his feet, balanced and ready.

The big beast was on him and lowered its head but stopped before jarring him, as if deciding what to do next, as if playing a game. Hannibal froze, the beast too close for him to run, to drop to the ground, to do anything.

Ashoka did not let the beast decide. He jumped off his horse and bounded between the elephant and Hannibal, shouting loudly enough for all to hear but in his language so only mahouts might understand, "Four Nails, stop. Stop now, Four Nails."

The giant lifted its massive head, his left eye and side toward Ashoka.

More softly, the last word almost merely a thought, "Four Nails. Be still now."

The giant exhaled, raised his trunk to pull in every scent, and moved his head from side to side, trying to take in all of this man so close, so bold. The giant grew quiet, only the ears flapping gently and the trunk out toward Ashoka. Ashoka touched the tip of the trunk, then up the trunk to the cheek with his fingertips, his hand, and patted the cheek. There he stood for a long time, the only sounds his and the elephant's breathing and the horses snorting and their hoofs still trying to back up. "Front foot."

The elephant bent its front leg to make a step at the knee. Ashoka grasped the top of the tusk and swung up onto the neck. The scar in the shape of a star, darker than the surrounding hide, had not disappeared but had lost all its redness.

The horses, even Ashoka's now with no rider, stopped moving their restless feet and watched as if in awe.

Hannibal slowly turned and eased to elephant and mahout, looked at Ashoka above him and said in Greek,

"Who are you, mahout?"

"I am Ashoka."

"How did you do that?"

"My family trained elephants that fought the Macedonian."

"How does this magnificent beast know you?"

"He allowed me to save him from mad men in mountains west of India."

"You called him a name?"

"Four Nails," said Ashoka.

"That's a strange name?"

"He has four nails on his front feet."

"So I see. Shall we give all elephants that name?"

"No, Master. We must not. Our elephants have five nails on their front feet. Some believe an elephant with only four nails is crazed and will kill for no reason."

"Do you believe that?"

"No, Master."

"This one could have killed many of my men, could have killed me, but chose not to. He waited for you."

Ashoka bowed as best he could while sitting on the neck of Four Nails. Any other response would demean the high compliment from this common soldier with the name that meant beloved of the most powerful god in the Empire of Carthage.

"I want you to call him Surus, after the Syrians who brought him to me. I don't want anyone thinking I ride a crazed elephant. Can you do that?"

"That will be his choice, not mine, Master Hannibal. An elephant will respond to more than one name if it has greater intelligence than most."

"Can you take him over high mountains covered in snow?"

"If the gods will it. My helper, Tilaka, has trained elephants in high mountains."

"Can you teach me to tame this wonderful elephant? To permit me to ride him?"

"If the gods of this elephant will it, if he wills it."

"Then ask these gods of your elephant, and then ask your elephant." Hannibal smiled widely with eyes sparkling. All at once Ashoka understood that this common soldier might indeed be the best leader of them all massed under and behind the five hills. "And come to the war council tonight."

Hannibal laughed openly, a laugh of joy and power. Then he whistled. His horse, waiting now fifty paces away, walked up cautiously. Again he mounted the bare back easily and turned to Ashoka. "Tell Surus I will feed him well and he can bathe today as long as he wants. He has not been cleaned by anyone in many days, perhaps since you were with him last, I think."

"Yes, Master."

Ashoka leaned forward and gave the one-word command for "go." Four Nails moved out with a massive power through the silent riders and many silent barely-moving footmen in the mock battle fields. Ashoka had no idea where the elephant bath or war council meeting might be. But he knew anyone would tell him.

He silently thanked all his gods and the spirits of Father's grandfather and Govinda for keeping him alive and guiding him back to Four Nails.

Part III

Over High Mountains

Chapter XXIII

Warnings

In the third month after Four Nails found Ashoka, a stranger on foot made straight for the mahout camp. Ashoka, resting from another day of mock battles, faced one of several fires for the mahouts and helpers. He didn't notice the stranger until the man spoke.

"Ashoka, tomorrow prepare them with the light platforms. You'll follow behind the dogs. Don't wait for our Supreme General. You ride Surus alone. Our Supreme General will send for you when he wants his elephant. He'll ride Surus for the adoring masses after he defeats the Romans. Now is no time to celebrate."

At last, thought Ashoka, Hannibal's army is readying to move. But how could he know this command came from Hannibal? No false pride in this common soldier, that much was true. Before Ashoka could ask more, the stranger left, disappeared into the forest of men and tents in the evening light.

Ashoka said to himself, "Elusive Hannibal, did that command come from you? Where are you?"

Tilaka, sitting next to him, said, "If what they say is true, that stranger could have been our Supreme General. He hides himself well."

"Hides himself?"

"From those who know him better than you."

"He can't hide from those who know him." The stranger did have the same stature as Hannibal. But the voice and words sounded unfamiliar.

"They say he changes his hair, paints his hands and arms the color of the ground, and puffs out his face with leather in his cheeks."

"So that was Hannibal?"

"Sometimes he rides with the best of the dark Numidians, and they don't know he rides with them."

Ashoka thought Hannibal must be like gods of India. They change who they are and take the form of different animals when they come to the earth. "Why hide from the men who worship him?"

"To listen and learn—and frustrate any assassin."

+ + +

Numidian and Iberian horsemen, more than nine thousand, led the army away from the outer gates of New Carthage. Hundreds of two-man war chariots followed the horsemen. Giant black dogs on leashes and the dogs' handlers trailed the chariots. Other dogs, riding in bullock-drawn carts, guarded weapons, sacks of silver and tin.

The worthiest fifty-eight elephants, with Four Nails leading, came after the horses and dogs. A mahout rode on the neck of each elephant, an archer on a light platform on the back. The helpers walked beside their elephants. One of the helpers was an old man aided by a stout stick. Ganesha rode the second elephant. Hannibal did not let him stay behind.

"Here he comes atop his mighty Surus... No, not him, not Hannibal," shouted the onlookers.

"There he is."

"Where? I see the beast but not him."

"No, he's over here."

None spotted Hannibal. Ashoka rode Four Nails alone.

The foot soldiers marched behind the elephants. Rumors put the number of footmen at sixty thousand. Citizens of Carthage and laborers from many lands cheered them off. Young mothers held babies high and yelled at the men, but the men looked straight ahead out of hard faces bent on war and plunder and whatever else lay ahead.

A supply train of more bullocks and carts, then cows, pigs, goats, leather workers and blacksmiths, surgeons, cooks, and unarmed laborers rolled up in an unruly tide for another day behind the armed men. Wives of some soldiers and women not owned by any man walked or rode in the baggage train too. The last foot soldier at the rear guard left the city two days behind the leading horsemen.

The army ground north along the coast. On the sixteenth day, it crept past broken walls on a hill rising out of the flat coastal plain. The men and some of the animals fixed their gazes on those looming walls. Everyone knew the story. In recent days of easy marching, Ashoka heard the story too, more than once.

For hundreds of years these walls had protected the wealthy traders, their families, and servants of a nearby city named Saguntum. The walls kept out pirates, Greek armies, and hostile local tribes—but no longer. One year before this army marching past, Hannibal and many of these soldiers had attacked the city down by the sea. All the citizens fled to the fortress on the hill carrying in carts or on their backs everything they could take, everything that could not be replaced after their homes were burnt to rubble. After a siege of eight months, the invaders breached the walls and charged through. The last survivors set a fire in the center of the fortress on the hill, a fire so great that sailors far out at sea called it the Volcano of Saguntum. The wealthy Sagunti flung their gold bracelets, then themselves into the flames rather than surrender. After the fighting ended, the embers stayed hot and smoke rose for seven more days and nights, the heat and stench so strong the conquerors did not approach the ashes until the fire had grown cold.

Nothing grew yet in the hollowed-out fortress. During the day a white mist of ash rose on the warm breeze up from Africa. In the damp evening air, bits of the ash settled far outside the walls. This day the Iberian priests started a chant in the language of the Keltoi, the main language in the interior of Iberia. The hymn quickly spread to everyone in Hannibal's army.

Women and children still wail
without end in the cold fire of the suicide pyre.
Their breath blows the ashes far over the broken walls
To search out every soldier who had done this.
If touched by the ashes of the dead,
The soldier will suffer a fate worse than the brave Sagunti.

The fighters from Carthage, Greece, and Libya, scoffed at the priests' message. But for the first time on this cloudless march, they pitched tents. No windblown ashes of the dead Sagunti must fall on them in the night.

Hannibal's war council met in the outdoor amphitheater below the fortress of Saguntum. Ashoka sat farthest from the center. He wished he had not been summoned, but as the elephant leader he could not stay away. The men talked of where best to pass through or over mountains ahead, whether the tribes in the forests would fight against them or try to join up with them. The Greeks among them called these mountains Pyrenees, after their goddess Pyrene beloved by Hercules. The locals gave them a name translated as "burnt rocks."

After a short time, only Hannibal paced and talked. He talked slowly allowing time for the translators to quietly change his words into Libyan for the leaders of his riders, into Greek for the leaders of his engineers and surgeons, into Kelto-Iberian for the local warriors who had lain siege to Saguntum with him.

"All the gods of Carthage and Iberia favor us. You see how the locals adore us, don't let us pay for fresh meat or eggs, don't challenge us, how the young girls cheer our men on."

From where he sat, Ashoka had a clear view of the other leaders and saw that most paid no attention to Hannibal. Some grumbled to their attendants, some looked out to sea. The spirit of the dead Sagunti had taken hold, or something else distracted them, kept their attention on things other than Hannibal's oratory.

Perhaps the chief of the local tribes now infected them. He lay sprawled on the amphitheatre's hard steps, up above the others. His unblinking blue eyes out of a steady frown fixed on Hannibal. His chest and arm muscles reminded Ashoka of wrestling champions in India. His long hair took on the color of gold in the evening light and his pale skin the sheen of a single layer of spun silk. He wore only his short sword, they called a falcata, in a leather scabbard on a leather belt and a gold ring around his neck. The rest of him was naked. His name was Sinorix.

In the months of training and this march, in the war councils held on most nights, Ashoka had learned about this Sinorix and his people. Most called them Keltoi, said they came from the far-away islands of Britannia and their related tribes spread to Iberia, to the plains north of Pyrenees, down into Italoi and east as far as Damascus. Everyone said their men fought like caged cats, that sometimes their women fought with them.

Now Sinorix spoke in a deep voice which made everyone listen, though Ashoka understood none of what he said. Another one next to Sinorix translated into Greek. "The dead Sagunti talked to me all the day. They warned me to not go on. They see the days and months to come. You, every man, and animal that goes with you dies on the march against Rome. You leave this land, and every living thing in the New Carthage City of the five hills this army left behind will fall to Roman hands, and before many more winters the whole empire of Carthage dies by Roman hands."

Hannibal stood on the level center of the amphitheater in front of a fire that cast its light up the semi-circular cement steps. He yelled, "Sinorix, you'll forget the skirmish over that little village when we, you and I and the men at this council, stand inside the gates of Rome, when we free its cheering people."

Sinorix spat to the side in Ashoka's direction though not close. "This was no little village. It was a city that welcomed all strangers. I and my men helped you turn it to ash and broken stones."

"And for that I am in your debt, but you and your men—each one of them—begged to come on this march—and..."

Sinorix yelled over Hannibal's last words even before his translator had started, making Ashoka and many others sit up, some stand, "The dead never forget. They speak truth and see what comes in days ahead."

Hannibal said flatly, "Sinorix, your guilt under the shadow of these walls makes you soft, makes you afraid. And I, all in this council, understand your guilt. Your men behaved worse than even Roman brutes."

Sinorix yelled each response louder than the one before, though he had not shown the respect to stand or sit up. "You don't know what my men did. You treat my men like dogs, treat all my people like dogs unworthy of any respect from almighty Carthage. You are worse than Romans."

"Sinorix, in every battle I let you decide where to place your men, let them lead or not as you like." Hannibal lowered his voice but projected enough for all to hear. "It's not been long since I married one of your people, since she gave me my first and only child. My fight is for my people and yours."

A hush settled over everyone. They knew, and Ashoka had heard the rumors of the Supreme General's marriage, his child, and everyone wondering if he had taken them along in the baggage train. No one could say with certainty.

Even Sinorix kept quiet after the translation this time, then, "You, you don't fight. That scratch on the leg kept you lazing in your tent while my men fought at the walls eight long months, fought for you and for Carthage." Many in the semi-circle snorted. Everyone knew that on only the fifth day of the siege of Saguntum's hill fortress, Hannibal, always in the lead, took a javelin deep into his thigh. It nearly killed him. "But the dead Sagunti have talked to me all the day... and they tell the truth."

Hannibal said calmly, "I offered them an honorable surrender."

"A fool's barter." Sinorix shook his waist-length wavy hair. He sat up, raised the oval shield from the step in front of him and struck it with the flat blade of his falcata sword. After the metal on metal clanging died out, the translators repeated for their groups. "You had no need to slaughter my good friends."

"Carthage has pleaded for an alliance with Saguntum since my father united all other people of Iberia. Saguntum chose Rome."

"Rome comes here in peace and to trade."

Hannibal extended his arms to point out over the sea and the last daylight glow. "The only peace Rome knows is the

189

quiet of our girls weeping after Rome's brutes have had their way with them. The only trade it knows is plunder—ripping for itself the bounty grown by people in the land it conquers. We all know what Rome did to our countrymen in Trinacria, made its young boys and old men slave in the fields and sent the girls and young women off to Rome. It will do the same in Iberia if you allow it one toehold in Saguntum or anywhere on this coast." Hannibal stomped up the steps to Sinorix, pausing after each step as if bracing for a charge, until their faces were not an arm's length apart. "Romans fight to rule the earth, to plunder and enslave. Rome will not stop until it has it all."

Sinorix stood up, a full head taller than Hannibal. "Your promises made my men crazy the last time. This time all you can promise is death to the fortunate and life as a slave to all who live."

Hannibal looked back at the others. By hand gestures and raised brow he invited any to answer. "I fight with noble warriors, or I fight alone. Take your crazed men home."

The others nodded agreement with Hannibal. For a moment Ashoka felt relief. This army would march on in the morning united. But then Sinorix spat. "My men are ashamed and will not tell their wives and children what you made them do."

Hannibal's voice turned sarcastic. "But they'll keep the treasures they stole. Your common soldiers will buy a good plot of ground with loot taken from the Sagunti."

"And they'll leave you to die in the mountains with your stinking elephants."

"That torc of gold around your neck, you stole it from Saguntum? You wrested it from the chief, who met you to surrender, to save his people—but then you gutted him."

Sinorix grabbed the thick, solid gold collar around his own neck. It was open at the front in the shadow of his chin.

Though Ashoka sat off from Sinorix, he easily made out the thick solid gold.

Hannibal said, "Throw it down, and your men will do the same. That will ease their shame at what they have done. We can use the gold to barter for food and beasts on our way to Rome. We'll cut it up to pay our soldiers"

Sinorix took hold of each end as if to pull open the collar and fling it at Hannibal. But he stopped before the split collar opened wide enough to remove it from his neck.

Hannibal moved up closer so their noses almost touched and said loudly, "You'll make a pretty feast for lions in Rome's Coliseum."

"You're the peril." Sinorix hissed.

"Joined together we'll have the strongest armies. Our people will live without war."

Sinorix again banged his sword on his shield. "Your elephants will run over you. You're mad to take them. You're mad to go."

Sinorix and his translator turned their naked backs to the war council, climbed the rows of the open theatre and up into the darkness. Sinorix yelled something, yet still faced away— the universal sign of disrespect. His translator turned back. "I'm tired of talking. You'll have our decision before the army enters the burnt rocks." Their backs remained easy to see until they crested over the top of the last row of seats.

Ashoka again puzzled at the naked Keltoi warriors who had marched this far with the army. Bare white skin was so much easier to see and lay open with any blade.

Hannibal sat down in front of Ashoka, next to a brown-skinned man with shaggy black hair. "Masinissa, your light riders and horses must separate from the horsemen of Sinorix tonight. Send your men to move them now."

Masinissa said loudly, "My men have tired of him. His riders make more noise than a tree full of monkeys."

Hannibal said, "Shall we heed Sinorix and send the elephants to help in the silver mines?"

Masinissa answered first. "My horses have been with elephants for many lifetimes and know their cunning, their strength. One tusk into the belly brings certain slow death. Roman horses and the tribes on the other side will run at the first scent of the noble beasts, at their first trumpeting. Our elephants will go as high as horses and men. They come from mountains."

Hannibal's three brothers, Mago, Hanno, and Hasdrubal, all younger than he but as strong and intense, spoke as if with one voice. "The elephants will help us against unfriendly tribes... and carry the supplies and siege rams better than any horse. The tribes in the Tagos valley ran from your elephant line."

The brothers looked at Ashoka and then said, "If prepared for Rome's trickery, our elephants will crush its mighty infantry as no man on foot or horse has ever been able."

Hannibal said, "Then let's move fast on this flat ground. Neither winter nor Rome waits for us."

The others murmured assent and quickly agreed on their orders through the Pyrenees.

Chapter XXIV

Gods and Mortals

As they left the council, Hannibal motioned at a little man, dressed all in black, to walk with him. The man kept a half step behind in a servant's place, though Hannibal had no servants. "Bogus, my wise priest, you said nothing after that blasphemy by the naked one. What does Baal El tell you?"

The little man moved up close to Hannibal. "Baal El has not spoken to me about Sinorix. Baal El has not told me the future."

"Then what has mighty Baal El told you?"

"How do you know he told me anything?"

"Your voice, your eyes."

"Yes, you must know. Baal El tells me to trust no elephant in war."

Hannibal had not expected this, did not know what to say or think. The power of this little man ran straight back to the Senate of Carthage. The Senate had selected him and placed him in Hannibal's army as the army's highest priest. Hannibal had not wanted to take any priest, but could not refuse, not before any smashing victories over Rome, before sending back to the City of Carthage enough plunder to provide for a generation. "Has Baal El been sleeping until now?"

The little man's voice turned gruff. "Baal El never sleeps, but he chooses when to talk to me. Until your army left New

Carthage, only you knew your plans for the beasts. Now you have taken them with us, and Baal El says not one of your elephants has seen real war."

"My elephants routed all the tribes in the West."

"The wild tribes of Iberia ran from them. Not one beast felt a spear deep in him or heard a thousand screaming hostiles."

The little man was right, but many people knew this. Hannibal could not help himself, had to test the priest in a small way. "Tell me, my wise priest, when Baal El talks to you about the wild tribes here, does he call this land Iberia or Hispania?"

"Ah, Master, surely you know better. Baal El is the Supreme God of Carthage. He does not use the names used by the Greeks or the Romans. He honors the locals here in the main colony of the Empire of Carthage, and speaks of their land as they do. Baal El speaks of this place as the land south of burnt rocks."

So, this little man was not so easily fooled, had been tested many times before and survived to rise to this high stature, and talked back to Hannibal as no other Carthaginian. "So I'll send back the elephants to work the mines and let Sinorix and his men go home?"

"Perhaps. Baal El doesn't doubt the elephants of our North Africa to carry heavy loads. He doubts them in war."

Hannibal and Bogus kept walking toward the forests of tents and men gathered around many campfires. "I should leave the mahouts and their helpers here too? What does Baal El tell you I should do with them?"

"I will ask him and pray he talks to me this night. The mahouts worship false gods." Bogus said the word *false* as if spitting.

They arrived at the first cluster of tents but hung in darkness at the edge. "Bogus, my wise priest, I'll leave you now."

"As you wish, Master. You will not tell me where you go?"

Bogus again said that with the arrogance of someone with greater power than even Hannibal, and Hannibal knew Bogus was right about who held the greater power. "I must get close to Sinorix and learn what he'll do before he tells me, and I best do that alone."

"And if they find you, Master?"

"How will they find me?"

"Master, many say you are our best spy, but here too many know you."

"Sinorix's men won't harm me, not while my army is all around them."

Hannibal was not troubled about Sinorix. Better he fight with loyal men than drag along fighters who didn't want to go. The greater trouble came from Bogus. If Bogus turned against the elephants, their drivers, against him, the little priest could poison the leaders on this march and then the Senate. If the Senate turned against him, he'd have to rely on plunder to feed and pay his army—it would take enormous fruits of war to satisfy more than sixty thousand hard men. Loyalty does not last long when the stomach is empty. Nothing to be gained by challenging the hunched little man now, better to try to play him. "Bogus, before I go, tell me more about the false gods of India."

Bogus moved close and talked softly, as if he did not want anyone else to hear, though there was no one near them. "Master, I have seen their icons, their little altars, heard their prayers late in the night. They worship false gods with many hands, arms and heads. Baal El and our other gods are angry. Mighty Baal El may throw clouds and rain, thunder and boulders, floods and all else against us if we keep them."

"Have you seen these altars and false gods in our army?"

The little man shrugged. "I will have to think on that."

"Thank you, my wise priest. Until we talk again on these things, until Baal El talks to you more." Hannibal picked up his pace so Bogus could not follow easily, and the little man did not try to keep up.

As he eased into the tent forests in the direction of Sinorix' camp, Hannibal thought more deeply. He had never seen any of his mahouts at an altar to their own gods, had never heard them pray. But he had heard of Buddha, the many Indian gods. Perhaps the mahouts did worship in secret.

Ah, the all-powerful Senate, its gods, its festivals. He shook his head as if the Senate sat in front of him, would have pointed a finger if he did not think someone might see him. All people worshiped gods of their choosing, went into battle following the orders of their chosen gods—and at least half the time lost everything. Who had the better gods? It never mattered. Battles and wars did not listen to any god. Some day he would leave the priests at home with the almighty Senate— but not on this day. Too much to do before then.

He walked fast to the camps of the baggage train. It was easy to find by sound—the only place with women's voices, laughing, shouting, crying, sometimes moaning in pain and pleasure and the voices of men responding as they do only when with their women. He knew the rumors, but his beloved Imilce was not among them. Beautiful Imilce, she wielded a sword as well as any man, ran faster than most men, and fought naked like all the warriors of Iberia, but she had stayed behind in New Carthage.

She had not told him until their last night together, and he would not have known she was with their child unless she had told him. They had talked about her coming with him, about her fighting side by side with him. Oh, the glory of that. He let that thought linger, though it would never be.

A pregnant woman or mother of a newborn had no place in this campaign, and no army of his would ever knowingly carry an infant. Some of the women in the baggage train might get pregnant, might produce a child—and he hoped they knew better. He did not know what he would do then, what he would do when the newborn cried out in the night—leave mother and infant with a friendly tribe and collect them after this great war was done perhaps.

For an instant Hannibal allowed himself to wonder about the age of his own child when he might see that child for the first time. Must not think about that, must let Sinorix and his men think about such things while he, Hannibal, shielded them, their women and babies from the Roman beasts.

He located the wagons with extra tents and bed rolls, told the guard he could not find his own bed roll in the dark, told him he had forgotten where he left it. The guard let him take an old shabby one and made him promise to return it in the morning. The guard of these supplies took him for a common soldier, and it was better that way.

Hannibal pretended to sleep on the ground in that bed roll not far from the main tent of Sinorix. No one slept in that tent, too many loud words and bursts of laughter, too many men coming and leaving all night. As the camp quieted, Hannibal shifted a bit closer and made out the louder shouted words, though all spoken in the local Ketlic-Iberian. He picked out *family, home, my farm, my village* spoken with relief. He caught his own name uttered in unfriendly voices, heard it often enough that he knew Sinorix's decision and was glad. A strong but disloyal soldier would be far more dangerous than no soldier at all.

Before the army reached the southern flanks of the Pyrenees, Sinorix and his seven thousand men returned to their villages, farms and families. Hannibal assigned eleven-thousand of his army, two thousand riders and twenty-one elephants to maintain the peace in Hispania and keep open the low trail through the eastern end of the Pyrenees. He left behind his brothers, Hanno to guard the pass and Hasdrubal to oversee all of Hispania until his return.

Thus the remaining armies of Carthage and thirty-seven elephants entered the last flat land on the way to the high mountains the Romans called the Alupae, after the name given to the she-wolf.

If the gods of Carthage or India looked kindly on his army, Hannibal would get through the high mountains before the snows sealed the passes. Then they would charge down the other side onto the fertile farms and cities of Italoi. The greatest of all the cities covered seven hills. It, called Roma, lay more than eight hundred miles away.

Chapter XXV

In a River Valley

The lookouts, those soldiers with the best sight, signaled and shouted and pointed at the boat approaching from the far side of the river. A crowd quickly gathered. Ashoka, one of the tallest in the growing half circle of waiting leaders and their entourages, pressed to the front. The boatmen raised the oars and let the boat ease to rest on the flat bottom. But every man on the shore stayed behind their leader.

Hannibal stepped forward to help a lone passenger out of the river boat, manned now by unfamiliar locals. Hannibal's oarsmen had taken this passenger and two others across earlier that day, but these oarsmen were not the same. The passenger, his back to the shore and waiting men, stood up too slowly, too awkwardly, as if he didn't know where he was, though the boat rested firmly on hard sand. Ashoka noticed the passenger's purple hands bound behind him in chains. He noticed more about this passenger and cursed, as did a hundred hardened fighting men. Two freshly dead heads hung against this passenger's chest, tied together by leather straps slung around his neck. The two heads soaked the stupefied man's tunic a dirty red across his hips and down his legs. Some waiting on the shore muttered the names of the two who had crossed to the opposite bank earlier on this day with only their bloodied heads to return.

Hannibal talked to the passenger quietly and braced against him, helped him turn around, and guided the man's foot up and over the boat's side lest he trip and fall. Hannibal and more men from the shore lifted the dripping heads off the man's shoulders and eased him all the way out of the boat, then held him upright, while Hannibal continued talking quietly into his ear.

This lone returning survivor, one of Hannibal's best in local languages, did not comprehend the burden he carried back to his master, did not understand the words intended for only him. They on the far shore had slit the center of his eyes, so that he would never see again to point a finger at the men who had done this. Hannibal eased his grip on the man's elbows but did not let him fall. The newly blind man staggered one step on the shore and collapsed to the gentle mercy of unconsciousness without having uttered a sound.

The boatmen sat unmoving on the boat's boards, heads down, plainly not allied with the tribe on the other side of this river, called the Rhone by the locals.

That tribe had slaughtered two of the three emissaries sent to deliver Hannibal's generous offer. For a bounty of silver and tin, Hannibal asked they let his army cross safely to the flat land beyond the far shore and then all the way to the high mountains. The tribe's rejection had now been conveyed with all finality.

At the nighttime war council, no one talked of the treachery against Hannibal's negotiators. Ashoka wanted to ask if Sinorix might have sent riders ahead and across the Rhone to poison an allied Keltoi tribe against Hannibal. Instead, Hannibal opened by asking, "Charon, you must build pontoons?"

His chief engineer said, "They'll break the current and shelter the small boats and swimming men and horses."

"The pontoons will keep up with the swift small boats?"

"Large vessels look slow on water but travel faster than small ones. And we'll need them to carry the elephants."

Ashoka caught his breath. No elephant would keep still on a small platform floating on water. No water platform could hold Four Nails. It was not his place to speak up, not now, but he had to stop this foolish plan.

Bogus, as if he had heard Ashoka's silent protest, said, "Every river is an instrument of the gods. Baal El rules over this river, and Baal El does not countenance worshipers of strange gods fouling his—"

Hannibal cut in. "Surely after all the help our gods have given the armies of Carthage, Baal El will not stop us now." He turned to Bogus, "Or are you saying all our footmen, riders, dogs and horses from other lands must sprout wings and fly across this river?"

That brought laughter and a collective relief from many leaders, their translators and attendants.

Bogus dug in. "Mine is not to order you or your army. Mine is merely to report what Baal El tells me when I sleep." He shrugged and smiled his wrinkled and unfriendly smile, as if his stomach gases pained him. The smile reminded Ashoka of the festival and the smiling children. "Do as you wish, but Baal El has told me your elephants will not do well here in his river and will do far worse later in battle." He shrugged and smiled that smile again. "Might be best to leave them here."

Ashoka had been studying the little priest. When he spoke everyone, even Hannibal sitting close to the little man, listened. When he finished, the little man looked at Ashoka, looked at him with an unblinking scowl. Ashoka waited for Hannibal, for anyone, to say something. No one did. Some looked at Ashoka now, but Ashoka kept silent, unable to utter a word, not daring to defy the one who seemed to hold as much power as Hannibal.

Hannibal rescued Ashoka by pressing Charon with more details about the vessels the army would need to cross the Rhone and surmount the tribe on the far shore. The leaders spoke about tricking the hostile tribe, about Masinissa ambushing them from the rear. Bogus did not interrupt any more. He had said enough.

+ + +

They took every moment of three days to prepare. Hannibal instructed the leaders of his supply train, Charon, and all his infantry generals to make the strategy obvious. He ordered his buyers to not haggle in the expected manner—usually over days, even weeks for more expensive items—but to quickly pay only a little less than the sellers asked for every stout boat and every timber of soft wood. His army would run out of time long before it ran out of the tin and silver it carried to barter.

At a good place on the shore, laborers worked day and night. They flattened and smoothed the dirt along the shore, removed rocks down to water until they created a wide beach, and then they pulled large stones and boulders out of the shallow water to make the crossing easier. They set many posts into the sand and built temporary piers out into the river at the crossing place.

On the fourth day when the sun had passed its midpoint, Hannibal rode along his army massed at the water's edge. He rode around and behind men and horses, from one end of the army to the other and back once more. But he had ordered Ashoka to keep the elephants far away from the water, had ordered them to not interfere, to wait for their time to cross. Ashoka and his mahouts now sat on fence posts and looked over the tide of men and beasts and out to the river.

General Monomachus, leader of Hannibal's infantry, rode on one side of Hannibal. Charon rode on the other. They stopped when they reached the upstream end of the waiting army. Here the largest pontoons made of logs with a flat deck waited. They floated in shallow water off the bank barely deep enough to keep the pontoons from sticking to the river bottom. Bullocks and heavy carts sat on the flat decks of the platforms. Not far north from this point the river narrowed and deepened and flowed more swiftly.

Hannibal raised high his right arm and ten ram horns sounded. The army up and down the river as far as Ashoka could see surged away into the water. Tens of thousands of soldiers and thousands of horses shoved off in hundreds of boats, in logs dug out by carpenters, and on the pontoons. Men who had grown up around water swam in light armor of leather no heavier than water. Others let their horses pull them across.

Four Nails leaned into the heavy logs of his pen but with less than his full strength. Ashoka and all the mahouts commanded the elephants stand still.

When the lead boats and men were too far out to turn back against those charging into the water behind them, a roar rose from the opposite side.

The rams' horns blasted again, and Hannibal's men in the river and those still waiting to plunge shouted and screamed back. As Hannibal's army reached the opposite bank, thousands came out of trees and bushes on the far shore. Ashoka spotted specks of bright color from plumed helmets, striped cloaks or bare skin painted in white and black, orange and red. Those on the far shore banged swords on shields so loudly that the clangs reached even Ashoka.

Hannibal's men and horses surging across the river did not pause. The first pontoons neared the opposite side in the lead, as Charon had predicted, but Ashoka could not see how close they were to the enemy, whether the fight had begun, how many on the far side challenged Hannibal's army. It was all too far away.

The sky told Ashoka the battle would be short. A billow of smoke, dark and uneven, rose out of the low ridge behind the clamoring tribe on the river's far shore. Another cloud of smoke and another then more billowed up until the grass and trees on the opposite bank struck a green line under the smoke-dirty sky. Fire-tipped arrows streaked upward against the smoky canopy, the signal to Ashoka and all the leaders that Hannibal's plan had worked. In the night, Masinissa and his riders had crossed the river far upstream and snuck down behind the hostile tribe.

The clamor from the opposite bank took on a different pitch—one of surprise, then fright, then panic, high and uneven. Soon the noise died. The entire line of colored plumes and cloaks turned and ran away from the far shore and back up the rise. They were trapped. Masinissa's light horsemen bore down on them from their own tent camp on fire, and Hannibal's army charged at them out of the river.

Most fled or surrendered without serious hand-to-hand fighting. Before full darkness, Hannibal's men secured both banks. But the army had no time to celebrate this nuisance victory.

+ + +

Hannibal ordered the mahouts and elephants to gather before sun up of the next day at the northern end of the crossing place where the three largest of the floating platforms waited. Each platform was eight paces long and four paces wide.

"Ready, Ashoka? Take them onto the platforms."

Ashoka had wrestled with what he would do, what he

might say, at this command. For days he studied the giant water platforms, watched Charon and his men work under torches and moonlight after the main army had crossed, watched them cover the pontoons with dirt, leaves, stones, and dead wood to make them look like dry land—and fool the beasts. Ashoka's anger rose at their ignorance.

Now, sitting on the neck of Four Nails, Ashoka shook his head and thereby disobeyed a direct command from the Supreme General. "Your elephants will not ride on the platforms. They swim or walk. It's easy for them."

"My engineers and your mahouts will keep them dry and safe." A frown betrayed Hannibal's doubt.

"Master, no elephant will step onto a big plate that rides on moving water."

"They must. The gods of Carthage command it."

"Master, the gods of the elephants command them more strongly than I can. Their gods tell them the greater peril is ground that will not hold them. Once stuck in soft footing, they die there, slowly. Vultures eat their eyes. They will not tread on unsteady platforms."

"Ashoka, do as the engineers command. They know the river and how to cross it. Surus will lead them onto the pontoon, and the others will follow him."

"Mighty Surus will die fighting you, me, all of us before he steps onto that water platform. If we are able to force him, he'll never trust me—or you—again." The elephants waited in a rough line facing the river, their mahouts and laborers on and around them. The elephants flopped their trunks up and down and sideways sniffing cool water. They were ready to plunge in if just one mahout nudged them to go forward.

Hannibal yelled at his head engineer. "Charon, let them ford the river. You know they swim better than men."

"If Bogus allows it, Master, the elephants—and the Indians—can go as they please."

In the last days, at every chance Ashoka had watched the little man who stared at him as if preparing to spit, who talked only to Hannibal whenever Ashoka came into view, who hated him with a religious hate. But now Bogus was nowhere in sight.

Hannibal said, "Charon, look at them. The noble beasts hear and understand us. They know more than we suppose. They won't go near the platforms but strain to run into the river. Most are from the coastal mountains above Carthage, and our gods know them."

Soldiers and laborers had run out of things to do. They stood around the pontoons and watched Charon, Hannibal and Ashoka haggle. Leaves, stones and sand or mud covered the pontoon decks. If these did not fool, adding more would do nothing. No one needed to say that the army had to push on and not wait one moment longer.

Charon broke the silence. "Leave them here then. They can make their way back to Hispania with a small escort of your laziest and weakest soldiers. Supreme General, you don't need them."

Hannibal motioned for him to wait and rode up to Four Nails. He said so only Ashoka could hear, "Ashoka, I know my elephants can cross on their own—easily. But Bogus has the ear of many senators. I need the senators now and in times to come. Soon I'll have to ask for fleets filled with men, supplies, coins and perhaps more elephants. Take your best mahout and your most obedient elephant and try once more to walk onto the platform. I can't leave you here, but I must not disobey Bogus, not yet. He's on the other side preparing our biggest and best bull for the sacrifice to Baal El, to give thanks for our victory—and we should be glad he's not here now."

The manner in which Hannibal spoke the words *I must not disobey Bogus*, the shrug of the shoulders, told Ashoka without needing to say it aloud, *We must try Charon's and Bogus's plan, even if it fails.*

Ashoka leaned over to the mahout on the other side. "Have Ganesha bring up his charge." Ganesha had drawn the oldest, gentlest, most servile female still with the main army. Ashoka hoped that even Ganesha's elephant would refuse to ride the pontoons, that Hannibal might find the courage to disobey Bogus and let the elephants plunge into the water and cross on their own.

But Ganesha and his elephant gave in. At last, two elephants followed down the sandy bank onto the pier and over to the first pontoon deck, then over to the second deck farther out on the water, and onto the third pontoon farthest out. Three elephants followed until each platform held two. Indian helpers and soldiers sat or stood along the edge of each pontoon. Every man held a wide paddle or pole.

Short ropes tied the three platforms to posts. Charon, waist deep in water upstream of the platform closest to the bank, lifted one of the lines off the platform post. His helpers loosened the others. Men in smaller boats out on the river pulled on oars and pushed poles against the river bottom. The long ropes snapped taut and eased the three pontoons off the bank.

Away from dry land not eighty paces, the lead platform veered downstream with the current and rocked gently. But that was too much. The two elephants on the platform stepped back toward the rear. The elephants on the two pontoons behind followed the behavior of the front two. The pontoons could not support two elephants crowded on the back edge. Their weight drove the back ends of the platforms under the moving water. The current caught the flat pontoon surface and pushed it down, twisting the whole pontoon while hoisting the front up out of the water. Elephants, men, dirt, and all the paddles, poles, and tools from three platforms spilled into the deeper current, at first slowly, then faster until all three pontoons upended crashing into the river. The nearest platform stuck up out of the water, its edge on the bottom, for a long moment until it too fell over. Heads and shoulders of men disappeared under the massive platforms and animals. The two lead pontoons were far enough out in deeper water that most of their men plunged out of sight. Some bobbed up, gagging, shouting, splashing.

Ashoka lost sight of Ganesha on the first pontoon to turn with the current, the first to tilt up in the water under the weight of its two elephants, the first to spill everything it carried.

He and Four Nails, followed by the others that had waited on the shore, powered into the river. Four Nails headed straight to the nearest struggling humans. They reached for his trunk or ears or tail. He did not mind.

The elephants on the pontoons found their footing on the river bottom and headed out to swim or walk across, away from the chaos, from the many shouting mahouts, helpers and soldiers thrashing and gurgling.

Not all the men knew how to swim. Some floated face down in the water. Others disappeared and came up later in a different place gasping, shouting, splashing and waving, before they disappeared again, swept by the current, pulled under by their clothes or by not knowing how to swim.

In a short time, every man on the river and some under the water were pulled out and, if alive, to safety. The tallest elephant, Four Nails, easily walked across except in the very deepest section. Thus the thirty-seven crossed the Rhone River.

Seven helpers and thirteen soldiers drowned. Two mahouts did not come out of the water. Ashoka knew they all swam well and must have been crushed under the massive platforms, the stones on them, or tumbling elephants. Tilaka helped by his walking stick made his way across with the rescuing elephants.

Ganesha was among the missing.

No one saw him again. Ashoka and Tilaka did not eat that night, did not talk.

The army had no time to linger or search for missing bodies. The bodies easy to find were burned and the ashes buried later.

The first battle on the way to Rome, but not against Roman soldiers, had taken five days to plan and prepare for, five days of no progress eastward to high mountains not yet in sight.

Chapter XXVI

Far From Home

When the cooking, eating and stories were done and the main campfires died down to a glow, new sounds filtered through the tent walls. Brief, like the snuffed out wail of a plant-eating animal in the clutches of a big cat crushing the neck, Ashoka thought the cries lived in his fear-filled dreams of Govinda, Father and sisters, and, late in the night, of Radha. Awake, he still heard those sounds, and from one night to the next they got louder and more constant.

After many days marching northward along the river so the army would not face an attack from four sides at once, Ashoka understood. Ointments and syrups made from the opium bulb could not blunt all pain, close all oozing skin and torn muscles, draw out all fever and bring quiet sleep. Wounded animals never complained aloud. In the wild, a cry of pain draws predators. All these cries and moans came from men and perhaps women in this army's far off camps.

By the middle of each afternoon, the army lay strung out over miles of unknown terrain, and small groups became isolated or lost. The advance scouts and dogs could not find all the ambushers. The locals let loose local bitches in season to distract Hannibal's big dogs away from men hiding in dirt and brush to ambush the most vulnerable.

At the last war council, Hannibal said with no emotion, but everyone let the words sink in, "Stay tight, together, and do not chase. They will set traps, and I will not send anyone to save you, will not slow to find you or barter for your freedom. No time for that. Winter comes to the mountains too soon. If we don't make it through the mountains before the deeper snows, everything will be for nothing."

Ashoka rode Four Nails leading the other elephants in the middle of the army but felt safe only when encamped at night, with sentries and dogs posted around the perimeter inside the ring of trip ropes and holes with poison-smeared stakes pointed upwards. Every night the laborers set holes at all likely points of approach if soft ground permitted quick digging, and tied ropes at knee height impossible to see after sunset. The army's dogs rested with muzzles and ears pointed outward.

Lesser rivers and streams now flowed into the Rhone from the east. The land began to rise, and colder water tumbled at them out of gorges, forests and meadows in higher hills.

Late one day from atop Four Nails, Ashoka spotted dust rising and the glint of sharp metal—another distant interruption or skirmish. Through the wind and the noise of many men and animals marching, Ashoka thought he heard words shouted in his language but was too far off to be sure, to make any sense of it. He might have dozed on the neck of Four Nails and dreamed of India. In this army only the other mahouts, laborers and translators, all behind him, spoke his language.

In the fading summer light, the army found an oak forest at the end of a field of grasses ready to harvest. The horns sounded once, the signal to stop, wait for the whole army to arrive, circle up in flat places and make camp. The army quickly trampled the field of golden grass and grain. The bullocks and cattle, horses and elephants ate every stalk down to stubble before penned or tied up for the night, still hungry. The elephants and large animals needed at least a day of grazing for every day's march to not suffer. Since crossing the Rhone they had not rested.

The mahouts and helpers ate their porridge and dried fruit quietly, some so weary they crawled straight into tents and sleep. Since the river crossing, some elephants had no trained mahout. Less experienced helpers took charge of the more docile animals. Random army slaves who understood the mahouts replaced the helpers who had become mahouts. From one morning to the next, all the elephant men were harder to rouse, slower to break camp and take their places in the masses of men, horses, dogs and carts.

As Ashoka prepared to enter his tent on this night, foot soldiers carrying swords and knives but not wearing armor—they expected no resistance in their own camp—approached. Ashoka stood up. The lead foot soldier spoke forcefully but in a quiet voice, though it would have taken more than loud talking to alarm any of the other weary men. "You, come with us."

"I must sleep now. The sun comes back too soon."

"Our swords will send you to a long sleep, Indian." Three of them raised sword points close to Ashoka's shoulders and neck.

"I'm coming too," said Tilaka, propped up on his walking stick at the tent flap.

"Quiet, old man, we'll take only Ashoka."

This stranger knew his name but so did many of the army.

Ashoka's thoughts collected up everything he could, everything he might do. He and his mahouts had camped at a good place for treachery. The stand of giant oaks with their low overhanging branches on one side of their tents and their elephant pens on the other side in the wheat field—what was left of it—shielded the mahout camp from easy view of the other camps. He could get out one loud shout before dying. Those nearby still awake would shrug and likely think he was dreaming, or someone in pain had shouted out. No sentries would come running. Hannibal posted them around the whole army's outside perimeter far from the mahout camp. Four Nails, if he sensed the danger, could not help him, his feet again tethered. This man spoke like the common men of Carthage. He and his men gave no sign they could be cowed by an unarmed Indian and an old man leaning on a walking stick. They were not bent on taking him far away on foot. This band of soldiers could not get past the sentries. Even if they did, the night in this strange land held treachery. If these soldiers wanted only to slay him, they would have waited until he slept soundly. Killing was not their purpose.

Ashoka said quietly, "Tilaka, stay here, but don't tell the others unless I'm not back at sunrise." Then to the men, "Let's go. Where are we going?"

"To the prisoners," said the leader when they were out of earshot of the tents.

At the metal and wood cages, Ashoka felt the presence, heard the breathing and saw the darker masses of chained men, many more than he had thought Hannibal would transport and feed and guard, hundreds. The army must have captured and kept alive many attackers after all—for their local knowledge, to trade for concessions or information, to labor when Hannibal's own laborers fell sick or wounded, and if they proved loyal perhaps to fight. No campfire near, the only light came from stars and torches in the distance nearer the perimeter.

Prisoner guards greeted the band of soldiers which had summoned Ashoka. The leader shouted into the prisoner cage, "You who claim to be priests of Buddha, come here." He spoke

Ashoka's language, broken and with a heavy accent but well enough to be understood. This startled Ashoka. Groans and curses came from the prisoners. The many dark forms stirred and rolled over, or, if standing, moved aside.

"We are here, all three of us," said the voice of an old man in the form used by the educated.

"Ashoka, ask them if it's true," said the leader.

"If what is true?"

"If they are Buddhist priests from your country..."

Ashoka made out the shapes of the three men standing inside the cage. He could tell their heads were shaved and they wore plain one-piece garments. "I will. But don't interrupt. It's rude to interrupt a priest."

He began in a formal style of a lesser man permitted to address a Buddhist monk. "How did you come to this place?"

One of the three standing at the cage bars responded. "There are more of us in this valley."

"More?"

"More of us trying to help others on their journey."

"You are priests of Lord Buddha—here?"

"We are, and here."

"How can that be? You are too far from India."

"You are here with all your mahouts and helpers. Why not us?"

"What caravan brought you here, when?"

"We took no caravan. Our Emperor Ashoka sent us to spread the teachings of the Veda and our Lord Buddha as far as our legs would carry us."

The accent was authentic. The words matched what the most devout Buddhist in all history—his Emperor Ashoka—would have commanded. The voice did not have the intonation of falsehood. "What may I call you?" said Ashoka.

"My name does not matter. Call me Buddha's Pupil if you like." The voice was of an older man, older than Tilaka, clear and strong. The spirit behind this voice had surmounted many obstacles to walk to this place and survive to this day.

"When did you leave India?"

"Before you were born, I think. What may I call you?"

"Please do not be angry. My father named me after our Emperor."

"Your father is not alone. That is good then," said the one who wanted to be called Buddha's Pupil.

"How do you live, how do the locals let you live?"

"They know we mean no harm. The people in this valley have forgotten how to make war. When we arrived, they thought us idiots. Here it is forbidden to menace an idiot."

"Then they are not like the people where we crossed the river?"

"They are not the same as the tribe your army slaughtered or chased off."

"And they allow you to teach them?"

"Sometimes, or help a sick child, an animal in distress. When we collect extra food or clothes, we give them to those who have less than we do. We've learned the language here well enough to spread the teachings of Lord Buddha."

"How did you come to be here—in this prisoner pen?"

"Travelers from the south and west talk of the coming great war between Carthage and Rome. A Roman army chases up the river behind you. Many talk of elephants and mahouts readying for war. I and my brothers wanted to learn if this is true."

"That's dangerous for unarmed priests. These soldiers know nothing of our country or Lord Buddha's teachings. How long have you been in this cage?" said Ashoka.

"We found your army today. It let us watch but not long enough for you and the elephants to reach us. Impatient soldiers afraid we might be ambushers"—the deep voice laughed—"brought us here."

"Tell me please, Buddha's Pupil, how I can help you return to wherever you wish to go."

"We are where we wish to be."

Ashoka understood the priest's next words even before he heard them.

"Young Ashoka, if we could persuade against such folly, such waste, then this life would have a worthy purpose. Our Emperor Ashoka grieved for all the lives his armies had slaughtered in the great campaign to unite India, for all the lives his armies had lost. Everyone for five hundred miles in all directions has heard of Hannibal's army and is afraid—or rushes to join it, thirsting to kill and loot."

"It's all true," said Ashoka, head bowed in the night.

"They say a mahout from our country drives the big Indian elephant of the general from Carthage. We came to talk to that elephant driver, pray with him if we might, if he would pray with us."

Ashoka remained silent for a long time. The three priests from his country that his Emperor sent out long ago did not move. They likely could remain still in deep snow, in the torrent of a flooding stream, in wind-driven heat. They would wait for his answer. "I am that elephant driver."

The priest who had been talking said, "You have great power then. They say the lead general himself wants to ride that elephant to the gates of Rome. If you persuade him to turn back, you'll save as many men—women and their babies—as have died in all battles in a hundred years."

For the first time, Ashoka felt the weight of heavy things that he had never considered—and shame for not considering them. He, out of the land of the Emperor Ashoka, who forbad the killing of any human unless under threat of death, now rode the biggest elephant of the largest army assembled since Alexander. That very army was headed for war and slaughter, and he had done nothing to find another way. At last he said, "He doesn't heed me, not even about how our elephants cross a shallow river. He'll send me back to the mines if I ask him to do what you want."

"Then you must not. Do only so much as you are able."

Out of guilt and shame, Ashoka had to finish. "I can't stop Rome's ambitions and slaughter. Hannibal is the only one who can control Rome. And, from what everyone says, Rome will slaughter or enslave us all if it can."

"Young Ashoka, serve as best you can and the path will be revealed to you. Perhaps your leader will let us speak to him."

The leader of guards bumped against Ashoka's back. In this night of no breeze, his breath carried the odor of young wine and as if he had not bathed since leaving New Carthage. "What's all the yapping like old women, too fast for me to understand. Enough. You must translate."

"They are priests from my country," said Ashoka. "They will not harm anyone or interfere with the will of any gods."

"Why did they sit and watch us?"

"They must have an audience with our Supreme General."

"Infidel priests, we serve Hannibal if we kill them now," the leader said.

"Death is nothing to them. You'll free their spirits if you kill them. Remember Saguntum."

"What do they want?"

"Our Supreme General will want to know what these priests know. They have lived in this valley for many years, and the locals tell them all their secrets."

"Did you hear that?" bellowed the leader to the other guards. Prisoners stirred and grumbled again and told the

217

soldier band to stop their noise. The leader laughed, and the other soldiers laughed with him. "What secrets?"

"A Roman army follows not far behind."

"That's no secret. The prisoners told us when we heated their tongues." He turned away from Ashoka. "Let's kill the infidel priests and this elephant driver. Baal El will be pleased."

Ashoka had checked the possible avenues of escape, measured the size and ages of the guards—the youngest and leanest would react most quickly—tried to position himself in the darkest places and as far from the members of this band as he could. And it all seemed futile. There were too many, the avenues of escape closed, and at least one kept a heavy hand on him.

He said quietly, "You'll have to kill all the prisoners, and all my mahouts, and all the other guards. And that will not hide you from Hannibal and his vengeance. You didn't bring me here to kill."

"We brought you because these infidel priests asked for you. Ask them why they want to talk to our leader."

Ashoka translated for the guards, who listened without interrupting. "There is an island a day's march from here where the Rhone is joined by two lesser rivers. These three priests and others live in a grotto not far from the river island. For many years the main city and all the villages in this wide valley have been ruled peacefully by a wise king and his father before him. The king died of old age last winter. His two strong-headed sons quarrel over who should succeed the father. We came here to turn your army around. That we now know we cannot do. But there is another worthy reason. The brothers sent us here to beseech your General Hannibal to listen to their arguments and mediate. We asked for the mahout who drives Hannibal's big Indian elephant—knowing that mahout will heed us and Hannibal will heed him."

All but two of the band left the area and huddled out of hearing. When they broke up, the leader said, "Ask them the name of the elder brother and how we can find him."

Again Ashoka translated. "The elder brother is Brancus. He is waiting for an answer from General Hannibal in the main house on the island."

"Ask him how he knows this."

The priest said, "Brancus and his brother are no friends of Rome. In his dying, the father asked about Buddha's teachings. I was by his side when he cast off this life."

"And if Hannibal decides for one brother and against the other?" said the leader.

"In the years of peace, they have amassed ten-fold supplies and weapons and clothes for every man. If the brothers are pleased, they'll give your army what they don't need. Their best guides will take you into the mountains."

"Ashoka, at first light take these infidel priests to Hannibal. We'll come with you. You tell him about these priests we captured for him," said the leader.

"I will if I can find our Supreme General. Now let them go. They mean no harm and will not leave before they have finished what they came here to do."

Released from the prisoner cages, the priests slept without blankets on the hard ground outside the prison fence.

At first light the meddling guards of the night led Ashoka and the priests to Hannibal's tent. The lead man entered the tent and soon beckoned for the priests. Ashoka was glad no one asked him into the meeting, that the lead soldier wanted to hoard for himself whatever glory came from introducing the priests to Hannibal.

+ + +

After one more day's march, the army stopped and rested for two days and nights. Hannibal helped the two feuding brothers agree on terms of a peace. Brancus became the new king and sent guides to Hannibal's war council on the last night. They reported that Brancus' younger brother was most pleased with Hannibal's assistance. The younger brother took charge of the counting house that kept coins and treasures stored by the ruling family, accepted the peace and promised to honor the new king until he might succeed him.

All the second day, a new clanging sound swept over the army. Hannibal's metal workers mounted new metal bands to heavy cart wheels so the wheels would not splinter on rocks.

The wagons left the valley filled with tightly-packed fresh hay for the animals and salted meats for the men. Ashoka wished some of that might be saved for his elephants. The weavers in the valley brought blankets that the army distributed first to the women and older men in the baggage train. Ashoka persuaded Hannibal to allocate four blankets to each elephant. They would not do well in the cold. Leather workers from the entire region brought the most valuable implements, though most of the soldiers did not know it yet— heavy leather and fur-lined boots. Ashoka had never seen footwear like this. Not even traders from the high mountains of India brought anything like this to his village.

Chapter XXVII

The Greatest Elephant Trainer

Cold showers mixed with thunder from clouds forming in a high blue sky. No trumpets, voices or laughter broke the crunch of footfalls and heavy breathing of men and animals. Though warm, well fed, and not under attack, every man knew their easy marching lay behind.

Ashoka wore the wool coat Nuur had given him. Riding on Four Nails he felt the colder blasts first and every morning saw the distant line of mountains, like jagged teeth on the land, before most foot soldiers could see them. With the passing days the teeth got closer, and the higher peaks looked down at them.

They followed a new river eastward. Soon the trail into the mountains steepened, and the river flowed faster making the noise of angry wasps. The men and women back in the baggage train, the riders, carriage drivers and mahouts walked or rode without talking, each one blunted into silence by the mountains looming larger every day. The inclines broken by fewer and fewer straight stretches had not slowed them. The months of training and marching had done that. Only the sick and seriously wounded needed help, and Hannibal allowed them to ride atop the carts and carriages.

Craggy, treeless and unfriendly, these mountains took Ashoka back to that last night with Sinorix, to his warnings, to the constant fear that elephants could never surmount them, and to Father's warnings. *Hairy men and animals live in snow, not our people with our smooth skin or our hairless elephants. Cold turns their ears to ice and brings them sickness.* Ashoka did not know what ice was until they passed through the high passes above Exandahar, but somehow he knew that in long spells of cold elephants struggle to breathe, fluid fills their chests, and more mysterious ailments kill them. Ashoka prayed the North African elephants would climb mountains higher and colder than their kind had ever known. He ordered the mahouts and helpers to cover the older and leaner elephants at night with stitched-together blankets.

Every evening the scouts searched out level areas next to the water for camp. After two more days into higher country and colder, thinner air, Ashoka kept the coverings on his elephants in the daytime. Ashoka did that not only to keep them warm but because of what he spotted in forests, on rocks and on the crests of hills in the distance. At first they seemed no bigger than fleas on a dog. Every day there were more, and they came closer. They sat or stood on the edges of cliffs and ducked around trees.

Soon everyone in Hannibal's army watched for these hairy little men above them and kept shields ready for arrows, spears and stones. Hannibal ordered that no one shoot back. Any arrow sent to a high target would lose all speed before it hit. That day or the next the same arrow would come back down at them. At the nightly councils, Hannibal said, "Tell everyone under you that the arrow which fails to strike carries far greater danger than an arrow not shot."

In recent days the hundreds of dogs stayed leashed. Left free, too many ran off and never came back. Other dogs crawled into camp at night on their bellies and died of poisoned meat. For the last two nights, laughter and strange words in a language Ashoka did not know heckled the army from rocks and trees above.

As the army neared the higher mountains, the sun stayed blocked by the great masses of trees, rocks, and snow. The strange faces now looked down close enough for Ashoka and others to see the paint, the wild hair, even the blue and green color of their eyes. From their voices and builds some might have been women, and not one showed any fear. Still Hannibal ordered that no footmen or rider break ranks. He said, "The pests in the hills will soon tire and leave us alone. Winter will not."

That night the army camped along the last open and flat stretch by the river. At the war council the head scout said, "They climb the cliffs like shaggy mountain sheep. We have one trapped, and he disappears. When we see him next, he's on the other side of a stream and laughs at us. But if they don't attack us, our fleet footmen and riders can reach the pass in half a day. On the other side of the pass lies a meadow big enough for us to camp and then days of easy marching."

Hannibal said, "And places on the trail for them to block us where we can't form up to fight?"

The lead scout hesitated. "The gorge pinches in before the pass, but there's no place for them to gather."

"Where are my other four scouts?"

Several of the scouts shook their heads and did not answer for a time. Then the head scout said, "They chased after two of them. We thought to capture one and bring him back. But our men did not come back. The rest of us heard nothing, saw nothing, and could not stay out there at night…" He looked down at his hands in his lap.

Hannibal said, "More of the little men wait for us. We must be ready for them."

Masinissa said, "Our Supreme General is right. Their coats and face paints are all different." He paused for the point to sink in. "Many tribes have been gathering for many days, watching us—but not as friends. How narrow is the trail by the river gorge at its narrowest?"

"Enough for a cart, maybe two side by side," said one of the scouts, "but not wider."

Hannibal said, "Ashoka, what is your plan for the elephants?"

Ashoka had asked Tilaka many times, had tried to remember Father's lectures about elephants in mountains. "We'll cover the eyes and legs and set the heavy platforms on their backs. If the Supreme General will permit it, archers with long bows will sit low on the platforms."

"Monomachus, what do you say?" Hannibal asked the general.

Monomachus, resting on his haunches like an old cat ready to spring, looked at Ashoka and back at Hannibal. His bald head carried only one ear, on the left side a hole. Many in the army called him One Ear, and Monomachus seemed to like that, as if his missing ear was a well-earned remnant of battle. His bare arms, though older and scarred, the strength of his large body reminded Ashoka of Sinorix. Like most of the older foot soldiers, he had no front teeth. "Let the Indian boy do what he wants alone. My men can't suckle him any longer."

Hannibal said, "The elephants protect your men more than your men protect the elephants."

Monomachus said, "One wounded beast will run back down the mountain and trample any of our men and horses coming up behind them."

Bogus cut in. "General One Ear repeats what Baal-El instructs. It's time to leave the elephants here. I was not with them at the River Rhone, but we all know."

Everyone waited for Hannibal, for Ashoka. After a time, Hannibal said, "Ashoka, what's your plan now?"

Ashoka fought to suppress a shudder and calm his insides, then his voice. Only one answer came. "We can stay here, can go on alone, can go first or last and ask protection from no one. Surus will lead our elephants—even if we must find a way home."

Hannibal stood up and walked twice around inside the circle of leaders, their translators and personal servants, more than fifty men. He stopped in front of the eight scouts huddled and cowering for having lost four of their own without good reason. "Can our horses and riders reach the heights above the tribes?"

One of the scouts said, "There must be a way. All the wild tribesmen, their horses too, came down from higher hills or high mountain valleys. They must live at a place far up from where they mock us."

Hannibal said, "The moon is full. Before first light, Masinissa, take your best mountain riders and follow the trails into the heights. I'll come later with the heavy horses. When the barbarians wake, we'll be above them. The army and supply train will stay here. One Ear, on the second day, lead your fastest infantry into the gorge but leave half to guard the supply train. That's what they want, and without it we are lost. Ashoka, wait here at this camp with your elephant men and elephants. You and your elephants will come alone. Wait for a rider to tell you to come up the pass after all my men and horses and my supplies and laborers have cleared through to the other side."

No one responded out loud. The plan made sense.

For the first time on the journey, Ashoka's stomach threatened to heave. The army would leave him and his elephants here, with orders to not move until the whole gorge was clear. He and Four Nails and all his noble beasts were useless to them now, ordered to come through last. And if they never made it through, no one planned to come back to find them, to rescue them. One last and final chance, he closed his eyes and thanked the God Ganesha for that much.

"One Ear, how are the food supplies? If we lose the baggage train?" said Hannibal through Ashoka's prayer.

They waited a long time for the second in command of the army to respond. "If we lose our supply train, we'll have enough meat to get to the other side."

Hannibal said loudly, "From where? Speak your thoughts."

"The guides Brancus gave us say the crossing from the first gorge takes five days. We'll find friends on the other side of the mountains. They hate the Romans as much as we do."

Hannibal challenged him. "The guides talked about fast riders, not an army—with slow carts pulled by slow oxen and followed by slow women. One day's climb without meat makes us go faster. Five days with no meat will make us crawl. Ten days without food and many will lose the will or strength to climb on."

"Supreme General, you're right. We must find meat for more than five days. Our scouts tell us the locals don't look well-fed. They want what we have more than we want or need their wretched stock. Their necks are swollen for want of fish and salt. But there is a way for us to always have enough fresh meat."

"Say it, One Ear," responded Hannibal.

"We can't sacrifice our hardy bullocks or donkeys or the riders their horses."

Hannibal looked at the large man still on his haunches in a way that invited him to say more.

"When the gods take the weak and the women are used up, we'll throw small pieces of the tender parts into the camp stews."

Hannibal sounded playful. "One Ear, when the plump chicken, the well-fed sheep is led to slaughter before your eyes, what do you think?"

"My mouth gets wet." Monomachus stood now, taller than Hannibal and as lean and strong, though two decades older. "I wish we had many chickens and even one sheep."

"And if the chickens and sheep knew your thoughts, what would they do?" said Hannibal loudly enough for all to hear plainly.

"Run, run fast…" Monomachus whistled through the hole from missing teeth. Some of the others snickered with him.

Ashoka caught Hannibal's direction.

"And you want all our fighting men, their women and baggage carriers and slaves looking at the wounded and infirm like you look at that chicken." All mirth gone, Hannibal switched to his general's proper name. "Monomachus, never talk of eating our dead again. Our men and animals must trust each other as never before. Do you understand me, Monomachus?"

The big man stared back. In the dark, lit only by firelight, Ashoka was not sure he saw the infantry leader react in any way to the humiliation. The stares of all the others told Monomachus to hold his tongue, and Ashoka was relieved this council meeting did not end on him or his elephants.

+ + +

Two days later, the last of the wagons, women, and men on foot left camp at sun up.

Now, past midday, all was too quiet. No gray and black mountain swallows swooped and chirped. No wind stirred. No crows waiting for food scraps cackled in the upper branches. The wagons and women should have been five miles or more up the trail into the gorge.

The army left Ashoka no food, no horse, and only archers and arrows to defend himself, his elephants and his elephant men. Hunched-over Bogus was getting his way. Ashoka felt shut down, frozen, as if this day might be the last, and he did not know how to change that. No leader of elephants and men, he was a beggar boy left out in the rain, on the street, afraid, reaching out a shaking little hand for a coin or piece of bread. Patience, he said to himself, one step and then the next. But his orders said to not even take that first step out of here until told.

From the trail up into the gorge came the sound of hoofs beating on stones and dirt. A rider on a foam-lathered, snorting, panting horse burst into the flat area. He yelled, "Elephant men, leave now. Don't stop for any man or beast until you catch our army."

He dismounted long enough to let his horse drink in the stream. Ashoka ran up to him, waited for his attention, waited to ask how far the army and last of the baggage train had gone, if danger lay ahead. The rider did not look at him, jumped onto the spent horse and rode back from where he had come. That answered every unasked question.

Four Nails led the thirty-six upward. The days of rest and foraging in pocket meadows and woods had restored them. Leather draped the foreheads, hind quarters and legs. Yet the beasts covered the steep parts of the trail and around the switchbacks faster than any armed soldier might have.

The drop to the river grew steeper. Ashoka did not look down there. One misstep, one unbalanced lean could be his last. If the fall did not kill, Hannibal had ordered no one to attempt a time-eating rescue.

What if they never caught the main army in these mountains? The elephants could strip bark and leaves and rip up brown grass, but not the mahouts and helpers and the archers. Patience. *Don't trouble about where to place the second step before taking the first.*

Four miles into the gorge, fields of stone, stands of pine trees and dead wood dropped down to their path from the right side. On their left a white waterfall crashed onto rocks. Its noise masked the heavy breathing of Four Nails.

The path suddenly became more difficult but not from steepness and narrowing. A stretch of loose rocks, some split open, others larger than three men could move, and cut trees lay on the path. Some of the trees crossed the trail entirely. Armored men, chariots, and ox-drawn carts could not have climbed over them. Hostile ambushers must have cut these trees and rolled down these rocks after the last of Hannibal's army passed—so it could never retreat, never flee.

Whoever had done this had to be close, might be watching them now, but no elephant's ears searched out strange noises, no trunk raised at strange smells. Without any commands, Four Nails and the lead elephants shoved the trees and rocks out of the way and kept the elephant line moving up the trail.

At a steep place where Ashoka could not see far ahead, the neck and ears of Four Nails suddenly told him someone was ahead. Four Nails climbed faster. The elephants behind copied their leader. The archers readied their bows.

After rounding one tight bend, then a straight stretch with dense pines on both sides, and another tight bend, two oxen, yoked together, came down the path at them. Long reins and wagon spars dragged between the oxen but no wagon behind them. In the place where a wagon should have been, three horses followed, their heads almost on the oxen's rumps.

Two spears dangled from the ribs of one ox. The skin on the lower front leg of the other ox had ripped away, raggedly. Arrows or short spears stuck out of the sleek necks, muscled upper thighs, and belly of each horse. Blood oozed from the wounds.

The pair of oxen slowed, braced on their front legs, skidded and slid, and stopped at the shadow and smell of the giant beasts. Four Nails stopped too, ears out, trunk tip searching out every scent.

The horses behind the bullocks could not stop as fast. They slammed and twisted into the backs of the stopped oxen. One of the horses reared and tried to lift its forelegs onto the stopped oxen. But there was not enough space, or it had lost its balance and strength. It rolled sideways into the gorge, hitting its back on the path's shoulder, and tumbled out of sight into the noisy watery mist.

Ashoka jumped off Four Nails and yelled back, "All but one on each elephant, get down and follow me. Bring your weapons."

Archers and helpers approached the stricken animals. Four Nails kept the other elephants from moving forward, and his mass forced the oxen and horses to stay put.

Ashoka tore off his shirt and approached the ox on the right. He talked to the animal, touched it on the snout, across its quivering cheek. He worked his hands gently but firmly down to the exposed foreleg, pulled up the loose skin and tied it in place with the strips torn from his shirt. The wounded animal did not resist.

He pulled the pins holding the yoke in place. Other mahouts helped lift the yoke off the stunned oxen and passed it back and out of the way. Prodding gently on the heads and necks and feet, Ashoka and another mahout turned the two oxen, one by one. Others grabbed the reins of the two horses, shuddering, nervous and in pain. But they allowed the men to keep them in place, line them up in single file and turn them back toward whatever they had fled.

Ashoka said to the mahouts next to him, "We'll walk the horses and the bullocks up ahead to the next place where Surus can pass. We'll meet many more wounded. And we'll meet the wild men who wounded these. Beasts or men up ahead must see and smell our Surus and our elephants before anything or anyone else. Tell the others." His orders quickly traveled to the last mahout waiting down the trail.

Ashoka now knew what he had to do. They must not stay here or return down the mountain to that last base. The local tribes would find them, watch them and in time lose their fear of the elephants, then pick them off one by one or overwhelm them. They must catch up to Hannibal—if he still lived—and the main army before the day ended.

Two hundred paces up the trail, the elephants had room to pass. The wounded horses and oxen stood aside obediently, trusting.

The noise of the waterfall receded, but new sounds came from higher up the gorge, at first distant and intermittent like the cry of a hawk, then more and closer, then plainly the cries and screams of many men and women, shouts and dogs snarling.

More horses, oxen, mules, and donkeys staggered or ran at them, fear and pain in their eyes, yellow froth mixed with blood running out of noses and mouths. Many limped. Every one of them bled from cuts or spears and arrows still in them.

Each time a stricken animal saw or smelled the elephants, it stopped and allowed Ashoka's men to turn it, if there was room on the trail and if it had the strength to turn around and head back up the hill. Some wounded animals lay down. Among their own and in the safety provided by the elephants, with all energy of fear and flight gone, they could not take one more step.

Farther up, the sounds of many people in pain grew louder, and the water flowed closer to the trail. The drop off was now less than the height of a tall man. The cries of the living— animals and people—no longer able to climb the short distance up from the stream joined the sounds of rushing water.

Ashoka made out some of the words in Greek or the language of Carthage. "Indian, over here. Your elephants… pick us up… Help me… lift me up. Throw me a rope… On your gods, help me… I'll be your slave all my life."

Bodies, mostly of laborers, slaves and baggage train women, lay jumbled in places where the water slowed and collected in pools. They draped over and around rocks, heads down, heads up with mouths agape. Other bodies, some wearing leather helmets, skirts, and coats of the infantry tumbled with the flowing water to places where the roiling river smoothed out. Frothy water, the color of pomegranate flesh, eddied around rocks in calmer edges of the mountain stream.

Whines of human pain and whimpering flowed out of deep stands of trees too dense to see far into. Many struggled to get up from the shallower water or from the rocks onto which they had pulled themselves. They limped laughing, gasping, some crying, toward the elephant line for a chance at one more day in this life. Ashoka and his men slowed for any who could reach them and keep their place on the trail, but they did not stop—too little time until darkness.

Still farther up the gorge, more cries came from ledges and crags and dense trees.

Overturned and broken carts sat in the gorge and in the stream upside down and at odd angles. Their cargo of clothes, weapons, salted meats, wine, coins, tin and tools lay scattered about. Empty crates and barrels washed downstream, perhaps already looted by the local mountain men.

Higher up the gorge, hostiles lay among the people of Hannibal's army. They too, if they could, raised a pleading arm or head and croaked for help in a strange language. Up closer now, Ashoka saw their necks, thickened and distorted from lack of salt and the magic potions in fish from salt water. They needed Hannibal's supplies and, most of all, his salt.

Ashoka, always in the lead, glimpsed painted faces in the waning light and shadows. Helmet-covered heads of hostile tribesmen flitted between the trees and on the ledges above them and on the trail ahead. Each time, after a moment's hesitation and recognition, the face or head or body fell back out of sight. And Ashoka knew. Those little men had never seen an elephant so close, had never heard them breathe, and did not challenge the big strange beasts with platforms carrying unknown threats.

At places where the trail allowed a view up to switchbacks and ledges, he spotted and heard North African light horses ridden bareback by Masinissa's men. The horsemen waved down at Ashoka and those following. Hannibal's riders had taken the higher ground and rained their own stones, arrows and spears on the ambushers. That told him why the locals had vanished so fast.

As evening neared Four Nails led many hundreds, then more than a thousand, broken and wounded men and animals up the trail toward the main army. Some could not keep pace after the first surge of energy and life. They slumped down on the path to wait for a stronger man or animal to pick them up or for the night and death. Some of the badly wounded, as if intentionally or pushed by those behind, fell sideways down into the river.

Gradually Four Nails caught up to laborers, merchants, women and soldiers exhausted but unhurt. Carts with one or more wobbly wheel pulled by tired oxen plodded uphill. Each time, the men and animals shouted and gestured in surprise at the sudden sight of giant beasts bearing down on them from behind. At first they tried to get away or turn and fight, though they could not. Soon they smiled and cried for joy and relief. The trailing monsters were their own strong elephants.

As day's light faded, Ashoka's elephants led more than two thousand people and a thousand animals into the forming camp on the far side of the crest in a meadow with a town in the center. Small mud huts had been recently lived in. Cows, horses, sheep, chickens and other farm animals stood in crude pens. Fires in the huts were still warm.

A full moon rose early over the mountain peaks. No rain or thunder storm slowed them. Hannibal held no war council this night.

+ + +

Early the next morning, Ashoka searched for the men who might give him the next orders or, perhaps, send him and his elephants back from where they came. He did not care about that. He would serve them and his elephants until he could not or until they no longer wanted him.

As he walked through the camp, soldiers and laborers, women and even prisoners tied to each other and to posts in the ground, turned his way. They followed him with their eyes longer than any needed to. They talked to each other and pointed at him. Some waved at him, then more joined them. Some said his name in many accents, then more, then many. Men came out to their tent flaps to view the commotion as the elephant leader passed among them. First one, then another, then many put together their hands at the height of their foreheads and bowed in his direction—the universal sign of gratitude and respect. Many raised their right hand, palm facing him, the universal sign of friendship. Soon everyone did so—to him, the elephant leader, who had saved them, saved someone close to them, or saved an animal they needed.

That night Ashoka dreamed of Govinda alive and smiling. Ashoka thanked him, asked him about the next day and the one after that, but Govinda did not answer.

Chapter XXVIII

Deeper Treachery

All morning the foot soldiers looked up, to the left, to the right, and back behind them. One-eared Monomachus did not see what they spotted or searched to find. His eyes did not allow him to see what they saw. But he read the tilt of their heads, the open mouths and stares betraying fear. The air had grown colder, the sky darker and the north wind gusted louder down the canyons, but these hand-picked fighters never feared weather or looming mountains. Other things drew their gazes.

They marched stepping with toes first and then set down the heels to not miss any crunch of pine needles in the dense trees by the trail, any stone dislodged, any hard breath or cough from strangers hiding in ambush.

In the days before the battle in the gorge, Monomachus had heard the loudest shouts and whistles rained down from the rocks and forests above them. Some of his men understood the insults but refused to shout back. No use challenging men they were not allowed to chase.

The dogs out in front told him he had not missed anything. The twenty big dogs Hannibal sent with him to warn of secluded ambushers did not strain on their leashes or pull off into the woods or up the stone fields. The dogs' ears drooped, and they kept their heads in line with their muscled backs. They heard no sounds and scented nothing worth chasing.

As a young man, Monomachus always spotted the distant enemy first. But for years—he had forgotten how many—smoke lived inside his eyes. At night he needed bright torch lights to walk fast on strange paths without stumbling. He told himself he saw well-enough for fighting, all the better to not see clearly the faces of men he had to cut down. On his left side he made out what anyone said only if they were near enough for him to see their lips move. In daylight he marched as fast and long as any man, but on this cold and damp morning his knees ached.

He ignored hunger pangs longer than his men, but if his legs refused to take one more step he'd have to eat or die at the place where the legs stopped moving, and that enraged him more than his eroding senses. Hannibal's stupidity, the stupidity of youth, could lead to the slow death of his army. Better lifeless flesh give strength to the living. Better to honor the dead by using their bodies to live another day than dying with the fallen.

Every day Monomachus wondered why the soldiers had acclaimed ignorant Hannibal as their Supreme General. All the glory of taming the tribes of Iberia belonged to Hannibal's wise father. Hannibal was a nine year-old brat when his father subdued the locals in Hispania. The Barca family's influence with the Senate and its wealth meant nothing when the fighting and screaming began. Surely he, Monomachus, could beat Hannibal in hand to hand combat with any weapon or no weapon. Yet none asked Monomachus to lead them, to challenge the upstart young Barca's rule over the armies of New Carthage, to halt the attack on Saguntum and this mad run at Rome.

Deep down Monomachus knew his jealousy came from old age and time running out, from the need to take control while he still could. Soon others would challenge his leadership of the infantry. A warrior who could not do all things better than his men did not deserve to lead one of them. Every day he prayed his god Moth would allow him enough time to finish what he had to do and, after doing it, lead the entire army back home. If Roman armies descended on Iberia or on the old City of Carthage on the north shore of Africa, far better to fight her there on home ground.

He could not grasp all the possibilities from right here and now to the end game, did not know them, but for days his insides told him Hannibal had misjudged. The local tribes of the mountains had been won over by the battle in the gorge, the thirty-seven elephants, Hannibal's counterattack from above, his razing of their main village in the valley not three miles from that first attack, and his army's swift recovery. That's what the local leaders said, as they paid their respects by bringing scrawny farm animals and tubers for gifts.

These local mountain people provided guides, now at the front of the long chain farther up than Monomachus could see. The guides had sworn to take them over the mountains by the safest and quickest route and left some of their own men with Hannibal's command to calm suspicions of treachery. The guides would not lead them astray or into a trap and certain death for themselves and the hostages, unless...

For the last three days, Hannibal's army marched through meadows and high forests without any interference. On this cool morning, Monomachus began to understand. The allegiance of the mountain tribes had changed too fast. Their rage and desperation for Hannibal's supplies cooled too quickly. Their behavior took him back to the day he lost his ear to a Libyan prisoner. As Monomachus twisted his long-bladed knife under the rib cage ripping the traitor's insides, the North African neither cried nor backed away, but pressed in toward Monomachus, clamped the ear with his teeth and ripped it off, though his hands had been tied behind him and even while his heart seized and he dropped to the ground taking that left ear with him.

In the gorge three days before, the little people of these mountain tribes had shown that kind of bravery. They ran at his well-armed infantry guarding the baggage train to fling a spear or shoot a crooked arrow at a horse or an ox so that the pack animals panicked and the cargoes splayed out over the trailside. The bigger mountain men, not afraid of dying, ran at clusters of Hannibal's men. They wielded axes well enough to take off an arm with one swipe before they fell. Though the boulders and logs they rolled down from above slowed the army, to get close enough to the prize the locals risked almost certain death. That kind of courage and rage does not melt into obeisance and gifts in one night.

On this day, the elephants led Hannibal's entire army close behind the new local guides riding small mountain ponies. The elephants cleared the heavier boulders and trees that had fallen or been placed across the path. The mahouts and archers sat high to see ahead better than footmen or men on horses. These archers were the best of the army's long bow marksmen. At the last war council, Hannibal had proclaimed, "The local guides fear our big beasts and will not lead them astray. They won't run from our archers any more. The elephants will clear the way for the carts and baggage train." Monomachus had turned away to not show his disbelief at what Hannibal said next. "I can smell the verdant farmland of the Roman peninsular. In three days we'll eat their plump chickens dripping in fat and all the eggs that fit into our guts." So far, Hannibal's predictions held true, but Monomachus' insides told him trouble lay out here not far.

As this advance column of elephants and infantry gained altitude through the tree line, no stray logs or boulders blocked their path. The elephants walked the fastest on big round feet that made little noise.

By midday the elephants' size blocking his hazy view, their odors and stepping around their droppings, began to worry him. The guides up past the elephants had been out of his sight for too long. He should have kept up with the elephants and mahouts and within an arm's length of the guides, but had been more concerned about any attack from behind or above that had not come. He gave the command for the men around him to pick up their pace.

At every council, Hannibal reminded them of the first rule of a large army marching in unfamiliar territory. Avoid isolation, never lose sight and sound of other elements in front or behind. But Monomachus and his men had already lost contact with the main group behind. By now Hannibal and the heavy horses, guarding the last and heaviest, the most desired, ox-drawn carts filled with supplies, were miles back down the trail. One Ear Monomachus had not seen Masinissa and his light riders since yesterday. They again sought the higher trails—if there were any—to protect the army from above.

The harder pace broke the group fear. The dogs raised their heads and once again pulled hard on their leashes. Monomachus and his men caught up to and passed the rear elephant and the others one by one at places where the path was wide enough and not slippery from loose boulders or muck.

Monomachus was not ready to pass Surus. He would stay clear of the largest elephant he had ever seen, as clever and mean as any man. That monster might charge or stomp on them if he came too close. He didn't trust the smaller, tamer elephants either, not any of them. One hot spear in the hide, one sword swipe across the trunk, and the beasts were as likely to turn on him and his men as to keep pushing against Romans. That Indian boy had too much influence. Without the infantry first clearing out the nasty little men of these mountains, all the elephants made fat and easy targets. Indian boy Ashoka had not seen a real fight, had not needed to control a wounded elephant. Monomachus wished he'd be far away, far clear of the big beasts when that time came, when they went mad with wounds and pain and a thousand armed men cutting into them. Hannibal was a double fool for taking them and would pay a heavy price for his elephant love, unless... Monomachus' own plan worked before then.

But... he saw no guides on ponies out past Surus. He should have, even with his bad eyes.

"What do you see and hear?" he shouted up at the elephant man and archers riding the beast behind Surus. "Where are our guides?"

"The guides are up there I think, sir," said the mahout in the language of Carthage with little accent.

"Do you see them, Indian?"

"Not now."

"Why not? When did they leave?"

"I don't know. The clouds have come down."

That explained why he could not see the mounted guides. The clouds on the ground must have hidden them. For years, he had not been able to tell when clouds came to ground. "You hear their ponies?"

"Not for a time, sir."

"So, they have abandoned us?" Friendly guides stayed where their followers saw them, talked to them, touched them.

"Their ponies' hooves are still on the trail."

Monomachus checked the ground around his feet. He led all the men, and only Surus walked ahead of him now. Here and there, he saw fresh horse droppings. Perhaps the guides were still up ahead somewhere. He said, "Have you seen others of the mountain tribes?"

The mahout raised a long wooden stick and pointed. "Not in the trees, not in the rocks. They're not here. And my elephant's ears tells me there's no danger close to us."

"What do you think, Indian?"

The mahout shifted to look straight down on Monomachus. "In my country, friendly locals always walk and talk with travelers from far away."

"Mahout, how close did the guides come to the elephants?"

"They've kept their distance all morning."

They kept their distance to gallop away before the attack came. Monomachus said, thinking out loud, "Tell me, mahout, will they attack us?"

"Not here. They believe elephants are gods come to ground."

"Do you think so, mahout?"

"Elephants are gods among animals. Our god Vishnu comes to us as an elephant."

Monomachus could not suppress the laugh. "What's your name, mahout?"

"Tilaka, sir." The mahout coughed, coughed again and wheezed in a deep breath.

Monomachus heard the cough well enough, even coming from his left side. That cough sat low in the chest, of a kind that caused worry for himself, his men, and anyone who came too near this Indian.

"Tilaka, you're too old. We should have left you in New Carthage tending the pets of a senator." Monomachus had guessed the age of the man from the sound of the voice, slow speech, and thin brown skin on thin bare legs. His eyes could not focus on the mahout's face, but the hair was white. When this old man died, he would not gouge out any of his scrawny muscles for the camp stew. He must listen for that cough and isolate or kill the old Indian before his cough spread.

This time the mahout laughed. "Ashoka took me from a senator's mansion. I'm older than any in your infantry but perhaps remember some useful lessons from my youth."

"What lessons could serve you now, old Tilaka?"

"I was born under the highest mountains, trained elephants there."

"These are the highest, old man. You weren't born here."

"In India, sir, the mountains are three times higher."

Monomachus had heard of a land to the east with mountains touching the moon. "Do wild men live in those mountains?"

"In the valleys, sir, like here."

"Do you see or hear them now?"

"No, sir."

"Tell me when there are no more fresh hoof prints on the ground."

"Yes, sir," said Tilaka.

Monomachus got all of it now, had seen it before and became angry he had been so easily fooled. The enemy, beaten but not destroyed, too suddenly bringing food, blankets and women, and then the attack at night on the lightly guarded camp of battle-weary men. These guides, if still at the front, headed them over a cliff or into a box canyon with no exit.

He had warned Hannibal, but Hannibal had refused to listen. Then again, Hannibal might have been right. They had to push on or turn back to New Carthage and disgrace—if they made it back. Winter raced in as fast as they raced to Rome. They had to trust the guides, or again beat back their tribes if it came to that, and then find their own way out and over the mountains. Hannibal or he, if not Hannibal, had to lead the whole army to the pass over this second range and down into Italoi. That was the only choice after all. He would push on for a while longer. Had old age confused his thinking, distracted him? He didn't know, and that made him angry too.

The trail crested and dropped to a valley large enough for the army to camp. Surrounded by trees, covered by dead grass rising to fields of rocks above the tree line, a camp here would be easy to defend, though he could not see to the ends of the valley.

The advance party of dogs, elephants and infantry collected up. No one took the protective leather coverings and platforms off the elephants. No one started a fire. The men and animals drank deeply from rivulets out of the rocks but remained anxious, alert. The mahouts fed the elephants balls of honey-soaked barley, while the men ate salt-cured meat and flat bread wet with olive oil they carried in their pouches and tossed the toughest scraps of meat to the dogs. Everyone kept looking around, walking around.

The pony hoof prints told them the guides had come this far and perhaps were near, resting or waiting for them to catch up, or alerting their tribesmen to attack. The lead dog handler pointed his charge at a pile of horse droppings. The droppings were barely warm.

The main trail picked up again on the far side of the valley. A jumble of rocks, rotted logs, and a washed out hair pin turn proved few had used this path to cross the mountains in recent times, perhaps not in years.

The elephants formed a loose circle. The soldiers with the best vision positioned themselves where they might see back up the trail that brought them here and spot the lead elements of Hannibal's main army, or an army of the mountain tribes. They saw no sign of Masinissa and his riders. The heavy wet air muffled subdued voices, cloaked the ground and hid all the features of the land beyond the immediate flat area and perimeter escarpments.

The answers came to Monomachus. The local guides had not led them into an ambush. They had separated the elephants and elite fighters from the rest of the army and baggage train.

"Sir, we must go, go back and go fast," said a voice in Greek from a tall man on his right side.

Monomachus turned to face Ashoka, standing close enough that he could make out the brown skin and black hair, the stature of a strong man but young and lean. He knew this Indian too well, proud and of great influence over Surus and hence over Hannibal, greater than even Monomachus himself after what the Indian and the elephants had done in the last ambush. Not a boy after all. "Ready your elephants, mahouts and archers. Tell them to eat and drink now."

The lead Indian elephant driver was right. They had to go back and fast.

Men and animals quickly formed up and headed back up the path. Monomachus felt soft snow flakes on his bare arms and face, tasted them. Heavy snows always started lightly. He forgot to listen for the old mahout's cough or did not hear it again.

Chapter XXIX

An Old Man Fighting

They headed back the way they had come but this time without any local guides at the front. Miles out of the hollow and up to the pass then down the other side, the dogs and elephants picked up the gait without any command. The footmen broke into a trot and ran to keep up. The dog handlers released the leashes so not to be pulled off their feet on the downhill run, to free their hands for swords and the shields they carried on their backs.

The dogs sprang forward, low growls rising, and disappeared around a wooded bend at the narrowest part of this, the second, gorge. They disappeared into the trees on the south side of the path and bounded to their quarry. Here too, loss of footing on the northern edge meant plunging onto rocks or into frothing water far below.

Up ahead a hairy local man, then another, broke out of the trees and ran away down the path. The dogs pounced onto the backs of men running away. One of the tribesmen tripped and crawled away on hands and knees. A dog knocked him flat. He jumped up and spun around to stab at the dog leaping at him once more. In midair, the agile beast twisted out of the way of the slashing arm and short sword. The tribesman's unstopped momentum carried him over the edge. His scream merged with the sound of rushing water.

The dogs found others hiding. Twenty strong jaws clamped onto necks and faces or the large muscles of the legs and arms and pulled the little men off their feet. A short way down the path, unmolested tribesmen vastly outnumbered the twenty four-legged fighters. But they could not easily climb through the wild trees and jumbled rocks to rescue their comrades hiding in ambush up the trail. The few who came running out from their cover and up the main path in the direction of their fallen mates froze.

The elephants, with archers set to fire from the platforms, trotted down the main path moments after the dogs had imparted the first shock. Four Nails stepped squarely on one fallen tribesman so fast and hard the little man could not utter even one scream. In one motion, with a sweeping trunk and tusks, Four Nails tossed another off the trail into the abyss. Wildly flung spears and stubby crooked arrows fell off the leather blankets covering thick hides.

Monomachus heard the dogs and the startled shouts before he saw any of it. He drew his broad sword, grabbed the man next to him and shouted, "Let's go. Stay to my left."

He and that soldier ran into the trees at the front of his elite men. They pulled each other through the pine stands and over the rocks where elephants could not go and, side by side, reached a tribesman who had not yet fled.

Four days before, in the ambush at the first gorge, Monomachus, through the fog in his eyes, had been able to spot the shorter and thinner men of these mountains. Some had shed their bulky firs and fought dressed only in loin cloths and boots, but their short stature, frantic motions and ceaseless shouting allowed him to fight them. The little men had proven no match in hand-to-hand combat.

The first tribesman waiting in the trail side trees ducked under Monomachus' sword and flashed a short pike at his gut, but Monomachus' first move had been a feint. He leaned aside to evade the jab of the little man and brought back his two-edged sword, taking off the tribesman's outstretched arm above the elbow. The disconnected fist clutching the spear dropped onto a carpet of pine needles. Monomachus brought his sword around a third time with a backward slice deep into the neck. His kill slumped to the forest floor at his feet. Stepping over him, he caught the odor of close fires in a rancid hut and the scent of fresh blood. That pleased him, made him move faster, made all his senses keener. He could still fight as well as any man.

He knew the tribesmen had no idea the enraged infantry leader could hardly see them. Had they crouched motionless in the darkest shadows of the pines and kept quiet, they might have killed him easily. Instead, those who did not run away brandished swords and yelled or stood up to try to aim a clear shot. Monomachus' skill, developed over tens of deadly fights and thousands of training exercises, gave the tribesmen little time or any opening. He and his fighting partner jumped from tree to tree and boulder to boulder and never stopped moving, turning, ducking, slashing.

The little men had no time to talk to each other or gather on a flat area before another dog took one of them down, another fighting man came at them, another elephant crushed any who lingered on the main path, or another archer sent an arrow into one who broke cover long enough for a clear shot.

Monomachus and his select men—bigger, stronger, faster—wielded swords of steel forged in New Carthage that did not break, wore light armor that crooked wooden, iron-tipped arrows could not penetrate, carried shields that deflected spears hitting at an angle. One by one, then in threes and fives, the tribesmen were cut down, scrambled out of the trees onto the main path into certain slaughter, or disappeared into the tree-covered slopes and around rocks. This battle ended quickly.

On a wide part of the trail, Monomachus ordered his horn carrier to blow one time. His men and dogs collected from the woods, from up and down the path. The mahouts halted the elephants, lined them up and waited.

Monomachus quickly counted. He missed five to six men and three dogs but did not wait for his own dead and wounded. If they were of any use, they would recover and find their own way. The mist would turn to rain, then sleet, and snow by morning. They had to press on down the trail to the main army while they still could.

He shouted, "This was nothing. Hold the dogs with all your strength. There'll be too many, fighting too close."

Then he said what he thought he would never say, utter blasphemy if Bogus could have heard. "Surus and his Indian must lead. The first wave of spears and arrows fell off him like pebbles. Let's find our brothers and save them."

Not far down the path the faces of his men alerted him to the screams and shouts drifting up to them. The elephants again picked up the pace, though the mahouts tried to hold them back, and the dogs on leashes pulled hard at their handlers. Monomachus ran again not caring about his loud footfalls, not looking around, leading again. The squeals of horses, shouts in his language, snarling of other dogs and yelling of tribesmen growing louder told him Hannibal's entire army just ahead was in its second fight for survival.

From behind him a trumpet blast, not from a horn but Surus, ears out, head and trunk high, shook the trees. He looked around and saw the giant beast rise up on hind legs. He squinted up the trail to try to make out what caused Surus to pull up, the entire line of elephants to slow, and the footmen on both sides of the elephants to bunch up and stop.

Less than two hundred paces lower on the switchback, a light horse out of North Africa, blood and dirt covering its normally gleaming black back, head lifting off the path and flopping down, lay in the middle of the trail, legs broken, its rider under it—a Numidian, one of their own—dead.

Six of Hannibal's soldiers, crouching low and ducking, tried to fasten ropes to the horse's feet, to stand it up, move it, or tie it down to kill it. Other men, but too few, tried to form a ring of shields around the horse and men to shelter them from spears and stones. Two other riders of their own showed their heads over the edge of a granite ledge above the trail and faded back. They could do nothing for their compatriot and his horse.

Beyond the fallen horse and rider, a multi-headed animal snapped its multiple froth covered mouths and surged up the trail in the direction of the fallen horse. The multiple heads separated to reveal two oxen pulling a broken cart up the trail, with Hannibal's men, shields held high, backs to the carts and animals, trying to protect them from wooly tribesmen running at them, spears and swords raised and then slashing.

Every man and animal in the chaos froze and stared in Monomachus' direction, not at him but at Surus and the line of elephants and archers behind. The long bow carriers on the front two elephants fired a volley and hit two of the little men at the edge of the trees. The other little men stopped fighting, charging, and fled. Monomachus thought old Tilaka had it right. These ragged little people believed gods had come to ground in elephants.

Monomachus and his men cut down the few who stood up and fought. The tribesmen beyond those who stood to challenge melted away before the dogs, fighting men, and elephants reached them. They left behind a wide string of chaos. The carts and their cargoes, the weapons and clothes of the dead, the meat of the dead animals presented a bounty they could harvest at leisure once the army moved through.

Slowly, steadily the elephants helped right turned-over carts, and, as they had before, by their massive presence, calmed wounded animals that snorted and stomped in pain but permitted men to aid them or end their suffering. The elephants helped hoist unbroken wooden barrels of tin and coins back into carts that could still be pulled. Some helped pull or push uphill carts whose oxen could no longer pull or were gone.

Monomachus said to his fighting mate, "Come with me now. You and I can do nothing more here. Help me find Hannibal Barca."

They worked their way down the trail for over a mile through the baggage train. Women and wounded soldiers huddled in carts that could not move because other carts blocked the trail or their own animals had broken down. Hannibal's foot soldiers hit and slapped with hands and whips and flat sides of their swords to keep the animals moving. Laborers and ox drivers lowered their shoulders and backs and on straining legs tried to become oxen and push or pull carts whose wheels still turned but no longer had animals to pull them. Other soldiers, their backs to the carts and animals, still fought straggling tribesmen in the trees. Some horses carried two wounded men. Other horses limped rider-less, leg bones exposed under ripped skin. Open-mouthed men sat by the trail too tired or broken to move. Other men carried one of their own on their shoulders. The entire army moved uphill as inexorably as a tide but no faster.

As Monomachus made his way down the trail, more than ever he had to see clearly, recognize others before they recognized him. No one stopped him, accosted him, acknowledged who he was, everyone fully occupied with their own safety, their animals, broken carts, or pain. Or perhaps his vision did not allow him to see quick nods, a flick of a hand from soldiers who recognized him in the gathering darkness. He hated Hannibal for his youth, and now most of all for sight rumored the equal of the hawk's.

Farther down in wider areas the trail became more crowded. Women past fear and shame no longer huddled in carts but, sobbing or silent, tended to their men or tried to help the animals. The largest baggage carts drawn by as many as six oxen stopped dead though pulled and pushed by scores of men. At some sections of the crowded path, Monomachus and his fighting mate headed up the mountain side into the trees and over rocks to pass around the clutter and misery. Local tribesmen no longer bothered to engage them.

More and more foot soldiers of his army crowded the trail below the heavy carts and oxen. He was among his own now. He grabbed his companion by the arm, "He must be close. Do you see him?"

His companion said nothing, stared at Monomachus, then past him.

"Monomachus, we've looked for you," said the familiar voice on his right.

Monomachus started to raise the sword he carried tightly in his right hand since his run into the battle but, before he could, felt a sharp blade on his wrist above the hilt.

Hannibal said, "Don't... you can put up your sword. You are among friends now. Your men and the elephants have opened the trail for us. Masinissa and his riders have chased them away."

Monomachus bowed his head. Hannibal had no need to tell him again about losing contact with the main army, about his failing sight and bad hearing, his aching knees, nor about his plans. Had he, Monomachus, been more careful, calmer, he would not have allowed the guides to race up the trail far beyond contact of the main army. Had he kept contact, the tribesmen in the woods would not have been able to set the ambush of the baggage train without first engaging the elephants and lead dogs and his elite fighters.

"Your men and the elephants have saved the army of Carthage this day."

How could Hannibal know this? The riders from the higher trail must have signaled the return of his men, his dogs and the elephants.

"We should have come back sooner, not lost contact."

"What did you find up this trail?"

"Over the pass and down is a valley big enough to hold us all. We can guard the perimeter from these stinking little men."

"Tomorrow we'll rest there and then to Rome," said Hannibal.

+ + +

The first snow of the year fell through the night. They built fires on the trail and tried to huddle around them. Their own dead bullocks and horses fed the weary men. In the morning, the lead elements reached the valley Monomachus had found the day before. The clouds lifted off the land. All could see the valley sat among peaks too steep and rocky for any but goats and unburdened men to scale. A rocky hill, modest in the midst of high mountains, rose from the middle of the flat valley. Foot paths, worn by tired or scared locals and travelers over uncounted years, ringed the rocky hill and wound into its caves. Multiple ledges at the top made a natural look-out over the whole valley. Heavy grasses, though dead for winter and covered by the night's snow, fed the large animals which scraped off the fresh snow.

For three days, Hannibal issued no new orders. For three days, more dogs, rider-less horses, oxen, men on foot and men on horses found the camp in the valley. Drawn by the glow in the distance and then the lights of large campfires and aroma of cooking meat, many came in long after the sun had left. Out of good fortune or instinct, they had not fallen off the trail, had avoided scavenging tribesmen and wolf packs. Wounded scrawny men of the mountains came in too, this camp their last chance for survival.

At first light on the third morning after the battle in the gorge, his sore knees woke Monomachus before any light penetrated his tent, his eyes. As if from far away, he heard the familiar voice, "Monomachus, get up. I need you."

He jumped up, over two men sleeping, threw on the heavy coat and stepped out the flap onto muck and dirty snow. Hannibal's stare made him forget the cold wet ground biting into his bare feet.

Seven local tribesmen, all small, lean, and giving off the same rancid odor of smoke and animals as the men he fought hand to hand, crouched together in one corner of Hannibal's large tent in front of a fire that warmed the inside. Their hands and feet were bound. Ashoka, Masinissa, Bogus, two other generals, and three common soldiers stood over them waiting.

"Monomachus, you'll break the tie. Should they live or die now? They say they'll show us the true last pass to the other side."

"But their brothers have already betrayed us," said Bogus.

Monomachus did not tell the priest he thought him stupid, but the priest's comment made his vote easy, "Ask them where the main trail over the mountains begins from this valley."

"No. The main trail is on the other side of the trees on the north side of this valley," said the translator.

Monomachus knew that was true, at least in part. The trail at the far end of this valley led nowhere. "If they show us the true path to Rome, they can live."

Hannibal said, "I think this time they want to live more than to betray us again."

The shattered army crawled upward again though not on the trail that headed off on the eastern end of the flat area. They climbed ever higher on steep switchbacks and ridges into air thinner than many had known. Men unaccustomed to heights struggled for every breath. The laborers had to level or clear sections of the trail with picks and shovels so the elephants and wide carts could move ahead. The trail became so narrow that they had to take apart the heaviest, widest carts and carry them piece by piece. Trees did not grow here to provide hand holds and shade from the blinding light and a safe trailside to lean against. Stones and boulders covered the loose gravel, shards of shale and granite. Cold leather boots found no traction.

By the second day, many developed early snow blindness—eyes that hurt as if rubbed by hot sand and hazy vision. Less than five men from among the thousands in Hannibal's army knew the cause or the remedy. These few carried and wore leather or bark eye coverings with a center slit and thong to tie behind their heads. The others had laughed at them that first day of full snow, but by the second day they showed the others how to make their own eye coverings and told them the gods will heal their eyes.

+ + +

On the fifth day after the battle in the second gorge, the lead elements reached the top of the main pass, with only one more climb ahead before heading down. The main pass flattened out in a desolate plateau big enough for the entire army to gather. One by one, hungry, spent, not sure if they were seeing or imagining, they looked out at the open sky to the south and east. Clouds lay beneath them and, through breaks in the puffy white carpet, the hazy dark green of a flat land called Italoi.

Chapter XXX

Fire and Vinegar

Cold wind stung Ashoka's face. Not one mahout or archer rode. They crouched low to their animal's side or behind them. Four Nails took one short step then another, slid on snow packed hard by the thousands ahead or on loose stones where snow had blown away.

For the past two days of trudging in the highest passes, many men flopped onto their bellies or dropped to their haunches so the ground might grab and halt the slide. Then they crawled, rose to their knees, to their feet and stood to regain balance under heavy packs and shields before they marched again. But the snow-blinded had to feel their way. They and the wounded stumbled often. When they lost footing at the wrong place, they took a long fall down ice, old hard snow, and rocks. Their slides stopped at the bottom of the abyss far out of sight.

Covered by long coats and thick caps, some survived the fall. Ashoka heard their pleas carried up the mountain side. The slope was too steep and slippery to climb, but he wanted to wait for them at least a little while. Firm orders commanded that if they could not climb back on their own, leave them, keep moving.

His elephants trudged up the mountain to their own voices. They stood still when a man reached for a leg or for the ropes tied to platforms on their backs. The animals cared more for their masters than the men cared for each other.

Hannibal ordered the elephants to come last. The big beasts had better balance than men or other animals. But if a fragile snow bridge covered the trail, better the lighter men and animals crossed first. Hunger slowed them more. They had not eaten in three days. The last of the hand-sized treats ran out five days ago. Four Nails could keep moving without food for many days more. Ashoka was not as sure how long the smaller elephants from North Africa would climb on without food.

Near the end of the second day on the highest part of the mountain, the elephant line bunched up behind men and horses. Everyone in front of them crowded forward to look, to listen at what lay ahead to slow the army. The trail ahead now snaked downward, but the entire line had come to a standstill.

Word passed up to Ashoka. He patted Four Nails, told him to stay, and walked to the elephant men behind them. "Tilaka, everyone, listen, and then tell those coming behind. We must turn around... maybe back to the last valley."

The old man shook his head, coughed, breathed in deeply and said, "Who leads them down there at the front?"

"Tilaka, teacher of patience, where is your patience when we need it?"

"What stops us... who says?"

"A boulder blocks us," said Ashoka. "Sits across our path, the mountain on one side, a long fall on the other side. No one knows..."

"What kind of boulder?" said Tilaka.

"I don't know, old man—a big one."

"I'll go to the front, Ashoka. I must see it."

The nearer mahouts and helpers shook their heads or looked down out of respect for an elder. On the march from

New Carthage, Tilaka's face changed into that of an ancient. His skin hung looser on arms and legs of bone. His cheeks had flattened, and his eyes glowered out of dark hollows.

"Why? You will push that rock down the mountain?"

"Ashoka, trust our gods if you don't trust me. Our fate is not to die on this mountain."

"You should have reminded our gods before they blinked and made the mountain side collapse." Ashoka patted Four Nails on the cheek. "From what they say, not even Four Nails can budge that boulder."

"Ashoka, every spring in our mountains we move giant boulders." Tilaka drove his walking stick into the slush piled on the trailside. "These men all around us are flatlanders. Not one has been in real mountains, not like our Indian mountains."

"Tilaka, they'll throw you off this mountain, me too."

"Let me do this one thing, and I'll never ask for another."

Ashoka wanted to tell Tilaka of the last time he had begged Ashoka to let him do one more thing, of the cross in the square of Carthage. "I'll take you down. But don't insult them if we get there."

The soldiers grumbled as they moved out of the way of Ashoka and his old mahout trying to squeeze past them down the mountain. But they let them through. Some helped the old man over difficult places without asking why. Tilaka's face had the look of a crazed old man who would not stop, flushed red, his eyes burning.

From up the trail, Ashoka saw Hannibal, Charon, Monomachus, Masinissa, and laborers. They appeared small at the base of the gray rock taller than two four-story buildings and as wide. It rested against the nearly vertical slope of a field of loose stones. On the downhill side, the boulder hung over a drop no one could survive. The engineers had built steps and a foot path into the mountain wide enough for an agile man to climb to the boulder's top. There a laborer crouched as if in deep thought or just struck dumb.

"My order did not reach you?" Hannibal yelled up at them.

"Yes, sir, I did receive it," said Ashoka.

Ashoka, still higher than the boulder, saw beyond it down the mountain. So close, were the fir tree-covered slopes down there. Warm air drafted up bringing the aroma of fertile dirt and vegetation. Winter had not caught hold down there.

Hannibal's face and eyes had taken on the same color as Tilaka's, and his voice too sounded like an old man— resigned, lifeless. The waiting men, draped in torn, muddy, and perspiration-caked garments, looked smaller, thinner against the boulder, more like the stinking little men of the mountains who nearly destroyed them.

Bogus—Ashoka had not noticed him until he heard him—yelled, "Take them back, take them all away from us. You and your foul beast are a curse on Carthage and this glorious campaign. We should have heeded Sinorix and the spirits of the dead Sagunti, left you behind, left your stupid beasts."

This outburst took Ashoka by surprise. Ever since his elephant line had cleared out the ambush in the first gorge, other leaders turned to him and listened when he spoke, though Ashoka seldom spoke up other than asking for blankets, food and treats for his elephants. Bogus no longer pestered him, though he had not given up his hard unblinking stare every time he looked at the lead elephant driver. Ashoka shouted back, "You, none of us, would have come this far without Surus and the others."

Bogus said loudly enough but not at a full yell, "Baal El told me in my last sleep on the mountain to turn you and your beasts away."

Ashoka, now closer to the rock and the group standing around it, said quietly, "They have served Carthage well and will again. You must talk to your Baal El about how our beauties did at the two ambushes in the gorge."

"Not here, not down there. The Romans are ready. They will kill them all in the first battle."

Foolish pride had made Ashoka challenge Bogus, and the priest might still be right. Later others would remember Ashoka's boast. His elephants had surmounted every test so far, but far more severe tests lay ahead now on this mountain and down there in Italoi. Tired, too hungry to feel hunger, worried about dying on the mountain and what might happen after that, Ashoka managed, "They'll work better than hundreds of horses and men and will not talk back."

The priest said, "Charon will widen the path around this sign from Baal El, wide enough for the men and horses. The men can carry the carts in pieces. But, no elephant can pass." He looked at Hannibal and said loudly, "Don't you dare dishonor Baal El again. The Mighty One commands this is the end for them and for their drivers."

Sweat dripped into Ashoka's eyes. Days before he had lost feeling in his feet. A hawk, circling below on the updraft, distracted him. All at once, he didn't care about the little priest, about the priest's warnings or hate. None of that would make a difference now, on this day, if the giant rock remained in place. As if from far away, he heard Tilaka, "Supreme General, there is a way for your elephants to reach the gates of Rome."

"Tell us, old man."

Tilaka's voice, raspy, still resonated off the giant boulder. His command of the language of Carthage made all those within hearing listen.

"I come from the highest mountains of India. When I was a boy, boulders such as this one, even bigger, rolled onto our pathways, into villages and houses, onto precious plots for planting. The big stones and boulders rain off our mountains alone and in crashing clusters. Waves of snow from mountains far higher than these," he pointed up and around, "thunder boulders down at us. We break every big one with fire and wine. My people live in the shadow of the mountains and have done that easily for thousands of years."

Bogus laughed.

Hannibal rubbed his chin covered with a three-day growth of beard. "Make it so hot it glows red and then drench it in spirits?"

"Yes, sir," said Tilaka. "And smash it with heavy hammers when the water smoke rises around the stone."

Hannibal said, "The Greeks teach that fire and water break any rock. Our metal workers break swords with water after fire. Charon, can you do this?"

The chief engineer said, "Supreme General, glowing rocks sometimes do break apart, and the pieces fly out when doused with water. If we crack them, they'll break open. But... we carry little wood for fires, only enough... to last until the trees below."

Bogus broke in, "This is the sign from the most high, Baal El. The Indian and his elephants must go no farther."

Tilaka said, "The elephants will haul all the wood we need."

Ashoka wondered if they had the strength, if the mountain trail would support treks up and down. But if the army turned around and went home... it must not. He must not think that, must not let his elephants read that in his thoughts. They had to do what Tilaka said, or his elephants would all die here on this mountain.

Hannibal moved up to the boulder and rested a hand on it. He looked even smaller than before, the boulder bigger. "Bogus, if the elephants help us break this, will that be a sign Baal El approves?"

"I'll pray that Baal El speaks to me tonight and will answer at sunrise."

Hannibal said loudly, "Monomachus, Masinissa, can we wait the night to do nothing?"

Monomachus said, "Another day of idleness on this mountain will have them eating each other, sir. My best men will form a chain down the mountain and relay wood and branches to the base. Ashoka and his elephants can bring it up to the pass."

"Ashoka, will Surus lead the big beasts once more?" asked Hannibal in Greek.

"The gods willing, yes, Master."

"Go then. Monomachus, send your men with him. Charon, your best wood cutters and sharpest saws have work to do. Gather up all the flasks of that sour vinegar we call wine. Masinissa, get the horses and bullocks out of the way at the open places. Nothing must slow the relay to this little stone."

The army took to the task with an enthusiasm not seen since its charge across the Rhone. Ashoka and Four Nails led the elephants back from where they had come until they reached forests. The best wood cutters loaded small logs and many branches onto leather side carriers and platforms on the elephants. In a continuous loop, the beasts hauled the wood from the other side of the mountain to the flat area at the top. From there soldiers passed the wood piece by piece down to the base of the boulder. Some said eight thousand men made up the relay. This mountain became easier to navigate the second time and a third. The wounded, lame, snow-blinded and the animals not part of the task stayed clear. Ashoka marveled at the stamina of the elephants but understood. They too knew good fertile soil, a quiet camp, and days of foraging sat not far past the boulder.

A fire burned at the base of the giant boulder that night, into the next day, and past the midday sun. The base of the rock turned the same shade of red as the wood embers.

Early in the afternoon of the second day, many men took turns running as close to the boulder as the heat let them and flung their bottles of vinegar or pouches of water to break or spill against it. Another group followed the first, each man with a long-handled mallet, and smashed at the boulder. The clang of hammers on stone joined loud pops of rock splintering and cheers of many thousands on the mountain. Section by section the rock broke into chucks. The chunks fell away or were thrown off the mountain. On the fourth day, nothing blocked the army.

+ + +

In two days more, the lead riders and strongest marchers reached level ground. They found grass still growing late in the season, fresh water, deer, wild pigs and pheasants. They came to rest in the middle of a valley cut by a river the Romans called the Padus. For two more days, late arrivals found the camp, even some who had fallen down the abyss.

After all the grass-eating animals had filled their bellies and rested, after the men on horse and hunting dogs had caught all the deer, pheasants, and wild pigs within easy riding, Hannibal ordered his leaders to report at that night's council the number of men available to attack deeper into the homeland of the Roman empire.

The army that crossed the Rhone with fifty thousand or more infantry now numbered twenty-three thousand. Masinissa lost a thousand riders and horses. Of four thousand heavy horses that started, two thousand remained. Of the five thousand big dogs, three thousand vanished or died. More than half the oxen, mules and donkeys that left New Carthage perished.

Ashoka brought across every elephant.

Chapter XXXI

Winter And Romans Closing In

A tired routine returned. The fighters from places far from Carthage again formed their own tent villages and camped with their own countrymen. The cloth and leather workers mended tents, clothes, and light armor. Metal workers built fires hot enough to pound out and repair shields, weapons and armor. The surgeons replaced stitches holding skin together and smeared honey and mud smelling of sulfur onto hot wounds. The line of men outside the surgeons' tents waiting for treatment was shorter than ever before. The surgeons dispensed fewer crushed poppy bulbs to be mixed with water or wine and drunk to blur pain. Not many of the severely wounded had survived the trek over and down the mountains.

Tilaka kept to himself. He coughed a deep ugly cough. Every child had been taught about these stronger coughs, to stay far from those who had them. Some coughs ended in days. Others never stopped but spread until all the weaker and older family members lay dead. By now everyone near him knew Tilaka's cough was of this kind.

He slept by himself out in the open under a leather blanket and rode the last elephant in line. That elephant had to lie on its belly, or Tilaka could not mount it. No one helped Tilaka, his face the darker color of fever. He strained harder to walk, to breathe. In recent days, Tilaka talked only through his eyes and gestures, the effort to form words and breathe too hard. Ashoka had not seen him eat anything since they reached the flat land. Father warned this kind of sickness would spread to the elephants if men and elephants lived too close.

Other mahouts took on the same hard cough. If the plague, it could weaken and destroy them all.

At first light thirteen mornings after they reached flat land, Tilaka did not stir. Ashoka washed him, combed his white hair, draped his body in fresh clothes, dragged it on a wooden platform behind an old borrowed horse, and burned it to ash downwind of their camp on a pyre some other mahouts built from scrap wood.

Ashoka stayed until all the embers died. He tried to say something to send Tilaka to his next life, a prayer of thanks for Tilaka's wisdom. Tilaka had helped Ashoka get this far, to stay alive. But no words found him, only what ifs. What if the cough dug into him, his other mahouts, or his elephants? What could he do? What if he ran away, out there into the flat plain or back into the mountains? As long as one other mahout, one elephant looked to him, he would stay. What if the cities of this land were too far away, their walls too thick, their fighters too strong for the tired army? What if no one, nothing, could help him find his way back home?

From day to day the sun swung lower across the southern sky, barely long enough to dry the wet grasses and melt the morning mists. The camp sat on a rise above the surrounding flat land. When a southern wind blew and cleared the air, Ashoka spotted smoke rising in the east and south and, at night, the glow against a dark sky from many fires. Others lived or hunted in this land below the mountains.

The air grew colder, the days shorter, and for a month fog shrouded them. The sun rarely shone, never long enough for wounds and boils to dry and heal. Tents and clothes held dampness unless strung over an open fire. Days of rain and sleet followed the days of fog. Ashoka's worry for his elephants and men never ended.

Hannibal's army moved three times, seeking the better position opposite a large Roman army. That army stalked them close for weeks. The Romans sent out horses and riders to test Hannibal's response. Masinissa's swift ponies always came back with few losses against the slower riders of Rome. They always brought back Roman horses and saddles. Those saddles, of stiff leather and with posts on each corner, were useless to Masinissa's riders. Any rider in those saddles lost all close body contact with his horse, lost all feel for the horse's balance and back. The Roman horses were smaller, slower, more like ponies. Reports spread about a second army headed north from Rome with orders to engage and destroy Hannibal's army before winter turned the land to muck.

After every war council, Ashoka talked of these things with his mahouts and helpers. They listened but said little. Theirs was not to do anything until ordered. They talked of the cold, the damp and how docile their elephants had become. Ashoka's reports grew shorter, his mahouts' questions fewer.

As winter bore down, many riders trotted at the camp from the direction of the Roman army. They came in lines across the plain and more of them behind the front lines. Some pulled small carts of provisions. They wore light armor and bright paint but kept their swords sheathed and their shields tied to their backs. They neither shrieked nor picked up their gait as they neared the camp. Seven thousand soldiers from Keltoi tribes in northern Italoi joined Hannibal's army on one day and more on each day after.

Ashoka and the other mahouts guessed that Hannibal's trek across the Alps, the elephants, or perhaps Roman treachery had brought the new tribes over.

The army moved once more, this time to an area of gentle rolling hills dotted by rock outcroppings, the rest covered by grasses. A meandering strip of low trees, dense thorn bushes, and sand bars of a water way, called the River Trebia, cut through the hills not far away.

On the far side of the Trebia, the Roman army camped behind a hastily-built dry moat and dirt wall. There it waited, perhaps for the second Roman army, for spring and firm ground, for Hannibal's army to starve, for the local tribes to tire of him, or for the stars to align so as to assure victory. No one in Hannibal's war council could say. In recent days the council met often, sometimes every evening.

"General Monomachus, how far must your hunters ride for deer and wild pig?" said Hannibal.

"All the deer and wild pigs within a day's ride are gone. All the farmers around have fled and taken everything they could carry. We've eaten what little they left behind."

"Masinissa, how far do your horses go for fresh grass?"

The leader of the Numidians had lost the cheerfulness of youth. His face, his voice had taken on the hardness of hunger. Ashoka saw the same hardness in the faces of his mahouts. "The horses can live in this valley, but my men can't eat grass and will not kill their horses."

"Will the new Keltoi fight with us?" Hannibal asked them all.

Monomachus answered, "They can't ever go back or lose a fight to the Romans."

Hannibal said, "They come to us well armed, and clothed and on good horses, but with food only for themselves perhaps for two more days. They'll fade back to their villages if we don't feed them."

Ashoka's elephants had been without dry grain and salt for longer than he cared to remember. Without lush green leaves and treats for good behavior, they grew less responsive, more listless by the day.

"What numbers are in that Roman camp?" asked Hannibal.

His head scout answered, "The two armies together make perhaps thirty thousand Roman fighting men, ten thousand or more locals, four to five thousand horse and riders... that we can see."

"Who commands them—the leader of the new army or the old?" asked Hannibal.

The head scout answered again. "Our locals tell us that Masinissa and his men badly wounded the leader of the first army. He led more than a hundred horses against our riders but was no match for our lead riders. The new general wants to return to Rome in triumph before snow keeps him here all winter."

"How long will that be? When do the heavy snows come?" Hannibal looked around. No one answered, no one could say.

Chapter XXXII

Hannibal's Best Spy

*I*t *is time. The waiting must end before we eat our horses and bullocks or die of starvation,* thought Hannibal. His army would not last many more days waiting. The dwindling food supplies were not yet the main reason. Idleness killed before famine set in. Soldiers without any enemy to fight fought each other, and every day the surgeons tended more wounded men. Leaders with no campaign to lead grumbled and made up useless drills for their men. The local Keltoi who joined his army grew more sullen by the day.

He had to know more about these Roman armies gathered across the river. Did the Roman leaders want to march at him before winter set in, or were they content to starve him out, to let him wait here withering away and then assault in the spring? He had to pick the place for the armies to fight—a place that gave his men and horses all the advantage, that might allow his elephants to shock the Romans—and he had to make the Romans attack soon.

He had to act now, alone, on this night of a good ground fog with enough light from a thin moon so that he could see his way but would be hard to spot.

He found the large tent where his army kept Roman saddles, weapons and garments to entice elephants and dogs into mock battles, give them the scent of Roman men and garments. Hannibal walked up to the old soldier who guarded these items, had remembered him and his name. He was good at remembering any name after hearing it one time. "Greetings, Kanmi. We must get ready to fight the Romans. Show me where you keep the better Roman clothes and saddles."

"Yes, Supreme General, can't see too well."

"Let's look with this torch." Hannibal grabbed the torch that sat by the entry flap.

The two rummaged through piles of well-organized but damp clothes. Hannibal tossed to one side leather vests, helmets, and skirts that might fit, then swords, gloves and sandals. He found a decent looking Roman saddle with its four posts and a Roman bridle with its ugly and sharp-pointed bit. "I'll take these for now. Thank you, Kanmi. If anyone asks, you have not seen me. Understand?"

The older man could not summon any words, only a confused expression and a deep bow.

Hannibal strapped on the sword and sandals. He lugged the rest a short way to the wooden enclosure that held the army's extra and unwanted horses. There he asked the guard to find one of the more docile Roman ponies, one that would obey the commands of a stranger. The selected pony did not resist the bridle with its sharp bit, seemed to welcome the familiar saddle and a rider. But still Hannibal stayed in his own clothes and with his Roman pony walked to the perimeter of the camp.

There the guards were alert, young, strong, but they and their dogs recognized their Supreme General and responded in a way that said they had seen him like this at other times and before other battles.

"Show me the safe path out," said Hannibal. "I must test this Roman nag, see how it behaves by smell and sound in the night. Watch here for me to come back before light, walking. Look for me and don't take me for a Roman. Don't let the dogs after me. I'd hate to harm them." He smiled. The guards knew better than to ask any questions.

Soon Hannibal was beyond his own sentries and past any traps in the ground set by his own men. He walked slowly, even in the fog stayed in the thin shadow of his horse. If a Roman night search party spotted him, he would send this rider-less horse at them and hide on the land until they were gone. But that was not likely. Romans were afraid of the night, avoided fighting at night. He worked his way down the gently sloping land and easily found the bushes and high grasses lining both sides of the Trebia River.

The foliage was taller and thicker than it looked from a short distance away, as was true for all river banks and flowing water, all cuts through the land. From a distance they always looked tamer. Bushes and dense grasses, not trimmed in many life-times, covered every space between the trees right down to the water. And the ground fog lay thickest on the river and foliage. If he stayed here no one would find him, but that was not his plan.

He tried several routes down to the water, always running into thickets impassable without an ax or heavy sword, without daylight and more time. There must have been paths taken by Masinissa's riders on their many raids of the Roman camp on the other side. But he had no time to find those paths. They might have been made at many places far from him up or down the river. He had thought of taking one of Masinissa's men with another Roman pony, but then his plan could never have worked. He pointed his pony across the river and loosened the reins. It soon picked a narrow path down to the water. Horses were good at finding the best path home, far better than men.

Hannibal tucked the Roman garb under the saddle and plunged in after the pony, letting it pull him across. The river was shallow, but he had to swim in the deepest part. Despite the bitter cold he moved slowly, made his horse move slowly. If a Roman sat on the edge of the river, no sense in drawing attention to splashes. Ripples and nearby sounds of ducks on the water made him go even slower. No sense in scaring many ducks to take flight at once—always a sign that something alarmed their sleep.

On the far side, he tied his pony to a stout bush, scooped up the cold mud and scrubbed his arms and legs, hair, neck and torso.

The water, colder and wider than it looked from afar, the thickets, denser and bigger then they appeared taught him more lessons. The army having to cross the Trebia before fighting would be the weaker, but these tall grasses and trees could hide many horses and men. More to learn on this night.

Cold and wet, he let the pony pull him up a narrow path on the side of the massive Roman army. The ground fog grew thinner, and lights from its torches, noises of men, dogs, and horses came at him. His horse pulled harder. Hannibal had to yank on the bridle and bit to slow it down. At a clump of trees, he made his horse stop longer than it wanted, long enough for him to try to figure out the main elements of the Roman camp and for his horse to get anxious enough to relieve itself.

He reached down into the soft and warm, almost hot, horse droppings and smeared his arms and legs, his hair and neck. *Here you go, Roman dogs, this is for you.* After dark dogs made far better sentries than men. They sniffed out the strange animal or man before anyone might see it. He knew dogs smell many times better than they see, especially at night, and they always bark or growl at any strange predator or unfamiliar man.

The scent of new Roman horse droppings would overpower any scent his body might now throw off. If the dogs caught the scent under the stench of horse droppings, smells of river mud should not provoke them to raise a challenge.

When he got close enough to the Roman encampment to locate the sentries on the towers at the ends of the dirt wall and above the ground fog, he stopped, put on the Roman garb, pulled himself into the saddle, and rode around the walled camp. His pony seemed to read his thoughts and wanted to move faster than he let it. Most of the horses and riders must have been kept away from the higher wall and over on the far side.

Then he saw them—too many horses to count milling in the rolling fields behind the main encampment, too far spread out to protect by any hastily-built earthen or wooden fences. Their feet had to have been tethered, and many more guards and dogs kept them together. Riders on horses sat around the edges, no doubt alert for another raid by Masinissa. The warmth of the many horse bodies and the dust they kicked up even in the night thickened the fog enough to prevent Hannibal from seeing far. And that was good. Anyone looking at him would not see him clearly either, and, if they saw him, had to take him for just another Roman guard in a Roman saddle on a Roman horse.

He focused on the men, some on foot, some on horses, some with dogs on leashes standing about the perimeter, talking, gesturing, sometimes looking out but not ever staring at him. Their dogs remained quiet, and he knew he had time to look for the last thing he needed from this night.

After a time of riding around the resting horses in the faint moonlight, he spotted it. There, off to the left and away from the horses and dogs and a bit closer to the camp stood a short line of men, waiting, moving, waiting once more.

He found the nearest cluster of trees with other saddled horses standing still. He tied his horse to the same trees, patted it on the neck and face. "Won't be long. You're a good one. Stay good a little while longer." If it got away, that would not matter. He'd have enough time to make it back to his army camp on foot before daylight. The ground fog would not lift until mid-morning.

He shuffled up to the cluster of men waiting in line. They were armed but not at alert, not wearing chain mail or other armor. Some in line turned to him, and he said, "*Culpa mihi.* Sorry, I must."

More than one moved aside. "*Tu oles.* You stink."

At the head of the line sat five stone latrines side by side with proper seats of stone with a hole in the right place, arm rests, jugs of water for each latrine, and stone sides for privacy when seated. Romans were good with stone, and this army must have taken with it more than one stone cutter. This army was well organized, didn't want to foul the whole countryside with the waste of its tens of thousands, and that was good.

The waiting line let Hannibal get to the front and use the first free latrine. He made all the proper sounds, mixed in with, "*Langueo expecto ad bellum.* Sick of waiting for war."

Several grunted approval and talked of boredom, waiting in the cold days for the battle with the *barbari* who had come over the high mountains. Hannibal picked up words of an older voice perhaps from near the back of the line. "*Ibumus ad bellum coram Luna tegit.* We go to war before the moon covers itself."

That made sense. The Romans made many decisions based on the position of one general's pet star or a priest's favored moon light. Hannibal groaned some more, washed, and quickly left while bowing thanks to the waiting line that had let him cut to the front.

He found his Roman pony, rode it to the river, crossed back over, shed his Roman garb and marched back to the sentries who had sent him off earlier in the night.

At the next night's war council, Hannibal said, "From now until we run out of food, every soldier and rider must eat the morning meal as if he'll not eat again. Before we roast the last pig, boil our last chicken, we'll rout the Romans, but only if every man is strong." He paused, waited for any response, any protest, and looked around at all his leaders. "I know the place where we'll fight them. I know how we will fight them. I know they'll run out of patience and attack us before the moon goes dark, as they say in their language, before it covers itself."

"Where is that? How do you know all that," asked Monomachus.

Hannibal turned to Bogus. "My wise priest knows many things, and Baal El is with us." That got them, made them think Bogus told him what to do directly from the mightiest god of gods. He waited for that to settle in then said, "South and east of here less than two miles, the hills flatten on this side of the Trebia. The river bed is dense with growth, the river deep. There we can hide our best and quietest horses. The Romans will run at us a short way downstream from there where the river is wider but much shallower. They will tire running through the cold river and its muck. After they have crossed, our hidden men and horses will come at them from behind up out of the river bushes and will destroy them."

Silence again. "Masinissa, every night you must raid them as best you can. If they come at you, run back here. Make them think we are afraid and will run when their main army comes at us. It will not take many raids to make the whole Roman army come at us."

No one protested the plan. They rustled and murmured with excitement. All the group leaders had made the calculation. The Romans had far more fighting men, almost as many horses. Hannibal's only advantage lay in his battle plan—and perhaps in using elephants to fight, the sooner the better.

Chapter XXXIII

Elephants in Battle

Ashoka sat on the neck of Four Nails, an archer in the howdah behind him. Four Nails stood at the head of a line of fourteen elephants. To the left of Ashoka's line of elephants, a thousand mounted riders on heavy and light horses waited. The front line of the horses stretched to fifty across, with those behind crowding up, stomping, neighing, wanting to charge out after months of cold idleness.

On the far side of the riders and horses, soldiers on foot spread across the plain. Though too far for Ashoka to see, he knew the recently-joined Keltoi held the center. They had insisted on that, and neither Hannibal nor Monomachus tried to talk them out of taking the most dangerous position in the coming fight, where evacuation of the wounded would be impossible and escape unlikely. Most of the Keltoi carried only shields and swords, wore only leather boots and metal helmets.

On the far side of all foot soldiers, another rectangle of a thousand riders flanked by another fifteen elephants stood ready.

Hannibal ordered Ashoka to hold back his elephants until four horn blasts signaled them to charge.

Ahead, Ashoka saw only gently rolling hills of dead winter grass, gray-yellow and wet, broken by rocky outcroppings rising into the misting morning. In the distance lay a gully that marked the Trebia River, too far for Ashoka to see in the dark morning, but he trusted it was there and Hannibal's trap set.

A faraway torch flame waved back and forth, the last relay signal. Before first light, the relay had alerted Hannibal's army that the Romans had broken camp, chased after the pestering riders of Masinissa, and formed up to move this way.

The mist turned to a steady rain mixed with snow covering all but the closest sounds—Four Nails blowing out of his trunk, the horses to his left snorting, neighing, stomping, his own heart.

From atop Four Nails, Ashoka was among the first to see them weaving up out of the hollow. Black-draped riders pressed toward him, black soot on their faces and arms and legs. Some carried spears or pikes in both hands and guided their mounts with their feet. Four Nails remained still, undisturbed by these familiar Numidians galloping at him.

After the swift riders, came the wounded—men slumped over holding on around the necks and manes of their mounts. Behind the wounded riders, men on foot pulled wounded horses by ropes around the horses' necks. They trotted or walked as fast as their horses could limp on. A few came running without a horse.

Now Ashoka heard noises unlike any other, a mixture of yells, trumpets' blare, the clang of flat swords on shields, horses squealing, and boots marching. The sounds of the Roman army shook the air and the earth. He tightened inside, not from fright for himself, but for all his elephants, who had never heard anything like this or seen what now charged at them.

The torchlight in the distance stopped moving and went out.

Then Ashoka saw it. He closed his eyes and opened them to be sure something so massive could be made of only men and animals. The Roman army seemed like a giant fat-bellied snake rolling at him. He leaned forward low on Four Nails' neck, trying to make himself small, to hide, and to give the archers behind him a clear shot.

The Roman horses were bridled and armored, and their riders sat high in those peculiar saddles. Behind the Roman horses, clusters of men carried large rounded shields. The footmen ran behind the trotting horses. They ran in square formations, each square at least eighty armored fighters.

Ram horns behind Ashoka joined the carpet of noise, but no four blasts. Hannibal's army moved out with a forward charge of the horses on Ashoka's left and tens of thousands of soldiers on foot.

Ashoka looked around for a place to run, to hide, to flee from the crashing, squealing, shouting, and growing screams that swallowed up all thought and left only fear of the now and what was to come next. There was no place, not the slightest opening for Four Nails to move in the jumbling mass of horses and men. He managed to yell into Four Nails ear to stay, to stop, and through it all, Four Nails remained still. Ashoka felt his calm, his patience, breathed deeply once, and the chaos in front of him slowed down enough that he could follow it. *Watch now—watch Four Nails under me, his ears, his shoulders. Wait—for blasts from trumpets. Look out—for a cluster of Romans to run down. Look for our men who need help from our elephants to chase off Roman foot soldiers.*

Ashoka could see the backs of Masinissa's riders leading Hannibal's army out. All at once, they rode off to one side as if running from the charging Roman horses, as if to concede defeat and let the closing Roman horses crash into Hannibal's foot soldiers. The Roman riders cried out so loudly Ashoka could hear them above the cries of all others, above the stomping feet. They kicked their mounts and came on faster. He ducked down and readied but did not know for what, helpless to resist any armed man.

The charging Romans slowed and then stopped. Masinissa's horsemen now rode at them from the side. The Numidian spears must have found the seams in the armor, the ankles, the necks and eyes that could not be covered. Many Roman horses fell hard. The edges of the Roman cavalry crumbled.

Not all the Roman horses fell. A wide front made it through to face Hannibal's heavy horses out past the elephants. Again Hannibal's riders, these from Iberia, avoided a head on collision with the tightly packed Roman cavalry. They too veered away, then wheeled back and thrust long spears and pikes from the side. Again the Roman cavalry was too slow, too stubborn, or too unskilled to evade.

Closer to Ashoka now, more Roman horses and riders fell, and more fell on top of them. Some Roman riders jumped off their wounded mounts and dodged around their own squealing, stricken animals. Others climbed onto horses that had lost their riders.

Ashoka felt and heard the whipped air of arrows shot from behind his head. These arrows plunged into the necks of the closer Roman riders and of their horses. The chaos of many fallen horses blocked the charge of Roman foot soldiers coming from behind them.

The battle, the yells, shouts, screams mixed with the high-pitched squeals from wounded horses were louder than he had ever imagined. The fallen, bleeding, crippled men and horses from both armies were nearly on him. And still no four horn blasts. Four Nails leaned forward, held his ears straight out and prepared to charge. Ashoka again shouted into Four Nails' ear and restrained him with tugs of the prong at the end of the *kole*. Ashoka's every sense knew he had only the archers behind him and the head, trunk, tusks and legs of Four Nails for protection. Fifteen elephants on his side of the army were no match for thousands of armed riders and horses and more soldiers on foot behind them. And if he advanced recklessly, Four Nails and the elephants waiting behind him might run up the backs of Hannibal's horses and men. He had to keep Four Nails here, if he could, if Four Nails let him.

After what seemed a long time, a clearing in front opened. Roman horses and riders trotted into it. They formed up to charge directly at his line of elephants and the few foot soldiers of Hannibal's army lagging back around the elephant line. Four horn blasts sounded from close behind him, so close he couldn't miss them. Ashoka, too confused to think, too overwhelmed to cower, leaned over and yelled, "Go, go, go fast."

Four Nails surged on the first "go", trotted, then ran at the Roman horses and riders, trumpeting as he ran.

At the first blast from Four Nails, the Roman footmen ahead of him stopped dead. The Roman riders among them yanked on their reins. The foot soldiers turned and ran back at their own soldiers and horses crowding up on them.

The Numidian riders now reinforced by Hannibal's heavy horses on the outside, Hannibal's foot soldiers with long pikes charging from the inside, and the strange monster elephants at the front hemmed the Roman riders and men into an immobile crushing mass. Ashoka yelled at Four Nails, "Stop, stop now." He saw his elephants had done all they could. They had to stay clear of the many swords and pikes, not get caught in the slaughter ground.

He tugged hard on the trunk with the hook at the end of the *kole*. Four Nails obeyed. He shook his head up and down, snorted and pawed at the mud under him, but stopped.

Two smaller elephants did not obey. They ran past Four Nails on the outside too fast for Ashoka to yell out, to try to stop them. They plunged into the fallen men, broken horses and riders still mounted.

A Roman horseman, then another and more turned to face that first elephant. Its mahout could not stop it, or did not want to. It charged into the waiting open-mouthed men, stepped on some Ashoka could not see. But he heard the screams. It knocked three men down and flung one man aside with a swipe of its head and trunk.

There were far too many Romans against two unguarded elephants. The first elephant limped once and again, nearly fell onto its side, then stood balanced on three legs. Shrieking, screaming men on foot and horse surrounded that elephant, its mahout and archer. It and they fell, engulfed in the melee.

Ashoka could not charge in, could not help. Any elephant made a huge and easy target for every arrow, spear and sword. He raised his hand for the other elephants and mahouts behind him to stay. He turned Four Nails and signaled the rest of his elephant line to follow back and away. He must not lose all at the start. They followed.

His line moved back from the main battle, moved in among the wounded and broken, moved far enough away that he might have time to run away if the Romans routed Hannibal's army. In the rain and gray morning, Ashoka could not see well, the colors too mixed and jumbled. Only the nakedness of the Keltoi and the loudest noises told him where Hannibal's main army held its line.

From behind, Ashoka heard new and louder shouts. A fresh Roman group, shields in their neat line, ran at him and at the few foot soldiers around him. He shouted at the mahouts to circle up and to stay together. Hannibal's men on the ground around him responded fast too.

The Romans crashed into Hannibal's men. Both sides fell back and reformed, chased a short way when a rout started, but soon had to reform again. Increasing snow blurred vision, splattered blood wider, and undermined footing. Increasing cold slowed every thrust. Deflected and weakened blows that might have killed in good weather prevented either side from gaining an advantage.

Ashoka looked for any opening in the circle of fighting men and horses. If the Romans got too close, one sword thrust into the leg of an elephant would cause certain panic. If they got too close, Four Nails had to lead the charge to a safer place.

All at once without reason the Romans stopped fighting. They turned and ran over their own fallen men and horses, ran away through the splattering brown and red mud. Farther off other Romans cried out, not cries of power and killing but cries of fright. Many fell blocking the muddy-footed Roman soldiers and horses crowding on and behind them. In a short time, all fighting stopped, all war cries faded, leaving only the sounds of men in pain.

+ + +

On the other side of the front, Monomachus's keen sword ripped through the leather skirt below the breastplate of another Roman legionnaire. He had not counted his kills and would have lost count by now. The scent of fresh blood mixed with the smell of cold air and sleeting rain, and it was good too, though this blood had a different scent than that of the dirty little men in the mountains, cleaner, not as strong.

The hand-to-hand fighting had lasted half the morning. At the beginning the Roman formations were as strong and impenetrable as any enemy he had ever encountered. But after a corner of the wall of shields crumpled under the hoofs of a horse or a charge by his men, the enemy formation broke.

The Romans no longer moved on fresh legs, no longer parried with their heavy shields. Hannibal had been right once more. The trap was a simple one, inducing the Romans to fight after running three miles or more in cold rain out of their warm camp before light, down the gully cut by the Trebia, through water too deep to walk across in the narrows but wide in the shallows, then run up the hills on the other side to challenge Hannibal's fresh and rested army, with horses and elephants all waiting for them.

Even so, these Romans, unlike any he had ever encountered, fought and fell but pressed on, fought and fell again, and more kept coming. Exhaustion gripped his own right arm, both knees and thighs. Neither line of infantry had forced the other to give way or retreat.

From his left, his nearly deaf side, he sensed the sky growing darker and his men turn away from fighting the Romans. An elephant, one of the fifteen elephants assigned to protect the left flank of the entire army, loomed over him and his men close to him. No mahout rode on its neck. Out of arrows, the archer in the howdah screamed at the beast to stop while he waved his arms and ducked low to avoid spears thrown up at him. The unguided beast charged into the line of foot soldiers it was supposed to protect, tromping, goring and flinging to the side Hannibal's own men.

Monomachus thought the red tusks would impale him next and in that same instant saw the arrow stuck in the beast's eye half way up the arrow's shaft to the feathers. He forgot about his sore knees and hips, jumped and lunged out of the way, stepping on the chest or back of a fallen soldier. As the beast passed, he cried out with all the strength left in his chest, "Kill it, cut it down. Do it now." His infantry heard. Despite the danger, ten or more swords and pikes and spears buried deep into the belly and muscles of the legs. The beast dropped to all four knees, waved its head from side to side at the jabbing thrusting men until it dropped to its belly, rolled over and lay still.

Monomachus heard but did not understand the shouts rising from a fresh legion, shields in their neat line, running at him and his men. The fallen elephant must have given the Roman infantry renewed strength, the symbol of Hannibal slaughtered. He braced himself and shouted at those near him to form up, though now he and his men had to look around for other elephants running amok.

The two infantries pounded and crashed into each other, neither yielding. Both sides fell back and reformed when pressed and chased when a rout started. But a heavier rain blurred vision, undermined footing, deflected blows that might have killed in dry weather and prevented either side from gaining a decisive advantage.

Monomachus did not hear or see the cause of the change that came upon the Roman fighters in the early afternoon. Without apparent reason, without having suffered great losses, they retreated and did not form up again. From behind them, other Romans cried out loudly enough for him to hear but not understand. The Romans closest to him now ran more frantically, over their own fallen men and horses, ran through the splattering mud. Many fell, blocking the muddy-footed, exhausted soldiers and struggling horses crowding on and behind them, all of them running away, fleeing, escaping in any direction. The fallen lay at the mercy of Hannibal's soldiers and riders. The battle ended in moments.

+ + +

That night at the council, Ashoka and Monomachus and all the leaders learned Hannibal had judged correctly. His fresh footmen and riders came up from their hiding places in the valley of the Trebia, came at the Romans' unguarded rear at the right moment. Hannibal's trap broke the Roman soldiers, already spent from their dawn run and morning-long fight. A heavy sleeting rain dropped like a curtain on the land as the battle came to a sudden end and allowed half the Roman army to fade away. The other half, fifteen thousand, lay dead, mortally wounded, or were captured. Hannibal's losses, less than two thousand, were heaviest among the naked hot-blooded locals at the center of his infantry.

Seven mahouts did not return after the battle. Four elephants without mahouts found the way back. Cut and stabbed in many places, they died in the night. Two elephants did not return at all.

At that war council, Hannibal asked for the report from Monomachus. The infantry leader described what he had seen and heard, made none of it up, lied about none of it. Near the end of his report, he stood up to his full height and waited until he had everyone's attention. He walked over to Ashoka hunched in a far corner of the large tent. He stood over him and yelled in a deep voice that carried far, yelled in Greek to make sure Ashoka understood. "Your elephants are of no use. They kill us before they turn on any Romans. They don't know a Roman soldier from one of ours. They are stupid, dangerous beasts." He turned part way around. "Ashoka, his mahouts, their strange gods and all their elephants must stay away from us." He stared back at Ashoka, pointed down at him, then out and away. "Ashoka and his mahouts and foul beasts must die quickly or leave. Fast. Before they kill us all, before their sickness spreads to us all, before they trample more of my valiant fighting men."

Silence. Then from somewhere in the large tent the voice of Bogus croaked out.

"Heed the warnings of Baal El, or die. That's the way of the gods of Carthage. Always has been, always will be."

Ashoka dared not move, dared not speak, though not from fear. He felt no fear, only a growing numbness, a not caring. He had cared too much but had misjudged badly. Saying anything now would not help, only hurt what little chance was left for the remaining elephants and mahouts to see the next sunrise. He felt nothing from the infantry leader's outburst. Any leader would have felt the same, said the same after seeing his own men attacked by a wounded elephant. And Ashoka knew from deep inside that this was the only way it could have turned out. Bogus' little rant had no effect on him either. He expected worse, but deep down understood that with the great victory by Hannibal's army, the foul moods against him and his elephants would soon fade out.

At last, Hannibal said, "I fear you are right, brother One Ear, and my wise priest too. But we will find good use for anyone in this army, as long as they are able, even for our elephants and their mahouts."

Monomachus again took his place in the inner circle. Hannibal asked for other reports.

At first light, Ashoka rode back to the killing ground scattered on the muddy field and all the way down to the river. Masinissa's riders already stood guard. Hannibal's surgeons and their assistants walked over and around the dead and dying. Women in heavy coats and head coverings searched for their men or for useful weapons and clothes to take from the dead. The cold and solid rain muted the smell of death but not completely. The missing mahouts, without weapons or armor, should have been easy enough to spot. But Ashoka did not find one. He prayed they lived and the Romans treated them with respect.

Chapter XXXIV

A Colder Rain

After the Battle of the Trebia, the surviving Romans not captured scattered. They did not flee back to their camp, could not. Hannibal's men and horses coming up out of the Trebia valley had cut them off. Hannibal's men would not follow the fleeing men through unknown terrain and bad weather, but they made good use of the many Roman horses left without a rider, the cows, goats, and chickens left behind at the nearly empty Roman army camp. All danger of running out of food in this winter had now passed.

The locals said this winter came to the plain below the high mountains earlier than any in memory. No new Roman army would soon reform and attack. Rome's intact legions were posted far south and would not march north through wet ground and days of sleet and snow.

The mahouts and elephants who had survived the battle stayed downwind from the strutting soldiers and riders, as far away as Hannibal and the camp perimeter guards allowed. All the mahouts and Indian laborers felt useless.

"Bandhu, you haven't laughed since we smashed the boulder," said Ashoka at the outdoor campfire on the first rainless evening.

"I won't again in this life," said the youngest mahout other than Ashoka. "My elephant has Tilaka's sickness. She

292

moans from pain in her chest. When I stroke her, talk to her, she doesn't rumble, doesn't eat. Walking is hard for her. She can't breathe."

"Mine too," said another mahout. Other mahouts repeated the two words.

"We must build a cover to keep them and the hay dry," said Ashoka.

Bandhu said, "The cold ground cuts her feet."

"Wrap them. Boil the cloth before you put it on again. Wrap every elephant's foot until they heal," said Ashoka.

"They huddle to keep warm and don't move, don't eat," said Bandhu. "The men who still talk to us, who don't revile us, say we can't stay here. More Romans are gathering. If we stay in one place, they'll surround and destroy us in the first days of good weather. We'll have to tear down and carry anything we build."

"We have enough time and men," said Ashoka. He wondered if other men would help, with the elephants now unable to carry heavy loads, much less fight.

Bandhu said, "All our elephants but Surus come from south of Carthage." He hung his head. "They don't know cold. I don't know cold. What will happen to them—and to us?"

Forty mahouts and helpers turned to Ashoka.

Twice he had tamed Four Nails. He brought them and their elephants across the mountains without losing one elephant. In one long day, the battle of the Trebia crushed all that like a strong hand crushes dry clumps of dirt.

Months of training at Mintho's camp and harder training on the plains outside New Carthage had not changed habits formed at the beginnings of their breed. A hundred mock battles did not change their instincts. Nothing made them heed shouted commands when the white hot pain of a spear's tip buried deep in them and the noise of thousands filled their big ears, their heads, their insides. Nothing could make them grow thick hair in a hard winter.

Sitting there in the cold darkness, all eyes on him, Ashoka was now sure of more. Hannibal had known, had known elephants would never fight like a fighting dog—helping their own, attacking only the enemy, and obeying its master's commands to the end. Hannibal used elephants for their size and shock against the Iberian tribes and against the little men in the mountains. But... he did not ride Four Nails in the battle of the Trebia or through any mountain passes where an ambush might wait. Hannibal knew the danger was too great, the nature of the elephant, even mighty Surus, too unpredictable in battle.

Bogus was right but for the wrong reasons. The river of life and the gods of the elephants controlled their path, not Baal El. In his way, Sinorix had it right too. The elephants did not die in the mountains, but they were dying now because Hannibal—and Ashoka—made them cross the mountains.

Ashoka knew the end, had known from the first days in Mintho's camp. And that made it all the harder. He could not blame Hannibal. He, Ashoka, knew the nature of these wonderful giants better than Mintho, Hannibal, and Bogus, better than any in the army. He knew the whole truth of their purpose and strengths, was sure of them from the days before he could talk but rode on an elephant's back, and yet did nothing to save them. Were he alone now, he might have started weeping and not stopped, might have walked far away into the cold night and never come back. He quieted himself, forgot about himself one more time, for them—his mahouts and for the elephants still with them.

They did not know about his promise to Govinda. They

did not know his family's elephant camp was likely gone now, his father dead. The mahouts did not know that his younger sisters had no dowry for a proper husband. But they all knew that their life's purpose had been smashed in the first real battle against Romans and one cold winter.

He had to say something. Their needy faces made him start, slowly, one word then another. "Our path is to serve. We've tried to serve our elephants. Every surviving elephant knows it. Our wonderful beasts are kinder and more generous than any man who might have made them do what we did. They will not fault us. Hannibal... I believe he will honor our service. Our gods know it. They will look over us in this life and the next. Let's put all the blankets we can on our elephants. Let's protect their feet. We'll build a roof to keep the straw dry. If we must move, we'll—our elephants—will carry the pieces, and we'll again build the cover at the new camp. Spring will come to this land, fresh grass will grow again."

They remained still for a long time, stared into the warmth and dying flames, then, wordlessly, found places to sleep. The mahouts who coughed slept far from the rest.

+ + +

Not everyone in the army so soon forgot Ashoka and his elephants. The carpenters shared their left-over wood. The metal workers gave them bent nails and metal straps. The mahouts and carpenters built a long roof over a high rack to keep fodder out of the rain and snow and a lower trough for water. Laborers brought carts filled with straw collected in the last dry days or perhaps stolen by soldiers from village hay lofts. In days, the elephants had a place to line up side by side and eat dry fodder under cover. But when they moved out from under the narrow roof, they were again helpless against the cold and rain.

The older, weaker elephants died first, one every seven days or so, then one every three days, then one a day. The rest stopped eating and stood by their dying and dead mates. They moaned over the bodies. Tears ran down their gray cheeks and hardened to ice in the night wind. Four Nails mourned with them but somehow knew to move away from the most sick, to stay by himself.

Some wandered away in the darkest time while the mahouts slept in tents. The army's perimeter guards and dogs did not see or hear them through the sleeting rain and snow. Perhaps they saw them leave and did not care. Perhaps if they cared and wanted to save them, they had orders to let them go. Thirteen mahouts and ten helpers followed their elephants out of the camp over several nights. Ashoka could not mount a search without horses. No search party could have saved the elephants. No one of influence in the army cared to save mahouts who had lost their elephants.

When the army next moved, it came upon three giant carcasses at the low point of a gully. Five mahouts and helpers, all dead, lay with them. The living mahouts and helpers tried to burn the bodies, but could not in the wet and managed only to bury the human bodies in shallow graves of the hard ground.

By the middle of February, the North African elephants, every one, had died or left to places where no one found them. Only Four Nails survived that first winter in Italoi.

+ + +

Every day a one-donkey cart brought fresh hay. Some men who had crossed the high mountains with the army came around. They didn't talk. They stood or squatted and watched a while. When their eyes met Ashoka's, they nodded, saying without speaking they too felt the loss of the gentle beasts, remembered the better days and took on a piece of Ashoka's sadness.

More local tribesmen joined Hannibal's army. They, hundreds on some days, found Four Nails and the mahouts still alive at the low downwind edge of the camp. They walked all around the biggest animal they had ever seen, talked, hissed and laughed at him over the heads of or through the protecting ring of mahouts and other soldiers.

Ashoka slept out in the open under heavy leather skins on all but the wettest nights. He wanted to see and, after it was too dark or he fell asleep, to be able to hear any menace that might come at Four Nails. He prayed for one more chance, for the gods of India to show him the next step on the path to making it right, to in this life or the next correct all the mistakes he had made.

+ + +

On a day when the air came out of the south and the fog lifted to a high sky, a new laborer brought dry fodder in a new small cart pulled by a donkey. Ashoka's group had shrunk to seventeen mahouts and helpers, silent, downcast. Many of them coughed the cough of Tilaka and kept away from the others. The healthy ones sat on animal skins by a fire under a small open wooden shed and paid no attention to this visitor. The laborer, as usual, spread the old straw far away on the ground and loaded the new hay into the feeding trough without their help.

When he had finished, this laborer came up to them. "How is Surus?"

The mahouts rose to their feet at the familiar strong voice. "He'll survive," answered Ashoka.

The cart driver leaned forward on the sitting board of the one-hitch cart, looked at them, at Ashoka for a long time in silence. Ashoka did not avert his own eyes from the driver. That driver, alone on the little cart, was no elephant man. He and all his advisors had been duped by High Senator Mintho and a dream of conquering Rome with elephants. The cold winds of winter took that dream to never return.

At last Hannibal said, "Ashoka, I did not know."

Ashoka's insides did not believe Hannibal. Nothing to be gained though by challenging what Hannibal did know or when he knew.

Hannibal said, "Ashoka, keep Surus healthy and in good spirits. I'll use him yet. You others, follow me. Idleness makes mischief. We'll soon all grow fat and healthy, and, if the gods favor you, you'll soon be training other elephants."

He waited for the other mahouts and laborers to gather up their bundles, throw their tents into the cart emptied of straw. Some of them looked back over their shoulders as they walked away into the center of the huge army camp behind the cart driven by the Supreme General, leaving Ashoka and Four Nails alone. Some of them, the sick ones, followed a good distance back, and Ashoka worried for them all.

Chapter XXXV

Too Far, The Gods of India

Spring swept north on the warm air out of Africa and up the peninsula of Italoi. More fighters from many tribes joined with Hannibal. The number of his footmen grew to fifty thousand. Riders under his control again numbered more than five thousand.

The mahouts—only six had not died or disappeared—and Four Nails did not go out with the marauders. They had nothing to do on the runs for plunder.

Every three or four days the camp packed up and moved, ever southward toward a range of mountains far lower and tamer than the Alps.

On a clear morning, the sun bright and the rolling hills green with new grass, Hannibal said to Ashoka, "We depart tonight when the moon's up."

"Yes, Master. We'll be ready."

"Leave your tent and the elephant shelter. Leave the fire burning."

Ashoka understood. Any Roman spying on the camp from nearby must believe Hannibal's army had not left.

Hobbled and out a short distance searching for fresh growth, Four Nails came over to the voice and scent of the man who brought fresh hay and was his sometime rider.

"The scouts report a Roman army stands in the easy passes to the south, and another is on the march against us.

We'll take cowherd trails over these hills and come out behind them. They say the trails end in high grass and wetlands that the Romans avoid. That grass will hide us until the main road south. Can Surus walk through high grass on wet ground?"

"Yes, Master. All elephants from my country know how to walk through high grass growing out of wet ground. He'll find the safe path or stop. He knows grass doesn't grow in quick sand."

"Then he'll lead my army."

"Should we mount the heavy platform?"

The old confidence and enthusiasm flickered across the lean face, the bright blue sky reflecting in his eyes. "Put up the light platform for one rider. I'll lead us through the gates of Rome on Surus. If we move fast…"

That night the men who had survived the march from New Carthage easily hiked up the mountain trails south from the camp, through birch, willow, and wild olive trees at the lower levels and fir trees higher up. The local fighters who joined Hannibal after the trek over the mountains lagged behind. After the first day, Hannibal made the dogs and Masinissa's horsemen follow the new men. They were afraid of black horses, brown riders, and big dogs, and kept up the pace.

The scouts had it right. The cow trails over these local mountains and down the other side did lead to high grasses that turned into swamps. Mile after mile the big head and wide belly of Four Nails swished through tall reeds and dense undergrowth in the direction of a sun barely visible through the wet air. The heaviest bullocks, built for any terrain and sensing the old cow trails, kept pace behind Four Nails. Light-footed and nimble, the lead footmen followed, and they too kept up.

But the thousands of boots and hoofs leveled all the raised paths and flattened the grass to wet pulp. By the time the local soldiers and the baggage train came through, the old cow trails had turned to muck. Mud clamped onto wheels and boots. The smaller hoofs of pack mules and horses sank up to their ankles and knees and sometimes their bellies.

On the second day when morning breezes stilled in the rising heat, the army understood why the people who lived here used these trails only in winter. The lead dogs yelped, ran back and forth, jumped high and snapped as if to snatch a bird in flight. Then they flopped down into the grass and rolled on their backs and bellies, jumped up, ran again and rolled again until exhausted.

Right after the dogs' wild behavior, men cried out and slapped at their own exposed arms, legs, faces and bellies, pulled out longer garments and hurried to put them on. Any skin uncovered by heavy cotton, leather or mud, turned to pink welts under gray layers of mosquitoes. They crawled into the folds of clothes, around uncovered eyes and eyelids, noses and lips, onto exposed fingers and ankles. Everywhere they landed, they drew blood and left red welts.

Ashoka and his five mahouts tried to wipe the mosquitoes off Four Nails. Their blankets turned red. They and Ashoka grabbed handfuls of mud, wiped their heads, faces and legs with it, but could not do that for Four Nails. Hannibal stayed on his last elephant, better up there than on the ground.

At night Four Nails rolled in the wet grass and mud until he shed most of them or stopped from fatigue and loss of blood. All the men, dogs, horses, and bullocks tried to do the same, to cover themselves, to move as fast as they could until they had to stop and rest.

After three days and nights in the swamps, the army emerged to the firm hills and rich soil of the west central peninsula of Italoi. Wheat already stood waist high. Neat rows of grape vines framed fields of barley. Olive and walnut tree groves covered many gentle hills. Hannibal's army again had open access to fresh farms and villages, all their animals and supplies, all their people who stayed to fight. The main Roman armies, so close days ago, now searched for a phantom on the northern side of the mountains.

Hannibal no longer rode Four Nails. Ashoka rode him alone in the middle of the baggage train well back from fighting men and far from any skirmish. Every night the shouts of men drunk with wine or plunder reached Ashoka. The men and women of the baggage train saw some of the bounty trickle down to them—a friendly soldier passing out brass coins or one gold coin to a willing girl. Some near Ashoka flaunted a fine shirt of leather or silk and talked of more wealth taken from big estates in the surrounding hills than any had ever seen.

One of the old carpenters who had helped the mahouts build their elephant shelter nudged Ashoka, motioned him to come over to his camp fire. The two sat for a long time until those near them had retreated into tents or fallen asleep on the ground. Then the old man reached into the deep pocket of his garment. His knobby hand pulled something out, and he opened his palm to reveal a gleaming green stone set in a gold ring. Ashoka had seen such things only at Uncle Vasavedu's house and never this close. The old man leaned forward as if asking Ashoka to say something. Ashoka knew he should have spoken admiringly, should have helped the old man share his joy and good fortune, but nothing came. He could only look at the old man with an expression that meant to say, *I am sorry you have this now, am sorry a family died giving it up, that a woman might have been raped after she yielded it.*

The old man said, "This is why we all fight. This will take care of me when I get home. Our Supreme General is most fair."

Ashoka left the old carpenter and crawled deeper into his place without light. For months now, he heard the shouts of victory joined with screams, loudest through the nights. From a distance he saw the drunken thousands stagger around the camp, watched them kill each other over games played in the dust with pieces of gold and jewelry looted from wealthy strangers.

Ashoka's numbness never left. Many nights he did not sleep. Many days he did not eat. He spoke in head movements and single words, refused to look any soldier or rider in the eye, afraid of what he might say or do. He let his nails and hair grow. Tears never welled up, the horror too great and constant. Anger never cried out, too useless the rage of one solitary young man from India.

The five mahouts came round from time to time. They sat with Ashoka and looked at him as a stranger might look at a torch over a village gate lighting the way to shelter in the night. He did not talk to them unless they asked and did nothing for them. Everything he had said to them in the years past, everything he had done for or with them turned to an early death. He knew only to withdraw from them. They came less often and did not stay long.

Ashoka overheard enough that he understood the larger scene. The first farms and villages and estates ahead of Hannibal's marauders failed to flee or had not been warned. Or if warned, they did not believe. Or if they believed such a fast-moving army lay so close, they were too sure that their own Roman soldiers had to be near and would protect them.

After not seeing him for a month or more, one evening Hannibal again drove the hay cart, again unloaded fresh grass. At the end he said, "Ashoka tomorrow I need Surus to lead again. He will serve us well. I know it. Prepare to leave at first light."

Ashoka wanted to ask why tomorrow, what was new about tomorrow, not another swamp infested with mosquitoes? But his numbness would not let him, forced him to pretend he did not care about tomorrow. But he knew he still cared to be of use, to exercise Four Nails, to ride him once again, and he would have Four Nails ready.

The next day, a clear warm day with a high blue sky, Surus, with Ashoka on his neck and Hannibal once more on his back, followed close behind fifty or so fast riders and a hundred or more trotting foot soldiers heading south.

By early afternoon they reached a hamlet that had not emptied out.

Hannibal said, "Take Surus up closer."

The band of riders, Numidians on bare back and locals in saddles on heavy horses, surrounded the village. Ashoka made Surus walk up to within earshot of the silent farmers staring at him over a wooden stake fence only high enough to keep out wolves and keep farm animals in. Hannibal raised his chin at the horsemen next to him. One of them yelled in a strange language and then translated the responses shouted back from one of the villagers on the wall.

"They can't send out their young men to join our army or baggage train. The Romans will kill or enslave them all if they help you, Supreme General. They beg you barter fairly for what little they have."

The faces of the villagers showed no defiance, only fear and bewilderment at these strangers in their peaceful land, at the brown men riding unbridled black horses, and at the monster elephant unlike any animal they had ever seen.

Hannibal said to the horsemen, "Return to camp and summon a thousand of our newest men. Tell them they can have their first rewards."

Ashoka tried not to listen, to not hear the command but Hannibal's voice, shouted out from behind him, carried to every member of this band.

Before full darkness that village was stripped of everything useful or alive and set aflame. Up high on the back of Surus, Hannibal attended the siege. Ashoka could not help hear the cries and watch riders chase down and drag back, by leashes around their necks, youngsters and women who had tried to flee to the next town.

Hannibal's marauders laid siege to new villages and burned them down every day for a week. The lights from villages set ablaze and smoke broadcast their presence and power far wider than they could ride. They rounded up horses and mules, bullocks and cows, pigs and chickens. Each day the army devoured scores of white cattle that grazed along the sides of dirt roads and kept the grasses around villages cropped. Each day Hannibal insisted he ride Four Nails and that Ashoka guide him. Each morning Ashoka vowed on this day he would refuse but gave in to the unspoken threat against the five other mahouts still alive. Without Hannibal's continuing favor, Bogus and many infantry would either kill them where they stood or banish them to the locals and the first Roman soldiers who might find them.

Returning to the main camp from yet another town savaged since emerging from the swamp, Hannibal said to Ashoka riding in front of him, "Ashoka, I have no taste for this. I can see in your eyes, in your shoulders, you hate this and hate me for what I do."

Ashoka could not see the face in the dark and did not turn around to get a better look, but the tone invited a response. After a long time he said as if to himself, "It is true. Four Nails, whom you call Surus, is feared, and you are despised wherever we tread and far beyond. When they see our dust on the horizon or the smoke from a village burning, they flee, taking with them everything they can carry. And not a single one joins you or offers you one sack of wheat, one chicken."

"You're right, Ashoka. They now flee before we reach them and leave behind less and less for my brutes."

At last the question, the only question that mattered. "Why then? Why do you do this, inflict this suffering on those who have done you no harm?"

Ashoka heard Hannibal breathe deeply, so deeply that he thought the Supreme General might be crying, but refused to look at him. No fighting man wants another man to see him break down. Hannibal sniffed and swallowed, then said so softly that Ashoka had to turn his head half way in order to hear, "I don't have enough men, horses, battering rams, or time to chase down every Roman soldier, lay siege to every fortification, or assault the walls of Rome as thick and high as the inner wall of Carthage."

Ashoka's lessons about Alexander streamed in. After many great victories far from home, the Macedonian had likely said the same in his India a hundred years earlier. The real campaign, just begun, seemed as doomed as the Macedonian's. Ashoka didn't want to say anything, not now, not any more. He wanted to save Four Nails and the last mahouts, nothing more. The words just spilled out as if on their own. "Master, perhaps your gods will help find a way with no more killing. Our Emperor prayed to our gods at his killing time, and our gods showed him the way to a lasting peace."

Hannibal scoffed softly. "India's gods are too far from here. Bogus makes us slaughter and burn to ash our best bull every night for our gods. Sometimes I can persuade him to select one we captured that day."

"The Romans do the same, they say," Ashoka said.

Hannibal laughed loudly now. "I know. I know. Men will decide this war, surely not your gods or ours. I must draw Rome's armies into the open, and these poor villagers must help me do that."

They rode on back to their main camp in silence. After a time Hannibal explained more, though he need not have for Ashoka. He must have needed to for himself. "The Romans are far worse than any army since man can remember. They are the biggest brutes. Everything they have and have built is stolen from weaker people. My Carthage has been a great trading power for over four hundred years—until the Romans ripped open many of our towns and cities and farms. When I was nine years old, I promised my father I would stop them. And now I am so close, but I can't stop them if they run from me. These poor farmers, whom I've made you see, beg the Roman legions to destroy me before another winter. That's why I always let some go, let some flee on foot or horse at each village."

Ashoka listened to every word, had wanted to know, and had to admit Hannibal made sense—if what he said was true. "Where are the Roman armies, then?"

"They chase us, but their generals are cautious and stupid." Hannibal sat up high now, presenting a silhouette against a rising moon and the light from another village burning. "They know that on terrain of my choosing, I'll kill them as the hawk kills a rat in a field of cut wheat. Then fortified cities will throw open their gates, turn on their Roman tyrants, and Carthage will let the common people live in peace for a thousand years. But I must draw out their remaining armies before any of that."

"If you must do all that, I hope it's soon," said Ashoka softly and ashamed for being there at that moment, for helping the unfolding horror, for not knowing any other path. He did not say that surely the Roman generals saw Hannibal's army could not remain intact another winter among people who fled from him, and that Hannibal's plan could work only if the Roman generals were fools.

Chapter XXXVI

Roman Fools

Heading ever south, Hannibal's army left behind crop land and swarmed into wooded hills. Stone ramparts, crowded with soldiers watching, sat atop the highest and least accessible hills. A big Roman army had found them or caught up to them and again stalked close. As daylight drew longer, Hannibal's men seized only abandoned farms and towns. They lived on the wheat and rice left behind and dwindling herds of cattle previously captured. The villagers and every animal they could take fled to cities behind stout walls and garrisons difficult to destroy without heavy machines throwing heavy stones or ramming stone walls over many months or years.

Ashoka again rode Four Nails alone in the middle of the baggage train behind the main force. On clear warm days the dust of many pursuers followed them. Hannibal refused to stand or fight in the day, and the Romans did not dare attack at night when they could not clearly see the enemy and the traps they might have built around the enemy camp.

At night Ashoka and the five mahouts slept fitfully. The baggage train was safer for them than the main army with Monomachus and his infantry, safer to be far from Bogus. But they knew the Roman army followed, and the baggage train was both defenseless and precious to the main army. Softly, as if wishing, they said to each other that as long as Four Nails stayed alive, as long as Hannibal rode him from time to time, he would protect them.

For three days the opposing armies marched over and around hills surrounding an inland sea so large that a man standing on the shore could barely see the other side. Every night the lake's cold water turned the summer air to a white blanket covering the lake and the surrounding shore and lakeside valleys. The fog did not clear until mid-morning, sometimes later.

On the third night the baggage train camped at the upper end of a flat chute between wooded hills running away from the lake. If the Roman army followed, the only way out was up those steep wooded trails between even steeper hills. Then the baggage train would surely be captured or destroyed by the far faster Roman soldiers. Hannibal's main army melted away on this night. The few soldiers of the baggage train lit the usual number of campfires and posted the regular sentries and dogs. But if the whole Roman army assaulted the camp, all would be lost long before morning and any rescue from Hannibal's riders or foot soldiers, where ever they were.

In the middle of the night, the fog from the lake rolled up their gully until they too were enveloped in the cool mist.

Ashoka and his mahouts did not sleep. Most in their entire camp sat or walked around deep into the night. Before first light, Bandhu said, "Where have they gone?"

"Perhaps they rushed ahead and are camping over the pass," said Ashoka. "They need what we carry."

"Perhaps the battle has joined up ahead."

"We would hear it, Bandhu. Rome is afraid to fight us at night."

Bandhu said, "Perhaps the Romans have outrun us up these hills, and night hides them until we walk into them."

"The two armies might just be staring at each other somewhere down by the lake," said Ashoka.

Hoof beats came at them from the direction of that lake.

The lead rider and the riders behind him were of their own. Their horses' sweat glistened in the fire lights. They circled the baggage train camp, its shabby tents and bewildered laborers, tradesmen, prisoners taken at the Trebia, local women and young men who, tied to each other by chains, came to the tent openings.

The lead rider shouted, "Hear me everyone. Break camp fast and head uphill. The Roman army is readying to move on you when they can see where to tread and ride. It must not catch you. Do not trouble to go quietly. They know where you are. Hurry now." He and his compatriots turned and rode away, soon out of sight and hearing, before anyone asked about the rest of Hannibal's army.

On the morning after the battle of the Trebia, the new prisoners tied one to the other had refused to move, delaying in the hope that the next Roman army might find and rescue them. Hannibal's footmen sliced open the belly of the most vocal and left him, tied to others, to die slowly. The Roman prisoners never again delayed in breaking camp, in marching out as ordered.

The bullocks and mules obeyed the commands and whips no matter who wielded them. The baggage train carts had not been unloaded except for tents and cooking pots. The men and women hitched the animals and ate their dry bread, fruit and salted meat in less time than it took for first light to become a full sunrise. When they moved out, Ashoka rode Four Nails at the very last—to see how close the Roman army and to turn on pursuers and wreak chaos with his last elephant if it came to that.

In the gray morning, no disc of the sun yet visible, two miles up the chute Four Nails heard or felt the earth quiver before any man or other animal. He stopped and shook his massive head, pawed the dirt and wanted to turn to face from where they had come. He wanted to return down the hill to the lake. Ashoka urged with his voice and hard prods behind the ears to keep him pointed up hill.

A sound welled up at them from the lake behind, first like new winter wind howling through trees. The cry of thirty thousand Keltoi and Iberians, Numidians, and thousands of riders rose into the fog from the lake and up to the baggage train. The sounds told Ashoka everything.

The baggage train had been a decoy for the impatient Roman army to chase into Hannibal's second trap. Under cover of the lake fog and darkness, his fighting men had peeled off into the trees and dense growth at the base of the hills leading away from the lake. They waited there in the night for the Romans to race out at dawn unable to resist the chance to capture mighty Four Nails and all of Hannibal's supplies within easy reach. The Roman generals must have guessed—wrongly—that Hannibal's main army was up ahead. Baggage trains always trailed a marching army. No army could have hidden in the steep forests at night, the Roman generals must have thought.

Ashoka did not need to see the arrows and spears impaling the Roman horses, the Numidians waiting in wider stretches to overwhelm the legions trying to maintain tight square formations but helpless without their own cavalry, sealed off by expert archers and spear throwers, by the dogs and fighting footmen in the narrow valley. Ashoka knew instantly that Hannibal had once again neutralized the enemy's far greater numbers and taken away the power of Rome's horses by teasing them to string out in single file between the steep hills with no place to form up for a mass attack. At the hands of the fit and disciplined army of Carthage, with its fine metal weapons and horsemen born to ride, the slaughter would be far greater than the backward little men of the Alps had inflicted on Hannibal using the same tactics.

The noises from downhill made everyone ahead of Ashoka slow down. The few soldiers and riders with him and up the trail now stared at the shouting too. They pulled their own swords and spears and threatened to poke the cart drivers and laborers on foot. They wanted, above all, to keep everyone moving away from the battle. Any lead elements of the Roman army that had broken through the gauntlet must not catch them.

All their escorting foot soldiers and riders, not more than twenty horses and fifty men, fell to the rear of the baggage train, the better place to defend now that they knew the Roman army was behind them.

In time the mist lifted. But no one, not a single Roman rider chased them. The baggage train waited at an open flat area large enough for Hannibal's army to camp and recover— or make a last stand.

By mid-afternoon the battle at the lake the Romans called Trasimeno had ended. The scavenging of weapons and armor and horses without riders, mercy killings of the severely wounded, and rounding up Romans within an easy distance continued through the night. Hannibal's war council met that evening, and soon everyone in the army knew.

Eighteen thousand Roman soldiers perished in that one morning. Hannibal captured an equal number. Over the next days he released all the Roman mercenaries and urged they tell the citizens in their villages and towns he meant no harm, to join him against their oppressive masters, and they would live in peace.

His army lost less than two thousand, most of them recently joined Keltoi from the north. They still fought their own way, charging in where wiser infantry would wait for friendly horses and riders to break down their opposite numbers, naked for freedom of movement and quickness but too easily wounded. Hannibal had stationed them at the likely places of first contact. The leaders of the Keltoi tribes again said they wanted to draw first blood and have the first chance to avenge Roman cruelty inflicted on their people over many lives.

After the rift between the hills had been made safe, Hannibal allowed his laborers in the baggage train to strip from the dead clothes or boots, helmets or hand weapons, rings and any baubles that his soldiers had not wanted.

Ashoka, the five mahouts and Surus remained in camp.

Ashoka no longer attended the war councils, had not since the end of winter. He had only Surus to lead and would not attend even if asked.

Loose talk came to Ashoka from soldiers he had known at the start of the long march. He tried not to listen, looked away from them. But they told him anyway, as if he needed to know and they wanted to tell an old friend. They said Hannibal's strategy was working. Town after town, even some walled cities no longer cleared out in front of Hannibal's army, no longer refused to join up with him in the remaining battles against their larger oppressor. But no one spoke with confidence of the final outcome. The city of Rome and the larger towns around it were protected by walls that no horse or man could bring down, and the elite Romans still commanded many more men than Hannibal. Rumors said that the entire northern section of the peninsular, both banks of the Trebia River were now back in Roman hands. A fleet of vessels from Carthage carrying men and supplies to reinforce Hannibal from the north never set foot on land, but had been out-sailed and out-fought by a Roman fleet.

Chapter XXXVII

Four Nails, Sometimes Called Surus

In this, the second winter on the peninsula of Italoi, Ashoka stopped caring about his other mahouts, about living to see one more sunrise, about anything. Noble Four Nails had taken on a sickness without cure, and it was breaking the mighty beast. Four Nails was dying.

Ashoka first noticed it seven days after the mosquitoes and the swamp, a raised pink crustiness over the left eye. It did not go away. From that day, Four Nails turned his head so that the diseased eye looked inward. After a time, the thinner areas of his hide broke out in sores like those over the eye, yellow. They did not dry.

When he lost his herd in that last winter, Four Nails never mourned as long as the other elephants. Four Nails led them, but they were not of his kind, from his land. When spring came again, he seemed to regain his power, his gladness to be with Ashoka, his curiosity for all things new, even his playfulness.

But after the swamp, his spirit died. The stinging air of the swamp attached itself to him. In the last weeks, he ate dirt and pebbles, tree bark and leaves, or nothing for days.

When left alone, Four Nails hobbled away to the river where they now camped. That river ran past a city not far from Rome and down to the sea. The city of Capua and its citizens had welcomed Hannibal and his army. Hannibal even rode Four Nails through the gates and once around Capua's coliseum. That was the last time Four Nails let anyone climb onto his back, not even Ashoka.

At night Four Nails pushed against the heavy wooden posts and rails of his pen until he fell to his knees. No kind of treats cheered the bull, not even celery sprinkled with salt. No fresh grasses or sugar cane restored his strength. At every chance, Four Nails walked farther from the camp. Ashoka knew that Four Nails searched for a dark place far from men and noise where he could stand in cool water up to his chin and die.

A drizzling darkness closed out one of the shortest days in the cycles of the seasons. It was a milder season than the last two. Hannibal's army had marched many miles to the south, but the milder winter did not matter to Four Nails. That evening Four Nails meandered down the valley into the mud and bushes. This time he refused to turn around, to obey Ashoka. He tried, but not very hard, to make Four Nails turn back. He felt what Four Nails felt, though his own body was free of boils and sores. After a time of cajoling and prodding, all without any effect, Ashoka followed Four Nails.

Far down the river from the camp, Four Nails stopped, held out his ears and raised his trunk. Soon Ashoka heard the shouts and horses. Four then six then eight Romans on fresh horses broke out of the high grass and bushes and surrounded them. They closed on Four Nails from the rear, from where Ashoka walked.

On the first charge, they knocked Ashoka down, and then again and again as he tried to get up, to grab at a rider's leg or belly. One of the riders jumped off his horse and pinned Ashoka to the ground with his pike pressed into Ashoka's left shoulder. Though Ashoka felt no pain, he could not move. He thought it safe here on these river banks so close to the city and Hannibal's army and had left his *kukri* bundled up where he slept with the other mahouts.

He could only watch, shout, and flail his legs and arms. Another soldier came over to him, grabbed his wrist, and tied it to the other wrist, laughing, spitting, making Ashoka lie still face down under the point of a dagger not a finger's width from Ashoka's neck. But Ashoka could still see and hear the savage attack on Four Nails.

The six other Roman soldiers cut the tendons on the back of Four Nail's legs. Four Nails dropped, and they plunged lances deep into the muscles of the shoulders. They laughed loudly, whistled, shouted, faked a charge and veered off to come back from another angle, both on foot and on horse.

Four Nails collapsed onto his side and dropped his head to the ground. One of the riders came up to him. His horse bucked and tried to not get close to the big elephant on the ground, but the rider kicked its sides hard. He held a long lance high over the massive head, over the good eye. The instant before the downward thrust, Four Nails rose up on his front legs and swung his head and right tusk deep into the belly of the horse. It fell sideways to the ground and toppled its rider. This horse knew but had obeyed its foolish master.

As suddenly as they had come, the Roman horsemen turned out and galloped away through the grass and down the valley of the river. They left their dying horse somewhere in the tall grass.

Ashoka jumped up to Four Nails lying on his side again. He wriggled out of the ropes that tied his wrists. He rested his left arm on the great face and patted and stroked the large cheek.

After a time, looking directly into his good eye, he said, "Mighty Four Nails, forgive my... stupidity for bringing you to this place. In the next life... when you are my master, I will serve you better."

Four Nails let out a rumble of contentment from deep in his throat, and Ashoka rested his head on Four Nails' bleeding cheek. He would talk to him through the night and the next day, as long as it might take, stay and comfort him until one or both crossed over to their next life.

In near total darkness, as in a dream, he heard the cause of the Romans' sudden flight—many riders on Masinissa's lighter horses.

He did not move. Four Nails needed him, and he did not care about the riders.

As if from far away he heard one rider dismount.

He felt two strong hands on his shoulders and a long arm rest next to his own on the head of Four Nails.

The stranger left and returned with a heavy blanket that he draped over Ashoka's shoulders. Only then did Ashoka realize his bare body shivered. He glanced at the shoulder by which they had pinned him to the ground, expecting to see wounds and blood. But there were none. Perhaps the Romans had wanted to take him back alive as a trophy or one more healthy slave and used the blunt handle of a spear or pike to hold him down until they tied his hands.

After a long time he looked up and around. By the light of one torch from one of the riders, he took in this stranger who had brought the blanket.

Older, leaner, with less hair, but the same silent Nuur stayed with Ashoka through the night in which Four Nails, sometimes called Surus, died not four days ride from Rome.

+ + +

They came down all the next day, other riders of Masinissa, then foot soldiers wearing light armor and carrying light weapons, then the generals, their hand servants and translators in horse-drawn chariots. When the larger part of Hannibal's army had assembled in the valley of the river, and the route down to the body of Four Nails was safe, citizens of Capua came too. They gathered on both banks of the river as the last elephant's once mighty body, soaked with oil, burned brightly.

Ashoka stood in the inner ring warmed by the fire. The heat melted all feelings until not one conscious thought intruded on the let-it-be.

Let the night, the air, the mist off the sea, the earth, the river of life and this life passing, the memories of Govinda and of that first night outside Exandahar and the smell of elephants, setting him free and finding him again, and all that joy and all that sadness and all he and Four Nails had done, let them all be.

The body burned down to ashes and bone fragments for burial deep in the river mud. That way the Romans could not dig them up and show them off, a trophy and symbol of the destruction of Hannibal.

After the citizens of Capua had left to safety inside their city walls, the soldiers had returned to their barracks, women, and games, and only the last riders remained with Nuur and the mahouts, Ashoka sensed another man standing next to him.

"We shared him for a time, for the best time," said Hannibal. "We would not have come this far without him."

Ashoka did not answer, his forming response to no purpose.

Hannibal said, "You have served as well as any man can or I have a right to demand. Listen to me one last time, and I pray you need never listen to me again. You and the other mahouts must leave before sunrise."

"We can do many things, make rope, drive bullocks. Some of us can ride," said Ashoka, bowing slightly.

"If you go back, you'll not survive the night. I can't put Monomachus and Bogus in chains."

"I'm not afraid of them."

"It is not they who will come near you. Monomachus has many loyal footmen. They're drunk and drunk with their power over everything they don't understand. They still blame you and your gods for their losses, their wounded, and their dead at the River Trebia. They do not care to remember the many you saved in the high mountains. A small boat waits on a beach down the coast from here and a fleet lies off the shore."

"Thank you, Master."

"Take this," said Hannibal, handing Ashoka a heavy pouch belt filled with coins, "And this too," a light flat pouch used for carrying sheets of papyrus.

Ashoka's silent face in the waning glow asked the questions.

"Show what's in this to any ship captain of Carthage, and he will give you free passage where ever he is going, and all your mahouts. Don't let anyone see what the belt holds until you come to a city that has a counting house and keep it safe. The pouch holds an epistle for the Senate, your first stop. The Senate will want it and will treat you well after the cargo the ships bring is delivered to them."

Ashoka felt the coins that weighed down the belt. He understood the Senate sat in Carthage, the city of Mintho and the festival, and Radha. But no feelings about them rose up in him, the numbness too great, the care about any of that too little. He had to serve once more, if only to help the remaining mahouts, and that made him move slowly, one step, wait, another step in the direction Hannibal pointed and a faint trail down away from the city and to the sea.

Hannibal tapped the belt that Ashoka still held out in front of him, stupefied. "Tilaka's reward for showing us how to break the rock, not much, but enough. Your belongings are on the boat. Go now. Nuur will take you."

Ashoka turned to Nuur. "How did this noble Numidian find us?"

"Nuur has been my best scout since he came to my army. He sees and hears and rides better than all others. He's watched over Surus—and sometimes over me when I needed him."

Nuur led Ashoka and the other mahouts to a secluded beach on the western shore of Italoi and south from the port city of Neapolis, still loyal to Rome. Small boats waited out on the water until three candles on the beach signaled that it was safe for them to come ashore, pick up their cargo and head back to the safety of large ships farther out on the water in the darkness.

Chapter XXXVIII

Old Men Hanging On

Hannibal spoke of a fleet, but only two ships waited. The small rowboats found the ships a mile and a half off the beach, and the mahouts scrambled up the rope ladders. The two ships headed away on a running tide. A gentle breeze blew across rolling swells from a storm long passed.

Crewmen on the single mast yelled down every time they spotted a light, a reflection on the water. The strongest oarsmen in the Empire of Carthage leaned forward and pulled back as one to beats pounded on goat skin drums. Two on each oar, twenty oars to a row, four rows stacked one above the other on both sides, they pulled for their very lives. These vessels rode high and leapt forward through the water with every stroke.

At sunrise a relief set of men came out of the deepest part of the hull. They took their place at the oars in an orderly exchange so the first set might drink and eat and rest.

In the morning Ashoka, his mahouts, and many of the oarsmen who were supposed to rest stood on the narrow platform running around the top of the hull. They faced backward to the north and the receding hills and mountains of Italoi.

Ashoka counted two sails chasing them and worried for Hannibal. These Romans must have launched the chasing ships in less time than it took to eat a long meal, after someone on the shore spotted the two unknown ships running south on calm water in the night. And that told Ashoka more. Hannibal's army could not soon expect supplies from across the water. His army could hold its own ground where ever it marched, where ever it camped, but never subdue all of the peninsula. It had to live off the land. If it did not soon turn the common people of the peninsula against a determined and wealthy aristocracy, the great campaign would trickle away as sand through fingers.

This vessel carried live sheep and chickens in coops. The twice daily stews of rice or barley contained great chunks of fresh meat, but Ashoka mostly picked at his food.

By the second morning, only the smoke and ash from a volcano south of the bay of Neapolis pointed the way to land more than sixty miles behind the sails. On the third day out, one Roman sail, a white speck on blue water, still tried to catch them but disappeared in the afternoon. By the fifth day at sea, Ashoka stopped searching for Roman ships of war, slept without jumping awake at the slightest strange noise. But it was a restless sleep filled with dreams or interrupted by the memories of screaming women and children.

The two ships did not sneak up to the island of Trinacria, formerly part of their domain but now overrun by Romans. After they passed that island, the wind stilled and turned. Warming air came at them pushing against the great square sail from the wrong direction, and that sail came down. The sky turned a brighter blue and the sun hotter. The days had grown longer and the nights brighter. The calmer water and migrating terns flying south signaled North Africa lay not far ahead.

That evening Bandhu announced, "I've decided."

The mahouts looked at him, eyebrows raised.

"I can't go home. My father beats me like he beats his dogs."

"He won't anymore," said Ashoka. "He'll have grown old. You've grown strong. He may need you."

Bandhu shook his head. "Then I will beat him, I fear. The wealthy of Carthage need servants more than my father needs me." He stood up in the tight sleeping space assigned to them, three cots on both sides of an aisle no wider than one thin man. "Their best servants come from India, and all their young men have left to join Hannibal's army or guard New Carthage."

Ashoka wondered where Bandhu had learned these things, but the others murmured agreement. They all looked at Ashoka on the bottom cot, stared at him to tell them his plans. All his possessions formed his pillow, the *kukri* still rolled up in his trousers with the money belt. When worn, it looked like an ordinary sash but weighed far more than mere cloth or leather. He had evenly distributed the tarnished coins among his six mahouts, guessing by weight and size, not recognizing their origin. The coins appeared as though they had little value. The pouch of papers was tied around his chest under his loose shirt. He sensed that the captain, his officers and many of the crew knew of the papers he carried for the Senate.

At last he said, "After I deliver these epistles, I pray our gods will guide me home. I'm the last son of many generations. Father promised my family I would come back with much gold in five years after he sold me."

"How long, Ashoka?" said one of them.

"Double that and more now." He tapped the rolled up money belt. "Perhaps I can earn my way on a caravan and keep a few of these coins. After my father passes, I'll be the ruler of the family. If I still have one. I must come home with something."

The other mahouts smiled a smile that wished him well.

That night for the first time, the crew lit torches on the bow and stern, and smaller candles in the center of wide bowls filled with water so that in a sudden violent shift the water would snuff out the flames. After dark the drummers slowed the tempo, and the rowers manned only two rows of oars on each side. They did that to not ram one of their own in the night.

The next morning wide cargo vessels and sleek war galleys bristling with oars, coastal fishers, and cargo barges moved out of their way to allow them to maintain speed to the entrance of the outer harbor of Carthage. As they passed between the high walls, many thousands cheered. Crowding mothers held babies and toddlers high. Clusters of the senators and magistrates in long white tunics peered at them from the best positions on the ramparts and docking areas. Agile boys, too young yet to become soldiers, watched from rooftops. It seemed every able-bodied man, woman and child had come out to welcome them home from the great war.

The second galley passed through the opening in the outer wall, but soon the shouts died out. The waiting masses must have realized these two ships led no victorious fleet or line of captured Roman galleys. The same crews and soldiers returned who had left Carthage not long before. The men on the ships lined the decks, but not one among them jumped, shouted or waved for a family to find him after a long time away. No wounded had returned. A restless, questioning murmuring descended on the harbor and spread through the City of Carthage. Why had these two great ships returned so soon?

The senators, magistrates and soldiers shooed back the many curious, so they might have an unobstructed view of the two ships coming in. Walking along the loading piers and docks, they followed the vessels to the merchant lagoon and into the circular harbor of the navy with the Admiral's circular building in the center. The two ships docked side by side in empty covered wharves arranged in a circle around the circular waterway. All the other docking areas were empty. The rest of the Carthaginian navy was out on water near and far.

After their captain and high officers strode down the gangplanks, soldiers on land beckoned for Ashoka and the mahouts to follow before the oarsmen and other passengers. Many more women and girls than men and boys crowded on them.

The mahouts set foot on land, and several soldiers surrounded Ashoka, separated him from Bandhu and the others. They motioned for only him to follow the senators. The soldiers cleared a path for Ashoka and the senators toward the city's dominant hill, but they blocked the other mahouts from following. The soldiers must have known he, and only he, carried epistles for the Senate.

Ashoka cried out in his language, "Bandhu, take them to the nearest inn. Stay together. Tell them Hannibal himself sent you back here. I'll find you. Here, take my bundle." He lost sight of his charges in the swelling throng that stretched into the city and up the hill.

As they marched, Ashoka looked out everywhere to spot everything. He hoped he might see his mahouts or other servants from his country in the many faces. He looked for Mintho in the line of senators and remembered Mintho's last snarling commands. For a moment he wondered if Mintho had died, and then he thought of Radha. For the first time he understood that thoughts of her did not trouble him the same way as back then. He no longer cared that she was a tanner's daughter. Her caste did not matter. He wished she lived in a happier house.

Most of the throng no longer paid attention to him or to the senators and soldiers ahead of him. They all fixed on twenty brown laborers emerging out of the second vessel. Those laborers also followed the little parade up the hill. The laborers carried five small wooden barrels. Each barrel hung from two long poles resting on the shoulders of two men at the front of each pole and two at the back. The weight of the barrels, made of wooden planks tied by metal bands, bent the poles in the middle. More soldiers than laborers strode on both sides of the barrel carriers. Brandishing swords and spears, they yelled at anyone who came too close. The street dogs, always trailing large groups for scraps, kept their distance.

At the entrance to the Great Hall of the tallest building on the highest hill in the City of Carthage, the guarding soldiers stopped. They allowed only the senators and their attendants, Ashoka, and the porters carrying the poles and barrels to enter through the wide door at the top of four flights of stairs. The soldiers had to help the laborers hoist the poles carrying the barrels up those stairs.

The door at the top of the stairs opened to the largest room Ashoka had ever seen, far larger than Mintho's main hall. He tried to look inside, but the soldiers blocked him, shoved him aside for the barrel carriers to pass through, until all five barrels were inside. A soldier motioned for him to follow. He entered the room and stopped.

The cargo barrels sat on a light stone floor in the middle of sofas and cushions. The laborers left through the main door, and the door closed behind them. Ashoka eased his way to the side, to see all he might as fast as he could and to keep the solid wall behind him.

Purple and red sofas drew his attention, not only because they stood out on the nearly white floor but because there were so many. He quickly counted thirty, one for each senator. All the senators, most sitting and leaning forward but some standing, peered at the barrels in front of them. Here and there slaves and advisors clustered around their masters. Older women in plain grey garments brought round bowls of grapes and open pomegranates, figs and dates, ewers and drinking cups and placed them on low tables between the sofas. As they left, they closed the doors to the side halls, to the porch, and the main door to the stairs. For a moment the giant room stilled without any talk, any cough, any shuffling of feet.

He saw Luli from the night of the festival, his black hair now flecked with grey. He was fatter and rounder.

And then Ashoka spotted Mintho, resting on one elbow, the hair whiter and thinner, the beard less full. Unlike every other senator, Mintho did not face the cargo. His eyes fixed on Ashoka, unblinking, and the mouth hard, telling Ashoka that his journey home would end before it began, would end in the night if Mintho had his way.

The senator with the most wrinkled face, clean shaven, clapped twice to interrupt the quiet. He stood behind one of the sofas close to Ashoka and turned to face the newcomer. "The captain of your vessel tells us your name is Ashoka."

Ashoka bowed.

"He says you led the elephants of Hannibal Barca."

"I rode the biggest elephant, sir. The other elephants followed wherever he led."

"Why aren't you still riding him?" The old man scowled as a father scowls at a lazy son. The other senators laughed. Some of their attendants laughed even louder.

"The elephants died, every one. General Barca asked I carry his letters to you."

"Yes, we know." He shook his head. "You would not have set foot here if we did not know. Give them to us then." The old man said it in a way that made Ashoka think he ought to feel stupid, below them all. But he felt nothing, remained calm on the inside but touched the *kukri* under his trousers on his right thigh.

A servant took the pouch from Ashoka and handed it to the senator. He held up the blue seal for all to see, inspected it, and smiled. "It is the Barca seal." He snapped the seal with both thumbs. He pulled out three sheets of papyrus parchment, each folded twice, opened each, studied them for a moment, held one up, again as if for all to see. Grumbling rose up. "Well... what does it say? Read it to us... so we all hear the same."

He began to read in the language of Carthage, slowly, deliberately. Ashoka understood every word.

Honorable Senators, I write this in the house of the Governor of Capua. Your army winters here after three great victories against larger Roman armies. This city, all of the southern peninsula, has sworn allegiance to Carthage, as has Persia.

Grumbles of surprise and approval. The old man read on.

A handful of trinkets from the great campaign should swell the Treasury beyond the City's and Empire's needs for many months. The wealthy land owners here have looted from too many for too long.

The senators grunted approval in unison this time. A voice, Mintho's voice, yelled out, "Hanno, stop reading. We must inspect what the Supreme General Barca has sent us. Perhaps he sent lead." The others laughed again.

Hanno motioned them to the barrels. Twenty-nine senators and twice as many attendants and slaves surrounded the barrels. Some had brought hand tools to cut the metal bands that held down the tops of the barrels. The senators lifted out gold bands and necklaces, rings inlaid with stones of green, yellow and deep red, vases made of gold. Out of silk blankets they pulled finger-sized vials of the deep blue extracted from murex shells and strings of pearls matched for their hues and sizes.

Soon the floor resembled a child's room strewn with toys, the senators as intent as children, holding them up, walking to the openings in the walls so that the bright sun hit the jewels, and points of light swirled on the ceiling. They set them down on the floor and reached deeper into a barrel, pulled out a blanket, and reached farther down for the next treasure. From the lower reaches of each barrel, they pulled out coins, round and rectangular, each the butter yellow of gold or of polished silver. All the while, they watched each other that none slipped a small piece under loose garments.

Hanno had not moved. At last he said, "Senators, Senators, we have business to attend, back to your places." The attendants repacked and closed the barrels, and the great room calmed down.

He continued reading, *Send your fleet and men to the north coast. It is open. Rome's navy follows me. Its armies shadow us and retake territory from which we have departed. I will hold the south but not the north without more men.*

A voice yelled, "We have done that—and lost many ships."

Another yelled, "What does he say about the City of Rome?"

Hanno held up his hand and raised another sheet, *Send siege machines with the fleet. The walls of Rome will not fall to spears and swords.*

"We must discuss this, how we might get him what he asks," said a voice.

"Not in the presence of a stranger," said Mintho. "What shall we do with him, eh?"

"Hannibal tells us," said Hanno. He lifted the last sheet and read on, *Ashoka and his mahouts have served the Empire as well as any of our own men. Without them and the elephants, not one of us would have set foot on Italoi. I give them their freedom and safe passage to wherever the ships of Carthage sail.*

Mintho yelled out, "Hannibal can't tell us what to do with slaves. The Senate commands him."

Before Ashoka could think about what that meant, how much time he had to react or to flee, Hanno said slowly and firmly, "We will do as he says. His army must defeat Rome. And we must help him in every way we can."

Mintho said, "Hanno, you change colors like the lizard. You, the one who wanted to wait for any attack on Rome."

"What is done is done, and we must make the best of it, Brother Mintho. If brash young Barca loses our support, he'll lose this war and we our heads. We'll honor Barca's wishes with this one and the other elephant men. It costs us nothing." He waved the back of his hand at Mintho.

Ashoka saw Mintho's momentary stiffening, that of a once powerful man now insulted in front of many, in front of the man Mintho hated perhaps more than any other in this life but could not harm here or now.

After a time Mintho said, "My men will put him on the best galley to wherever he and his mahouts want to go."

Hanno said, "Thank you, Brother Mintho. Ashoka, take this last sheet. It gives you and your mahouts safe passage wherever our ships go. Wait on the first level. Eat and drink until we're done. Tell the vendors that the senators will pay them well. The Senate thanks you. Mintho's man will take you to the next ship bound for where you wish. The gods of Carthage be with you." Other senators grunted approval.

Ashoka left the great room alone, thinking, remembering Tilaka's lesson that first night mighty Mintho came to his elephant camp. Not one senator would challenge Mintho's account about the death of a solitary useless mahout, even one who had served so well. He had little time and no one else to help. Hannibal was too far away to shield him. As he left, he caught Mintho whispering something to his attendant. They both stared at him.

+ + +

Mintho's attendant did not run out of the Great Hall to chase after the brown messenger. That would have been too disrespectful and alarming. But he walked as fast as he could without drawing attention. After all, Ashoka had been ordered to wait on the first level of the building. When Mintho's man arrived at the lowest level, Ashoka had disappeared. Mintho's man asked the soldiers surrounding the Senate building if they had seen a tall Indian, which way he went. The soldiers grumbled they were watching the crowds, keeping the rabble away from the entrance. "You want that Indian elephant driver, you find him," said one of them, and the other soldiers laughed.

Citizens, laborers and slaves crowded the city streets and alleys all that day and into the night. Their mood had changed when the barrels came out of the depths of the hull. Only gold, the heaviest of all metals, could weigh down modest containers so as to bend thick poles and take four men to carry each barrel. The senators and magistrates spread the news of victories and treasures returned to their rightful owners. They gave a few of the smallest new gold coins to shop owners and wine makers. Spontaneous celebrations sprang up throughout the city.

+ + +

Late in the day, Mintho silently raged, though smiling and nodding at the adoring citizens. He and his attendant asked at every inn and on every street of shops if anyone had seen the tall Indian man, the one who arrived on the first ship that morning, the one who marched up the hill behind the five barrels. Mintho had a message for him from the Senate and had to find him.

Many said they knew of him, the mahout who had driven Hannibal's elephant. Some said they knew where the other mahouts might have found a room and had heard the other mahouts looked for work. One said he had glimpsed the mahout leader on the street but that he suddenly vanished. No one knew where he might have gone, if he had left the inner City or already fled on a ship bound for the eastern territories and Persia, an ally again.

Enough loyal men to blanket the City once swore allegiance to Mintho, but the drought and the war had taken them away. Many good men of the City of Carthage left for Iberia in the months before Hannibal sacked Saguntum, and many more in the last five years. The exodus cut by more than half the markets for crops from Mintho's farms, orchards and vineyards. After he fed his tenant farmers and the servants of his estate, the leftovers fetched a few coins for broken down old soldiers not fit for any long march, for blacksmiths and weavers with crippled hands, inexperienced stable boys and dog handlers. In recent times he had to sell many of his healthy horses. He no longer found buyers for pups out of his big dogs.

Once he could have ordered strangers to torture other strangers who might know the whereabouts of the elephant man, but no one would obey such orders now and might report him to another senator. His reputation would fade further, and in the next election he might become merely another ruler of another crumbling estate.

He did not believe Ashoka had left the City, had taken a vessel to a far shore. Someone would have seen that. He knew to a certainty beyond conscious thought that this Indian had to see her, talk to her, be with her if she would allow it. If they found each other before he found them, his own stupidity was to blame. He had let all his servants, even her, leave his estate and come down to the harbor to welcome the returning vessels of war. When the two ships docked, he had to attend the Senate meetings lasting well into the night and no longer owned enough soldiers to round up his few servants—or Radha. If he found them together, no one in the Empire would blame him for what he would do to them both, but he'd have to do it with his own hands after he himself found them. And he knew he could not do even that, not enough strength in those hands.

Standing in the city center, still nodding and smiling at people staring at him and smiling back, he whispered to himself, "Oh, Moth, god of all revenge, help me one last time."

Time to get home, to play with his sons and give them something very special. Tomorrow he would renew his search for the insolent Indian.

Chapter XXXIX

Love In A Hollowed-Out Tree

Ashoka scanned every building, every sign to find the nearby inns, to fetch his bundle and make a plan with the other mahouts. The crowds down the hill from the great Senate building, crowds almost as happy as on the night of the festival, might protect him for a little while but not long if Mintho bellowed at them to take the tall Indian.

From the street to his left, someone hissed his name. There in an alley stood Bandhu motioning for Ashoka to come quickly. Bandhu said, "Don't ask. Just do as I say and follow me, fast, fast like your best elephant follows your commands."

Bandhu ran down the alley to a door in a broken wall. On the other side of the wall, a covered cart and mule waited. "Jump in. Your bundle is here. Cover yourself. Don't look out. Your black hair and brown skin will give you away. Do not be afraid when the cart lets you out and go with the driver. Good-bye Ashoka. Our gods go with you."

The cart stopped after what seemed like a long ride, and a strange voice said, "Sir, get out with your things and come."

They were in the courtyard at the place Ashoka had last seen in the night of the festival, the days of summer rain, and his last meeting with Mintho. The cart driver, walking fast, led him to the same main building though not to that great room, but to a smaller room on the same level as the ground.

"Wait here." He pointed to a chair. "Sit, you are safe here. There are things to arrange that may take some time." The driver backed out the door but did not lock it behind him.

After a long time alone, footfalls on floor tiles, footfalls of a woman, made Ashoka stand up...

The sight of her took away the first words practiced, changed and practiced again, and then memorized. Gone was the child with downcast eyes in the tanner's shop, the girl on the caravan and at the auction, the new mother screaming a curse at Mintho for the slaughter of an unwanted but cherished child out of her womb. She strode into the room and looked directly at him as an equal and spoke first with the authority of a Brahmin.

"Have they taken good care of you? We can still find tea in the shops," she said in the dialect of Lalput.

He looked past her, unsure of how to address her, where to look, how to begin. Her talk of tea made him lock onto the plain brown pitcher of sweet tea and cup he had drained in one long gulp. The pitcher and cup on the floor next to the bundle of the wool coat and all his belongings disturbed the tidy and dust-free room. Perhaps he should offer to take the pitcher and cup back to the kitchen area if she told him the way.

She must have taken in all his thoughts, his confusion. "Soon the shops will run out of tea, I fear." Her slight chuckle told him she could survive far greater hardships.

At last he said, "How did you find me?"

She, not two arm lengths away, laughed a soft laugh that reminded of Indian women, a laugh that chided him for asking questions the answers to which did not matter, for not keeping still and letting this moment and the next unfold uninterrupted by inadequate spoken words. "You and the other mahouts stood out like hawks among crows. The greatest ships of Carthage had barely tied up before everyone in this city knew Mintho's elephant trainer had come back." She shook her head. Her hair, soft and hanging down to her waist, flowed in the same rhythm, and its sweet scent drifted to him. "You were the last cargo my mistress, or I, expected on the great ships from this war with Rome."

She beckoned him to sit on the comfortable leather and wood chair. He did not have the courage to ask her why he had been brought here, to the den of the lion which hated him.

She also sat down, cross-legged, on the layered cotton rugs in front of his chair. Shafts of golden light through the openings in the south-facing wall came to rest on her sandaled feet, on her ankles and calves as smooth and slim as that day on the platform of the auction at Seleucia. She, sitting like that so he looked down at her, brought back the old feelings of caste—and of yearning. In his home country, he would not have been allowed to be alone in any room with her, this close, unless she were his servant. Her shoulders and long strong arms, the smooth neck and brown skin down to the white tunic, tied at the waist, flowing over the curves of her body disturbed him for those and other reasons, universal, not influenced by caste.

She looked up at him, at his face, across his shoulders and chest, down his arms and legs. He wished that what she saw pleased her.

A horse neighed over voices of children playing, another horse snorted, and hoofs on dirt approached. He, looking again for all possible paths of escape or hiding that he had already studied, started to rise out of his chair.

She said, "Mintho will be with the Senate until night, and his one loyal servant isn't allowed in here."

"The Mintho I knew goes where he pleases."

Radha's voice turned hard. "Not any more. The brother of my mistress owns this land, this house now. It's been in the family since the founding of the colony by the people from the eastern shore. Everything Mintho ever owned came with my mistress or her family. And this, you and I, are in her private area."

"Are you—?"

Radha's full smile melted years from her face and calmed him more than he might have imagined. "No, I'm not a free woman. I serve my mistress, and she is still Mintho's wife. Since that little uprising by your friend, then our great war against Rome, he has lost all power. Only one last manservant fully obeys him."

"Tilaka was my friend."

"He leaves me alone... most times now, adores our sons, his last sons." She shook her head again, ran her long fingers up through her hair and leaned back, both hands resting behind her on the rugs.

He looked off to her side or would not have heard her next words, her limbs, her face, her torso too alluring for him to hear, to bear and do nothing more.

"Servants have become the masters, rule all the wealthy households. The best men of Carthage, the young men are scattered by the wind. Women ride horses, drive oxen and hammer out weapons. We suffer the indignities of our old masters, but they do no harm, not like when you were here last, when they treated us worse than they treated their cows. Without us the old men are helpless, and they know it."

"Why did you bring me here?"

She sat upright, hands in her lap, looked into his eyes until he blinked, embarrassed, and gazed away. "Dear Ashoka, in our country I could not search your face, could not talk to you for fear of a beating. I could not touch you for fear of stoning."

341

He remembered what Madan had said. "Our carriage had a guru, a cook—"

She held up her hand to quiet him. "I summoned you because I had to tell you... From the first time I saw you in my father's shop, no not in it, you and the high castes did business with my father from the street. But you were different than the other boys. The other boys taunted and kicked our beggars. You never did that. You left food for them."

"Mother made me do that at first, and then I wanted to." He smiled. "But she never let me talk to them."

"Do you remember the foot races down our street?"

He raised his eyebrows and wanted to clap. "I do, I do. That street is the longest and straightest in all of Lalput."

"You won every time, even against older boys, and I wanted to shout for joy, but couldn't, but then I could not help shouting. Sometimes I nearly fainted for holding my breath to suppress my shouts."

This time he looked into her eyes, and she looked away. "Had I only known then?"

"As you grew into manhood, the men talked of your way with elephants as a gift from the gods."

"The gift was Father's."

"You were the one thing in a good young life before my father died that made me wish I had not been born a *sudra*."

"I watched you too—many times—though I shouldn't have."

"When they dragged us out of the cart... and took my mother's head, I saw you as close as the soldiers who had done that. I died twice that day."

"You were the fairest, saddest girl I had ever seen."

"At my auction I saw you and Nuur in the braying throng. I wept many nights because you witnessed me being sold on that day."

Ashoka said nothing for a long time, not sure whether to move closer or away, whether to kneel down to her or pull her up to him. He remained still. "I was young and stupid. I should not have asked Nuur to take me to the sale of women. I had to know—if you were among them. I made Nuur leave before the bidding for you ended."

Now she waited, fighting against emotions. "I saw you next the night they took my son."

"Dearest Radha," he said, addressing her by name for the first time, "the gods brought me to you on your saddest days, and I had no way to take away your sadness. Had I been wiser, I would not have let a boy from your village add to your suffering."

She blinked. Moisture covered her eyes. She closed them and turned away. Until this moment her direct gaze had presented a barrier as strong as a metal shield. The shield had dropped. He slid out of the chair to his knees. Slowly he reached forward until his fingertips touched her cheek. She leaned into his hand and held it to the side of her face, rocking forward and back, weeping. Through the tears she said, "Ashoka, you must go now, we... must not."

He did not answer, did not want to say what he knew he had to say. Her wet gaze forced him to utter slowly, "I know. I can't stay in this city, can't stay here. And I know you must... But in my dreams you are always by my side. Every mahout travels with a helper."

She took his hand in both hers, their faces close enough they each felt the breath of the other. "Ashoka, my karma was to be born of a tanner's wife, to come here and give Mintho his last living children and to stay with my sons until they need me no more. I cannot leave them and go back to where I am but a tanner's daughter."

He laughed at his next thought, but not loudly. "Come with me. No one will know. I'll tell them you're a princess from Tamil." The childish words echoed off the bare walls.

She laughed too, wiping tears with the back of her hand. She said between deep breaths, "No princess from the south travels with a lone elephant driver, without marriage, and servants, guards and fine carriages. I brought you here for another reason, not just because I had to see you and tell you."

Ashoka waited for her this time, though he had no thought about what she might say.

"I brought you here because my mistress knows you are a good and kind man. She has suffered Mintho for too long, and now wants to do this—wants to help you find your way home."

Ashoka closed his eyes, too many things, too sudden. Home... Was that possible?

Radha interrupted his thoughts. "You need to go now, before the Senate meeting ends, before his servant pays beggars to kill you. Men of my mistress and her family will take you to the harbor, to merchants on their way to the eastern shore and Persia. They'll give you clothes and a suitable head covering—so you look less like you."

"I can't," he said though he meant to say more. "Not until my other mahouts are safe."

"Ashoka, let Carthage go. You're done here. Mintho will forever try to find you and with his last coins pay beggars to kill you and feed your body to the street dogs. Bandhu, they tell me, can work in the stables here, and the other mahouts will find a household in this city or over in New Carthage if they want. Or they can leave with you."

She stood, lifted his hand for him to stand, and led him to the portico outside the room.

Flowers, in shades of deep red, orange and pale pink covered a fence or wall. An opening in the bushes led to a

344

grove of palm trees. On flat dirt in the shade of the biggest palms, two boys, naked to the waist and bare legged, threw spears at tree trunks. Ashoka guessed their ages at perhaps six and eight. The spears, short but full sized and too heavy or too blunt for the youngsters, hit their mark but did not stick. Shouting, the boys ran to the spears and threw them again and again. Ashoka thought soon those youngsters would throw spears in earnest, would have to.

Radha said, "The older is Arabo. The younger is Bostar. No harm will come to me so long as I keep them safe. They are healthy and will become honorable men. I'll grow old with them."

Ashoka tightened his grip on her hand. She lifted it to the center of her chest and held it close.

"Dear Ashoka, remember this beating heart. It beats stronger for our paths having crossed, for having come to know a good man who feels about me as I do about him. Our paths will cross in all our future lives and, if the gods smile on us, will come together as two paths come together in one."

This time Ashoka held back tears. "When your sons are men and can travel to India, to our village, tell them to ask for me. If my time in this life has passed, tell them to ask others in the village about their mother, a beautiful tanner's daughter, who once looked with love at an elephant trainer. When I get home, all the villagers will know about her. I promise you."

The spear throwers stopped. They looked at their mother and the tall man standing by her side in a manner of no other man. Arabo yelled, "Mother, who is that?"

She said quietly, "Children have no manners," then loudly, "A man from my village has come here so he can tell them what fine boys you are. Take your brother and wash before you come in for the night."

345

"Yes, Mother," said the older one. He put his arm around the younger, picked up both spears and headed into another part of the building.

A familiar voice from behind them interrupted. "Radha, he must change his clothes and we must trim his hair in the shape of a trader. My husband must not find him. The horses are ready, the tide is right not long after sunset, and the galley will not wait."

Ashoka turned to face Mintho's wife. He bowed. "Thank you for your kindness and for having become Radha's mistress. I will remember you as long as I live. If the gods are kind to us, we will meet again, all three of us, perhaps as eagles or lions..."

He reached behind. His fingers found Radha's and intertwined for an instant.

He did not look back as he walked into the room, grabbed his bundle, slung it over his shoulder and followed an attendant waiting, the empty pitcher and cup still on the floor.

+ + +

"Come talk to your father," said Mintho. "What have my favorite children been doing while their father attends to business?"

"Fighting with spears," said Bostar.

"Did you slay many Romans?"

"Many, again and again," said Bostar.

"Look what I brought you." Mintho withdrew two gold rings from a deep front pocket in his tunic and handed one to each son. The weight and color of the small round circles gave them pause, as if they thought nothing so small could sit so heavy in the hand.

"Tell me, did you meet any interesting people while I was gone?"

Bostar blurted, "How did you know, Father? Mother was with a man from her village in India, browner than this," pointing to his tanned forearm. "Mother said he'd tell her village about us."

Mintho, lying on a sofa, reached out and tousled the youngster's black hair. "He will, I say."

Mintho did not sleep. Thoughts about whether Ashoka had left, how much time he had spent with Radha, what they had done, whether they had concocted a false story kept him awake. Long ago he might have beaten Radha to tell him the truth, given her to lust-maddened soldiers if he sensed any lie or treachery, but now he could not. She was his wife's favorite, mother of his only sons. He had no soldiers or money to pay them, and his own hands and arms were too old and weak. His hands hurt when he picked up a simple plate or cup. His shoulders cried out when he lifted his arms higher than his head. And if he did attack Radha, Dido's brothers would surely kill him.

Deep in the night, he struck the floor next to his sleeping mat with the side of his fist until his hand hurt, then harder until he thought he might split his brittle old skin. He said, "Moth, give me a sign that my son told me the truth, that the insolent leech-eating whore Indian came and left without... Or I will find a way to make her suffer worse than the smallest street dog in heat. Moth, protect me from seeing him ever again, that he is truly gone."

347

Chapter XL

Home

Hawkers, carrying wicker trays and baskets on their shoulders or heads, crowded around Ashoka and everyone getting off the great ship from Persia. They peddled candy, flowers and leather straps embedded with cheap metal studs, dried fruit and bits of salted meat.

The ground swayed. He lowered his bundle and regained his balance, took off his sandals and dug his toes into the warm red dirt. He laughed inside at the shouting people so close to him. They spoke in dialects he understood without straining. Some looked in his direction, right at him but then past him. He wanted to wave at them as if to an old friend, talk to them no matter their caste. He was no longer the stranger but one of their kind in this, the port city of Mumbai on the west central coast of India.

By grace of the letter from Hannibal, his passage had cost nothing. From here, he would have to pay or work for everything. Counting houses, the tallest and most ornate buildings in the area, stood side by side across the crowded street from the harbor. He chose the middle house, the largest, where two guards in full armor looked over a long line of patrons waiting outside the tall entry door.

Ashoka approached the back of the line, but before he settled a guard came up. Ashoka patted the belt on his waist to reveal the outline of coins and said with a raised voice to throw off any lurking beggar or bandit, "I need to change these. Cheap coins of Carthage and Rome are useless here I am told."

"We don't know you. Strangers are searched before they enter."

Ashoka held out his hands and arms, inviting a search. "I'll leave my belongings by the door if you would allow me. They're not much." Other sacks, tools and even weapons lay on the ground by the door. The guard took the bundle.

When one patron came out, the guard let another in. Many from the Persian ship stood in this line, and it moved slowly. Ashoka did not mind. The air felt thick with water, and the sun pressed down hard, the same air and sun as in Lalput.

Once inside the heavy door, the line moved slowly too. Ashoka had time to take it in. A high ceiling, clear water pond in the middle of the room, and two servants wafting large fans over the pond eased the heat. Light came through narrow openings in the four walls. Only one or two people at a time were allowed deeper into the room. At a long table up ahead on the other side of the pond, two men examined whatever customers brought in. Now and again coins clanked onto the table top. Behind the men stood shelves of bins, bottles, and unmarked containers.

At each side of the table hung what Ashoka took to be a scale—a pan at the end of a long level bar suspended from the ceiling by a chain and hook. He wondered if his coins might be weighed, if they were worth only as much as their metal melted down. From their weight, heavy for any common coin, Ashoka had often wondered if they were cast of lead. They did not look like Tilaka's or any other coins he had seen.

Each patron left with a clerk's paper. Those who left seemed pleased and did not grumble.

Ashoka got to the front of the line and dumped out the coins from his belt. One clerk looked at him closely, then at the coins, then back at him. "I've not seen you before. I've not seen such as these. What do you want?" The clerk said it as if he had seen many coins from many places but never these tarnished round things.

"I must change them to the common coins of our Empire, *panas*, if you please." Ashoka spoke formally, as might an educated Brahmin, and the words came to him easily.

The clerk looked up, this time with a slight downward tilt of the head. "Yes, Master. I don't know how much I can give for these. But I will do what I am able."

Ashoka relaxed. He was no longer a slave, no longer a boy. In the eyes of this counting house clerk, Ashoka was a high caste to be reckoned with. At once, it did not matter how much these coins might bring. He now knew he could find his way home. "If they have no value, I'll give them to the nearest orphanage."

The clerk picked up one of the coins and squeezed it between thumb and forefinger. That one, thin but half as large as the palm of his hand, was the heaviest. The clerk's practiced fingers crimped one of the edges. "Master, I think you may not be giving these to an orphanage." He pulled over a glass bottle and bowl from among many on a shelf behind him, placed the smallest coin into the bowl and poured a clear liquid over it. Bubbles engulfed the coin. The rust coating vanished to reveal the shiny yellow metal that no solution can tarnish. Faster than the eye could follow, the clerk's fingers arranged the other coins in a line by weight, ten in all counting the one still in the cup. "Master, whoever smelted them didn't want anyone to know."

Ashoka said under his breath, "Plundering armies." He thought to leave them on the table. Without any gold stolen from dead Romans, he had survived far worse than what might lie ahead. But he could not return them to their rightful owners. Leaving them to this counting house would dishonor Tilaka and even Hannibal. "Exchange the small one, please. It might bring enough for passage to the interior?"

"Yes, Master."

"I'll keep the other coins as they are until I get closer to my village."

"Yes, Master. That is wise." The clerk employed the scale once more and noted the place on the bar where the hook and ceiling chain held it level. He gave Ashoka a stack of local coins and a piece of paper with notations of the trade-in value, and the gold coin disappeared.

Ashoka did not question the amount he received back. This counting house would not last two cycles of the moon if one high merchant accused it of cheating.

+ + +

The past had collapsed as if he had left before last year's monsoon. On the Emperor's main roads, caravan drivers shouted and whipped mules and oxen to get to their destinations or to higher ground before the rains began. During some nights, big cats grunted and roared. They stalked close enough to the caravan circles, to the horses and bullocks huddled inside them, that their eyes reflected the fire light.

Alone with his thoughts, Ashoka thanked his gods for the days of quiet travel, nights without killing, and time with his memories. Excitement did not well up. Too many questions blunted it. Was Father still alive and with Mother, had the two older sisters and Sanju married, where was Red Eyes? Whatever the answers, he knew he would accept them. Nothing on the road ahead would disturb him as much as his journey of the past eleven years.

Far out of Mumbai, his caravan stopped to unload its cargo and travelers, take on new cargo and return to Mumbai.

But this last stop was days from Lalput. Someone pointed Ashoka to a much smaller caravan also unloading, said it might go where he wanted.

He found the driver. "Sir, I am from Lalput. I am told you are going there."

The driver looked him up and down. "I have no more room for anything and no time to haggle about a price."

"Sir, I ask only room for me and will pay any fair amount you say."

The driver frowned. "Then what business do you have in Lalput with nothing to trade?"

Ashoka had found the right caravan, though it had only five carts and four armed riders to protect it. He accepted the caravan leader's probing. Fools and bandits came in many forms. Ashoka pulled up to his full height. "My family owns the elephant camp down the river from Lalput, has since the time of Alexander. I have been away for a time, and my journey takes me home."

The caravan driver grew still. No part of him moved. He looked at Ashoka, into his eyes as no one since Ashoka had set foot in India. At last in a low voice, he said, "I'm going to Lalput. I'll take you there for nothing. I knew your father."

Ashoka jerked inside but tried not to show it. This man might tell him much more, but. . . he had said that he *knew* Father. "Thank you. That is most kind. How, may I ask, did you know him?"

The head man pretended not to hear the last, turned away, shouted instructions to one of the laborers loading one of the carts, then pointed. "You can ride on the front of that one if you make yourself small. Help us set up and break camp for your food."

Ashoka exhaled, and all anticipation flowed out of him. He bowed and mumbled, "Thank you."

He asked no more about Father then or at any other time on this last caravan ride. If the caravan driver had wanted to answer, he would have... Father was dead, and the caravan driver did not want to talk about that death. More questions piled in but no use to pry for answers... He would find answers soon enough.

Thirty days after leaving the ship and deep into India, a thickening sky promised rain. The sun dropped behind the same distant forest trees as it did on those nights when he was a boy. Familiar shafts of smoke rose above the jungle, banana plants and cultivated fields. This smoke came from cooking fires and metal worker ovens, not the black billows from a plundered village burning.

They crossed Lalput's river, running low, at the usual place. The village wall was smaller than he remembered, but it stretched farther north too. Farmers cleaning dead leaves and grass cuttings out of the ditches around the wall brought back the feelings from Govinda's last night. The trees rimming the open area had grown taller, but the river looked the same, with the same brightly-clad women pulling clothes out of the water and calling their youngsters to stay close.

Two hundred paces from the village wall, Ashoka jumped off the cart and ran to the nearest gate. Guards looked him up and down, making him slow to a walk and feel silly. A young man did not run like that unless something very strange or bad had happened. They let him pass. Their duty was only to keep out bandits and predators.

Inside the gate, for a moment he was lost. The streets extended beyond where they had ended back then, and the nearest houses and shops were new. Two taverns, not there back then, sat on opposite sides of the street closest to the gate.

It came back as if it were yesterday. That last time he had run around the corner down the street to the crowd wailing.

Govinda… his father kneeling, his mother and sisters huddled. He trotted around the same corner and stopped. His house stood small, timid, not the house of a warrior class family or the owner of an elephant camp. Smoke rose from the cooking fire in the same place. A middle-aged woman, with toddler under foot, tended the fire in the same manner as his mother had then, but these two were strangers.

The woman said to the naked youngster, "Get inside. Now. Or I'll tell your father and he'll strike you." She said it as if she had often felt the father's strike. The little one ran into the house to noises of other children. The woman did not notice Ashoka or, if she did, ignored him.

The house walls crumbled where its corners met the ground, the roof straw had rotted, and the chicken coop at the side was gone. All was not well with these tenants or with the only home he had ever known. His insides told him to leave alone this poor woman and her children. They could not help him. His insides told him it would be best that no one knew he had come home. He needed to find a place to sit, to watch, to ponder, to let the next step come to him.

He moved on as if he had a place to go. In the growing dusk, he did not see anyone he remembered. No one shouted out to him. Here and there a villager looked at him, but no one challenged him. Now was not the time to find the elephant camp by himself. He wondered how many others from back then had gone away. He retreated to one of the new inns and left his bundle in a small room. He had enough coins to easily pay for a room and food for as many nights as he might want.

After dark he talked to beggars and drunks. It did not take long to find several who knew of Uncle Vasavedu, knew he owned many houses, knew where he lived in the wealthy section. Some knew Uncle's servants, but, from their descriptions, none of Uncle's servants was Ashoka's mother or sisters. No one said anything about an elephant camp, about his father, his mother or sisters. But that did not add to Ashoka's worry. His family never talked to a beggar or street drunk.

Uncle's house looked and felt the same as back then. It sat away from the street behind a stone wall and another wall of bamboo behind that one. Banana trees and flowering bushes filled some of the gaps. Thorny bushes spilled over the stone wall in some places. Ashoka found one unprotected section of the wall and hopped up onto it. He sat and listened and watched deep into the night. Once or twice a dog sniffed below him but moved on. No light from the houses of the estate shone brightly enough for Ashoka to make out any people. The only sounds in the quiet night from the estate were voices of a man and a woman and horses snorting.

He thought about what his guru might have instructed, what Father would have said, what Hannibal might have done to find his family and keep them safe from their uncle or whoever owned them now. An easy next step came to him. It would not take many evenings or cost much to gather the garments, pile straw into his hair, and dirty up his face and arms.

She turned away from the beggar. Her attendant stepped between her and this stranger reeking of cow dung. But the odor reached around her attendant and through the silk shawl that protected her from view of commoners.

The beggar, head bowed, said something. She refused to listen. He said it again, the words of an educated man in a familiar voice. He did not ask for a coin, or begin a story of bad fortune and the good karma bestowed on those who give to the poor. "Your nephew Ashoka sent me. He has been away for a long time."

Her eyes could not make out his face well enough in this light of late afternoon and through her shawl. She scoffed, "I... many have that name, too many for me to know them all."

"He says he is your nephew by your husband's brother, the elephant man."

Her attendant, hand on the hilt of his sword, stepped in. Others should not see her talking to a beggar. She said, "Out of the street, come over here."

She stopped close to the entrance of her estate. She did not want him to follow any farther, though no doubt he knew where she lived and had waited here for her to return. As they moved off the street and onto a neighbor's land, a dog on a long leash approached growling. Her attendant said, "Quiet, Little Tiger. It's us." The dog wagged its tail and lay down facing them.

The three huddled where garden growth shielded them from easy view of anyone on the street. She said, "Where is this Ashoka?"

"He is close by..."

"How do I know any of what you say is true?"

The beggar shrugged. "He wants only to see his mother and sisters, to know they are well after the death of brother Govinda, to take care of them and his father's elephant camp."

She gasped and put her hand to her mouth. Only someone who left the region soon after Govinda died would know about that nephew's death but not what became of the elephant camp, what became of his mother and sisters, and only one man alive would care about that camp and those women. She said no more, not now, not within hearing of her attendant, paid by her husband. She mustered up her strongest voice and turned to her the attendant, "Go over there. Make sure no one approaches from the street. I will call for you when I'm done with this beggar."

The attendant stood away from them and out on the street where he could see them and keep others away.

She felt her neck and chest tighten, the same as when her husband came home drunk and angry. She did not fear this beggar. She feared what her husband would do if any of this beggar's story was true.

This stranger, now much closer, did not smell of cow dung after all. He did not smell of anything. She must have imagined the stench when she first saw him. He stood up, much taller than she. She said, "I will tell this Ashoka what he wants, but only him."

"You are. I am he, Aunt Dur..."

Her eyes darkened over. She heard nothing and felt her knees buckle. She needed to lie down, to sleep, to vanish. A strong hand and arm kept her from tumbling in her fine silks and lowered her to sit on the ground.

After a time—she did not know how long—the firmness of the ground, stones digging into her thighs and buttocks brought her back, and she remembered what he had just said. Only the elephant man's family had ever called her by that variation of her name. She whispered to herself, to the ground under her, "Lord Vishnu, save us from Shiva's wrath."

Before she could say more, the beggar grasped her hands and helped her to her feet. They stood there, him holding her, she holding onto him and not afraid to lean into this man whose voice, whose scent did seem familiar, comforting.

He said, "I left two days after the cobra. Tell me please where I might find Mother and Sisters."

She brushed the dirt from her garments. If he were Ashoka, if Ashoka found them or didn't find them but learned what happened to them... too much to think about. But she knew she could not lie, not to him, not about that. If she lied, bad karma would follow her through all her lives. "Ashoka, if it is you, you should know, and then I pray you find them but never bring them back..."

"I must find them."

"I took Ashoka's—I took your mother and sisters away from here on the night of the first full moon after the monsoon ended, after Ashoka's... your father died. I gave them all my hidden *panas* and all the bread and clothes they could carry."

"Took them where? Please tell me."

She sighed. "No, that is not right. I didn't take them. I sent them to my family in Ajanta, over there where there's honorable work for everyone. That was the last I saw them or heard of them."

"Why, why did you send them away?"

She must not answer this. Nothing good could come of the true answer and worse if she lied. It was all past now, but... she had to. This one person needed to know. "My husband thinks they fled on their own. I don't know what he thinks about them leaving without telling him, without them thanking him for having taken them in. I had to save the girls from him. Go now. You're in danger if he finds you, if my man standing out there tells him about you. You must remain a strange beggar as long as my husband is alive. He has great power in this village, in this region."

She pushed away from him so that they no longer touched. "All the gods of India go with you."

"And with you." The beggar or Ashoka disappeared into the darkness.

Chapter XLI
Good Sister in A Past Life

The first drops of the monsoon fell the next morning. After three days and nights the rain lashed at the houses and jungle, fields and animals. It swelled lazy rivers to torrents. Only wide waterways and paths of stone allowed easy travel. Ashoka's destination, the city of Ajanta, sat astride one of the newest sections of the Emperor's Road many days travel from his village.

The Magistrate of Ajanta shook his head. "They would not have used their own names. More than a hundred families in Ajanta have your aunt's family name."

"In my region the magistrates keep records of new people. If they used another name, I might know it. May I look at your registrations?"

"If you are fleeing a powerful uncle, would you make it that easy for him to find you? Your mother and sisters would not register at all. Besides, too many laborers come and go without registering. We're much too big and busy to find them, try to record their names and where they come from. In the dry season we have work for everyone."

Ashoka said, "Perhaps you can point me to the dwellings of some of my aunt's family."

The Magistrate gave Ashoka directions to a few people he said who might be connected to Aunt Durga's family. The Magistrate walked outside with him and pointed down streets telling him where to turn next and after that to perhaps find someone related to his aunt.

While all nature drank deeply, and man rested and prepared for the planting and growing, Ashoka wandered the city of Ajanta and nearby villages. He pressed through the rain, the mud which at times came up over his ankles, the streets flowing with brown rubble-filled water and often empty except for him.

Starting with the names and general direction of people the Magistrate had given him, he asked for those with the same names as Aunt Durga's family or his family or for anyone who had seen a mother and three girls wandering.

After many days, he found an old woman in an outlying village whose family had taken in a mother and three girls some years back. Now this woman lived by herself in a small house of several small rooms crowded with straw bedding, stools and utensils for cooking and tilling soil. One of the rooms clucked with chickens. The roof leaked in many places from the warm rain, but the woman did not seem to care. In years past it must have been an inn or the crowded home of a big family, all of whom had left or died leaving their belongings behind. The woman told him, "Yes, we rented a room to four women, a mother and three daughters."

"When? Where did they go? Tell me more please."

She shook her head. "They were proud. The girls were pretty, and the mother worried about them. They stayed with us for... then after my man died... I don't know, not long. They came back once or twice in the rainy season when begging in the city was bad, and the great Buddha work had stopped. We shared what we had, but it wasn't enough, never enough, and they did not have money to pay rent. They knew when it was time for them to go... Proud, so proud... of the warrior class, I think. At least that's what they said."

"Do you remember the name they used?"

She shook her head.

"Where did they go?"

She shrugged and raised her hands palms up. "They didn't want us to know." She cackled. "They didn't want anyone to find them."

When the rain eased, newcomers arrived in Ajanta. Ashoka made out that these were low castes, tenant farmers who could not pay the rent, widows of poor husbands, orphaned children too young to have a trade but old enough to labor. They streamed in to work on the Emperor's project started many years before. Ashoka joined them. Someone might remember something. Mother or his sisters might be among them.

Not far outside the city, he came upon the crescent-shaped gorge carved through steep hills covered by jungle growth. He stood looking at it for a long time, at the people near him and far down the gorge.

Along the top a hundred or more laborers toiled in a line that reminded Ashoka of the relay to bring firewood to the rock. They swung machetes at the surface growth and picks at the dirt and loose rocks. Others carted the loose diggings off the hill, and a trail grew down the canyon wall.

At the far end of the canyon, the work had progressed the most, perhaps for years already. There, many hammers hitting spikes and the spikes hitting solid rock echoed up to him. There, stone cutters shaped the stone gorge into the top of a big chamber. Everyone seemed to know that in time this gorge would house many statues and paintings in caves to celebrate the life of Lord Buddha. Monks, revealed by their shaved heads and occasional commands, worked among the stone cutters and directed the whole effort.

"You there, stop staring and get to work." A gang leader handed him a dual-headed pick shovel and pointed for him to join another man already bent over a new trail section.

Ashoka said, "Forgive me." He swallowed words about his search and that he was not here to labor.

Not many had the strength and stamina of Ashoka. He became the leader of a gang of ten. He and all the workers received two large portions of a rice stew and all the flat bread they could eat every day. At the end of seven days, they got a few coins and a ewer of rice wine. They slept in communal camps separated by sex, married couples in their own camp.

A swift flowing stream cut through the bottom of the gorge, and little water falls burst out of the cliffs. Up from the stream women carried jars of water on the tops of their heads. Boys and girls hauled away dirty clothes to be washed in the river, dried in the sun and brought back to the workers.

On that first day and every day, he studied the faces of women and girls as best he could without holding up the work. He had not intended to help carve this gorge into giant icons in caves. He did not need to labor for the few coins, enough to buy food and clothes but little more. His reward from Hannibal was safe in a counting house in the center of the city.

But all spirits instructed him to stay here, to wait here. When the rain was too heavy to work or the labor camp rested on a festival day, he wandered again to places he had been, asked those he had already asked until they avoided him when he approached.

Over the days, then weeks, the sweat covering his arms and chest and running salty into his eyes washed away the grime of his past. Clearing an area no bigger than a small mat, then building a short section of a trail down the face of the hill, then reaching the hard stone underneath and clearing more area for the stone cutters made good toil. It calmed his memories and eased his longing. The frenzy to find his family melted to acceptance of this work, this day, and whatever the next day might bring.

He knew nothing more to do.

+ + +

On a day no different from all the others, he heard the song. He stopped the steady swing of his pick shovel. He stopped to make sure the words—*baby elephant chases the little boys and girls, it wants to play with them, wants to play*—and melody were not sung by the breeze, by his own yearnings. Many women hummed or sang softly as they worked. But not one of them would know this song. Mother made it up and sang it to each of the children.

He found the singer pouring water into the cups of men down the line from him.

She came closer. It seemed her movements, the way her hands and delicate fingers moved, were familiar. But he was not sure. She might have copied the song from a friend. She did not look at him, at any of the men, only at the mouth of her jug and the cups that sat on the ground near each man, or that each man held up for her. She, perhaps sixteen, tall for her age and lean but to be desired, bent over Ashoka's cup.

And he knew though he did not know how he knew. Perhaps her face matched the memory of Mother, her mouth the line of Father's mouth, the hues of her skin and hair the same as Father and Mother's combined. He feared his heart might stop, or, if not stop, explode. He was not sure words would come out of him, but they did. "Sanjushree is your name, I think?"

A deeper sense made him place his hands under her water jug as he spoke. Had he not, it would have toppled to the hard ground and shattered.

She put both hands to the sides of her face, to her mouth as if trying to keep words from flying out. "No, that's not my name, sir. I must not talk to you. It is forbidden."

Her voice sounded the same as Mother's when Mother was young. He smiled widely and thought his heart might sing too. "Don't worry, Sanju. An unmarried maiden can talk to her older brother. Uncle did not send me."

"What uncle?"

"Uncle Vasavedu."

She leaned in toward him ever slightly, looked down. "Lord Vishnu, father of all creation in this life and all lives, send me a sign I am not dreaming."

He became aware of others in line behind him stopping, rising up and staring at this young man and woman, at their intense exchange. He felt they would not interfere for a little longer. He had earned their respect. But they did all stop working, and soon a leader would scold them and shoo the girl away.

He set the ewer at their feet and took her hands. "These are my hands, my arms—even my wrist that is still missing what you made for it. You're not dreaming, sister Sanju. Aunt Durga said you had come here."

Sanjushree now looked around too, moved to pick up the ewer and continue her task. She stopped and looked up, closely at his face, into his eyes, as might anyone pulling up images from many years before. And her expression—wide eyes, a smile of joy and tears welling—told him she understood this was indeed her last brother. "When... you?"

"At the beginning of the rains. Lord Vishnu and all our gods did not let me leave here until you came to me. Go now, but wait for me by the bread ovens when our day is done."

She moved to the next man in line, looked back at Ashoka, closed her eyes and stammered through her tears, "I must have been a very good sister in a past life."

+ + +

After their day's work, after thanking their group leaders and asking permission to leave and not return, brother and sister left for Ajanta. On the way, Sanjushree said, "Mother toils in the place of the last days of our sisters. She could not help them, so she helps others who lived and suffered like our sisters did at the end."

As the last light faded, they made their way deep into the area of the city assigned to the unclean. Sanjushree led him to an alley covered by a straw roof. The alley ended at an alms house.

Every few paces along the alley, candles set on posts cast enough light for him to avoid stepping on limbs or feet. Hollowed-out eyes followed him. Fly-encrusted mouths asked them for anything. Bony fingers and hands with sores or no fingers reached out to them. These people came here because they had no other place to stay out of the rain and sun and away from the shame heaped on them by those more fortunate.

He had smelled death and human waste many times, in houses and ditches, in fields covered by the dead and the dying, in camps of many thousands, but never this odor, the smell of old bodies sweating, and diseases rotting parts of bodies still alive, and the living slowly dying. Ashoka snarled inside at Uncle Vasavedu. He would make that right. And he thought of his other two sisters, their lives ending in this place.

At the entrance to the alms house, two women stood over a pot on a stone fire ring. One ladled out portions of hot rice into little bowls handed to her by the second woman. Beggars lined up waiting. With knobby fingers, each scooped the rice out of the bowl and ate hungrily.

Sanju said, "Wait here. Let me talk to her first lest she not believe or, if she believes, lest she die of happiness."

She made her way past the crush of the waiting and leaned close to the woman ladling out the rice. That woman stopped, stood up straight, listened, and looked down the alley in Ashoka's direction. More words passed between them. The old woman kept ladling but slowly shook her head from side to side. Sanju motioned for Ashoka to approach.

As he neared, the old woman said, "You're bigger than my son. Say something that tells me who you are."

The last years had become many more than eleven in her. Her face was that of an old woman, her hair all white, and her voice out of a mouth with few teeth had aged more than the rest of her. But even in this dark alleyway, the light from her eyes, the wisdom of her words, were the same he remembered. He reached out and pulled her into his shoulders as he had on that night Govinda died, and it felt good. "Mother, all the gods of Carthage kept me away too long. But I have come back... I have come back... come back as Govinda said he would."

She relaxed and dropped the ladle but made no move to back away. Three beggars near the front of the line dove at it. Two wrestled for it until the stronger one tore it away.

The other woman yelled, "Stop, you ungrateful dogs. Give me that." The culprit did as she asked.

Mother eased out of his arms. "Wait until this pot is empty."

She took back the ladle and continued filling bowls eagerly handed to her. She looked at her pot of rice, at him, back at the rice, and Ashoka saw a slight smile. She said, "You must tell me about where you have been, what you have seen, how you have grown, until I fall asleep in peace for the first night since your brother left us."

Chapter XLII

Ruler of the Family

Aunt Durga's warning had sunk in. Ashoka left Mother and Sanju at an inn one town to the west of Lalput. He rode with local caravans back to Lalput three times in the next two weeks but stayed only one night.

It did not take Ashoka long to find a trustworthy courier, common in India to convey negotiations for transactions of commerce and marriage proposals. Strangers would never know and neither side would lose face if negotiations failed.

Ashoka asked his courier to contact Uncle Vasavedu, to tell him Father's last son had returned and now claimed his entitlement to Father's house, elephant camp, and whatever else of Father's the uncle had taken. If all went well, the Emperor's Magistrate and the town judge would sanction the agreement, and the family property would once more be held roughly equally by the living male rulers of the two family branches. Under all law and customs in India for more than a thousand years, Uncle held Father's house and any remaining gold, chickens, furniture, and the elephant compound only as a caretaker until the eldest son might return. That son had now come back.

After seven days, Uncle Vasavedu sent a message back through his own courier. *All the gods of India rejoice in your safe return. After I take inventory, I will advise what is rightfully yours and trust we will quickly reach a fair division of your and my rightful property. You will, of course, have to establish you are who you say you are. Imposters and thieves are everywhere.*

Every night he was with them, Sanju and Mother slept deeply in the small room on the other side of the curtain. Candles at each end of the hall running along his and every room on the upper level of the inn cast a faint line of light around his doorway. On this night, seven days after Uncle's last message, the carousing in the tavern below quieted at about the usual time. Customers left or lost their struggle against cheap spirits distilled from rice, sugar cane or wheat grass.

The long trail to Rome through hostile territory, the nights sleeping but alert to any strange noise heightened Ashoka's awareness of unseen threats, of men in hiding, of quiet words, of movement in a bush not caused by the breeze. His senses and the events of the last days told him to stay alert a short while longer. On this night, the leaf-soft fall of a bare foot outside that door roused him. Perhaps the wood planks had creaked or a new odor wafted into his sleeping place by the door. He sat up fast. The narrow strip of soft light under the door wavered more than from flickering candle flames. Someone stood out there.

Noiselessly, he rolled off the cotton mat, spread out his wool coat and clothes to simulate a human form on the mat and, naked to the waist, crouched behind the closed door and next to the curtain into his family's sleeping area.

The frame of light around the door fell dark. Whoever was out there must have doused the candles on the walkway. Scratching noises came from the latch on the door, a latch that could not be opened from the outside if anyone occupied the room. The person outside moved on.

Ashoka stayed awake until morning, thinking, planning. Had Uncle sent someone to make trouble, to scare him off, or had a drunken guest tried to enter the wrong room? But whoever was out there had doused the candles.

In the morning, he left for Lalput again but only after moving Mother and Sanju to another inn.

His courier rushed up to him smiling. "Ah, I have another message and am glad you came so soon."

"An inventory of what my uncle took from my father, I hope?"

"No, no, but perhaps something better."

"Oh?"

"Master Vasavedu proposes to meet face to face... wants to meet at the house of the town magistrate, and, as you know, that rarely happens without friendship and agreement."

For a few moments, Ashoka was unclear if he heard correctly. It was too soon for this, but the courier's smile and excitement matched his words. "He proposes a meeting for tomorrow, if that suits you."

Nothing felt right. It was too fast, too honorable, too open for Uncle Vasavedu. He collected his mother and Sanju and returned to Lalput once more. He did not want to bring them, but they insisted on staying together, losing face together, even dying together.

The day came up cooler than usual under a bright blue sky. Ashoka wore a cheap cotton coat over his cotton shirt. The Magistrate's house sat on the main street, the street of the foot races when Ashoka was young, the street of traders and Radha's shop, now occupied by another tanner. The Magistrate's house, of two stories, was the most imposing in the village center.

Uncle Vasavedu, an attendant, and Lalput's Magistrate all waited in the main room downstairs. A servant showed Ashoka and his little family into that room. Another stranger was there too. Several smiled and looked self-assured, satisfied.

None rose from the seating cushions. The Magistrate, Uncle Vasavedu, and the stranger looked at each other with smiles and nods, as if they had been talking, their happy talk interrupted by these visitors.

Not many grown men had too much to eat at this time in this village, but Uncle Vasavedu's face was puffed, his chubby hands resting on an ample belly. Ashoka bowed in his direction, as was required for an elder of the same caste. The two women stood in back against the wall—as if they were not there.

They all waited for the Magistrate to speak first, and he did, but did not rise. He spoke in the direction of Ashoka. "Sir, we thank you for coming, and for bringing the two women." Now he stood up and came closer to Ashoka. "You might wonder why you were asked to come here without an established agreement." He waited for any reaction from Ashoka, but Ashoka stood still. "There is a preliminary matter we must address before any agreement can be discussed." He smiled, almost laughed, and the two others sitting laughed with him. "When we get that out of the way, we will drink tea and talk of more substantial things."

Ashoka bowed to him slightly. "I am happy to discuss any preliminary matter."

"Well, then," said the Magistrate, "you will be able to establish you are Vasavedu's nephew, son of the elephant man. You must, you know."

Ashoka was driven into silence of words, into blank thoughts, away from any fear or emotion except his guru's command to keep still when the fire threatens, when the trees fall, when too many attack. His deeper sense had to show him the solution. Suddenly he understood the presence of the stranger in the room, likely the same man who had slunk around his inn in the middle of the night, now ready to give false reports to the most powerful man in Lalput. No anger rose in him. He already had found a way to confront the threat. "In time, if need be, I can do so. I can establish I am the last son of the elephant man of Lalput."

"Please proceed," said the Magistrate. He glanced at Vasavedu.

Those two had their arrangement worked out in every detail. Ashoka stared at both in turn. They did not flinch or look off. He said, "You may ask my mother and my sister. They know me. They know Father. They know Uncle."

The Magistrate flicked his hands as if brushing dust off the table in front of him. "At this time, there are so many who go by the name of Ashoka, so many young men out of work, but strong and able. They do all look somewhat alike. So many beggar women roam the cities and towns that their lies can be bought for one piece of bread." Uncle Vasavedu, his attendant, the Magistrate's servant, and the stranger all laughed at that last, laughed too loudly and long.

Ashoka heard Sanju make a sound of anger and disbelief. He thought Mother might not have been able to hear well enough to understand and was glad for that.

The Magistrate turned to the stranger. "Sir, tell us please what you witnessed."

The stranger, a rail thin older man with a beard, dirty garments, no teeth and finger nails longer than the matching fingers, stood up and bowed to the Magistrate. "I sometimes, when I have a few coins left over, take my evening meal at the Inn of The Half Moon. A few nights back, I heard a woman and man talking. They said things that were not right, not just. I glanced at them. They are this young man and the old one back there. I felt it my duty to report them. One never knows in these times what crimes others plot." He paused but did not look at anyone other than the Magistrate.

The Magistrate said, "Well, go on."

"I heard this man and the old woman over there say they had found a way to get a great house and the land of an old elephant compound—but the man had to pretend to be her son." The stranger looked down. He was done.

They all waited. They all looked at Ashoka. Sanju breathed heavily and held her mother. Vasavedu scowled at Ashoka and then smiled at him through his scowl.

The Magistrate looked satisfied. "I believe, whoever you are, there is nothing more to be done. Vasavedu is kind and merciful. He will not demand that you and those two women be thrown in jail if you withdraw your treacherous demands and never set foot in Lalput, in the whole region, again." They all waited for Ashoka to respond.

He did not feel hurried, angry. He felt the power of being right in the face of evil. "Master Magistrate, Uncle, witness and attendants, I will go gladly after you allow me to present one more thing. It will not take long."

The Magistrate looked over at Vasavedu and shrugged. The uncle shrugged back, as if to tell him to let the young fool try to escape this. The Magistrate said, "Be quick. I have other pressing matters to rule on."

Ashoka, pointing, said, "Please, all of you, gather around the rug here. Sit or kneel as you like, but sit so you can all together see what I will now show you, and allow me please to ask Uncle my own preliminary questions—so the Magistrate may rule correctly."

The Magistrate looked puzzled but directed them to all sit in a half circle at the place Ashoka had indicated. Ashoka knew he had to agree, had to hear both sides before he ruled with all finality in this dispute between two high-caste men.

When the five men were seated, Ashoka waited until he thought Uncle Vasavedu was ready to burst, the strange witness ready to flee, and the Magistrate to shout out. Only then did he begin. "Uncle Vasavedu, would you happen to know the trade of your father's father?"

"What difference does that make?" He looked at the Magistrate, but the Magistrate seemed interested. "Well, yes. He was a warrior and a champion wrestler."

"Would you happen to know if he passed anything small and precious to his son and then to my father?"

Again Vasavedu turned to the Magistrate before he answered. "There are rumors, all rumors, of a piece of jewelry or a *kukri* or something such as that."

Ashoka reached into and under his coat and down the left leg of his *dhoti*. He quickly untied the long string that held the *kukri* to his thigh and brought it out, black scabbard and long strings, and set it on the rug in front of him.

Vasavedu made a scoffing sound, but the Magistrate held up his hand for silence.

Ashoka said, "Father gave me this the day before I left. It is made of the finest metal in all of India. Its first owner was indeed a great fighter, with his hands, with this knife if needed, with elephants. I have carried this every day of the last eleven years, and it shouts the truth for all of my family."

Silence, the silence of minds taking it in, of trying to find words but unsure if the words would trap them. The Magistrate's face became stern, and he looked at Vasavedu.

At last, Vasavedu laughed, "Why that *kukri* could belong to anyone. This is a child's game." He slapped the rug. "A fool's game."

Ashoka raised his hand this time. He pulled the *kukri* out of its scabbard. Even indoors the shiny blade seemed to sparkle. "Uncle, you and everyone in this village will recognize our family seal right here." He pointed to the thick part of the blade under the hilt and the blackened etching of a round seal.

"Each of your houses, and Father's little house too, shows this seal on the main door and on the main foundation stone."

Vasavedu began to shout, flap his hands in time with his jowls. "You, you thief. You stole that *kukri*, and it must be mine now."

The Magistrate frowned more deeply and stood up.

Ashoka sensed now was the time to end this. "No man alive would steal this great *kukri* from its rightful owner—and then bring it back to Lalput, to the only town in all of India, to the only family in all of India who might recognize it. Only its rightful owner would do that, would be so foolish."

The Magistrate clapped his hands once in Vasavedu's direction. The Magistrate's attendant stood up behind Vasavedu. Two other men, each in light armor and carrying long pikes, entered the room from interior doors. One stood over Vasavedu, one over the stranger who had spoken lies. The Magistrate said, "Thank you, Ashoka. I believe you have satisfied the preliminaries."

Vasavedu jumped up and tried to push away from his shoulder the strong hand of the guard behind him. He shouted, "This is blasphemy of the worst kind. Enough." He pointed at the Magistrate. "You will hear from me and you will not be pleased with my anger."

The Magistrate blocked Vasavedu's route to the door. "Must I compare the seal on the main door of your house to the seal on this *kukri*?"

Vasavedu stomped his foot and sputtered. "I don't need to answer that."

The Magistrate, taller and stronger than old Uncle, moved closer to him. "When we take this to the head judge, you will need to answer that. For now, it is best you each remain in the jail until we get this sorted out. Ashoka, take your women back to the inn from which you came but do not leave."

The next day, the town judge interviewed the strange witness. As he had harmed no one, the judge sentenced him to mere banishment, but only if he confessed fully.

Vasavedu had hired the poor street man to track Ashoka. Vasavedu did not tell him what to do if he found Ashoka alone, just that there would be a reward if Ashoka made no more demands for property that did not belong to him. Vasavedu thought the false story of an overheard conversation between the old woman and Ashoka would be enough, that Ashoka would never be able to prove his entitlement.

After a fair hearing with other witnesses, the Judge of Lalput gave Uncle Vasavedu the choice of punishment for what he had done to his brother's family and for letting go of the elephant camp. He could spend the rest of his days in the village jail with drunks and thieves or leave the region within seven days and never come back. Vasavedu chose to leave. Ashoka persuaded the Judge to let Aunt Durga stay. She had not done anything dishonorable, but Aunt Durga left with her husband. She belonged to him and always would.

+ + +

Ashoka kept his promise to Radha. He gathered the leather workers of Lalput in the main street outside their shops and beckoned them to sit. He looked at them all directly, touched them, laughed and clapped with them as he told them about her good fortune. They remembered well that Radha and her mother had been taken away by Syrian soldiers, Radha twice and the mother once. When they asked about her mother, Ashoka shook his head, and they asked no more.

Starting with one aged female elephant he found in the jungle not far from the village, his beloved Red Eyes, Ashoka reopened the family elephant camp. In a short time word of his way with the beasts spread through the region and far beyond.

The compound on the river became too small for him to accept all new clients, though many offered extravagant sums to train their elephants.

In the third year after Ashoka's return, Sanju married a good man. She brought a dowry of clothes, cows, and horses.

In that same year, he took a wife—a beautiful woman from one caste down.

Mother told her grandchildren many true stories about the deeds of their father and Uncle Govinda and about an elephant with only four nails on his front feet.

Ashoka never again moved away from Lalput and died there of old age.

In later generations, the people of Exandahar told their children and sometime strangers of a young bull elephant marked for certain slaughter but saved by an Indian boy. Travelers through that valley from the West said they too had heard tell of that very mahout and elephant with a star-shaped scar high on its neck, that the boy had grown into a leader of men and beasts, that the elephant had become a majestic fighter, and that united again the two achieved great glory in the lands on the far side of Macedon.

THE END

Author Notes

These notes I give to any reader who wonders, did this happen, in this way, really? Although Ashoka and his family, Radha and her mother, their home village of Lalput, the caravan and its men, are fictional, most of the main events did take place. The main background characters lived as they do in this novel.

Throughout this story, I have tried to remain true to the events historians of the time have passed down, and to what coins and other physical evidence from back then tell us. I have walked in a number of the places Ashoka rode or walked. Where I am unsure, I have portrayed what seems reasonable based on all accounts available to me.

Perhaps the biggest unknown is how Ashoka and those around him spoke. Roman historians, writing decades afterwards, have given us their recreations of some of Hannibal's speeches, but not more. Common people in ancient India, Greece, Carthage, Assyria, Italy and the many Celtic (or Keltoi) tribal regions intermingled as friends, traders or adversaries, but their dialogue is not preserved in any record I have found.

Below I sketch some of the history before and after the brief span of my novel.

Ancient India. At the time of this story, India was at peace. Connected by raised roads from one end of the subcontinent to the other, it might have been the greatest power on earth. In math, science, literature, and poetry as well as farming, raising animals, production of cotton, spices, tools, weapons and jewelry, India had no peer.

In often brutal campaigns, its Emperor Ashoka had subdued most rivals. In mid-life he became a devout Buddhist and, it is said, cried every night for the many soldiers and civilians his armies had killed. He decreed the practice of *ahimsa*, a devotion to all life, non-violence and a vegetarian diet.

The caste system was strictly adhered to. How a person spoke, the family name, clothes and facial markings projected one's place in society. Often the only escape from generations of hardship and abuse was to serve other masters far away. The great households of Europe desired Indian servants and laborers.

Icons of Buddha dating from back then have been found as far away as Southern France.

In the early nineteenth century, a British tiger hunting party stumbled upon magnificent carvings and fresco cave paintings honoring the life and times of Lord Buddha cut into a gorge overgrown by centuries of jungle outside Ajanta, India. Tourists from around the world visit them today.

The dominant predator of India has always been the tiger, but lions still live in some protected areas. Indian lions were far more plentiful at the time of this story.

The spread of Buddhism peaked soon after Emperor Ashoka's reign. Late in the twelfth century, Afghan armies of Islam invaded India and in successive years won battles that opened the north central plains, the center of Buddhist universities and monasteries. In one day the Muslims slaughtered four thousand Buddhist priests waiting to surrender peaceably. The Muslims set to the torch hand-written manuscripts containing more than a thousand years of India's teachings preserved in the libraries where the priests had gathered. Buddhism never again achieved significant influence on the subcontinent of its birth.

Carthage and The Punic Wars. Historians closest in time to the strife between Rome and Carthage wrote not only from the point of view of Rome but also decades or centuries after the events they portrayed. Hence, it is not known how much they exaggerated or unfairly demeaned Rome's greatest adversary.

Carthage began as a one-town colony in about 600 B.C.E. on the present site of Tunis in North Africa. It had the best sailors and ship builders and became the strongest seafaring empire of the Mediterranean. At its height, it controlled all of North Africa west of Egypt, all of Iberia, and islands in the Mediterranean, including Sicily (called Trinacria by the ancients). Accounts close in time to the events of this novel portray a greener coastal strip of land than what we see today on the North coast of Africa. That fertile strip ran up to 100 miles inland along the Atlas mountains and supported large swaths of farmland irrigated by mountain streams and springs. The North African leopards, lions, and docile elephants are all extinct today.

Carthage built a second city center, New Carthage, on the present site of Cartagena, Spain. There Hannibal collected his army and from there launched his astounding invasion. Today some of the walls erected by Carthage still look down from the hills of Cartagena.

Carthage exploited servants and mercenaries from many lands, and that was both a strength and weakness. Decades before the time of this story, the mercenaries revolted and the empire almost collapsed. Full-blooded citizens of Carthage managed to muster enough of a loyal army and crush the revolt, killing fourteen thousand or more.

The gods of Carthage influenced every aspect of its culture. In Tunisia and other Phoenician centers, small urns hold the skeletons and ashes of children and babies. It is not certain what proportion were sacrificed or died of natural causes. But festivals organized around religious sacrifices of valuable animals and sometimes children of noble families were common. For those interested in reading more, including accounts of massive child sacrifices and the belief systems that spawned them see, Charles-Picard, Gilbert and Colette, *Daily Life in Carthage At The Time of Hannibal* (translated from the French), The Macmillan Company (New York 1961). Some ancient historians, perhaps biased, report Carthaginian nobles used slave children for this purpose.

Rome and Carthage fought three wars. Hannibal Barca led Carthage in the second of the three.

At the beginning of his march, the Iberian Keltoi joined him with great enthusiasm. The year before, they helped his siege of Saguntum. But soon some seven thousand left Hannibal and returned to their homes and farms. I have not found the name of their tribal leader and have given him the name Sinorix.

Many of the Celtic tribes from Iberia and elsewhere fought wearing only shields, a helmet, and weapons. They wanted freedom of movement in a fight and to run fast. They believed dirty leather or cloth thrust deep into a wound would more likely lead to a slow death than a more direct wound.

After Hannibal took his army out of Iberia, a small Roman force attacked the city of New Carthage. It surrendered in days. The soldiers Hannibal had left to guard Iberia lingered in the interior never expecting a direct attack on the well-fortified city.

Hannibal roamed Italy for sixteen to seventeen years, inflicting serious damage but never able to fully turn the local population against its rulers. In time, the treasury of Carthage was emptied, its mercenaries no longer loyal, and Hannibal retreated back to North Africa.

Masinissa saw the tide of war would turn against Hannibal. In the end Masinissa and his men rode for Rome and helped defeat Hannibal in the final battle of the Second Punic War on plains west of the original Carthage. Rome installed Masinissa as Supreme Ruler of North Africa.

The main battles between Hannibal and Rome are recreated in text and diagrams by many writers of military history, and I have stayed true to those reports in the two battles of this story. Some military historians suggest Hannibal led out with his elephants at the battle of the Trebia River. That is possible but unlikely. Thirty thousand well-armed Roman foot soldiers and many thousand more riders would have quickly slaughtered thirty or so elephants, no matter how great the initial shock imparted by the big beasts. Hannibal's war tactics were never foolish. Most of his elephants survived that first big battle but not long after.

Roman fighters employed bows and arrows relatively late in life of the Empire, but the Assyrians, Greeks, and Indians had used the bow and arrow for centuries by the time of the second Punic War. Hannibal's heavy reliance on mercenaries from other lands makes it somewhat likely that he did as well.

Hannibal was captured by the Romans and lived into his seventh decade exiled in Tyre, close by the site of the Phoenician city that had sent its young queen to found the original colony of Carthage. The Roman guards assigned to Hannibal allowed him to take his own life rather than answer a final summons to Rome.

After many years of an uneasy peace and unbearable tribute paid by Carthage, Rome started the Third Punic War. Historians are divided on whether Rome was provoked by some dishonorable act of Carthage or decided to eradicate its rival while still weak. Rome prevailed once more. This time it knocked down every building, confiscated every item of value and burned to ash all else in the City of Carthage. It tilled salt into the soil so that no living thing could again grow out of that ground.

The empire of Carthage lasted more than four hundred years. But its people showed no urge to record their own exploits and wrote sparingly on other subjects. Or, perhaps, at the end of this third Punic war, the Romans destroyed all writings by Carthage.

The Greek Polybius finished a multi-volume history of Rome not long after the third war. He retraced Hannibal's route over the Alps, traveled to North Africa and for days interviewed the aged Masinissa. But he too wrote for Rome.

In time, Rome subdued all the tribes of Iberia and Gaul and the Alps.

"Punic" is derived from the Latin word for a person of Carthage.

The Routes Described in This Story. Alexander the Great founded many towns on his campaigns into North Africa and Asia. At small villages on trading routes, his men built walls, installed loyal rulers, and intermarried with the locals. He tended to give each village his own name. Alexandria in Egypt became its capital and a great city, Kandahar in Afghanistan an important stopping point.

The local tribes around Kandahar could not pronounce "Alexandria" and changed that to Exandahar, later shortened to its present name. The village where Ashoka first finds Four Nails is not meant to describe Kandahar of that time, but any village on the old silk and spice trading routes in the high plateaus below the highest mountains on earth.

The trading hub called Seleucia had a peak population of over 600,000. Not far from modern-day Bagdad, it sat on a reservoir of oil that seeped to the surface in many places. Locals used the tar to hold street cobbles in place.

The town of Sagunt, a short ride by car or train from Valencia, Spain, lies under imposing walls atop a craggy hill. The oldest sections of those walls were built by the Sagunti people before Hannibal's siege. The walls have been added to, first by the Romans then by the Moors.

When Hannibal's army reached the Rhone, he tried to make peace with the tribes on the far side. Historical accounts about the details of his emissaries' failed mission are murky, but they were rudely rebuffed. Beheading the dead enemy was a common practice of the Keltoi in this and other regions. Hannibal's army swiftly crossed the Rhone and easily defeated the tribal warriors amassed on the far shore. His army built floating platforms to transport his carts and animals. His elephants would have none of that. Chaos ensued. But all the elephants made it across the river.

Before heading into the Alps, Hannibal did mediate between two brothers of the ruling family of a friendly tribe. The father had died, and neither brother could decide who should succeed the father. That tribe did provide Hannibal's army with many valuable provisions and guides.

Some historians say the St. Bernard of the Alps is the product of Hannibal's mastiffs and the local mountain sheep dogs.

Hannibal's path over the Alps is not certain. A number of modern-day explorers have walked possible routes (and tried to match the features of the terrain to the accounts of Roman historians). To them I am indebted. Bernard Levin published photographs and wrote about much of the way in his delightful, *Hannibal's Footsteps* (Jonathan Cape 1985). Mr. Levin gave me the name of Hannibal's hunched-over priest, Bogus. A wonderful first-hand account of Hannibal's possible routes by John Prevas is *Hannibal Crosses the Alps* (Da Capo Press 1998). Mr. Prevas and others describe two mountain ambushes of Hannibal's army by the Ligurians or other Celtic sub-tribes in the Alps. The Ligurians were no friends of Rome, and in the end probably helped Hannibal find the best route across the mountains.

On the way down the mountains, a massive boulder blocked Hannibal's path. A relay of eight thousand men brought wood to its base so the rock might be broken up with fire and bad wine.

The ancient world knew tuberculosis too well. Families, villages, cities and larger regions fell to it. Isolating the sick was the only known remedy. Elephants suffer from it too. Surus was the only elephant of Hannibal's 37 that crossed the Alps to survive the first winter in northern Italy. I am not sure the other elephants all died from wounds in the early battles or from this disease and the cold winter. A combination of these causes is likely. In later years Hannibal received more elephants by ship from Carthage, but these too were not of much help in war.

The Romans used the measure of a mile. The Roman mile was probably slightly shorter than the current British mile, but the difference is not significant to the distances in my story.

A Last Word About Four Nails. In the century before this story, India had driven away Alexander the Great. Both sides used Indian war elephants to good effect. In Europe, the first use of elephants in battle is attributed to Pyrrhus of the Greek city-state Epirus (located in today's Balkans). He defeated Roman armies in 280 and 279 B.C. but took such heavy losses the term "Pyrrhic victory" bears his name. After those battles, Indian elephants and competent mahouts were prized in that part of the world, a world almost constantly at war.

Hannibal rode a giant Indian elephant. He named it Surus, for the Syrians who sold it to him. Most or all of his other elephants came out of the mountains and hills of North Africa. These, a different breed than the larger elephants from south of the Sahara or from India, were shy and not suited to war.

Surus died of a mysterious illness contracted in the swamps of the Arno River. Today the swamps have been drained and the river channeled, but mosquitoes still plague parts of Italy.

This story is no more about people and wars of the past than it is about the wonder of elephants, probably the smartest of all creatures large and small. Their senses of hearing and smell are extraordinary. Elephants screamed and ran uphill away from the tsunami of Thailand in December 2004 well before people reacted to that wall of water silently rushing at them. Elephant rescues of humans and other animals are legend as is their clever brutality when mistreated.

Of the many pieces on elephants I have read or watched, one stands out. *Elephant Gold* by P. D. Stracey (Weidenfeld & Nicolson, 1963) describes how wild elephants were hunted, captured and tamed. It tells about the "four nails" myth making Indian elephants with only four nails on their front feet reviled, worthless. Some Indian elephant merchants glued an extra nail on each front foot to fool the unwary buyer. Mr. Stracey's parents were Indian and British. He started his career as an elephant catcher and rose to Chief Conservator of Forests in the Assam region of India.

About the Author

G. J. Berger's debut novel, *South of Burnt Rocks West of the Moon*, was selected as the best published historical of 2012 by the San Diego Book Awards. *Burnt Rocks* is the sequel to *Four Nails* and tells the mostly true story of the youngest daughter of Sinorix after the empire of Carthage has finally fallen to Rome.

Both *Four Nails* and *Burnt Rocks* are Writer's Choice selected historical novels. G. J. Berger is a member of this international writers' co-operative which helps its members produce the best possible historical fiction through careful selection, reading, editing, proof reading, design and layout.

G. J. lives in San Diego with his favorite tango dancing partner and grammarian. He reviews for the Historical Novel Society and is working on two other novels.

G. J. welcomes hearing from any reader, admirer of elephants, or others interested in this time and place. Contact him at gjberger@hotmail.com.

+ + +

If you enjoyed this book perhaps you might write a review for Goodreads or Amazon (either UK or US). You might also enjoy other Writer's Choice novels. Check out the following at the major sales channels (Amazon, Barnes & Noble) or the website (http://www.writerschoice.org):

- *A Woman Transported* by Sharon Robards
  - Amazon best seller
- *Unforgivable* by Sharon Robards
- *South of Burnt Rocks West of the Moon* by G.J. Berger – winner, San Diego Book Awards for best published historical fiction of 2012.
- *Jacob's Ladder* by p d r lindsay – short listed in the UK unpublished novel competition
- *Tizzie* by p d r lindsay –short listed in the MM Hubbards Historical Fiction Award, finalist in the Wishing Shelf Independent Books Awards
- *Women Waking Up* by p d r lindsay – prize winning short stories
- *Blokes Muddling Through* by p d r lindsay - prize winning short stories
- And five short stories in the Writer's Choice Shorts series.

Made in the USA
Monee, IL
21 May 2021